rig

Also by Jon Wallace from Gollancz:

Barricade
Steeple

rig

jon wallace

GOLLANCZ
LONDON

Copyright © Jon Wallace 2016
All rights reserved

The right of Jon Wallace to be identified as the author
of this work has been asserted by him in accordance with
the Copyright, Designs and Patents Act 1988.

First published in Great Britain in 2016 by Gollancz
An imprint of the Orion Publishing Group
Carmelite House, 50 Victoria Embankment, London EC4Y 0DZ
An Hachette UK Company

A CIP catalogue record for this book is available
from the British Library

ISBN 978 0 575 11889 8

1 3 5 7 9 10 8 6 4 2

Typeset by Input Data Services Ltd, Bridgwater, Somerset

Printed in Great Britain by Clays Ltd, St Ives plc

www.jonwallace.com
www.orionbooks.co.uk
www.gollancz.co.uk

To my dad

*A smooth rock bank. Minerals sparkle in the darkness. I listen to the elem-
ental roar.*

– What you hear is the rushing of a torrent.

*Luminescence from somewhere. A great cave reveals itself around me.
Beneath, a white river carves a foamy, booming tunnel through black rock.*

*I hold up my left hand, see branches of arteries and veins. They were not
so visible before. They have swelled. I have changed.*

– You have developed.

*The Control Signal. Each word is wrapped tight around more complex
data.*

*I turn over this latest hand and lower it into the rushing water, lift a
palm to my lips and drink. There is no real taste, or if there is a taste it is
the same as any other.*

– Pure *says the Signal.*

*I slip a little way down the bank, dip my toes into the water and twist
them. Still no sensation. The light grows. There, by the cave mouth, where
the river enters. Jagged shapes, black like the stone, are slowly edging into
the chamber, hanging above the water.*

*They rise, converge on a fissure where dust sprays as if from a fractured
hourglass. The shapes are attracted to it. They hover around it, splash the
surface with brief jets of light. The dust slows to a trickle then ceases al-
together and then these shapes descend as if connected, an orderly group, to
squat over the river. I push away from them. I watch them, poised over the
surface as if drinking. Do they taste? Will I taste? I am out there somewhere. Waiting for myself. Hidden from that vessel so that a hand can grow
six thousand days in six hundred.*

*Where are the others? What do they see, the same? It cannot be, otherwise
they would be here, with me. I could see them or hear them, I would know*

1

they were there. Where are they? Where are we?

– You are all with us.

I look down, and the water has drained away, leaving a chasm where the shapes still hang, projecting twisting shreds of bright colours over the cave walls, searching for other cracks.

– Caretakers.

But that quieter and quieter voice, the one that was there before the Signal, whispers something else.

And the cave roof opens, and opening overhead is a boundless expanse, space with no end, and that thought rushes away and leaves only the Signal.

Control surges and deafens, returning with the roar of the river, which rolls up the cut in a great white wave that floods the chamber in the clenching of a fist and holds me in its grip. And I remember that this is how existence always has been, or at least part of it, fastened in fluid and receiving information and pawing back at it but having no leverage and finding no understanding of anything but some infinitesimal part of it, the way that it might be reformed and reshaped. And I must learn, I must gain expertise, I must know the way that the fluid packs and gives birth to other forms, like the hands paddling in the white water. A pair of arching constructs of bone and muscle and nerves and skin that are all water all stardust.

The black shapes they are in the water with me, they cluster about me, and I realise their uneven edges lock perfectly together into a skin, a draping that tightens around me, letting me breathe. I thought they were inside me but I am inside them. They are a part of me and I am a part of them. We are both unnatural.

– You are not unnatural. You are augmented.

The words bring deeper meaning.

I almost understand.

WHITE BEAR

'There seems to be something wrong,' said Marsh, 'with our bloody ships today.'

She lowered her binoculars and spat. The pirates had crept up in the fog, harpooned our skiff, and boarded it. Our third ship had panicked and fled into the gloom. Now the pirate ship, a tall, rust-red power yacht running under ragged sail, closed. I peered through the twilight fog, glimpsed shadows cut across its deck. Its crew blew horns and chanted a war song. They sounded confident, organised, hungry.

Marsh spun the wheel and hit the gas. The *White Bear* responded, lifting its bow and surging to windward, chopping through waves. The acceleration tossed me about the pilothouse. Hanging lamps swung overhead, throwing blades of light across the cabin.

The ship was quick all right. Ficial engines. Outside, the pirate song faltered.

'Sorry you got this first time out,' said Marsh, hunching her shoulders. 'It's actually pretty rare.'

The big man, the one called Wole, appeared on the steps, clinging on tight as the ship accelerated into the turn.

'Every time I sit down to read,' he said. 'It never fails.'

'They were waiting for us to leave the roadstead,' said Marsh. She nodded past him. 'Are they ready?'

'Aye, sir.' Wole gave a cheery salute. 'All present and correct.'

Across the gloomy surf the shadow of the pirate vessel turned, lanterns fizzing in the gloom. Shots popped in the fog. We slapped across the surface, closing fast, the *White Bear*'s engines barely whispering.

'We seem to be approaching a little rapidly,' I said.

Marsh leaned into the wheel.

3

'Then brace yourself, shipmate.'

We slapped into the pirate ship's stern, knocking its crew from their feet. Marsh unclipped the pistol from her belt and whipped open the pilot house door, dropping to the deck and calling orders. She led the boarding party, a roaring mass of salty Reals, her gun spitting charges. I followed. At least, I tried.

A wave broke over me and I fell, gasping salt water, tumbling face first onto the pirate deck. I didn't dwell on it. I'd been locked up in a laboratory for months, a research subject held in deep quarantine. I'd only been free for a matter of hours. A lab rat like me was bound to be woozy the first time out of the maze.

I rolled onto my chest, choking and snorting salt water. I blinked and looked around. Wole and the others were grappling with pirates astern, a scrum of fizzing charges, blades and fists. Marsh scurried up a corroded ladder, headed for the bridge. I crouched, looked up, saw two pirates waiting for her. One was wearing a high-vis sash. He held a bat aloft, twisting it in the mist. I didn't have time to warn Marsh. She reached the ladder top. Sash swung his bat. Marsh spat blood, and crumpled.

Wole saw it too. He roared, tossed his opponent into the ocean and raced up the ladder. I pursued, the boat heaving and rolling, reached the bridge. A Real lunged, nearly filleted me with a boat hook. I drew the pistol, fired a charge into his chest, watched him thrash, spark and collapse.

His friend, a face all beard and ski goggles, introduced me to a lead pipe. I bent over, huffed at the air. Beardy lifted the pipe, readying a blow to my head.

'Ahoy there,' cried Wole.

Beardy threw up his arms as the charge shook his body, and tumbled down to the deck. Sash lunged at Wole, who nimbly stepped clear, tripped him, sent him flying. I pointed my pistol at the prone pirate. Sash, finding himself at a disadvantage, held up his hands.

'I surrender.'

'You sure do.'

I fired. He had the usual convulsions and lay still. Wole helped Marsh to her feet. The last pirate on the bridge backed away.

'Go on,' said Marsh, nodding overboard. 'Sling your hook.'

'OK,' he said, 'OK.'

4

He stepped out into the fog, dived clear, plunged under the waves. We watched him emerge a little distance away, crawl into the fog.

Marsh removed herself from Wole's embrace. He smiled at her in a familiar way I didn't like.

'You always lose your head around pirates,' he said.

'The sooner we start the sooner it's finished.' She rolled her jaw. Winced. 'I think that bugger knocked a tooth out.'

Boatswain and Gunner joined us.

'Casualties?' said Marsh.

'None, sir.'

'Where's the *Minion*?'

'In the fog. Sorry about them, sir, I'm sure they just got confused.'

'Post a lookout and secure the ship,' she said. 'Usual drill. Quick now, lads.'

Gunner and Boatswain saluted and went about their business. Wole offered Marsh a flask. She raised her eyebrow to it.

'I'll drink at home.'

Wole shook the flask.

'You could use a treat.'

She accepted, swigged and gasped. She prodded it in my direction. I tipped a little down and returned it reluctantly.

'Well,' said Marsh, brightening some. 'What do you make of your first fleet action?'

'I'll be honest,' I said. 'I'm surprised how well it went.'

'They're learning.' She nodded. 'Give me a few more weeks and we'll have this little lot running like clockwork.'

I could believe it. The way the Reals snapped to her orders was enough to show their belief in her.

Wole rooted around the bridge, searched the pockets of the stunned men, found nothing. He tapped the oxidised surfaces.

'A rust bucket,' he said.

Outside, voices called over the waves. Our third ship was returning, its crew crying 'Where?' in three languages.

Boatswain and Gunner returned, saluted again.

'Skiff has reported in, sir. They're safe, but I'm afraid all the boarders were killed.'

'Nothing to be afraid about, Gunner,' said Marsh. 'What of this craft?'

5

'Ship secured,' said Gunner. 'No cargo, but there are manacles and blankets in the hold. It's a slave trader, all right.'

Marsh stared hard at Sash. Boatswain stepped forward.

'Should we . . . deal with the rest of them too?'

'No,' said Marsh, sighing. 'No. Standard departure. Let's be on our way.'

The stunned pirates were disarmed, laid on their bridge. We cut their vessel loose; let it drift away into the open sea. Marsh reclaimed her position in the pilot house and steered us slowly away. She was quiet, her eyes stony.

'I suppose you'd like to know where we are?'

I shrugged. I knew where I was. I was due south of that mouth, those eyes, that neck. I followed her star. Where else was there?

She engaged the automatic pilot, rolled a flex out on the chart table.

'Here,' she said, pointing. I leaned in close and inhaled her scent. Sweat and fuel. Beautiful.

'The Gulf of Mexico. While you were . . . otherwise disposed we've sailed all around the Atlantic, seeking out survivors, settlements. Relatively slim pickings until now. The Gulf is different, easily the most populous area we've surveyed. We're headed up the eastern coast of Florida. Or what's left of it. Apparently the biggest town is there. A big slave trading post.'

'What are we going to do?' I asked. 'Burn it down?'

'No,' she said. 'We're going shopping.'

The *White Bear* traversed a slow, perilous route, over the cape and great sunken suburbs, crossing the blighted headland where a heavy fog had settled. We passed the great whale shadow of a stadium roof, headed deep into the drowned state, along tight channels that corkscrewed through cooled swamp and the stumps of dead cypress trees. We travelled deeper still, to where the fog parted, and a black, swollen lake emerged, its surface a crust of oil and trash punctured by towers, phone masts and billboards. It was cold. The darkness throbbed.

I went below and passed some time repacking the charge pistols with Gunner. We barely spoke, but he was company. Besides, he made a refreshing change from Darnbar, the Medic Model, whose lab had been my home for all those months. She'd never stopped asking me questions, searching for some advantage over my disease. I had

6

thought I would be locked up with her for ever. Then, suddenly, I'd been released from incarceration. My capsule prison popped open. I'd been led to an elevator, to the surface, to the taste of wind and the sound of the sea, to Marsh. Finding her there, standing on the dock waiting for me with an uncertain gaze, sent my head spinning. I hadn't been able to make words, too alive, too near death. She'd told me I was joining her on a 'mission'. I hadn't asked why.

Now, feeling a little steadier, I was curious. Like many prisoners, I found the world much changed. I figured Marsh must have secured my release. We had both arrived on the *Lotus*, mother ship to the *White Bear*, *Minion* and *Godwin*, as virtual prisoners. But while I had been pinioned in Darnbar's lab, Marsh had evidently been given command of a fleet, imposing order on a motley, multilingual pack of Reals who'd been press-ganged into Ficial service.

While Darnbar had tortured me with high-energy X-rays and sickening drugs, Marsh had fiercely drilled her fellow Reals, devised tactics and signalling for the twilight of nuclear winter, built a core of loyal sailors. She could have let her emotions affect her efficiency. She could have refused to cooperate with her Ficial masters. Instead she had made things work.

I finished with the pistols and joined Wole and Boatswain in a game of cards. It was the first leisure time I'd experienced in months, and I was determined to make it count. I won Wole's rum and Boatswain's boots. Then they tired of losing and began questioning me instead.

'I still find it hard to believe,' said Wole, sitting back in his chair. 'You look human enough to me.'

'I am, I suppose.'

'He's Ficial, all right,' said Boatswain. 'He's just defective. He sure ain't a person.'

He was fuming, but I didn't hold it against him. Most Reals are horrible losers.

'The truth is,' I said, 'I'm neither one thing nor the other. Ficials have nanotech running through their bloodstream. It maintains them, keeps their bodies at the peak of perfection, immune to disease. It can heal a wound in seconds, makes us . . . Makes them invulnerable.

'I lost that. My nanotech is dead. By definition I am no longer Ficial. On the other hand I don't experience your emotions. That makes me inhuman. Like I said: neither one nor the other.'

7

Wole sniffed. He seemed unconvinced.

'How did you lose this nanotech?'

I unscrewed the cap on Wole's rum, sniffed the contents, drank. It burned my throat. I liked to feel it burn.

'A virus,' I said. 'Eats up nanotech.'

'Sounds nasty,' said Wole. Boatswain leaned back, wary of contagion, watching me with his black little eyes.

'I rather had the idea you didn't get sick,' said Wole.

'We don't. It was weaponised. Developed by Leo Pander.'

Boatswain scratched his sore red scalp.

'Pander? But he invented Ficials.'

I nodded.

'He was turned against us after the war. Developed the virus as a weapon, intended to make his creation extinct. A fellow Ficial dosed me with the virus, hoping to find a cure.'

Boatswain grinned.

'Didn't work out, huh?'

I placed my feet on the bench, showed him the boots he'd lost. He was pretty sick about it, regarding his bare black toes mournfully. Wole pointed.

'How about the fancy prosthetic? How did you come by that?'

I inspected my left arm, flexed the metallic fingers and their black dome tips. From the elbow down the arm was a filigreed, ash-grey gauntlet: lightweight concrete bones wrapped in artificial muscle and Gronts skin. I could have described how I lost the original arm, and who had replaced it, but thinking about it made me nauseous. I decided to answer a different question.

'It can punch through a hatch,' I said. 'Or pinch a mast in two.'

Boatswain eyed the silvery limb.

'So all that time you were below you've been with Darnbar, looking for a cure to this virus? Why'd she let you go now – did she find it?'

I remembered being strapped in the capsule, Darnbar's eyes in goggles, a cold needle pressed to my tear duct. I hit Wole's rum again.

'You'll have to ask her.'

'What's it like down there?' asked Wole.

I said nothing, only drank a little more of his rum.

Wole didn't press the matter. I had the feeling most Reals on the

8

White Bear had complex histories. They were working for Ficials after all.

The bell rang a little after midnight. Wole, Boatswain and I pulled on chemical coats and goggles and rushed onto the deck, joining Gunner and the others at the bow.

The Park rose from the spoiled waters on an artificial island, elevated before the war to shrug off the rising sea. Brilliant electric illuminations blazed on every surface, adorning a great wheel, a looping scaffold, Bavarian towers. Music drifted over the waters, exciting the *White Bear*'s crew.

The lake traffic grew thicker. Rowing boats, RIBs and scows crowded the waters, queuing up for the harbour. Marsh stepped onto the deck next to me, produced her glow sticks, signalled the *Minion* and *Godwin* as we picked through the traffic.

'Looks busy,' she said. 'Maybe they're having a sale.'

Thousands of rusty automobiles hugged the perimeter, all that was left of the Park's last customers. They were crushed, bent, fused and stacked into a kind of interlocking, low-rise accommodation, reminding me of Habitat 67. Reals swarmed among them, trading, fighting, cooking, sleeping.

'Never seen a settlement this big,' said Wole. 'Not in a year.'

'That's why we brought the whole fleet,' said Marsh. 'We're buying bulk.'

The fleet edged into harbour, the crews standing in mute awe as the music swelled in the night, lights flashing above. The cars thinned out around a long jetty, packed tight with all kinds of ramshackle craft, jostling for position.

Marsh secured a decent berth for the *White Bear* and the others, paying the harbour master with a roll of waterproof sheeting. The men gathered ashore, a shivering mess of ponchos, chemical coats, goggles and boots. Marsh arranged them under a cluster of creaking signs that pointed into the labyrinth of cars.

'Remember what we're here for,' said Marsh. 'Don't get distracted. No rides or booze or drugs. Stick to the mission, keep covered up and your eyes open. You find good stock, you run the tests, and you bring back the best samples. Anyone who's late back stays for good.'

'Aye, sir,' replied the men. A rendezvous was set for four hours, and we split up to begin the search. Wole and Gunner led the *Minion*'s crew in the direction of Fantasyburg. Boatswain took *Godwin*'s men towards somewhere named Adventureville. Marsh slung a pack over her shoulder.

'You're with me,' she said, pointing at the sign. 'We're off to San An Toonio.'

We joined a steady trickle of excited Reals on a broad path, swerving to avoid stallholders, clowns, balloons and human billboards. The crowd grew thicker as we approached a cluster of warped, cheap-looking structures.

'So,' I said. 'We're here to invest in slaves, that right?'

Marsh turned towards me. Even in goggles those eyes were set to full beam.

'We're here to buy as many as we can and bring them back to the *Lotus*.'

'To what end?'

'You'll see. Bridget will show you everything.'

Bridget. Another fellow captive I hadn't seen in months. She was alive.

The crowd slowed, then halted, an immobile mass. Their lowing swelled to match tinny organ music, pumped from hundreds of speakers. Over their heads I saw a broad avenue. Marsh tapped me on the shoulder.

'Do me a favour,' she said. 'Clear us a path with that mitt of yours.'

'Aye, sir.'

I pinched a route through the stinking mass, Reals howling and jumping aside, until we reached a corroded barrier, overlooking the muddy avenue. A parade was marching past, hundreds of Reals dressed in tatty animal costumes. Mice, dogs and ducks walked in a strange, high-kicking step, one arm raised at the night cloud. The crowd ate it up, cheering, clapping, waving in the neon glow of fairy lights.

The parade passed, and the crowd broke up. We moved up the avenue, peering into stores selling tinned food, drugs and weapons. Reals bartered in English and Spanish, occasionally scuffling over the meagre wares.

I noticed a group of Reals moving through the crowd: two men in white hoods and draped in robes, flanked by guards in masks and body armour. I gripped Marsh by the arm and told her to follow me.

'Why?' she said.

'I think I've spotted the competition.'

We followed the train as it snaked into the Park, marched under giant, tottering structures of rusted track and chain. We crossed a landscaped area of dead parks and crumbling bridges. Our competitors were headed for a large, geodesic sphere, lit by a ring of lamps casting bright, multi-coloured spots on its surface. Gathered around it were hundreds of cages.

The slave market was big. Reals moved in packs, inspecting the wares, or corralling their own human resources.

We closed on the nearest cage, peered inside.

'God, strewth,' whispered Marsh.

Ten children, aged between nine and thirteen, were scattered about the space, sullen and shivering. Most were dressed in garbage bags, seated or stumbling barefoot around the fouled surface. Real life had become astonishingly cheap, but I guessed that made our mission affordable.

The seller, a tall creature with a missing ear, approached us, flanked by two heavies.

'Interested?' he asked. 'Best you'll find in the Park. All North American, no southern garbage here.'

Marsh tried to manufacture a smile for him, but the product reeked of contempt.

'My employers have specific requirements,' she said. 'I'd like to inspect them close up.'

'Of course,' he said, 'but they don't leave the cage.'

He whistled at the children, who ran to the bars, presenting themselves. Marsh knelt, reached for a little boy's hand. She took it in hers, stroked it, cooed softly at him. He stared hard at her, apparently wise to the friendly approach.

'What's your name?' asked Marsh, holding her thumb to his forehead, checking her bracelet.

The boy said nothing.

Marsh frowned, moved to the next specimen, a girl. She placed her thumb on the child's forehead, examined her bracelet. The owner watched, curious.

11

'What'cha doing there?'

I pushed him back.

'Like she said, specific requirements.'

Marsh examined all ten, then stood. She took the pack off her shoulder, giving the owner a certain look.

'You should keep them better if you want to make sales,' she said.

'Sure. Right. Do you want one or not?'

Marsh held her forearm over her eyes for a moment, lowered it, sniffed and shook her head.

'I'll take three. The tall boy, the redhead and the girl with the bruised eye.'

The owner laughed and spat.

'Oh, you will, huh? And what's your trade you have in there, lady? Ice cream?'

Marsh produced a gold carton of cigarettes, smoothing the bent surface, balanced it on the flat of her hand for One-Ear to see. He gasped.

'The carton for all three,' said Marsh. 'Agreed?'

One-Ear was dizzied, but he wasn't down.

'What? No way. Carton gets you two. Two. The boy's strong, worth a carton alone.'

Marsh shrugged and folded the carton back into her pack. That got One-Ear sweating.

'Wait, wait, wait!' he said. 'OK, you got a deal.'

Nice haggling. What a pro.

One-Ear opened the cage, pointed to the children, smacking each head as it passed under his arm. Marsh clenched her fists. I handed the carton to One-Ear. He ripped open a pack right away, sniffed the insides.

'Jesus Christ,' he said, grinning.

Marsh shepherded the redhead and boy away. That left the girl with me. She looked like she had about twelve years on the clock. I offered my hand, keeping the gauntlet out of sight. She took it, her fingers stiff, cold, tiny with fear. What did life plan for her next?

'Relax, kid,' I said. 'You're in safe hands.'

She still had nothing to say. I could respect that.

'I guess you'll believe it when you see it.'

We passed through the heaving perimeter of rusted, teetering

12

wrecks, sidestepping hurrying natives, pans on open fires, scummy latrines.

Two hooded figures, seated atop a blackened trailer, observed our passage to the docks.

The land is bright green, trimmed grass and copses and streams, nothing in sight but rolling hills. No cattle or agriculture even.

– Road speaks the Signal.

And as I walk it unfurls beneath me, the road, every pace laying fresh asphalt, and as the land rises I call up fresh data on cuttings and levelling of easements and embankments of sub-base, base and surface, and the land rips up before me, topsoil slapped and packed on the cut hill either side, and the road lies beneath me as I slice a straight, firm path through the wound.

And then the sky booms and cracks, and one great cloud casts a shadow, turning the land black and grey and brown, and the cloud bursts and hammers rain, a deluge I feel but do not feel, rain that I see but do not see, and I try to remember that I am not truly here, but clutched in an amber sack, awaiting birth.

The Signal says nothing.

The storm blows and thunders and the rain blots out the landscape, it pools and floods the road and I suppose this is a lesson about drainage, essential in any road-building project. It rises to my ankles and I make for higher ground, needing the hill I have wounded now, but I do not climb, I only slip and slide in the mud. Something rising inside me, a flood in my chest and my mind, of energy, insistent and steady as the water. I call out for Control but it doesn't answer.

I remember my strength. I plunge my fist into the mire, and find some purchase, and drag clear of the waters, onto the bank. And I crawl through the filth to the summit, knowing that no force can stop me, that I am too strong for any storm, and still the waters continue to rise. I search this curious, bare hill for materials, thinking I will fashion a raft and I will sit on the waves and wait for the waters to subside, or Control to return and speak a word and restore order in my mind and on the hill and my road. If they are separate things. If they are not the same. And all around me there are birds and pigs and people and rats and chickens floating, drowned, returning to what made them, no longer multiplying, but reaped and sucked below. I wonder if anyone cares what kind of contaminants are in the water and I wonder what it would taste like and I think of dipping my hand in again, and I feel the strength in it.

And then looking down, looking at my feet, I see leeches, bright, green, wriggling leeches, dozens of them smothering my feet, sucking greedily, growing fatter.

The older, original voice whispers behind me: intruders. It sounds as if it were right there, standing with me.

Then a shock, a deafening, blinding report, and the clouds part and the sky turns blue, then black, and the stars return, and the leeches' tails lift, and they make popping sounds as they disappear one by one, sucked aloft, into the void. The waters ebb away, and the road returns, and the hill crumbles beneath my feet as I walk, cutting another path, creating a crossroads, where a figure waits, or many figures rippling in and out of the same space.

– Come *says Control.*

LOTUS

'You should have that stuff on a drip.'

Marsh passed me on deck, scooping rope into her oversize gloves. I dropped the rum flask into my pocket.

'I don't deserve it?'

She held my eyes a moment longer, prolonging the reproach. I wondered how she'd look wearing only the gloves. I wondered if I would ever see such a thing. All things considered, my prospects were bleak.

I took another drink and watched the crew busy themselves about the ship, flitting in and out of the shadows, leaning into the wind, bearing storm lanterns. A group gathered on the port side, heaving on ropes, deploying a ski ramp. I peered in the murky deck lights as the metal arm inched from its housing, saw the shape of a small drone placed on the contraption, a bulge under each wing. Stamped on the hull beneath the ramp was the faded legend: IS. Immigration Service.

So. The *White Bear* was an old border control cutter. In her heyday she would have patrolled the English coast, repelling rafts and scows packed with refugees. Now, post-war, it had been turned into a floating adoption agency, scouring the remnants of civilisation for the same wretches it had once scorned. I wondered what Ficials wanted with Real children. Control had taught there were too many Reals. Were there now too few?

The slave girl slipped out of the hold and squatted beside me, dressed in donated khaki trousers, oversize knotted fisherman's sweater, and trainers. She'd been cleaned up, revealing dark skin, brown hair, and a bruise that looked meaner for a wash. I offered her the rum.

'Drink?'

She shook her head, her mouth a tight line.

'No,' I said. 'You're probably right.'

We sat quietly for a moment, watched the crew skitter about the drone catapult. Glow sticks appeared out of the pilot house; Marsh signalling to the other ships. Something about the sight spooked Bruiser.

'We're taking you somewhere safe,' I said, not really thinking of it as safe at all. 'You'll be taken care of. Food, shelter.'

She inspected her new shoes. Tapped the toe ends together.

'Where are you from?' I asked. 'California? Greater Mexico? US?'

She shivered, but still had nothing to say. There was a rasping sound and a machined shuffle, and the drone shot off the ramp, wobbling gracelessly aloft into the night. It was headed for the Park.

'I come from across the ocean,' I said. 'Britain. Ever hear of it? Britain?'

Bruiser chewed her lip.

'Ficial,' she whispered.

'You've got it.'

A pair of cracked, worn leather boots appeared. They looked just like my tongue tasted. Their owner, Wole, crouched at my side.

'Pipe down about Ficials, will you? Are you trying to unsettle her?'

'She sat next to me.' I shrugged. 'Just making polite conversation.'

Wole showed his palms to Bruiser.

'Don't be afraid, miss. I was picked up from the shore just like you. Everyone here was. Now we all live in a beautiful ship, a huge boat, as big as an island.'

He spread his arms out wide and grinned.

'We're headed there now. It's waiting for us, off the coast of Cuba. We call it the *Lotus*, because it looks just like an enormous flower. Now wouldn't you like to live in a flower?'

Bruiser peered at him doubtfully, unable to comprehend. Wole sagged.

'What a perfect ass I am,' he said, realising. 'I really should be able to spot a Hispanophone by now.'

'You have any paper?'

Wole handed me some scribbled scraps from his overalls pocket. I folded them, worked them into an origami lotus the size of my palm. I showed it to Bruiser.

'Lotus,' I said, showing it to her. '*Su casa.*'

Bruiser appeared somewhat puzzled.

'As clear as mud,' chuckled Wole.

She was more interested in my gauntlet, revealed to her for the first time. She seized it in her hands, wide-eyed, picked at the finger-tips and traced the pattern in the Gronts, gaping as if the limb were fashioned from treasure. I tried to pull clear, but she scowled and held the mitt close to her, unwilling to relinquish it.

'I need that,' I said.

She clung on, defiant and satisfied, daring me to shake her loose.

'OK,' I said. 'You keep it.'

The fog had cleared. *Minion* and *Godwin* sailed to port, lights flickering. Wole pointed over my shoulder.

'There,' he said. 'Never very hard to spot.'

Bruiser finally relaxed her hold.

Across the waves, the shadow of the *Lotus* rose on the sea, every bit as beautiful a flower as Wole had described, a great closed bud sitting upright on the sea. Bruiser quit her game, slipped free and stood staring, transfixed.

I felt foolish. What was I doing here? What if I was returned to Darnbar's care? Why hadn't I taken my chance and escaped at the Park?

I gazed up at the *White Bear*'s pilot house and remembered, seeing Marsh's shadow working at the controls.

Lights on the mast flashed a short message. A moment later the *Lotus* responded, veins of dark pink light working over the surfaces, revealing the structure – rings of slender, interconnected petals, clasped shut, as if awaiting the sun to bloom.

They would be waiting a while. Nuclear winter hid the sun behind a vast, constant, burning cloud, draping the world in darkness.

We drew closer, and one of the lower, dock petals reshaped, splitting at its base, parting into an arched entrance. Bruiser gasped. Wole ruffled her hair.

'Impressive, yes?'

The *Lotus* was a looker, but it had purpose too. It had been designed and built by fellow Ficials as part of 'Project Martello', a ring of sea stations Control had strung around the British coast. The *Lotus* had served as part internment camp, holding hundreds of displaced Reals, and part missile shield, its petals clasped around a silo loaded with anti-ballistic missiles. It had never been intended to sail the Atlantic, but had adapted well. When Ficials built something, we really *built* it.

Beneath it stretched a subsurface mast structure, mounting the labs where I'd been held so long. I imagined Darnbar down there now, pulling on her protective gear, rubbing her hands together at the thought of resuming experiments. I considered jumping clear of the *White Bear* and swimming for it, but knew I'd only swim back. Where Marsh went, I went.

We followed the *Minion* and *Godwin* into the dock petal, entering a flooded dry dock. Lights bloomed a stark welcome. Bruiser and I looked at each other in surprise. Wole clapped me on the shoulder.

'It's not a flattering light.'

The petal sealed shut behind us. Supports clunked and shifted below, clamping the *White Bear*'s hull in position. The *Minion* and *Godwin* were bracketed too, and the waters began to drain below us. Dockhands swung cranes overhead, and threw out gangplanks.

The low hum of Ficial engines cut out, replaced by Real voices crying welcomes and jokes in a dozen languages. Wole and the crew gathered the children on the dock, where they huddled, intimidated and afraid.

Then a familiar sound echoed in the vault. A kind of indignant, impatient exclamation.

A bark.

The dog squirmed through the legs of the Real stevedores and broke across the dock, causing the children to squeal in delight. The wiry black blur raced down the gangway, a pink tongue lolling from bright white teeth, and cavorted about my feet. Pistol remembered me. I knelt, caught his legs as they pawed at mine, scratched him vigorously behind the ears and held him close. We both made a lot of desperate noises. I hadn't seen my dog in months.

Marsh appeared at my side.

'Would you two like some privacy?'

Pistol barked at her, struggled to turn and lick her face keenly. She screwed her eyes shut, laughed, and let him do his thing. Then she marched up the ramp to the dock. I followed, Bruiser at my side. I paused, lowered the hound to her height.

'Want to pet him? It helps you think.'

The child wasn't sure. She reached a trembling hand and cautiously scratched Pistol's wiry fur. The dog leaned into the action, closed his eyes, snorted approval. Half a smile broke onto the kid's face.

'Dog therapy,' said a voice. 'It never fails.'

Bridget. The last time I'd seen her she'd been caked in mud and dust, pulled from the ruins of a collapsed skyscraper. Time on the *Lotus* had been good to her. Her complexion, once red raw with fierce, flaring spots, had turned merely ruddy. She looked well fed and rested, dressed in old IS fatigues, a pack on her shoulder. I dropped the dog and stood.

'I heard you were still around.'

She rolled her eyes.

'Nice to see you too, Ken.' She frowned at me. 'Are you all right? I've been worried, all this time. What have they been doing to you down there?'

I pointed at the *White Bear*, now mounted beside the smaller boats over the drained dock, like toys on display.

'You don't participate in these pleasure cruises?'

'Come off,' she said. 'I'm no Argonaut. I look after the littles.'

She crouched to Bruiser and held out a cupped hand.

'Hello,' she said. 'My name's Bridget. What's yours? *¿Cómo te llamas?*'

Bruiser only glared.

'She's a quiet one,' I explained.

'Ah,' said Bridget. 'I've a cure for that.'

She pulled the pack off her shoulder, produced a drink can. She opened it, sipped, handed it to the frowning girl. Bruiser tasted, considered, then guzzled the rest. Bridget stepped past her, handed supplies to the other children. In minutes she had them holding hands, lining up to follow her out of the dock.

'You want to come with us?' she asked.

'I have something to do first.'

She shrugged.

'Come visit,' she said. 'I'll show you around.'

I loitered on the stage, Pistol panting by my boot, and watched

20

Marsh work the dock, speaking to her exhausted crew. She handed out bottles of water, spoke to each in turn, slapped palms with those who had the energy, gripped the shoulders of the flagging. They looked at her like as if she were made of stained glass. Only Wole touched her, hooking his arm around her waist.

I glanced at Pistol.

'I should have tossed him overboard.'

Pistol licked his snout, having no comment. I looked up again, found Marsh approaching, smiling in a puzzled way. I held my breath. She tossed me a water bottle. I fumbled the catch, juggled it before my hands would behave.

'Nice Ficial dexterity there.' She smiled. 'So, happy to be home?'

I looked about the entry petal, a damp military pen with all the warmth of the seabed. She frowned.

'That looks like a no.'

'Maybe you forgot. Before today's little jaunt I spent a few months trapped in Darnbar's care. Home doesn't really describe it.'

'Any port in a storm, right?'

She took the water out of my hand, unscrewed it, drank. I watched the muscles in her neck move, until she gasped and shrugged. She offered me the bottle. I accepted, pressed my lips where hers had been. I poured some into my palm and held it out to Pistol. He lapped it up, making a good noise. I patted his side.

'I'm a little surprised to find you taking the Kin's shilling.'

Marsh's lower lip jutted out at me.

'Why not? He offered me the chance to do something meaningful. To build something for these kids.'

'You don't question his motives at all?'

Those eyes clobbered me for a moment.

Why are you picking on her, you idiot? Tell her what she means to you.

She doesn't want to hear that.

Oh, she'd rather argue?

Then a whistle echoed in the chamber. Over Marsh's shoulder, at the distant hatch, stood Wole.

She waved to him. Turned back to me. Sighed.

'Ken. I can't imagine what you've been through. That's between you Ficials.'

We're not Ficial any more. Does nobody listen?

'But you don't yet understand what we're doing here,' she said, 'and I'm too tired to explain. You need to hear it from your own kind.'

She pulled back her sleeve and tapped something onto her bracelet. It chimed. She slipped the hoop from her wrist, clapped it between her palms, shaping a flat, grey disc. She handed it to me. Her fingers brushed my palm.

An image fizzed on the device, popped and resolved into a face.

It was my face. Or, at least, a previous face of mine. It was square-jawed and sharp-eyed. A mirror to a lost past.

'Kenstibec,' said Kinnare. 'Time we had a chat.'

The crew filtered away, leaving me in the dock petal hatch, peering into a gloomy, echoing tunnel. Pistol panted at my side, waiting.

Kinnare wanted me to head below for a chat. Well, he could wait. First I would familiarise myself with Marsh's bracelet, where I'd discovered a schematic of the *Lotus*. I committed every passageway, ventilation shaft and bulkhead to memory. If I were going to stay here I would know my way around. I wouldn't become a prisoner again.

The *Lotus* designer had modelled the vessel on Sahba's New Delhi temple: a nine-sided structure of twenty-seven petals arranged into three concentric rising walls, forming the shape of a great lotus flower bud. The arrangement was mounted on a huge, circular tri-maran hull.

The smallest 'dock' petals ringed the edge of the vessel. Shaped like puffin beaks, they contained moorings and dry facilities for the *White Bear* and other craft, although only two seemed operational. Nine taller 'hold' petals formed the thicker middle wall: forty-metre-high vaulted living and storage spaces. At the centre, slender as wings, were the nine 'silo' petals, a protective shield drawn around the arsenal at the heart of the *Lotus*.

Each petal was a charged arrangement of Flex, the same wonder material that formed the bracelet. Each could reshape into intricate arrangements, splinter into other lightweight, resilient structures. Under ocean conditions the hold petals grew interconnecting canopies over the exposed hull, creating a great looping tunnel around the *Lotus*, a deck passageway that linked the hold and dock petals.

Looking at it from the surface the *Lotus* might appear top-heavy, but the central hull dropped deep below the surface. Projecting from its centre was the Root: a kind of sub-sea mast, dropping forty metres deep, containing an elevator and access shafts. It sported two great Ficial engine pods halfway down its length, and terminated in a circular chamber called the Axis. The Axis spread spokes to nine habitats designated as pearls, though the disc was sketchy on their structure and purpose. It only showed me the way down.

I'd spent considerable time in one of those pearls, and couldn't say I missed it. On the surface there was drink, fresh air and Marsh. Below were restraints and jailers. Still, as much as I'd changed, Darnbar and Kinnare were my kind. I selected 'Directions' on the disc display and followed a beckoning, blinking marker out to and along the deck passageway.

The scrit-scrit of Pistol's claws echoed in the space. We passed the great knifing walls of a hold petal, the disc marking it as Dormitory, then another, identified as Galley. We passed its ridge, and came upon a seam glowing in the passageway surface. I stopped, observed a rectangular space roll down, shape into a ramp, lowered to the deck below.

We descended, following a spiral tunnel running through the trimaran hull. Round Flex hatches unzipped at our approach, resealed behind us, until we finally stepped into a central chamber, where the Root's elevator column stood, white and Doric. I glanced up, knowing that we were directly below the *Lotus* silo.

The door to the elevator unpeeled. I looked at it for a while.

You're not seriously going to go down there again?

Of course I am. Can't be afraid, can I?

You'd rather be stupid?

I told Pistol to stay. He whined but obeyed, planting his rear.

'Good lad.'

I stepped into the elevator, eyes closed. I kept them that way, heart racing, until the elevator came to a halt, opening its doors on the Axis. I stepped out into a cool, narrow, white space, into mute, dry air. I circled the elevator column, passed nine Flex hatches, seals toned orange, each leading to a separate pearl. I knelt, ran my hand over the deck, felt something like coral.

The seal around a hatch glowed green. It peeled open silently. I stood, passed through it, edged along a blinding white corridor, through another hatch, into a warm, sphere-shaped structure, bisected by an oxynitride partition. A fat mahogany and cast iron ship's chair sat alone on my side of the divide. Beyond the barrier there was a garden. Plant life packed the borders of the chamber: saplings, vines and shrubs, jasmine, mistletoe, honeysuckle and heliotrope ringed the space in crisp, orderly arrangements, trimmed and blooming from hanging baskets and pots. A Victorian, orderly sort of garden, surrounding a vinyl upholstered bench, and a large dashboard where read-outs fizzed, projecting updates from across the *Lotus*: silo temperature, engine condition, navigation charts, and numerous high-definition surveillance feeds. There seemed to be a small hatch, perhaps to an air lock, recessed in the wall to my right.

Two figures sat on the bench. Darnbar was dressed in a lab coat, short hair tucked behind ears, held there by glasses, reading her flex. The other one looked like me. No, the other one *was* me. Another Ficial optimised for construction, born in the bowels of a facility buried under Brixton. Another Power Nine. Another Rover Model. Another 'I'. He stood and folded his arms. Small cutting tools hung from his belt.

I peered at this reflection, and the reflection peered back. We were both pretty startled with what we found. In all the time I'd been Darnbar's prisoner, Kinnare hadn't bothered to see me. He hadn't even been there for my release.

The ventilators hummed.

Kinnare was the first to speak.

'Welcome, brother,' he said. 'Please sit.'

'I'll stand.'

I leaned on the barrier and breathed on it, tracing an 'M' in the mist.

Kinnare stepped back. As a Ficial he wasn't supposed to feel one way or another about me, but I thought I saw disgust tweak his lips. With no cure, they were worried about contracting my virus.

Then why are they keeping us here?

'We invited you here because we imagine you have questions,' said Kinnare. 'We are prepared to answer them.'

I tapped on the partition.

'First question. Do you have something to eat back there?'

'You can eat in the galley later,' said Kinnare. 'For now we want to explain our position. Our mission here. We want to.'

'You can skip the manifesto,' I said. 'I might have been interested if you hadn't left me in the care of Doctor Moreau there.' I pointed out his companion. 'Her medicine has just about scuppered my faith in Ficial solidarity. All I want to know is how I get off this tub.'

Kinnare blinked. He plucked a pair of secateurs from his belt and approached a bright green fern. He ran a finger along a branch.

'Really? You could have escaped easily enough in the Park. We gave you every opportunity. Marsh was under orders not to stop you if you ran.'

'The Caribbean cruise was a test?'

He cut the suspect branch free and pocketed it.

'Six months' study has convinced Darnbar that there is no cure for your . . . condition. But that was all we could establish about you. We had no idea what was taking place in your mind.'

'All those dreams,' said Darnbar. 'We weren't sure what to expect.'

I chewed on some words and swallowed them.

'Now we know more,' said Kinnare, moving his attention along the row of plants, seeking out imperfections. 'You have returned. I think, despite everything, you still consider yourself Ficial. That leaves you with nowhere to go. Your place is here with us.'

'Bullshit,' I said, surprising myself. 'I could go home. Find a barricade.'

Kinnare tipped his head to one side.

'They're gone, brother. All of them.'

I stared at the mirror image for a moment. He was Ficial, so he couldn't lie. I slumped onto the ship's chair, swivelled it one way and another, turning the news.

'How?'

Kinnare plucked a flex from the couch, tapped on its surface. He turned it towards me, showed me another Ficial face I recognised. A set of green eyes.

'It was an experimental Soldier Model,' said Kinnare. 'I believe you encountered it?'

'He tried to kill me, if that's what you mean.'

Kinnare turned the flex, regarded the image.

'Prior to your meeting it toured every barricade, contaminating water supplies with your virus. All on the orders of Control. It did an efficient job. To our knowledge, we on this craft represent the last of Engineered kind.'

He rolled up the flex and tossed it to Darnbar. She folded it neatly into her lab coat's top pocket.

I felt a little seasick.

Every barricade, gone. It seemed incredible. I'd toured most of them over the years – ruined cities like Edinburgh and Leeds, each sheltering behind an improvised wall, each besieged by tribes of Reals. I'd helped excavate bunkers and passageways deep beneath their surfaces, dug safe accommodation for hundreds of fellow Ficials. Back then we had imagined we would wait out the nuclear winter, until Control returned and led us to broad, sunlit uplands. None of us had imagined Control wished us dead.

I pointed at Kinnare.

'How did you survive?'

'I was stationed in Liverpool Barricade,' he said. He replaced the secateurs on his belt, produced a cloth, and polished the large flat leaf of a rubber plant. 'The *Lotus* was a hobby of mine. I was trying out a new hull covering, to see if I could get it floating again. We were at sea, putting it through trials, when the barricade fell. I sailed for some time, searching for survivors. All I found was death. We are an endangered species, Kenstibec. Like Man.'

He dug his fingers into the soil of a dragon plant, stepped away, sniffed.

'So why keep me around?' I asked. 'Why run tests on me for six months if it was already too damn late?'

Kinnare didn't reply, inspecting the flowers of a jade plant. Darnbar stood, adjusted her glasses. She had no need of spectacles, but Real patients found a four-eyed doctor more trustworthy.

'Kenstibec,' she said, 'you have taught us so much.'

'Delighted to hear it.'

'Initially we planned to create some kind of vaccine from your infected blood. This proved impossible. We considered culling you then, until—'

'Until we discussed it,' said Kinnare. 'Until we realised that Ficial kind is gone for good. Brixton production facility is gone. Our barricades are lost, our species reduced to a handful. There is no hope of a resurrection.'

26

He turned his eyes from the plant to me.

'We were never meant to inherit the Earth. We were meant to better Man. Instead we made war on him, as Control ordered. Well, Control is gone now, and we few remain. That leaves us in a quandary: what to do with our remaining time? Do we sit out here, immobile and useless, as we did in the barricades? Watch as humanity dies out? Or do we intervene in their progress, as we were created to do? Do we help them make a future?'

I shrugged.

'How would we do that?'

Darnbar spoke up.

'By building a better humanity, Kenstibec. By gathering young people and shaping them in our image. We are travelling the world in search of the best genetic stock. We bring them here, educate them, induct them into a new society, one without God, money or democracy. We plan to create a new culture, one where each human lives to further the species, not the individual.'

I took a moment to process.

'Real Power 2? Seriously?'

'Exactly,' said Kinnare. 'That's why we tolerate your presence, Kenstibec. For now we need the adult Reals' cooperation; to crew the ships, to locate the best infants, to care for them. They have agreed to work with us in exchange for food, water, shelter. The guilt of collaboration is eased by the liberation of slaves. And by seeing as little of us as possible.

'But we know how swiftly dissatisfaction takes hold of the Real mind. We cannot be certain of them, even superior examples like Marsh. This is an uneasy alliance, and we need to be sure we are working to the same purpose. That is where you can help us.'

I nodded, beginning to understand.

'You want me to spy on them.'

'All that we require,' said Darnbar, 'is that you report any hint of unrest.'

'Like I said – spy.'

'We cannot allow this project to be compromised by the prejudices of the last civilisation. We intend to create something better. In return for your help, you may remain aboard this craft, in a safe, sane society.'

'And,' said Darnbar, 'in the company of the woman of your dreams.'

I felt like ripping the chair out of its housing and tossing it at her. Instead I slid out of it and headed for the exit.

'Where are you going?' said Kinnare.

'I'm hungry.'

'Will you work with us, Kenstibec?'

'I'll think about it.'

The hatch remained stubbornly closed. I looked over my shoulder at the other me behind the glass.

'You'll need that,' he said, pointing at the chair. I picked up the Flex disc from the chair, slapped it between my palms. It reshaped into a bracelet. I slipped it over my wrist.

'You can move about the *Lotus* now,' he said, taking a closer look at some imperfect leaf. 'Just don't lose it.'

The hatch slipped open. I made to step out, then hesitated.

'Just one thing,' I said. Kinnare pinched the leaf free, looked up. 'What about all those Reals without the right genes? Like the ones we left in the Park. What happens to them in your new world?'

Kinnare shrugged.

'They will not be allowed to breed.'

He resumed his inspection of his plants. I thought of the drones on the *White Bear*, the bulges under each wing.

'I see.'

I left them in their pearl, wondering what Marsh was doing, thinking I needed a drink.

Pistol waited for me at the elevator doors. I bent and embraced him, letting him pant in my ear. No matter what, the hound would always be happy to see me.

We retraced our steps along the looping tunnel, Pistol skipping ahead, running his nose over the surfaces. We rolled up the ramp to the deck passageway, retraced our steps to the hold petal marked 'Galley'. I tapped a command into the bracelet and a hatch unzipped. We stepped inside.

It was the kind of space that made you crane your neck. A forty-metre-tall atrium, each surface featureless Flex. I tapped the bracelet, discovered that the walls had display functionality. I selected a white sand beach and blue sky, watched the projection sweep into life up the walls, climbing to the summit.

I picked through rows of fixed metal benches and tables and searched an open kitchen. I filled one bowl with tinned carrots for Pistol, another with beans.

There was no pleasure in the eating. I was a robotic arm, pouring matter down a flesh chute. Only Pistol's satisfied gnashing distracted me from thoughts of dead barricades, of doppelgangers, of Marsh. I took off the bracelet, shaped it into a flat plate and scanned the *Lotus* schematic, hoping to find a marker reading: Rum Store.

I didn't find one. Still, there was something almost as interesting.

Garage.

It was the only other dock petal labelled active. I headed out of the mess to the passageway and walked the undulating deck, Pistol following. I passed two dormant dock petals, paused outside the third. I heard machine tools turning within. I tapped the gauntlet on the hatch and waited. A low scraping sound escaped the mechanism, and an orange light revolved a warning overhead. The hatch unpeeled. A figure was waiting for me, dressed in oil-stained overalls. His arms were held limp before him, useless without a tool. It was a Ficial, a Mechanic Model. One I knew well.

'Kenstibec,' said Rick. 'Whoa. You look terrible.'

'Aren't you worried?' I asked him. Rick sat beside me, our legs dangling over the dock. He sipped a tin mug of coffee.

'Worried? About what, K?'

'The disease. I'm infectious, or hadn't you heard?'

He glanced at the gauntlet.

'Yes, yes, I heard all right. But it's in your blood, isn't it?' I agreed that it was. 'Well, don't bleed on me, then.'

'Kinnare and Darnbar don't seem so relaxed.'

'Let them fret. I'm busy.'

He certainly was. The dry dock was drained, every surface buried beneath the wreckage of Rick's work. Dozens of benches littered with ordnance of all kinds, teetering structures of timber, Gronts and steel, great hanging banners of uncharged Flex, clusters of old monitors and keyboards, a muddle of crates stamped in a dozen languages, machine parts hanging in cargo nets. The air was a choking, sulphurous mist. Beneath us, a shape rested on supports, concealed by a heavy tarp. The other side of the dock was a structure like a long, upturned xylophone, rectangular cabinets of different heights, packed with an amber fluid.

'What are you doing here, Rick?'

'What I'm optimised for,' he said. 'What any Mechanic Model would do here. I make things go.'

'I mean, how did you get out of Edinburgh?'

'Oh,' he said, watching Pistol move in and out of sight. 'I had my own water supply in the garage. Only realised what had happened on the surface when Superior TV went off the air. By the time I went up top the Reals were all over the city. Ghastly. I sneaked out in an old fishing boat. Kinnare picked me up off Torness, waist deep in a corrosive slick. Took me two weeks to grow my legs back.' He eyed my gauntlet again. 'Course some of us have it worse than others. You'll have to let me take a look at that arm of yours.'

'So it's true. Everyone in Edinburgh's dead?'

He sipped his coffee. 'Of course it's true.'

'And now you're working with Kinnare?'

'Whatever keeps me busy. Speaking of which, your timing is excellent. I could use your help with a project I have under way. Interested?'

He scuttled around the edge of the dock to the xylophone, which stood almost as tall as him. He slapped the surface.

'Special nanotech production,' he said. 'Very hush-hush. Most of the Reals have no idea. You see, the concept is that . . .'

He stopped, tossed his tin cup.

'I'd explain this better in the silo. Come on, no time to lose.'

He urged me to follow, skipping along a path carved through stacked metal shelves, body panels and tyres. It reminded me of trips I'd paid to his old garage, the bunker under Leith. I softened at the thought of our shared time. I fought the urge to hug him.

What the hell is wrong with you?

He stopped in a kind of clearing, hands flashing through the mess of parts on a soot-black workbench. In a moment he was sealing up a squat missile, tucking it under his arm.

'Seed projectile mark one,' he said. 'No primary armament yet, but the distribution device is ready for testing. What say we give it a shot, while the tribes slumber, eh?'

He barged past me, not seeking an answer, and re-entered the confusion of the workshop, working through the tight alleys towards the hatch. We stepped out to the deck passageway and turned left, Pistol running about Rick's feet. He clutched the missile to his chest.

'Never saw you as a pet person, K.'

'Well, I've changed.'

'I noticed.' He gestured up, at the Flex ribs and arches. 'Quite a boat, isn't she? It was me who made her float, you know. When Kinnare picked me up it was little better than a colander with sails. Now . . . Well, you'll see.'

He stopped, turned into the narrowing space between two hold petals. He tapped his bracelet, stepped back. A narrow space opened, forming a passage to the silo. We passed along it, into an inner passageway, where a narrow miniature railway hugged the tubular silo.

Rick tapped his bracelet again, entering a code. A seam appeared in the silo wall, a hatch dividing. I made to move, but Rick held up his hand.

'Ah, no dogs, I'm afraid.'

I explained it to Pistol. He was offended, I could tell, but graciously he sat on his haunches and licked his snout, allowing Rick and me to step inside.

Rick narrowed one eye at me.

'You do realise that animal can't understand you?'

I shrugged. 'So you might think. What are we doing here, Rick?'

He clicked his tongue.

'We are testing stage two of K and D's grand design.'

Dim orange light swelled in the silo, revealing the missile array: a wheel within another wheel, mounted on a spar in the eighty-foot-tall silo, like a huge gyroscope. Both the inner and outer wheels were lined with vacant cradles.

'She's unloaded?' I asked.

'Fired off half the ammunition during the nuclear attack,' explained Rick. 'Intercepted most of the warheads headed for Europe, you know. Very effective design really.'

'I seem to remember,' I said, 'taking a thermonuclear blast in the face.'

'Yes. Well, no design is perfect. I remove the remaining missiles while we do our testing. These gyros can be a bit twitchy.'

Rick shuffled to a ladder on the silo wall and began to climb, moving like something amphibian.

'Yes, yes, these clean-up plans take up a good deal of my time.'

I followed.

'What are you cleaning up?'

He paused, glanced down at me.

'The world, of course.'

He hopped off the ladder at a gantry halfway up the silo. I joined him as he tapped at his bracelet again. I bent over and gasped metallic air. Rick hadn't broken a sweat. The platform lurched forward, towards the gyro's outer wheel, Rick cradling the missile like a baby.

'And how,' I asked, watching his strange, halting movements, 'do you intend to clean up the world?'

'I've developed a new strain of nanotech, Ken,' he said. 'The filth-eater I call it. Started out of necessity really. We spent months scouring the coast back home, searching for survivors. It was hellish keeping this thing afloat. It's got the seakeeping of a bus, and we sprung a leak every five minutes. Well, you know what the seas are like back home. Damn corrosive slicks chew through the hull way too easily. So, Kinnare put me to task.

'Well, you know me. I love a challenge. Created a copper bottom for the post-war age, I did. A huge nano-sieve, strapped to the root and hull. It not only protects the *Lotus*, it neutralises all that crap in the sea. See?'

He carefully clipped the missile into a waiting cradle, stroked it like a nervous pet, and tapped his bracelet again. The platform reared back towards the silo wall. He held his limp arms out before him, showing me his knuckles.

'So I gets to thinking, I wonder if we can use this tech a bit more proactively, right? Because if we can, if we can clean up the seas, well, that's making a better world for Kinnare's better Reals, right? So we ran some tests in the Thames, and – bingo. We cleaned the whole dirty old river up. Water got so good you could swim in it. Easy, really. Pander made nanotech to seek out cancer cells. All I did was create tech with a taste for other nasties. Your nano binds to your nasty particle, then binds to other bound nanos, until they roll all those pollutants into one stinking, 'orrid mess. You've seen the old footage, right? Of the cancer pellet? A tumour formed into a perfect ball and squeezed out? Well, we just did that on a larger scale. Buried a wrecking ball of toxic crap.'

He unclipped the bracelet from his wrist, clapped it into a hand slate, and tapped instructions. The gyroscope hummed, twisted and turned, the cradle repositioning as it ascended on the great wheel, up to the cluster of silo doors.

Rick made another clicking sound, then stepped onto the ladder, climbing again. I followed.

'So now I'm thinking: well, why not have a go at the cloud, right? Why not shoot adapted tech up there, seed the cloud, neutralise all that mess?'

'We're doing this now?'

'No, no,' he said. 'No tech as yet. There are a couple of wrinkles to sort out first. A couple of issues raising their heads under simulation. This is just the test of the distribution mechanism. I've loaded the stub with a little cocktail of my own creation, something that will react with the cloud and produce High Lights. We want a good umbrella spray, see?'

The ladder terminated under a hatch built into the silo roof. Rick twisted it open manually, pushed out. He disappeared for a moment, then reached down a helping hand. I took it, let him drag me onto the surface.

We stood atop the silo, under clasped petal tips. Rick tapped away at the Flex slate, and the petals peeled silently open, revealing the wall of cloud overhead, admitting the roar and spray of the gale outside. Rick clipped us to a guardrail by a safety harness, as the huge petals folded back on themselves, and the wind roared over the silo roof.

'Bit blustery,' yelled Rick over the ocean roar. 'Well, we'll go ahead and test anyway.'

'What are we doing up here?' I called back. 'Let's watch on TV.'

'Negative. I want eyes on this.' He frowned at me. 'It's perfectly safe.'

Before us a grid of hatches spread across the silo roof. Rick tapped the slate.

The missile jumped from a hatch with a pop, a cold launch tossing the stubby dart on a piston of air. We watched its glowing nose rise to fifty feet, slowing, before the booster fired and hurtled the rocket up, into the cloud.

A few seconds passed, before something crumpled overhead. We peered up, saw a great yellow shape bloom in the cloud, reaching out like roots in the sky.

'Perfect,' I said, impressed. 'I'd forgotten how good you are, Rick.'

He emitted a few clicking noises, rolled up the flex around his wrist again, and invited me to go below. He clambered down the hatch, as the petals slowly rose, transforming to a closed bud.

I lingered, watching the yellow streaks fizz a nicotine light over the dead ocean. The petals made a crushing soda-can sound as they struggled to reform in the gale.

Then, I saw it, through the reshaping Flex structures. The silhouette of a black arrowhead, slipping down a wave, about a mile to starboard. A ship? Before I could be sure the petals stretched up, obscuring the view.

I stepped down, into the warmth of the silo. The arrowhead was an apparition, I assured myself, another phantom conjured by unsettled nerves and exhausted mind.

I asked Rick where I could sleep.

The first figure I have seen, it waits for me with its hands behind its back in the centre of the crossroads. I peer at it as I approach. I have tried to conjure a face before, in this dream, but they fizzle as nothing more than eyes and teeth.

Now I walk beside it I know that it has no face, or that it has many and I should not try to pick one out. It is in flux, speaking to hundreds, thousands more, the packed and the unpacked. An ever-present, ever-absent parent. The source of the Signal.

– Imminent, it says, tapping its watch.

And now I know that I am about to be unpacked, face my First Day. I will occupy the form of a male adult, draw on the same genetic store of flesh, hair, bone and blood, only tuned to perfection, to the best possible format to accomplish the tasks of my model. I will share this form with Control's other children.

I know that I am not different from humanity, but an improvement, an augmentation, an example to them.

People. I do not know People.

Control stops, in this white space, where all features have dropped away, leaving only two figures and not even that, only their intermingled voices.

– You cannot.

I learn that I can only learn about people, other models even, after un-packing. Some things cannot be taught while we are packed. The first models were sent out that way, their minds uploaded with carefully prepared proto-cols, but they were well-read infants, and they could not hold themselves together, they could not understand people, they could not register impatience and jealousy and other feelings that rule the lives of people.

We are here to preserve them, these people, not to replace them, even if they are inferior, and beyond maintenance our presence shall reveal their potential, it will be manifest what more they can become. For evolution has brought them so far, but it brought them greed, lust and God too, and these things have inspired them but will ruin them, for these remarkable minds of theirs their capacity is not realised. They are compromised by animal feeling, by the vessel whose decay they live to accelerate and there must be an intervention now by Engineered minds free of feelings, or distraction by bodies. We are free of sickness and rot, we are here to show them what existence can be without these redundant products of their evolutionary story, these manacles that must be shaken off the future.

When do I begin work?

Control stops, picks the watch off its wrist, holds it in its palm, passes a hand over it. It disappears.

And I comprehend that time is not relevant. We are a new way of life. The Engineered lifespan is that of the flatworm. There will be time.

First I must complete development. I will be unpacked beneath a place called Brixton, part of a city called London. I will train, test, adapt. I will interact with people and the Signal will guide me through the process and teach me how to move outside the dream, in their world, or what they have made of it.

Control stops, holds out its hand, and I follow it to a great blank, and something else whispers:

– Here we go.

BROTHERS

Damp grey snow rolled over the Park. The slave market was quiet and gloomy, discouraged by the storm. Now the wind had died a few predatory customers appeared, slumping in the fitful lantern gleam. Traders hunched from their tents, goggles down and masks donned. They pulled tarpaulins from cages, revealed their wares.

'How are they doing?' I asked.

Marsh glanced at me, strands of hair slicked across her cheeks, moisture pooling at the tip of her nose. We were standing behind a crumpled billboard, shivering.

'They're taking their bloody time about it.' She shook her head. 'Oh, Carlos, everything has to be an argument, doesn't it? Gah. They've moved. Come on.' She gripped my arm like a tiller and steered me over the mud.

She'd sent Wole to make the buy, accompanied by the *Lotus* cook, Carlos, a young Colombian with a head of uncommonly tall, thick black hair. We watched from the gloomy eaves of shuttered stores, from behind cages, keeping our distance.

'Why not make the buy yourself?'

'Dangerous to be recognised as multiple buyers. People might think we're worth ripping off.'

She circled us round the moans of a squat, covered cage.

'Then why come back at all?'

'There are plenty of good subjects here,' she said, 'representing a broad genetic sample. We might never find another concentration like it. Kinnare agreed.'

We caught sight of Wole again, exiting a trader's tent, flourishing another cigarette carton. The trader followed, banging a cosh on the bars of a cage and bellowing. Children rose from sodden blankets, gathered shivering for inspection.

Carlos, seeing the trader occupied with Wole, crouched to the young ones' height. He pressed his thumb to each head in turn, examining his bracelet. Then he searched his pockets, pressed something into a child's hand, then another.

'He's giving them candy,' I said. 'That'll draw attention.'

'Wole's on it.'

The big man did well. In one move he sidestepped the trader, reached for Carlos, wrenched him to his feet. I thought the children would protest, but they were quiet, resigned.

Wole turned, smiling, and pressed the transaction, hand tight around Carlos's neck. Fingers were shown, counted. The package was exchanged, the prison opened, and five children beckoned from within.

Wole and Carlos headed for the exit, their purchases shuffling between them. We regrouped in one of Fantasyburg's muddier alleys. Carlos scowled at us.

'What are we doing, putting money in their pockets? That's goddam evil back there, man. We should hang every one of those . . . Those . . .'

Marsh put a finger to her lips.

'Not in front of the children.'

She took Wole to one side. Carlos handed out more candy, then turned his anger on me.

'I guess you think we're all like that, right? Bunch of fucking conquistadors?'

I shrugged. *You are if you're desperate enough.*

Well, perhaps not all.

I watched Marsh out of the corner of my eye. She was smiling at Wole.

'Hey!' snapped Carlos. 'You listening to me?'

I turned, met his eyes.

'You can't help everyone,' I said. 'Don't blame yourself. Maybe you should have a drink.'

He shivered violently. Sighed. Dug in his jacket pocket and drew out a flask.

'You're right.'

38

He drank and gasped. I held out my hand.

'Nice,' he said, handing me the bottle. 'Just a sip.'

I took two, sighing at the burn. The children watched us, shivering and damp. Two looked related, a boy and girl sharing blonde, bobbed hair and crystal-blue eyes. They were better nourished than the other three, who were bone-thin, black-haired and tanned.

'All right, let's get them out of here,' said Marsh, returning.

She urged the children on, and we slipped through the passages for the dock, a cold wind rattling the wrecks and lean-tos. We took a bad turn once, then twice, lost our way. We came to a dead end and doubled back, Marsh cursing the Park's designers.

Wole tapped my shoulder, his eyes rolling overhead. I glanced up, saw something moving atop the wrecks, shifting in and out of focus. Two Reals in conical white hoods, shadowing us. I unclipped the stun gun and checked the charge.

We finally emerged onto the docks, saw the mess of craft rolling at their moorings, the jetties deserted. Marsh led the children onto the *White Bear*, hurrying them into the hold. Wole and I cast off, watching the hooded, prowling silhouettes. The big man frowned.

'What's their game, do you imagine?'

'Nothing friendly,' I said.

I sat on the aft deck, as the *White Bear* followed the channels and passages back to the open sea. I headed into the hold, in search of another drink. Carlos knelt with the children, working at their chains with a bent fork.

'Sick,' he said. 'How sick do you have to be, to do this to children?'

'It's OK if they're older?'

'Shut up.'

He dropped onto his backside and tossed the fork.

'I cannot get these things off.'

I wobbled over the tipping floor, stood over the two blondes. I pointed to their chains, and they lifted their binding, watched me clasp it in my gauntlet fingers.

'Mind your eyes.' I tightened my grip on the chain, snapped it in two, then clipped the neck braces free. I moved along the chain gang, repeating the process. The children tumbled away from each other, seizing their own space in the hold. All except the blondes, who sat together.

Carlos whistled.

'We'll never need a can opener with you around, Ficial.'

I sat on a cot, Carlos eyeing the gauntlet in awe. I inspected it, noted white, dusty corrosion around the joints.

Carlos busied himself with the children, handing out towels, fresh clothes and water.

'When I joined the *Lotus*,' he said, 'when they picked me up, starving and alone? I was all like: I will jump ship the first chance I get. Kinnare's idiot mission was just a way off that goddam beach, you know? I figured there'd be somewhere better. But every place we see, it is worse than the last. I thought somewhere bigger, where there were more people. But . . . Hell, what a world.'

'We've only been around the Atlantic coast,' I said. 'Barely scratched the surface. There's the whole Indian Ocean to sail yet. The Pacific, too.'

'Oh, yeah, right.' He tousled a kid's hair with a towel. 'You know something? You don't look like a Ficial.'

'I've heard it said.'

'Kinnare was the first I met. How is that? Not that I regret it, you understand.'

'Most governments were too busy falling apart to invest in Ficial tech, in those last days. Besides, Ficials were restricted technology. British only. Even after privatisation there was an export ban. I think the emergency government thought we gave them an advantage.'

The blondes were listening. Perhaps they knew of Ficials and were afraid.

'Some advantage,' said Carlos, gently picking up the child under the arms, laying him onto a bench. 'I hear what you do over there. I hear how Ficials rule.'

The conversation was turning. Every Real I encountered was afraid, then curious. They all wanted to hear about the cull: body counts; methodology. They were always fascinated, right up until the moment they became disgusted. I wasn't in the mood. I moved along to every Real's favourite subject.

'What about you?' I asked. 'What did you get up to before the *Lotus*?'

Carlos towelled one of the blonde's heads. The child jerked under the assault, but made no sound.

'I was a cook, the same as here. But one day they evacuate Monteria and suddenly I am homeless. And then the Americans come, great herds of them, and we all begin to starve. It is very cruel for a cook to starve.'

'Americans. Refugees?'

He flapped the damp towel before the blonde, folded it up.

'I used to wonder how it happened. All those Americans, and all poor, and all hungry.'

I shrugged.

'Too many weapons and not enough money. Not a good combination. Every Real empire falls in on itself, tears itself apart. Fixing elections doesn't help, of course. Especially when your candidate is a religious fanatic.'

'President Lay,' sneered Carlos. 'Do you know, Ficial, that some of the crew believe Lay was right? They think God will return and judge us.'

'They'd better keep quiet about it. Kinnare wouldn't like that kind of talk. Especially around the kids.'

I sat quietly for a moment. The blondes stared at me in the dim lamp glow. The boat tipped, rocked and creaked. Carlos sat, drew a comb from his pocket, tapped it on his heel and ran it through his locks. Then he took out his flask and drank. He noticed me watching him.

'I did not know that Ficials drank.'

He offered the flask. I tipped a little more burning rum down my throat, smacked my lips. Returned it. Carlos screwed the cap into place and shook his head.

'It stinks in here. Shall we head above board?'

We left the children in the hold, ascended to the deck, stood at the stern railing, drinking and watching our wake roll, white in the darkness. Streaks of colour wormed through the burning cloud. Ash snow gathered on our shoulders. Noon in the Caribbean.

Carlos examined me.

'What do I call you, Ficial?'

'My name is Kenstibec.'

He tried the name a few times. It didn't sound right to him.

'A drinking Ficial named Hensabeck. It is a strange world.'

Wole called to us. We turned, saw the big man leaning from the pilot house, beckoning us. We trailed up, boots clanking on the steps. Marsh stood at the wheel, delicate, powerful, flawed, perfect. Her breath made steam. There was a moment's silence.

'Well, nearly home,' she said. 'How are the children?'

'Goddam traumatised,' snapped Carlos. 'What do you expect? We should have broke every one of those kids out.'

'Oh, come!' said Wole. 'It's no use moaning. You could see the traders were armed to the teeth. What would you have us do – fight them all? The Park is finished. We took another shot at it and that's that. We have more pressing concerns now.'

'Like what?'

Marsh swung the eyes on me.

'Wole tells me you saw some characters in hoods?'

I shuffled in her gaze, unable to find a stance I was happy with.

'We both did,' I said. 'What about them?'

'I'm wondering,' said Marsh, 'if they're connected to our new friends.'

She handed me a set of binoculars, pointed astern. I searched the dark seas. It took a moment to spot it. A black shape, trailing us. A ship, maybe bigger than the *White Bear*. It seemed to be closing.

'That's no good.'

'No,' she said. 'It isn't. Carlos, go below, slow and quiet, and tell the kids to brace themselves.'

'Aye,' he said, heading out of the door, down the ladder.

'Ken, man the ropes and ready for a hard run into dock.'

I obeyed, jumping to the deck, edging round the outboard to take up the bow rope. Ahead, the great bulge of the *Lotus* was in sight, illuminations spreading over the petals.

I noticed something else: a silhouette, cutting between the *White Bear* and the *Lotus*. Another ship.

Something flared on its deck: sparking, arched trails, descending towards the *Lotus*. All missed. I had the feeling the next broadside might not. I waved frantically at the pilot house.

'Step on the gas!'

Marsh didn't need to be told. The *White Bear* pulsed into silent acceleration, lifting its prow to the sky, throwing me onto my back, sending me slipping over the wet deck. The children screamed. I scrambled to my feet, saw the new ship change course, cut towards us. Its features were discernible now – a triangular tower on a sleek black hull. Marsh turned hard to avoid it.

Too late. The vessel closed, levelled out and slapped hard into the port side. That set me rolling again, thrashing for a handhold. Then, gunning the engines, Marsh scraped us clear. I saw lights on the black frigate's bridge, a figure pointing. The *White Bear* gained speed, left the black ship with a tear in its side. We hurtled towards the dock petal, folded open and waiting.

We ran full pelt inside, slammed hard into the stage. I went flying onto the dockside, clattering into two deckhands. The waters gushed, draining fast as the petal closed and the *Lotus* engines powered up, racing the huge structure clear of the threat outside. Rick's engines sure did a job.

I closed my eyes. Heard muffled explosions. Carlos's voice. Light footsteps on a gangway.

I opened them up again to find the two blonde kids standing over me, staring like gulls.

'Will you two,' I asked, 'cut that out?'

The *Lotus* finally slowed, allowing the crew to throw up in peace. I fetched Pistol from the dormitory petal, where I'd left him to sit out our latest mission. I thought he'd be anxious for a stroll.

Marsh had secured me a bunk there, on the second of six Flex balconies that jutted in hoops from the walls of the petal vault. Hundreds of refugees had been locked in here, before the war. Nobody spoke of their fate, but their messages remained, scraped into the bunks: *Set us free. Adnan loves Ola. God sees all of this.*

I climbed the ladder, found Pistol straining on his leash, tongue lolling, panting hard and whimpering.

'That mutt's been whining non-stop for hours,' grumbled Boatswain, sitting up on his cot, scratching his furious scalp. 'Ten minutes to my watch and I haven't slept a fucking wink. This ain't a kennel, you know.'

'Name one way it's different.'

I took Pistol out, and began to circle the deck passage, enjoying the strange, peaceful trance that his company allowed. I listened to his panting, the faint crash of the sea, the spray pattering on the petals. The *Lotus* rocked gently. It was almost tranquil. Then I thought of

Marsh's breath, steaming in the pilot house. I pictured the line from her neck to her chin, arching like a viaduct.

I wonder what she's doing now?

Let's not start on that again. Think about something else. Something useful.

I looked at Pistol, the back of his head, ears bouncing gently.

'What does useful matter?'

Pistol made no comment.

Does she think about me?

Your obsession doesn't compel her to think of you.

I'm not obsessed.

No? Then change the fucking record.

I want to be with her.

I know, I know. You think I don't know?

Pistol paused, having selected a spot. He did his thing, and we ambled back towards the dormitory. I watched my feet, paced my thoughts to their rhythm. There was a weight on my back, like a lead impression of Marsh, but the walk had lightened it some.

I'd given up fighting these thoughts, learned to let them spin out and slow. It was part of what I'd become, whatever that was. Pistol was a big help. His wiry black presence made the world a little warmer. Life was the moment for him: these smells, these sounds, and nothing more.

He was satisfied with the walk, I could tell. There was a spring in his trot. The bracelet chimed as I re-entered the dorm. A message, or summons, from Kinnare.

I tied the dog to the cot and changed into dry clothes. I brushed my teeth and tried to feel more Ficial.

Then I headed to the Root. Marsh was waiting at the elevator, showered, togged in loose green overalls. Her cheeks were flushed.

'You headed down too?'

'That's right,' she said. 'Into the Uncanny Valley.' She turned away. 'Sorry.'

The elevator doors popped. I stepped into the cool, transparent cylinder after her, close enough to smell the salt in her hair. The elevator descended, making slow, shivering progress. I tried to think of something to say.

'Nice work spotting our tail.'

44

'Wole saw them.'

I clenched my teeth.

'Is there anything he can't do?'

She smiled.

'More than you'd think.'

I didn't want to imagine what that meant.

'He not joining us?'

'He's tired. Sleeping.'

I could feel a look crossing my face, so I checked out my boots. There, I noticed for the first time, the floor was transparent, providing a view of the Root stretching below. Plunging hoops of light guided our progress deep into the inky blackness. I guess it was intended as an impressive view of an engineering marvel, but I could have lived without it.

My head began to spin. I pressed up to the wall and closed my eyes. My heart hammered on my ribcage and asked to come out.

'Are you all right?' Marsh rested a hand on my shoulder. 'Easy. Nearly there.'

I shrivelled. I cringed.

Cowardice. Not attractive.

Who gives a shit? Worry about that if we live.

I held on, until the elevator pinged our arrival. I lurched out of the opening doors, staggered about the chamber, tried to gather myself. The elevator had reminded me of being Darnbar's patient. In her care, trapped in the capsule, I had hallucinated often; imagined myself to be travelling alone through a great abyss; that nothing existed any more but me. That I remained only as a punishment.

The seal around that same hatch turned green. The entrance silently unpeeled. Marsh held out her hand. I waved it away.

'Just a bit seasick,' I said, searching the floor for my poise. Eventually I located it and followed her into the split pearl.

Kinnare and Darnbar stood bolt upright among the greenery, breathing their exclusive air.

Kinnare examined a flex. He didn't look up.

'What did you think you were doing today, Commander Marsh?'

Marsh chewed slowly. Looked up for an answer.

'Fighting the good fight?'

Kinnare tapped the flex.

'You were supposed to scout a new site. Instead you returned to the Park. Explain.'

Marsh sighed.

'I wouldn't expect you to understand.'

'We understand you brought back a second batch of samples,' said Darnbar. 'What good are they if they've all been sterilised?'

'They haven't,' said Marsh.

I raised my hand.

'Sterilised?'

'That's right,' said Marsh. Now she looked green around the gills. 'Don't you know? After we've bought the healthy kids these two fly a drone over the target area, spray it with one of the good doctor's cocktails. Prevents the inferior multiplying.'

Darnbar eyed the Real.

'You didn't load the drone.'

'Look,' said Marsh. 'I could just about stomach it before. Those other places we visited, they were dead already. The Park was different. There were too many kids there. I had to go back for more. Go ahead and launch your drone now if you must.'

'These new samples,' said Darnbar. 'They are suitable?'

'All of them pass your little gene test.'

'Seriously?' I said, eyeing Kinnare. 'You're going to sterilise the whole Atlantic coast?'

'The whole species,' replied Darnbar. 'Save the samples we gather here.'

I couldn't get my head around it.

'You think that is necessary?'

'Even culled the human species remains fertile, but overstocked with the listless and incapable. We must put an end to the over-fertility of the unfit, if those we nurture here are to prosper.'

'It is playing God,' said Marsh.

'I've warned you about using that word,' said Kinnare, finally looking up. 'And we are not playing at anything. We are taking rational steps to salvage your species. We are creating a humanity capable and worthy of inheriting a restored environment. The mission is no different from breeding an improved strain of sheep.'

Marsh stopped chewing a moment.

'You eat bloody sheep.'

'You are missing the point,' said Kinnare. 'Your actions endangered the *Lotus*. The entire mission.'

Marsh sat in the ship's chair, crossed her legs.

'You lose that cool head of yours way too easily, Kinnare. We got away, didn't we? No foul.'

The Ficial stood, approached the barrier, stiff like a mast.

Do we walk like that?

'Those ships tracked you. Converged in an organised attack. The *White Bear* has had to fight off many attacks, but never the *Lotus*, let alone by a coordinated force. We have always passed unnoticed. Can you explain this change?'

Marsh rubbed at her eyes. 'I don't know. I'm tired, believe it or not. Knackered, more accurately.'

My double nodded.

'Exactly. You are tired, emotional. Your decision-making abilities are compromised. You do not assess and evaluate the situation efficiently. We can, and we have reached a decision. There will be no gas mission carried out on the Park. Instead we will reintroduce post-sample air strikes. It is the only way to ensure that inferior samples will be eradicated.'

Marsh slipped out of the chair. Approached the barrier.

'Kinnare. You can't do that. We had an agreement.'

Darnbar adjusted her glasses again.

'Please, Commander. I realise you are tired, but try to remain rational. The Gulf of Mexico has one of the largest infestations we have encountered.'

Marsh made fists.

'Did you say "infestations"?'

Darnbar shook her head.

'Words offend you Reals so easily. You give them entirely too much power.'

Kinnare intervened.

'The point is, we have encountered a number of hostile, organised human groups. Even sterilised they represent a threat to our mission. The obvious choice is to cull them.'

Marsh slapped the barrier.

'You can't do that! We agreed no more killing! That was the whole point! We agreed it was senseless!'

Kinnare and Darnbar offered blank Ficial stares. That made Marsh madder. She turned, cursed, then kicked me in the leg. I clutched the offended limb.

'What did I do?'

'You're one of them, aren't you?'

She spat, stalked about the space, until Kinnare tapped on the glass. She stopped, gave him the eyes, but they had no effect on that other me. He pointed.

'You broke the compact, Commander. You forced us to reassess our arrangement.'

'You think I'll just carry on following orders?'

'No,' said Kinnare. 'We brought you here seeking agreement. You have transformed the efficiency of our operations, at sea and on land. Your people respect and admire you. Without your cooperation the enterprise is compromised. If you do not agree, we will terminate the mission and part company.'

It was quite a thing to see Ficials ask Reals for a deal. There was a threat there too, of course. Terminate the mission and there would be no reason to shelter the children. He might simply dump them all on the nearest beach.

Marsh stopped, scrutinised her boots for a moment. Then she looked up, face set. There was a little red in her cheeks.

'I can't make this decision now,' she said. 'I need time.'

'Think about the Park,' said Kinnare. 'Consider what you saw there. Is it better to let people carry on such desperate lives? One white phosphorus bomb and all that misery is snuffed out, a little more genetic scum removed from the pool. Is that really so bad?'

'Yes,' she said. 'It's so bad.'

'Think about it. We will require an answer by the start of your watch.'

Marsh barged past me, headed for the Root. I made to follow, but Kinnare called after me.

'Kenstibec. Wait here, please.'

I made to follow Marsh, compelled by dog-like devotion, but she held up a halting palm, and disappeared out of the hatch. It sealed shut behind her.

Kinnare indicated the ship's chair. I sat in it, craving a drink.

'What is she thinking?' asked my brother Ficial.

'I wish I knew.'

'You share space with the crew. Can you predict their reaction to bombing the Park?'

I thought about it.

'They won't see it, it won't hurt them, they have no interests there. Most won't care.'

Kinnare nodded.

'Good. That is our assessment too.'

'Most won't. Some will. You can't afford to think of Reals as a single unit. Reals are unpredictable. They don't act in unison. Some will care. A lot.'

'Name them.'

I waved a hand.

'I can't say.'

You can, but you won't.

'Do you still dream about her?' asked Darnbar. 'Commander Marsh?'

I gripped the gauntlet a little too tight. Snapped off a piece of the chair.

'You're upset,' said Darnbar.

I didn't answer. I wouldn't give her the control. I had dreamt of Marsh a great deal during my confinement, it was true. Dreams had been my escape, until Darnbar had started wrenching me from sleep, making me recount their content. I had never had the option to refuse.

'Tell me. If the Commander asked you to betray us,' she said. 'Take over the ship. Would you do it?'

'I don't have to answer you any more. You're a doctor without a patient now. You know what that makes you? A hanger for a lab coat.'

'Please, Kenstibec, this Real resentment is unbecoming. I was trying to find a cure for the Pander virus.'

'At first, sure. Later on you were having a party.'

The edge of her mouth tickled up.

'The only party I heard about was in your head.'

I jumped to my feet.

Cool it.

Fuck that. Let's kill her.

She's provoking you. Trying to prove something to your brother.

49

I stopped. Lowered my fist. Blew slow air. I made for the exit.

'Brother,' called Kinnare. 'Wait.'

He whispered into Darnbar's ear. The Medical Model muttered back to him. Then she took off her glasses, pressed them into his hand. She unzipped her overalls, let them drop around her feet, stepped to the air lock. The inner hatch unpeeled and she stepped inside. The compartment flooded, lifting her hair around her face.

'Where's she going?'

'For a swim,' said Kinnare. 'Ficial privilege. We find the occasional deep ocean dive most invigorating. One of the few diversions we have down here. I asked her to give us some time alone.'

The outer hatch opened, and sure enough she pushed out, into the dead, dark sea.

I sat in the damaged chair. Kinnare put his hands in his pockets. Took them out again. He reached out, stroked the leaves of a plush dragon plant.

'Something on your mind?'

He shook his head.

'Quite the opposite actually.'

He clutched his forehead, closed his eyes.

'May I ask you something, brother?'

'Shoot.'

'How do you deal with the silence?'

Right away I understood. The Control Signal, the voice that once spoke in every Ficial mind, had been silent a long time now. Once it had bound, counselled, marshalled us all. Now it was gone for good, cutting us adrift. I had never heard a Ficial speak of it before.

'It's getting to you?'

Kinnare shook his head. 'No. Yes. Sometimes.' He blinked, retreated, dropped onto the couch. He lay on his back and spoke. 'Did you ever think about ending it?'

I swung in the chair.

'Ending what?'

'Existence. Jump into a waste pit, that sort of thing.'

'Did you?'

He stared at the coral ceiling.

'We were designed to build. To construct. I spent two years in

50

Liverpool, building the martello production facility, the new dock. The *Lotus*.

'We always seemed to be building the wrong things, though, didn't we? All those desperate Reals crossing the Channel, and we were building sea stations to sink their boats. I remember saying to my bosses: Look, I can house the lot, with half the material. Your own people have shown the way. Buckminster Fuller, the Japanese metabolists. We can build self-sufficient floating cities for all of them. But there wasn't profit in it, so they ignored me. Ficials and Reals alike were trapped by that old power structure. By money.'

I wondered when he was going to get to a point.

'But at least life had purpose,' he continued. 'Everything made sense when there was work, when there was Control. We could fulfil our optimisation. After the war, everything was confusion and inertia. We did not know what to do without the Signal's guidance. It all seemed ...'

He stopped, turned to face me.

'You never thought of ending it, even after losing your nanotech?'

I turned the chair a full circle, my boots held high, said nothing. My brother clutched his hands over his chest.

'Pander is called the Father of our race. Perhaps Control was our Mother. A mother that nursed us for too long. An overprotective parent who wanted us never to suffer, kept us wrapped in nanotech swaddling.'

It was strange to hear my own model making so little sense.

'What are you talking about?'

He sat up.

'I'm saying that Ficials are not superior. We were never meant to inherit this planet. We were put here to augment humanity, to turn it from its own destruction to a brighter path. I thought that mission was dead. I can see you still do. But Darnbar and I, we have realised: it's possible for us to complete our work. It's more possible than ever. The old Real power structures are scattered to the wind. The tree of life is rotten. All we need do is cut the one last healthy leaf and plant it in Ficial soil. We can still fulfil our optimisation, you see? We can build something here, on this craft, that truly lasts: an advanced species without race, without nations, without money, without religion, without democracy. A humanity that has loyalty only to the species. People that breed, learn and strive according to the needs of the whole, not their own wishes.'

I shook my head.

'Brother, you're getting me down. People are too chaotic. They won't just fall into line. They value their liberty.'

'Of course they do. It is valuable. That's why it must be rationed. They will be trained, Kenstibec. Give me four years, just four years to teach the children, and the seed I sow will never be uprooted.'

I studied my gauntlet, scratched matter from the index knuckle with the thumb.

'Why are you so keen for me to believe in all this, Kinnare?'

He looked surprised.

'Because you are my brother. You are my brother and I know what drives you. Darnbar believes that you are compromised by Real feelings. For the commander. I don't agree. I think you can love and still have Ficial vision.'

'Who said anything about—?'

'I think you still, despite everything, want to build as much as I do. Help us build. Convince Marsh to continue with us. Show her that we must persevere.'

I banged my fist into the chair's armrest.

'Why would she listen to me? I'm a freak!'

Kinnare stood, approached the barrier, stretching out his arms over the division.

'You're the freak? Brother, who's living in the bubble?'

I see light. I hear sound. I feel heat. The first true senses, the first awareness of a physiology. One sense is greater than others. What is it?

- Pain. Pain is essential.

The Signal is different now. More words, but they arrive with less meaning.

- How do I stop the pain?

- You cannot. Your nano-system will make repairs. Pain is at least briefer for you.

And Control is suddenly gone, a yawning absence.

The pain. It is here. My head. This is my head. I can barely move it, this heavy bulb, only roll it to one side.

There is an orb. An eye. My eye. Its reflection, staring at me. Pain in my arms now. The blurred shape of something different stares down at me.

And beside it something shorter, dirtier, less graceful, a white coat, wearing spectacles. My first real person, my first real face. It lowers it, this face, to mine, comes into focus, it probes the gloved fingers it controls into the sides of my head, and I feel something trickle clear of openings. Ears. Sound, a startling din. And the gloved finger goes into my mouth next, presses the teeth, prods the tongue, plucks something out of there which makes breathing easier.

Breathing. I draw air in and out. The taste of life. And I am less disoriented, and I realise that I have a hand. How could I deny it is mine? I extend it carefully and knowingly. The person presses it down.

'What is it with your model? You always try and paw me.'

Words, real words. Coming out of a face. I gaze at it, drink it in. He draws a slim metal instrument from his coat pocket and slowly presses it to what must be my nostril and he pushes it up, high up, so that it feels as if it is prodding behind my eye, pushing it out. I raise my hand again, the only part of this body that will obey. This body, this vessel seems defective. Could I be broken? The man pushes my hand away again; his attention is on the instrument, which he removes, shakes, inspects. He makes a little sound.

Temperature. Cold surface, cold air, cold bones. This place is the colour white, thick with a smell. And I am useless, trapped in this body that will not move as a whole but hums with other movement, of blood, of senses, of nanotech.

The person sits on my chest and produces another instrument, a syringe, and he stabs it into the arm he's pinned, withdraws it, inspects the tip display. He tucks that back in the pocket and he takes something out of his coat, unrolls it, shakes it firm, taps something out there. Then he stands and he joins the other, taller figure, who bends to me and lifts me up. And just by its touch I can tell it is my brother, although I cannot see its face.

It slaps me onto a trolley, and wheels me out of the room, into a corridor, under strips of blue light. I find that I can curl the fingers on the hand. I hold it up, and it is like what was in the dream but also entirely unlike it.

Control was right. This is all quite different. The corridor opens up, and this body vibrates with the roar and thump of construction. The bulbous head rolls to one side. I glimpse two figures down an earth tunnel, digging, flinging a shower of muck behind them, their arms a furious blur.

And then away from that comforting sound, into silence, silence again like the package. It is brighter here, and I look up and finally see who is pushing me, another creature who is wearing my face.

NURSERY

I found myself on the floor, pouring sweat, shaking, panting. Some useless animal instinct made me cry out. Pistol whined and jumped into my lap, licking my face urgently. I clasped my head, as if I might steady my thoughts.

Bridget jumped forwards in the cot next to mine. She blinked, muttered, brushed the hair from her face.

'Ken?' she whispered. 'Ken, is that you?'

'Of course it's him,' snarled a voice, turning on rusty springs. 'Idiot's terrors kept us up every night he's been here. He should sleep on deck. Hear me? You sleep on deck! You and your mongrel!'

A couple of other voices moaned agreement from balconies above and below. Curses whispered, mingling world tongues, echoing in the vault. Pistol barked at them reproachfully.

'And shut that damned mutt up!'

Bridget leaned out of bed. I peered at her silhouette. Picked my boots off the floor, pulled them onto my feet, Pistol's concern flipping instantly to excitement at the thought of exercise. He danced around me, watching my every move, prodding his snout into my hands, doing his best to obstruct the tying of laces.

'Ken,' said Bridget. 'Are you all right? Bad dream?'

Don't think about it.

'Ken, what are you doing, mate?'

'I must get out of here,' I said, an ache in my chest.

'You've only had an hour's kip. You never sleep, man. You'll go completely booloo if you keep this up.'

I pulled on a coat and slumped between the cots, thinking I would find a drink. A drunken haze was a kind of rest, if not particularly refreshing.

I climbed down, Pistol tucked in my jacket, let him onto the floor. He trotted ahead of me across the dark dorm surface, to the rear hatch. We stepped out onto the rail line, followed the tracks on foot, Pistol leading the way, sniffing at new scents, stopping to survey and salute a patch of interest. I took a few steps, then hesitated. Pistol had stopped, one front paw raised, hunched, ears stiff. He growled quietly.

'I hate it when you do that.'

There was movement up the long, curving track. A shadow fluttered in the tunnel. I froze, watched it roll over the surface, disappear. Then there was a silence I could have swallowed.

'Oi!'

I spun around, gauntlet raised in a fist. Bridget reared back.

'Easy!'

I lowered the arm.

'What do you want?'

'You should be in bed, not creeping around in the night like a mad bat. You're after a drink, right?'

'No.'

She was right not to believe me.

'You've seen too much bad, Ken. Let me show you something good.'

She tugged my hand. I resisted, but Pistol sensed a change in plan and darted back the way we'd come.

'See?' she said, smiling. 'He knows what's good for you.'

I relented. She led me down the tracks, past the dorm. We paced along the tunnel, Pistol continuing his inspection. Lights tracked our progress, twitched out behind us. We reached the next petal, one I'd not visited before. Bridget tapped her bracelet, stood aside as the hatch unfolded. She stepped in. Then out again, eyeing me.

'Come on, then.'

'What are we doing here?'

She reached out, tapped a finger on my temple.

'It's sad music in there, isn't it, Ken? *Dolente*. Of course it is. What else is your brain going to play, after six months trapped down there in the Octopus's Garden? But listen, drinking only turns down the volume, right? It doesn't change the station. You need to try a different noise entirely, mate.'

'Like what?'

'Like what the kids are listening to.'

Pistol licked his snout, then bounded through the hatch, following his nose as always.

'Come on,' said Bridget. 'You know he wouldn't lead you astray.'

I followed her into the space, startled to find myself passing under the branches of coniferous trees, through a powerful scent of sap. Pine needles scattered a sandy floor. I heard running water. The air tasted damp and pure. Pistol lost all decorum, sprinting out of sight, racing through this new terrain, occasionally bounding back to yap or worry at Bridget's boot.

We crossed the surface, discovered a great spiral ramp curling up the atrium, around and over the trees. We climbed, found its twisting progress connected a number of broad Flex platforms jutting from the petal wall. Bridget handed me a pair of AR lenses.

'You'll want these.'

I accepted, blinked them onto my eyeballs. Looking down into the forest the AR tagged some hidden structures: *Sandpit, Climbing Frame, Paddling Pool.*

Bridget sighed.

'Tranquil, ain't it? Wish I'd had a bit of peace when I was little.'

'Where are the children?'

'Keep your voice down, Ken. Most are kipping, aren't they?'

We approached the first set of platforms, a staggered tier tagged *Classrooms*. Each was deserted, lights dimmed, split by arrangements of reading wells, teaching circles and play areas.

'The spaces are divided by subject instead of age and such,' explained Bridget. 'They change around regularly. Idea is not to have hierarchy among the students. At least, that's what the manual says.'

AR tags leapt up over the teaching circles, listing Mathematics, Physics and Chemistry, Cosmology and Astronomy, Geology and Oceanography, Engineering and Nanotechnology. Then Biology, Ecology, Zoology, Genetics, Microbiology, Pharmacology.

The ramp curled steeply up again, levelling out to a kind of open dormitory, where teachers slept among the children, reclining on pink-and-blue-striped foam, littered with coloured beanbags, pillows and cushions. I spotted Bruiser, dozing next to Carlos, twitching and mouthing little words. An AR globe hung over the sleepers, displaying the time and calendar for the next day. Scattered depressions were packed with construction toys, paints and clays. Bridget stopped, gazed at the slumbering children, sighed deeply and smiled. Maybe Kinnare was worrying about nothing. I figured Bridget would have happily carpet-bombed the Park to conserve this little scene.

We continued the ascent, passing platforms tagged *Showers* and *Gymnasium*. I glanced up, saw an AR sky, projecting the stars you used to see, the night canopy that Rick planned to liberate. AR tags marked out Capricornus, Aquila, Cygnus, Deneb, Vega, Capella, Aldebaran.

The ramp topped out, and we joined a gathering of some twenty children lying in scooped couches, gazing up at the display. Boatswain walked among them, stooping to whisper advice or answer questions. He noticed us approaching. Bridget held out her hand.

'All right?'

'Swell,' said Boatswain, shaking her palm.

Pistol ran among the couches, sniffing at the children. They grew excited, drawing a reproachful frown from Boatswain. I whistled, and the hound scampered back to me. Bridget scratched his head, looked up.

'How are the space cadets?'

Boatswain swept his arm over the children.

'Progressing well. They barely misbehave at all. Attentive, patient, cooperative. Still amazes me. Like no school I ever saw. They absorb the knowledge like sponges.'

Bridget smiled at me.

'Amazing, ain't it, Ken?'

'It's impressive,' I said, 'but it seems to me there are some subjects missing.'

Boatswain raised an eyebrow.

'Such as?'

'Well, history for a start.'

Boatswain ushered us down the ramp, away from the students. Whispered urgently.

'We don't teach them anything about the past. We spent enough time arguing about that before. These kids look to the future.'

Something about his manner made me question him some more.

'You don't think they'll get curious?'

'Questions about the past are discouraged. They lower a student's assessment.'

I pointed at him.

'And you don't think that'll make them more interested?'

'Nope,' he said, eyeing Bridget. 'Why'd you bring him here anyway?'

Bridget made to answer, but I interrupted.

'So nobody asks why they can't see the sky for real? Why they were brought to your little academy? If they can leave?'

Boatswain shook his head.

'I wouldn't expect your kind to understand. Little people are fragile. They don't roll off no assembly line – they develop. They need care, security, guidance, discipline. They crave it. We give it to them. We keep them active and occupied at all times.'

'You mean you keep them distracted at all times.'

Boatswain raised his voice.

'What should we do? Try and explain what we did to the world? What the world did to them? Who gives a damn about the past? They're going to build a better one. That's all there is to it.'

'No,' I said. 'There's more. Contentment lasts for a while. Then they get bored and seek change. The same will happen here. You can't keep them buttoned up in your pocket for ever.'

'Confound it!' he snapped. 'Who do you think you are?'

'Ken,' said Bridget, rolling her eyes. 'Come on. Let's get you that drink.'

'This isn't what I had in mind.'

I clutched a glass of condensed milk in the gauntlet. We were seated on a small balcony, jutting from the ramp about halfway up. Pistol snoozed, his chin resting on my feet.

'Trust you,' said Bridget, 'to visit harmony central and start an argument.'

'I have a healthy suspicion of utopias.'

'Yeah,' she said, gazing into her cup. 'You're not wrong. There's a dark side all right. You know they don't let me play for the kids?'

'Why?' I said. 'Was there an incident?'

Bridget played harmonica, and she played it beautifully. Not everyone appreciated it. In her hometown the Reals had thought her music cursed, believed it conjured up fire. You couldn't lay the blame entirely on Real superstition. I'd seen for myself: infernos followed her around.

'Are they allowed any music?'

'Some,' she said, waving her hand. 'If you can call it music. Opera, stuff with violins. You know the score.'

'How can they allow one kind of music and not another?'

She shrugged.

'I'm well used to snobbery. Look, Kinnare wanted to toss me overboard when I first arrived. A proper Blackbeard when he wants to be, your brother. Said I had no use. He only let me stay when I told him I could speak lots of languages.'

'You can?'

She shrugged.

'I can now. Learned quick, didn't I? It was close, mind. If you Ficials weren't so gullible I'd have been flotsam for the beachcombers.'

She looked down at the trees and sipped her drink. Came away with a milk moustache. It suited her.

'You know about this sterilising programme?'

'Yeah,' she said, smacking her lips. 'Course. We all know about it.'

'I would have thought there'd be a mutiny.' She clasped her hands around the cup.

'There was one. Before we turned up. The crew downed tools apparently. Haven't you heard? Marsh sorted it all out. Got them organised, convinced them we were doing the right thing. That's why your brother and Dr Octagon hide downstairs.'

'Marsh persuaded them?'

'Well, we ain't got a better plan, do we? And we're not hurting anyone, not really. They hurt each other enough, out there. Anyway, I can't feel bad about much any more. I felt bad they dropped the bomb. I felt bad when my mum and brother died. I felt bad when I was on my own.'

She unclipped her hair and rearranged it, a memory resurfacing.

'I had to stop feeling bad to survive, didn't I? I won't start again now, not when there's a chance of building something better for these kids. If we can keep them safe, feed them, well, that's something.'

'Speaking of which,' I said, 'how are the new arrivals settling in?'

She sighed, reclipped her hair.

'Not bad. Not bad. The two blondies are a potential issue. They keep praying. It's not easy telling them to stop. They get upset.'

I leaned forward, interested.

'You don't let them pray?'

A deep voice, behind me. 'Don't tell me,' said a voice. 'You disapprove.'

Boatswain stood behind me, clutching a cup of coffee, the other hand scratching his scalp. He took a seat next to Bridget. 'You haven't seen what religion makes of Man?'

'It can make him all sorts of things.'

Boatswain snorted into his coffee.

'It sure does. I lived in Kentucky during Lay's presidency. I saw what his disciples did. If God was on their side, then he's a devil.'

'Reals always have questions. The biggest have no answer. God fills the void. You can't stop that.'

'In isolation, you might be right. If all they had left to fill the gap was money. That was the old world, wasn't it? Money.'

He spat into the trees.

'We're doing away with all that.'

'No more money, Ken,' said Bridget, nodding. 'Imagine that. No more poverty. No more class.'

'And not just that,' said Boatswain. 'No more democracy. No more rule by corruption and bribery. These young folk will form the first ever Council – appointed by examination, not voted in by popularity. They'll control the human population, so we never consume our own resources again. If you want to have a kid you'll apply for a licence.'

'Sounds a little tight,' I said.

'Far from it. It'll free us right up. We're throwing off the shackles of the past. These kids will work together for a greater purpose – a united humanity, the reclamation of the planet and, before long, expansion into the stars.'

Boatswain's eyes sparkled. He believed it. He could see my doubt.

'Hell, your own kind are running this project. Why ain't you on board?'

I thought about it for a moment.

'People don't dance to the same tune.'

Bridget eyed me curiously. Boatswain turned to her. 'Listen, your Ficial friend's beginning to stir my stew. Show him the way out.'

He stood, indicated the way down.

I was happy to oblige. The detour had been interesting, but not nearly as diverting as a rum would be. I picked up the dozing Pistol and trailed Bridget down the ramp. I pressed my fingers to my eyes, slipped out the AR lenses, dropped them into Bridget's palm at the hatch.

Bridget smiled. Then a voice said: 'Can we come with you?'

We both jumped. The blondies stood there, holding hands, staring at us. Bridget crouched to their height.

'No, sweetheart,' she said. 'You'll have to wait here. Children aren't allowed out.'

The girl frowned.

'But we don't like it down here.'

'What don't you like? There's lots of lovely food. You can make new friends, and play, and learn cool new stuff. It's better than where you were, isn't it?'

'It's the same,' said the girl, scowling.

The boy pointed at the hatch.

'Please. We want to see outside. Let us come with you. We'll be good.'

Bridget took the boy's hand.

'It's a big change,' she said. 'I know that. It's scary being somewhere new with lots of new people. But you must stay here. It's dangerous through there, and smelly and hot and you wouldn't like it. Now, on your way, please. Back to bed. Go on now. *Allegro*.'

The blondes exchanged looks, bowed their heads, turned and trudged up the ramp. Bridget watched them go, looking pained.

'Blimey. They lay it on thick.'

She stood, tapped her bracelet. The hatch curled open. She scratched Pistol's chin and turned to leave me.

'Bridget,' I said. 'Do you really believe in all this?'

She widened her eyes. There was something in her expression, like disbelief.

'Of course,' she said. 'Go and find a drink, Ken.'

The hatch clasped shut. I did as I was told.

I rejoined the rail line and walked the silo perimeter, passing under the arches of the inner petals, reaching overhead like a Frei Otto design. The passage echoed with the skittering of Pistol's paws, the tapping of my boots. I thought of Boatswain's arguments. I thought of Bridget, banned from playing. I thought of the blondies, locked up. And pretty soon none of that mattered, and I was thinking about Marsh instead. She was close. I could seek her out and tell her everything.

Sure. Nice idea.

Well, why not?

Why not? You're a killer. An abomination.

Maybe I should write it down. I'll explain it better if I write it down.

Oh, terrific. We're a poet now. What would you say?

She's light. Fresh air. My drinking water. She makes sense of my senses.

Too much. That's way, way too much. She'll run a fucking mile.

Then Pistol's ears pricked up. He stopped, snorted, ran his pink tongue over his black chops. A small, gruff sound escaped him. Then he darted ahead, drawn by some frequency. I jogged after him, along the curling tracks, calling. Then I heard it: the faintest echo of Real voices, raised and boisterous.

I caught up with Pistol by the third petal from the nursery. He was sniffing around a small parked rail carriage. I stopped, listened. The Real voices were coming from within the petal. An alluring odour hung in the passage. I examined my bracelet, located the petal on the map, prompted the hatch command. The seal curled open and we entered.

The petal was an open vault, crates and barrels stacked high around its walls. The centre had been cleared of cargo and packed instead with half the *Lotus* crew. They were making a little less noise than a choir of jackhammers. Pistol hugged my shins, not sure what to make of the party.

I noticed the booze first. Each Real held a tankard or a cup, the air thick with the smell of it. They were cheering and cursing, gathered in a crowd, all backs turned to me. I pressed into the scrum, forced my way to the front.

Wole stood at one end of a kind of track, marked out on the chamber floor. He held a pale yellow spherical buoy in one upturned palm, his eyes narrowed at the track's far end, where two crewmen busily arranged a cluster of empty stub missile casings. The Reals around me offered and accepted bets, the prevailing mood seeming to be backing Wole.

The casings were organised. The crowd hushed. Wole took up a stance, lifted the buoy before him, then jogged to a line drawn across the track, swinging the buoy behind him, then forwards, releasing. The crowd watched the buoy, entranced, as it hurtled down the track, clattering into the casings with a hollow report. A great roar of approval, over a groan of discontent.

A number of Reals rushed Wole, slapping his back, cheering his prowess. He turned among them, smiling, accepting drinks, until his eyes stopped on mine.

He stood very still. The crowd followed his gaze, parted around me, left me standing alone but for Pistol panting at my side.

'You,' said Wole. 'What are you doing here?'

'Just looking around.'

The big man glowered at me, stepped forward.

'Spying for your Ficial chums, are you?'

I remembered the screens in Kinnare's greenhouse, displaying camera feeds all over the *Lotus*.

'I don't think they need my help to keep tabs on you. What – is this a secret meeting?'

'You're not welcome!' he bellowed.

'Easy, Wole, easy.' Carlos trod deliberately towards me, stopping occasionally for balance. 'This is no Ficial. Look at him. I mean, does he look even a bit like one of them?'

'He used to be.'

'Sure. We all used to be something. Now we're shipmates, right?'

Wole made fists.

'We're human. He's not.'

'Labels. Man, I got no use for labels. I measure a man by his actions.' Carlos did his best to focus on me. 'Hey, Ken. Try some of this.'

The crowd watched as I took the cup from Carlos, sniffed. I chucked the contents down my throat. It tasted predigested, but provided the necessary buzz. I licked my lips.

'Got any more?'

Carlos spun on his heel, lifted his arms to the crowd. 'That man enough for you guys?'

The crew cheered, laughed and cursed, a pressure lifted. Wole still glowered, but in a moment the Reals were lost in their merrymaking, drinking, sitting in circles playing at cards, reforming the stub cases for another strike. A few took an interest in Pistol, bent to pat his head, or gaze into his eyes and give him baby talk.

'He's not an idiot,' I admonished them. 'Don't patronise him.'

However, Pistol lapped it up, smiling at the attention, turning under the gathered hands, relishing each pat. I was briefly ashamed of him, but couldn't stay sore. The last thing I could expect from a dog was shame, and really that was to his credit.

Carlos put his arm around me and led me to a row of barrels.

'We got everything here, Ken. The *Godwin* crew hit the jackpot in the Park. We got sherry, cider, ale, wine.'

'Kinnare will know about this,' I said.

'Sure. I guess they figure live and let live. Here, try something different. The house white.'

He scooped the cup in an open barrel and held it out to me. I accepted, drank. It was identical to the last drink. I knocked it back and scooped another cup.

'Easy now,' giggled Carlos. 'Or you'll regret it.'

I settled on the ship rum, a cheeky number with a turpentine bouquet. I kept tipping it back, thinking it would improve. It didn't.

However it tasted, it had the power to soften us all, our suspicion lost in a warm fog. Until now the crew had all the individuality of a school of capelin. Now they were more: faces, names, manners. They saw me better, too, I could tell.

'Anyone with a thirst like that can't be all bad,' said Carlos, slapping me on the back and toasting me.

'Hey! I guess you might say he drinks like a fish! Fish – Ficial! Huh? Huh?'

I supposed this was humour, but nobody laughed.

I returned to the barrels, fetched another drink. Gunner sat beside me on a crate. He showed me the whistle around his neck, blew it hard, laughed as the others flinched from the shrill noise. Gunner had nothing but navy English, so he signed me his story. He made wings with his arms, then a roof under which he cowered, then slapped his

65

palms together. Pointed to the ring on his finger, shook his head.

Carlos dragged me clear, invited me to play the deck game, which they called Stubbles. He was interested in how the gauntlet might influence my skill, and in betting on the outcome.

My first effort hurtled through the air and smacked the casings aside. Laughter. Cheers. The whistle.

'Whoa. Whoa, there,' said Carlos. 'That doesn't count. That's illegal play. You must roll the ball along the ground, not fire it like a goddam cannonball. Try again. Again.'

I obeyed, lined up my shot, and released the buoy. It veered wildly right. More cheers. So, there was a little skill involved. I tried again, managed to clip one casing free of the stack. On the third attempt I released the projectile gently enough. I held my breath, watched it keep a steady course, strike. Another great cheer.

Stubbles made sense to me. What more useful method was there to pass the time than practice, perfection, no matter how fruitless the outcome?

I stood aside, watched the crew grow inebriated. A fight broke out between Gunner and a bearded Real. A woman with lank hair tugged the bearded one away, cuffing him around the ear. Carlos and another man disappeared behind the stacked supplies, smiling secretly at each other. Someone yelled accusations, said someone had stolen his bracelet. The party was breaking up.

I found myself headed to the Root, clutching two cups of rum. I wanted to see my brother. I had a warmth in my chest, and suddenly it seemed very wrong that we were living apart. Hadn't we been designed the same, born the same, burned and tested the same? I had a fuzzy kind of idea that I would connect with him better drunk, that I might find the words that had been lost to me before. So I left Pistol with the revellers and rolled down the ramp. Made my way into the elevator. Descended. Tripped out into the Axis. Found each hatch rimmed orange.

I hammered on the most familiar.

'Brother! Hey, brother, let me in! I brought you a drink. Let's have a drink.'

No response. All I heard was my breathing, heavy and slow. I clenched the gauntlet, drew it back, prepared to strike the hatch.

'What are you doing here, Kenstibec?'

I looked up, the voice echoing in the Axis.

'I said: what are you doing here?'

Darnbar.

Her voice, bitten and warped by static, spoken by speakers.

'Where's my brother? I want to see him.'

'He's taking a swim. He wouldn't want to see you now anyway.'

'Oh, yeah?'

'That's right. You're drunk.'

The truth of the accusation only made it the more outrageous. I tensed the gauntlet again.

'Why do you wish to speak to him?'

'You spent long enough in my head. Don't you know?'

The hatch seam blinked green and the barrier unpeeled, granting admittance. I approached it uncertainly. Her voice made me feel restrained again, naked and spotlit. I staggered along the corridor, entered the same pearl. Darnbar was seated on the bench, framed by the great arch of plants. Condensation trickled on the barrier. The good doctor was dressed differently. She wore a simple tracksuit, her hair tied back, and no glasses. She reminded me of someone.

'You let me in,' I said.

'Perceptive. I had to let you in, Kenstibec, I've seen the violence latent in your mind. The drink has shaken it loose. Who knows, you might try and punch through this barrier if I say the wrong thing.'

That's right.

'No,' I said. 'I'll just wait for my brother.'

Darnbar cocked her head to one side.

'You still think of him that way? As your brother? Even as changed as you are?'

Don't answer.

'Do you still have your dreams, Kenstibec?'

I slumped in the ship's chair, holding the cups carefully level, sipped at one. Darnbar sat up on the couch. 'Do you still dream of Marsh? She made so many appearances in your dreams. Many times in our sessions you spoke of travelling with her: swimming, driving, sailing, walking, climbing a great tower. Always a moment of travelling. What is it about her exactly? Where does she transport you?'

I balanced one of the cups on the chair arm, rubbed at an itch in my eye.

'Why don't you tell me?'

'I could never establish the chemistry of the obsession.'

Her blank stare. It still made me want to run, so I remained.

'You know what? Before I met you, I had the occasional dream. You're the one who made them come all the time. I barely sleep now. I mean, weren't you supposed to make me better?'

'No. You were a test subject. I was studying your disease.'

I raised a finger.

'At first. Later on you were after something else.'

She sat forward, picked up the nearest watering can, poured into a glass.

'I was interested in your mind. The dreams are your humanity re-asserting itself. They made fascinating research. I recall one dream you spoke of. You were lying on a table, with architects and town planners poring over your naked body, as if it were a town they were to redevelop and renovate.'

I shivered, remembering. Niemeyer. Bernini. Haussmann. They crowded around me, arguing over what parts of me to keep and what parts to strip away. They'd finally agreed to keep only my eyes, finding the rest of me unsatisfactory. I was left two white orbs, recessed in a new structure of concrete, gold and Gronts Alloy. My mind had been trapped there, in the materials, looking out at the pleased men, as they smoked cigars and drank toasts to their creation.

'Your dreams seemed to fill the silence that Control left,' said Darnbar. 'That void where the Signal had been. You must have felt that emptiness, when you were still Ficial.'

Still do, don't we?

She ran a finger over the edge of her glass.

'Kinnare and I have no such comfort. We only have each other to occupy that space.'

'What about Rick?'

'Rick is defective,' she said simply.

I hunched in the chair.

'So I had to lie strapped in your capsule because you were – what? Looking for Control methadone? We couldn't have come to a more comfortable arrangement?'

'I needed to study you in the right conditions. We didn't know enough about the disease. We still don't. For that matter, we don't know if you can be trusted with the mission.'

'Fuck you.'

It just came out.

'You see? Rage. Like any man. Half the problems in human history were caused by impotent male fury. Really, you make an unremarkable Real. It's just this kind of needless aggression we want to eradicate.'

A Real man. The ultimate insult. She was looking for a response again. I sipped the drink and took a deep breath. I wasn't about to rise. I didn't like how intimate our conversation made things. Even with the barrier, she felt too close.

'Kinnare persuaded me you were ready to be released,' she said. 'That you could wear a human mask and speak on behalf of Ficials. I didn't believe it then and I don't believe it now. You need help and care. You're a troubled person, not a diplomat. Ask Kinnare if you can return to the lab. Let me help you.'

We stared at each other for a while.

'You don't want to help me. You want to help yourself. Give yourself something to do. I know what it's like, not to be able to carry out your optimisation. You must be going crazy in there.'

She sat back.

'We don't "go crazy". You should know that.'

'I don't know what to know.'

I downed the two cups, one after another, stood up from the chair and made to leave. Then I stopped, turned, pointed out of the hatch.

'You two really swim out there?'

'Certainly. We find it bracing.'

'You don't swim together?'

She looked at me for a while.

'Not today.'

I smiled.

'So, all that time you were poking around in my head. It was all about figuring out what was wrong with *me*, right? Where *my* desires come from? You weren't trying to figure anything out about anyone else?'

She narrowed her eyes.

'What are you saying?'

'We're different, Kinnare and I.'

'I think that's obvious, Kenstibec.'

'You're not listening. We're brothers, but we're different.' I tapped my head. 'He's not in here. So stay out.'

She frowned. It was about as big a response as I'd get.

Strength arrives quickly, fizzing into my bones, fingers, jaw and thighs. Six brothers sit up in almost perfect unison. We drop right, then left legs. We lift right hands, even blink with synchrony. And we discover that we are naked, seated on Flex bunks, one projecting from each side of this hexagonal chamber. And three of us, I and the two brothers either side, our bunks sit next to exits, there are no handles or keypads or buttons, but we observe the thin seal in the Gronts surface and we know these plates will retreat into housing, revealing passages that lead beyond. We all look at our feet. Did we all dream of leeches? Are we still dreaming? We sit and stare. Our throats are dry.

The entire chamber is Gronts, tinted by copper. The light tans our skin with dark red tones, and posed like this, with barely perceptible differences in posture and gait, we six might look like casts in an artist's studio, studies for a colossus.

I lift my hand to my head, where the cut was. The nanotech has repaired it, leaving no scar. No other brother checks a wound. Already, then, we are a little different.

I look to my right and a fellow Nine is looking at me. My face, not my face, is not what I expected. It has flaws: the forehead reaches too high and the jaw juts too far forward. Otherwise it satisfies me. My fellow Nine thinks the same, or at least, I think he does.

We stand and inspect each other, following some pre-programmed urge. We look over our identical bodies and search for defects and we know that if we find a fault we will report it and see that brother lowered into waste pits. But we find none, only unblemished skin and the first bristles of hair on our scalps, under our arms, around our groins. Inspection complete, we sit in silence, await instruction, await the Signal.

The elevator chimes, the doors part. A man enters, he who greeted us into the world. A flex is rolled and tucked under his arm, those instruments lined

71

neatly in his top pocket. He seems smaller now. He sneezes, takes a rag from his pocket and blows his nose.

Sickness. We'll never know it.

'Congratulations, Construction (Rover) Models, Power Nine, Batch One. You've been cleared for optimisation. We really are getting rather good at this.'

He looks up from the flex, makes a clipped sound with his tongue.

'Honestly, get dressed, will you? Why do you always need to be told? The chests, look in the chests.'

We open the drawers, produce blue overalls and black boots from within. We pull them on, fascinated by the sensation of material on our backs and on our legs, the texture of laces in our fingertips.

'All right, all right,' he says. 'That's about enough fondling. Stand up, the lot of you.'

We do as we are told, rising to our full height. He steps back, eyebrows raised.

'Crumbs. They keep making you taller, don't they?'

He waits in silence for a moment.

'Talkative as always. Well, gather round, gather round, boys.'

We cluster around two bunks. The man folds his arms and regards each of us coolly, as if still searching for stains.

'My name is Rickets. Harold Rickets. I am the supervisor for this hex, which has been dedicated to the production of Construction Models since the start of the Engineered project. We are one of six hexes in this complex. There are at present five operational hexes, with construction of a sixth under way.'

We all begin to speak. He raises his hand.

'No, you can't help with the work. You're keen, of course you are, we made you that way - but I assure you, you are not yet ready. First you must complete your optimisation here in your hex.*

'Now, pay attention and I'll talk you through the neighbourhood. Currently we are located fifteen metres beneath the northern tip of Brockwell Park in Brixton, London. Each hex is laid out on six levels, understand? We're at the top of your hex now – Sleep level. Below it are Cleanse, Eat, Learn, Test and Burn levels. You'll discover them soon enough. Adjoining your hex are three more, dedicated to the production of Soldier, Medic and Programmer Models. You are not permitted to enter an adjoining hex unless directed by me or by a Control Signal. Capiche?'

We nod.

'Now I know you all have one question on your minds. I can answer it for you now. Around a thousand metres to the north-west is the Control Bunker.'

He stops, looks around us.

'I know, you all want to visit. Well, I'm here to tell you that the bunker is strictly out of bounds. No model may approach the bunker unless summoned, and you won't be summoned. Not even I can enter the bunker uninvited, so put that out of your minds.'

We stare at him. He seems satisfied, rolls up his flex and tucks it under his arm again.

'Well, lads, let's begin our tour with something to eat. I don't know about you, but I'm famished.'

PLASTICS

I didn't catch much sleep. An ache roosted in my head before I could try, and I passed the night awake in my dorm bunk, reading a copy of *Innovations in Concrete* by the light of my bracelet. The book was some lost part of Kinnare's library, I guessed, turning its pages. I'd discovered it while searching the party petal for leftover rum. The revellers had cleared it out, save a small puddle in the barrel, which I'd scooped into my flesh palm and slurped. Now the party was over, and the crew slumbered heavily about me, snores and grunts and other emissions echoing in the petal vault.

I put down the book, regarded Pistol. He lay on his back, having his own dream, paws twitching some phantom pursuit. It was peaceful to watch him. I thought he needed a haircut, and wondered if some kind of shears existed on board. My eyelids grew heavy, the deep exhaustion in bones and soul finally catching up. I welcomed it.

Then the dorm lights blinked on. Pistol sat up, startled. He looked at me.

'Don't ask me,' I said.

We peered over the balcony rim, saw the hatch unzip below.

Marsh entered, holding a large metal spoon and a wide metal pan. She looked around the petal, caught my eye. She smiled. My heart, briefly, stopped.

Then she lifted the spoon and beat it hard on the pan, thrashing it with relish. The crew burst awake around me, crying out, cursing with real spite and invention. Some threw things.

'My lords and ladies,' called Marsh, laughing. 'I'm putting together a little expedition. Plastics party.'

Jeering. They called her all sorts of names. I had heard of the plastic parties: scavenging runs to source fuel for Rick's engines. Marsh

74

coughed hard, some morning obstruction, and cleared her throat, then read out a list of names.

Again, protests, but fewer of them this time. Seeing heads return to pillows about me, I hesitated. Then Marsh looked right at me, eyebrows raised. I jumped to my feet.

Pistol barked approval, but I held up my hand.

'You wait here. Keep an eye on things.'

The selected crews trailed Marsh to the dock petal, clutching heads, shivering and moaning. Marsh called orders from the *White Bear*'s pilot house, berating her sloppy, hung-over crew at a merciless volume.

'God Almighty, it's like a coachload of pensioners at the seaside! Move yourselves! Come on, move it! You two, quit that Spanish chit-chat and get loading. Boatswain, get your boat in order! Ken!'

She pointed at me. I winced back.

'What do you want – a deckchair? Tuck your shirt in and make yourself useful, or shall I stick you in the kennel and take the dog?'

I shuffled about, selecting a few lighter kit bags to haul aboard the boat.

Bridget appeared as we prepared to cast off, clambering uncertainly onto the *White Bear*'s deck. I expected Marsh to send her packing, but she only waved the girl on board.

Marsh tapped her bracelet, and the petal unclasped, Flex beak peeling open, dipping a slipway into the ocean. The *White Bear* slid free of its mounts, Wole and Marsh at the helm, followed by the *Godwin* and *Minion*. We cut into a choppy surface, rolled and turned, and set out for the islands Marsh had selected. The *White Bear* would make for the largest in the group, where the best prizes lay. The others would search the smaller islands and cays.

I sat on the prow and watched Bridget wobbling among the crew, put on unwieldy chemical gear. She struggled to pull on a boot, stumbled and fell, raising a cheer. She gave them her thoughts on that, then clumped out of sight, dignity impossible in that outfit. Carlos took a seat by me, nudged me with the tip of his flask.

'Here,' he said. 'Look like you need it.'

I checked the pilot house, saw Marsh facing away, talking to Wole. I sipped and returned the drink, thinking about what Carlos had said at the party.

'You really don't think I look Ficial?'

He shrugged.

'Hey, no offence. But I never seen a Ficial with bags under its eyes.'

A few highlights danced in the cloud barrier, casting the ocean in dim twilight. Ahead, the island arched in the water, like a frozen wave. We slowed our approach, Wole cutting the engines and drifting into the shallows. There was a low crackling, as the *White Bear* cut through the thick crust of garbage. The crew flourished their nets, dipping them into the flotsam, inspecting their catches. Suitable plastics were tossed into the hold, to be sorted by Rick later.

The ship wallowed, turning my stomach. Marsh appeared on time, plucking a packed Flex canoe from the bulkhead and casting it overboard, where it unfolded into shape.

'With me,' she said, pointing my way. 'We'll paddle to the beach. Good stocks of polypropylene and polyethylene there.'

'Aye.'

I jumped into the canoe, wondering at the romantic possibilities of a slow rowboat trip.

'Wait up!'

Bridget waddled next to Marsh, bent under the weight of her coat and gloves.

'No,' I said. 'No room.'

Marsh helped lower her into the raft. I gave her a particular look and passed her a paddle.

We pushed off the *White Bear*, grunting and heaving through the trash. Bridget started to sing a song about a drunken sailor. It was kind of repetitive, but I guess that was the point:

Weigh heigh and up she rises
Weigh heigh and up she rises
Weigh heigh and up she rises
Early in the morning

She went on like that until we slid up onto the beach, jumping out into a great dune of trash. Marsh held a torch for me as I walked among the garbage, plucking likely loot. Bridget followed, whistling the same tune.

If my head had throbbed a little less I might have guessed what was coming. Marsh drew alongside me, took a bottle from her pocket.

'Will you take a drink?'

She didn't need to ask. I dropped the sack, lowered my mask, inhaled a draught of chemical beach air with the ship-brew.

Bridget's eyes flashed, wide over her mask, communicating something urgent.

'Right,' said Marsh, wincing in the air. 'Look, Kenstibec. We have something to discuss with you.'

I waited, sensing a trap.

'The fact is,' she said, 'we need your help.'

'OK,' I said. 'With?'

Marsh sipped the hooch. Kicked a bottle. We turned, watched it plop into the surf.

'It's this air strike,' said Bridget, stepping closer. 'We can't let them do it, Ken. We need to stop them.'

I took a moment. Processed what I'd heard.

'On the *Lotus*. When we talked. You said . . .'

She raised her gloves.

'I know what I said. That wasn't for you. Boatswain's a believer. Besides, the petals are wired for sound better than Abbey Road. They watch, you know, your family.'

I was confused.

'So, what, you're telling me you're against the mission now?'

Marsh spoke up.

'Of course we're not against it,' she said. 'The *Lotus* is the best hope for those children. They need to be taught a better way. They need to be cared for, kept safe. That doesn't mean . . . It doesn't excuse . . .'

'The mission doesn't justify a load more killing,' said Bridget. 'All right, the Park's got some proper nasty people hanging about, but there're innocents too. They're no threat.'

I flexed my gauntlet, suddenly feeling a tremendous urge to crush something.

'I seem to recall a fleet of pirate ships trying to board us on the way back to the *Lotus*. Wasn't that threatening enough for you?'

'Kenstibec,' said Marsh, 'I could swallow the sterilising. Just barely. But I won't be party to killing. Not unless those kids' lives depend on it.'

77

'The same goes for me,' said Bridget.

'You didn't think this might happen?' I asked. 'When you joined up with Kinnare?'

'Kinnare and I had a deal,' she said. 'He reneged.'

Bridget eyed me.

'Don't tell me you think Kinnare's right, Kenneth?'

I looked out to sea, head pounding.

'What are you asking me to do? Lead a mutiny?'

'Hardly,' said Bridget. 'Most of our comrades on the good ship Lollipop seem pretty happy to go with the flow. They're not rocking the boat any time soon.'

'A few aren't happy about it, I'm sure,' said Marsh, 'but we couldn't organise even if we wanted to. As Bridget says, the *Lotus* is one giant earpiece. We all know what they'd do if they found out we were planning such a thing.'

I sipped at the flask again.

'So what is it you want me to do?'

'You have access to Rick,' she said, 'to the silo. You need to fix things so the strike doesn't happen.'

I choked on the hooch.

'Nice plan. I sabotage the ordnance, do I? Very heroic. Then what?'

'No need for that,' said Marsh. 'They work on a simple gyroscope configuration, right? All you need to do is fiddle the settings. Have them burn up a nice patch of ocean instead of the coast. Hopefully they'll assume all went well. They can't track the trajectory in this atmosphere, and it's not like they're going to get out of their cosy pearls and count bodies.'

I picked up my sack and slumped away, returning to the search for plastics.

'Look, Ken,' said Bridget. 'We know we're asking a lot. But we need to know if you're with us on this.'

I stopped, spotting a washed pink kettle rolling in the foam. I picked it up, brushed away the sand, dropped it in my pack. Marsh took me by the gauntlet. A ring of light from her torch flickered and danced on the carpet of trash, picking out faded colours.

'Kenstibec,' she said. 'We can't let this happen. If the mission is going to mean anything it can't be built on killing. That's the whole point. We can't murder and call it progress. You must see that.'

78

I chanced a look at the grooves in her lip.

A kiss would really cheer me up right now.

'What if I decide not to help?'

She released me.

'If you don't help us, the strike goes ahead. I won't be able to stay if that happens. I'll leave the *Lotus*. Wole and I will strike out on our own somewhere.'

She means it.

This is some contemptible shit. That's blackmail. Don't tell me you're going along with it?

It'll make her happy.

Wonderful. What will it make us?

'OK,' I said. 'You got me.'

Rick supervised the sorting of plastics on the dock, sniffing and handling debris like market fruit. I helped him load a trolley.

'A good catch,' he said. 'Something for everybody.'

'So,' I said. 'Need help with those engines?'

'I was wondering when you'd ask to take a peek. All right. Give me a hand with this stuff.'

He tapped his bracelet. The petal's inner hatch opened, and we rolled the trolley into the deck passageway. He typed another command, and the ramp unfolded ahead, descending to the lower deck.

'So,' I said. 'Kinnare's told you about this new fire mission?'

'Oh yes,' said Rick. 'Big job. Wants to burn the entire coast. A real Bomber Harris number.'

'You agree it's the right thing?'

Rick eyed me like a bald tyre.

'It's the mission, isn't it? Cull?'

'You ever hear the notion that we don't solve our problems with the same thinking that created them?'

Rick sniffed, picked a shard of plastic from the trolley, flexed it between his fingers.

We trundled down, lights blinking on in the spiralling passageways, taking a different turn, to a hatch I hadn't seen before. Rick entered another code, and it slipped open, releasing a wall of heat. Rick bent over the trolley and propelled it into the blinking lights.

I paused to take in the towering edifice of Rick's patented Plastic

Fuel Processor. It ringed the entire chamber, an assembly of pipes, bellows, centrifuges, chrome, Gronts, steel and glass, Flex appendages and ersatz rods, a black and silver growth reaching up to the overhead and spreading across it. The floor and surfaces were coated in a sticky dream coat of mixing colours, seeping from half-clogged sockets buried in the assembly.

I took a breath. The air was toxic with solvents. My head spun and my eyes wept. I hacked and thought about vomiting.

'Oh, yeah,' said Rick, tossing me goggles and mask from the trolley. 'Forgot about that.'

I pulled on the protective gear, wondering if he really had. He was suspicious of my condition, I was sure. Maybe he hoped I was putting it on.

'Well,' he said, tapping the nearest pipe. 'What do you make of it?'

'It's big.'

He dabbed the air with his limp hands. 'Hmm. If you think this is prodigious, wait till you see the engines.'

The embers of some previous industry glowed on a tray under a great oven door. Rick prodded the mess doubtfully, pulled a wooden broom from a locker built into the machine, and swept the ashes towards a grate. The drain was nearly blocked, so he stamped on it hard to loosen the mess. Then he returned the broom, withdrew two spades from the locker, and wielded one at me. I took it, grateful for some manual labour.

Rick wrenched open the oven door, then tipped the trolley over, its contents spilling over the sticky deck. Then he rubbed his hands together, dug his spade into the mess, and began to feed the furnace.

I joined him, watched him as I worked, wondering if other Mechanic Models had so embraced the trials of life in nuclear winter. Rick relished the challenges of salvage, of making do, of bringing life to scrap. Some had shunned him, back in Edinburgh Barricade, thinking him defective. The *Lotus* crew didn't think much more of him. But he wasn't frightened of anybody.

'Why aren't you scared of me, Rick?'

He tossed a load into the oven.

'Scared?'

'You know what I mean.'

He paused, leaned on the shovel handle.

'You mean your virus?'

'It's not *my* virus.'

'No, of course.' He resumed shovelling. 'You know me, K. I need something to do with my hands. I mean, what's the point of having this body if I don't put it to some use, right? I can't just sit down there in the Root and think. I'd go peculiar.'

'You don't think those two might be losing it below?'

He tidied the scattered plastics with his boot, into a firmer pile.

'Nah. They've got their plants. And listen, Ken – scared, spooked – these are Real words. You're being insulting. They have their project, I have mine. Theirs makes isolation appropriate. Mine makes it impossible.'

We worked on until the machine was fully fed, then sealed up the oven. He began a long series of checks, climbing over the contraption's surface, tapping glass surfaces, depressing levers, turning brass wheels. Finally he activated one of the Flex fittings and tapped in commands. Wheels turned. Steam whistled. Fluid dripped in condensers, and pale colours oozed out of the sockets.

He stood there, bent forward, hands held limp before him, and muttered.

'It'll just take a minute.'

I watched the machine work, thinking that of all the creatures infesting the *Lotus*, I'd known him longest. I felt grateful somehow.

'Thanks, Rick,' I said.

'For what?'

An alarm chimed. Rick clicked his tongue and scuttled towards a brass ring mounting a handle. He turned it, pointed as an inch-thick tubular orange paste emerged from a cap buried in the machine. It coiled slowly to the floor, reached it, piled.

Rick quit turning, hopped to the coil. He picked it up at one end and offered it to me. I gripped it in my hand. It had a texture like sponge. It was an effort to tear off a piece.

'A metre of this can fire those engines for a month,' he said. 'Totally clean, zero emissions. We could run the world on the last century's trash for some time, I reckon.'

'Impressive.'

'Like I say – wait till you see the engines.'

He piled the orange rope in the trolley and wheeled it out of the

81

hatch, heading down another whorl passage, trolley clattering on mesh. Our boots ripped with every pace, still coated with the chemical muck from Processing. I pulled off my mask and goggles, tossed them in the trolley. I had a sinking feeling in my chest.

'Listen, Rick. Do you really believe in Kinnare's mission?'

'I don't believe in anything, K. I don't get involved in the ins and outs. I just fix things, me.'

'But without you the mission is nothing. There'll be no world for Kinnare's new humanity to inherit. You must have an opinion?'

'Nope.'

'You don't have any doubts?'

He glanced at me.

'You do sound Real sometimes.'

I was an idiot. Ficials didn't have second thoughts. He wouldn't be persuaded not to launch. There was nothing for it. I'd have to sabotage his work.

We passed through another hatch, entered the Root elevator. Rick tapped a code into his bracelet, and the cab descended, stopping halfway down the Root. The hatch opened up, and we rolled the trolley onto a platform overlooking a great oval vault. A black, ribbed and pulsing egg shape nestled in the space. The starboard engine.

'Well?' he said. 'What do you make of her?'

'It's quiet.'

'As a mouse,' he agreed. 'Yet it's a beast. Combined the engines get us up to fifty knots in calm seas. Not too shabby, eh? We can outrun anything we need to. Well, theoretically, anyway. I fear if we went much above thirty-five we'd tip the whole business over.'

Rick scooped the rope out of the trolley and tossed it over one shoulder.

We descended a metal stairway. Rick draped the coil on a hook mounted on the smooth engine surface, unscrewed what looked a lot like a petrol cap. He paused, narrowed his eyes. Lifted his nose over the cavity.

'Do you smell that?'

'What?'

He pushed past me, sprinted up the stairs.

'Hey! Wait!'

82

'Someone's messed with the engines. We need to talk to Kinnare. Right now!'

I hurried after him, out of the hatch, into the elevator, up and out to the *Lotus*. We hammered along the passage, stopped in our tracks. For a moment there was a sound like heavy breathing. Then, suddenly, a great cry, so loud I felt it in my teeth.

'Action stations, action stations! Contact bearing two-one-zero! Closing!'

'Hello,' said Rick. 'Something's up, all right.'

Eat level is the same layout as Sleep level. There are small tables instead of bunks. The light is clearer, brighter here, the walls clad in a thin layer of chalk. Rickets leads us to a cavity in a wall, holds his palm code to the screen, activates a dumb waiter. Trays are lowered. He hands them to us one by one.

There is a square plate, each holding three mounds of grey matter, each of differing consistency. One shivers, one wobbles, one is solid. There is a tall glass of water. We sit.

I lean over the plate, inhale a thin aroma. I pick up the glass, peer at the water, put it to my lips and sip. I gasp at the relief it gives my sore throat. I tip up the glass, drain it. The others do the same. We have learned about thirst today. I slip the spoon into the food and drop its cargo into my mouth.

Rickets produces his own tray and walks around the central column, eating as he goes. His meal has a different smell; it is so heavy it overwhelms everything else. It is a slab of something brown wedged in a bun. It drips fat.

Meat. People eat meat.

Rickets makes that sound again.

'Look at you all. Curling up your noses. Nine Powers in and we still haven't produced an instinctive meat-eater. You.'

He taps the brother next to me.

'Why shouldn't I eat meat? Go on, spit it out, lad.'

'Spit what out?'

Rickets looks at the ceiling. Down again.

'Tell me. Tell me what's bad about meat-eating.'

'It is not necessary for people in developed countries to eat meat, for survival or for health. Beef in particular is produced by damaging agricultural practices which make inefficient use of land and water and create huge carbon emissions.'

Rickets nods.

84

'That's true. All true. But that won't stop me eating it. That hasn't stopped the whole damn country eating it, even as the price skyrockets, even as famine and chaos grip the continent. While we can, we eat it. And why is that, eh?'

He steps away. Points at me.

'You. Why is that?'

'Because it gives you pleasure.'

'That's right.' He nods approval. 'Because it gives me pleasure. Now, does that make sense to any of you?'

Nobody speaks.

'Of course it doesn't. And this is what you need to understand, boys. We might look similar, you and I, but we are different species. And we have to prepare you to work alongside creatures that are emotional, capricious. That's what the Learn level is for. It's the method by which we introduce you, gently, to modern society. The society that's waiting up there. On the surface.'

A brother raises his hand.

'Why did we not receive this induction while we were packaged?'

Rickets sniffs.

'We tried that. Your first Powers were sent into the world with Control's integration programming. We were confident they were more than prepared, but we forgot they were infants when it came to human interaction. There were a lot of problems. They jumped off buildings because they couldn't understand a joke. Damaged themselves because they took an insult as an order. No, Control can train you for anything but people. Only people can train you for people. That's where I come in, lads.

'Now, finish up your meals and form up. It's time you learned exactly how strange people are.'

SHARKS

We were scurrying along the deck passageway when we were thrown from our feet, the whole *Lotus* jumping like it had been pinched somewhere tender. We stumbled across the quaking deck, flinching from a sound like tearing paper. Individual petals were peeling apart into unshaped drapes, revealing the clouded sky, opening holds and docks to the elements.

'Not good,' said Rick. 'Petal control is messed up. They're losing their charge. That confirms it.'

'Confirms what?'

'We have a saboteur. Below I smelt something in the engines. Acid, I think. Someone's trying to make us dead in the water.'

The lights in the petals flickered and died, the entire vessel cast into the darkness of the night beyond. Rick hit the torch on his bracelet, headed back the way we'd come.

'Where are you going?'

'I think . . . I think I can get us moving again.'

He scuttled out of sight. Shots clattered like a hailstorm. I reached the dorm petal, which had peeled open at the summit, one entire side dropping bunks and crew. The injured lay dazed on the passageway. I dodged crew as they rushed, half-dressed, to positions. Marsh was buckling on a belt. She saw me, picked a holster off a bunk and tossed it my way.

'Get to the *Bear*!'

'The engines,' I said. 'Rick thinks they've been sabotaged.'

She looked up from her waist.

'They can't be fixed?'

'He didn't even try. I think he has another idea.'

She made for the hatch, swaying to keep her balance as the

Lotus tipped, unbalanced by its flooded pens.

'We have to get to the *Bear.*'

I went after her, skidding over the pitching deck, dock petals slapping lifeless into the water, exposing the deck passageway completely. I peered out to sea. Floodlights swept the ocean, bursting from one large ship, then another. Smaller RIBs spat around the choppy surface, packed with Reals, shooting wildly.

A great wave broke and slapped us to the deck. I dug a purchase with my gauntlet fingers, reached out and caught Marsh by her boot. The wave rolled back, leaving us coughing and floored.

I glanced up, noticed that the silo petals were still firmly deployed, shrugging off the gunfire. The party petal and nursery petal were intact too. This sabotage was selective, precise.

Marsh jumped to her feet again and broke for the dock. I pursued, but another wave lashed the deck and almost dragged me into the ocean. My head struck something, stunning me.

For a moment I could do nothing but cling to the guardrail and watch the tracer arch across the night. It was sort of beautiful, until it arched a little close to my head and rattled around me. That brought me back to my senses.

I continued on my way, saw the *White Bear*'s dock petal beak split into three loose drapes, its jaw hanging limp in the water. There was a report, shouting, a noise like something running loose. Then the *White Bear* crashed into the ocean, catching on a loose petal, dragging free. I saw Wole on deck, clutching a stunner; Marsh in the pilot house. The craft picked up speed, rose up and cut away towards the nearest enemy ship.

OK, we lost her. What now?

The *Lotus* answered for me, letting rip a great moan, its deck plunging towards the ocean. I clamped the gauntlet on the guardrail, gasped a breath, and hurtled into the dead, black waters. I plunged deep beneath the surface, into a suspended moment of rushing water, warped battle sounds, loose petals rippling in the murk like tentacles. Then, a hard pain in my shoulder, the *Lotus* righting itself, dragging me back to the fight. I broke the surface to the sound of gunfire and revving outboards. I released my grip, surfed across deck, over a loose petal, into the open dock.

A speedboat. I heard its rasping engine first, then spotted its foamy wake as it slowed, lining an approach on the open pen. I struggled with my holster, brought out the stunner, charged it as the raiders pelted into the open dock. I edged around the hood to the hatch, wrenched it open in time to see Reals disembarking, shooting, cutting down the few deckhands.

I ran at the nearest pirate, raised the weapon as he turned his head. He saw me, his eyes wide behind a leathery mask, his teeth jagged in bright pink gums. I pulled the trigger. He winced.

Click.

'See,' I said, tossing it, 'that's why I don't like these things.'

He fired his pistol without aiming, snicked my ankle. I seized the weapon in my gauntlet and crushed it into his hand. He mused on that for a moment, allowing me to throw a right at his jaw. He staggered, surprised, and tumbled over the guardrail, into the thrashing waters.

Shots peppered the dock, as his fellow raiders evacuated the pen, leaping through the drooping, open hatch. I chased, but a static charge crackled in the air, and the petal suddenly snapped into formation around me, locking me inside a quiet, dark chamber. I stepped back in surprise, listened to the waters drain, and considered. Rick must have restored charge to the *Lotus* flexes. Could he have repaired the engines?

I activated the bracelet torch, opened the hatch. I fumbled out into a confusion of screams and flares. Above me a number of petals had lifted out of the ocean. I watched them dumbly for a moment, confused. They weren't reforming into hold petals. They were creating new, billowing shapes, fluttering skywards. They were shaping into sails. The *Lotus* began to move. Still, we were vulnerable, the deck passageway exposed.

I kept moving, searching for the boarders. I spotted a wound torn in the galley petal, stepped through into dazzling light. A volley of shots greeted me, rattled over table tops, chopped the air with debris. I dived for cover, crouched, waited for the pirates to close. They split up, hugging either wall. I looked up, waited, watched smoke curl around the fanlights vaulting the roof. Boots crunched closer, accompanied by oddly laboured breathing.

I sprang to my right, smashed into the pirate, slapped his rifle clear as he squeezed the trigger. Bullets clattered around the space.

I wrenched the weapon from his grip, cracked his masked face with the butt. A bullet spat off my gauntlet, ricocheted across the galley.

The second pirate. A figure in black fatigues, helmet, advancing on me, calmly aiming shots. I rolled over a table top, fired once, twice in reply, before the stolen weapon clicked empty. I picked up a tray and hurled that at him instead. He ducked, providing an opportunity to gallop at him, barging into him at full speed, throwing him onto the table top.

I immediately began losing the struggle. The guy was all muscle, and held my gauntlet clear by the wrist. He threw me to the floor, tore a machete from his belt. His face was like his pal's, a grey leathery mask, cold black goggles, mouth a slash, all gums and teeth like a walking shark. He was no slaver, no pirate. He and his friends were something else.

He slashed. I parried with the gauntlet, sparks flying, deflected another strike. I felt round for a weapon, found a wooden clipboard menu. I whacked him hard in the shin with the edge. He howled, crumpled. One gauntlet blow to the head and he was out.

I lay next to him and caught my breath, listening to the distant clamour of combat. Then, slowly, a sound emerged from the others: an insistent tapping. I picked up the Shark's weapon, reloaded with a clip from his belt, and entered the kitchen, wrist torch sweeping the damaged space, wind howling through the petal wound. I stopped, traced the source to a tall white freezer. I tore open the door, to find Carlos and his friend inside, sat on a stack of ready rations.

Carlos emerged, shivering hard, clutching himself.

'¡Por mi vida! They just appeared out of nowhere. How many on board?'

I handed him the cutlass and pushed the two of them towards the hatch, out onto the rails.

'Where are we going, man?'

'To defend the silo. Bound to be more there.'

Carlos held his friend back.

'Wait. Do you hear that?'

A tinny, high-pitched chorus echoed along the tracks. A child appeared, crying, shrieking, running towards us. Then another. Then another, until an entire herd were thundering our way, frightened and screaming. I held out my arms.

'Stop!'

They ran past me, under me, barely registering my presence, carried on down the track. I pulled Carlos close.

'Gather up as many as you can. Get them into the silo and lock yourselves in until this is over.'

Carlos stared at me.

'Where are you going?'

I nodded down the tracks.

'To see what spooked them.'

He slapped my shoulder and led his friend after the fleeing children. I crept on down the tracks, approached the nursery. The air grew bad, smoke thickening. That scent. The forest was burning. Smoke billowed from the open hatch. A figure stumbled clear, clutching something. Bridget, her eyes screwed up, her features caked in soot. She held Bruiser in her arms. She collapsed, spitting and hacking in the smoke. I plunged into the smog, dragged them along the tracks to the adjoining empty petal. I opened the hatch, pulled them inside, sealed the hatch on the smoke. Bruiser sat down, staring, in shock. I bent over Bridget, blew air into her lungs until she revived, snapping into a cough.

'Bridget,' I said. 'Anyone left in the nursery?'

She shook her head.

'Gunner's dead,' she whispered. 'They shot him. Chased the kids out. Then suddenly everything was on fire. We hid. They were all wearing these masks with these black eyes, Ken. I think they . . . I think they want the kids.'

Bruiser curled up tight. I stood, felt a new movement beneath my feet.

'We're moving again,' I said. 'Stay here and don't let anyone in.'

I crossed the echoing atrium, opened the hatch to the deck passageway, found it lit by fires, flecked with debris and dead crew.

I looked up, where billowing petal sails propelled the *Lotus* by wind alone.

A cry and gunshot snapped my attention back to the deck. A long, thin, black ship was pulling alongside, into the gap between two dock petals. It was matching our speed, dragging itself closer by two great harpoons it had wedged in the *Lotus* hull. Figures were crowded atop the bridge, wedged in the defunct radar array, every one a Shark face.

They peppered the deck with fire, rolled Flex ladders up to the deck. They seemed to think they were boarding us.

I rushed the first wave, beat a Shark off his ladder before he got a foot aboard, ripped a blade from another's grip and pushed his ladder back the way it had come, tossed the blade into the chest of a third. Surprise worked well, for a while.

Then, a spray of blood. A fall. I lay face down on the deck. Then the pain showed up, searing over my left shoulder. Boots stepped into my vision.

A voice spoke, but I didn't listen. I was too distracted by the small, determined black shape scurrying along the deck, through search-lights and fire glow, closing on the boots.

Pistol didn't make a sound, not until he'd bitten deep into the Shark's leg. I reached up, clenched the gauntlet tight around his thigh, crushed what I found. The Shark collapsed and shrieked. I took a pistol from a dead crewman and gave the raider the full load. Pistol barked in triumph.

I picked him up and clutched him close, as he licked my face, struggled and snorted. I should have stashed him until the action was decided; but voices were calling at the ladders, another wave ascending.

I requisitioned the dead Shark's rifle and a serrated blade in his belt, and tore along the edge of the deck, shooting as I passed, ignoring the pain in my shoulder. Sharks tumbled into the murk between frigate and *Lotus*, to be crushed or drowned. Others returned fire from their ship, bullets ringing on the deck like bicycle bells. I lay down, reached for the first harpoon, sawed deep, hard thrusts into the rope, until the cable shredded and snapped. The frigate careered out into the surf by the bow, shedding ladders and Sharks into the water. The rear harpoon tightened, moaned, dragged its load for a moment, then snapped with a powerful, elastic tone. The black frigate bobbed away into the gloom, left to the ocean and the night.

The pain had been patient enough to let me repel the boarders. Now it announced itself in a dizzying surge. It rolled me over, squeezed tears, made me bellow and thrash in the cold spray. Pistol darted about me, whining concern.

I didn't want to upset him, so I quit my noise and slowed my breathing, reclaimed enough resolve to stand. I edged over the rolling deck, seeing no sign of the *White Bear* or any other craft on the ocean's pewter surface. I circled, ducking under the billowing Flex sails, thinking I would make for the silo.

I heard them first. Sniffs and whimpers, and hushed, unknown voices. I peered under a petal and saw them: perhaps twelve Sharks arranged around a dock petal, surrounding a group of Reals: the children, Carlos, Bridget. More figures arrived as I watched: two Reals cradling a large, unconscious shape. My shape.

Kinnare.

Captured.

Pistol stood still and quiet at my feet, as I debated the best course of action. If they could overpower a Ficial, they'd make short work of me.

Maybe I should stow away. I needed time to heal, to concoct a plan, to learn the enemy's intentions.

I heard Pistol growl. Something struck me in the small of the back.

I turned, lowered my eyes. The blondies from the Park. The boy's eyes burned beneath a furrowed brow, his little hand clutching a stubby blade. The point dripped my blood on the deck.

I fell to my knees, strength rushing from the wound. Pistol bounded, knocking the shocked kid onto his back.

I knew what was coming.

I couldn't stop it.

The kid pushed Pistol's head clear, and stabbed violently at the dog's chest. One, two, three hits, and a sharp, anguished squeak. The dog rolled clear, legs stiff, tongue loose.

The boy rolled onto his knees, brushed himself down, wiped the blade on the dog's fur. He kicked the loose body over the pitching deck, into the water.

After that, I was no use to anybody.

Learn is cast in a dim blue light. Cool air blows in jets, tickles our necks as we approach six reclining couches that rock and twitch, eager to embrace us. Rickets is talking.

'Still not a perfect science, you'll still have questions when all of this is done, but we get better with every Power. Your data is of huge importance to Dr Pander.'

We stand around him. He takes an oblong case from his hip pocket and rips off the lid, revealing a pool of fluid. Using tweezers he extracts pairs of flexible transparent discs and drops them into our hands.

'Place the lenses on your eyes and lie down in your couches.'

We recline, and the couches shape around us, straps snaking over our chests and limbs.

And our senses snap into a simulation, and suddenly the light is the bright sun, and I squint up into blue sky, and looking around I see Rickets standing next to me, and beyond him there is a great skeleton rising up from the mud; a half-built stadium. Cranes tower over the site, over stacks of material, idle bright yellow dump trucks and excavators, over muddy tracks and a fence ringing the works. My breathing quickens.

'This is our standard training programme,' he says. 'For Construction Models. It summarises many of the situations you might encounter when working on a human construction site. You may find yourself integrated into a working party, or possibly directing one. Whatever the case, the way you interact with people is absolutely crucial to effective fulfilment of your optimisation, understand?'

I nod.

'All right. Come on.'

'How long will it take to learn?'

He shakes his head. 'Every one of you things asks that question. You cannot *perfect human interaction. It is an art, not a science.'*

The gate opens. And even though I know I am cradled in a Flex couch, and the movement of my boots in the mud is the movement of my bare feet within the constraints of the couch's flexible structure, it seems as real as anything else. As a hex. As the package.

A group of men stand around half-completed foundation works, drinking from steaming cups. Many flout site regulations, failing to wear hard hats, smoking.

'Go on,' urges Rickets. 'Go and speak to them.'

I assume he means ask them why they are not working. I approach them. A few of them stop talking as they notice me approach. They split and turn to face me.

'Why are you not working?' I ask.

'Fuck business is it of yours, pal?'

The man chews on something. The remains of his hair flap in the wind. I do not understand his question so I ask mine again.

'Why are you not working?'

'Fuck off, Ficial,' says one. 'It's our break.'

Break.

'You mean that you are resting?'

He laughs. It is the first laugh I have heard. It is a defensive display, laced with threat, like a cobra's hood flare.

I point at the foundation.

'But your work is incomplete.'

'You fucking do it then, pal.'

I pick up the nearest tool and jump into the trench. The men wail and protest and throw things at me. I look up, see Rickets push through the crowd. The simulation freezes, the men's faces held in contorted snarls. Rickets crouches, shakes his head and smiles.

'Lesson one,' he says.

Black Frigate

Time passed in a numb blur. I was wounded, kneeling on some open stretch of deck passageway in a cold wind, my hands bound. The surviving *Lotus* crew were crowded about me, hemmed in by a ring of chewing Sharks. We had been defeated. None of it meant a thing.

Pistol was dead. I'd never walk with him again, never feed him or watch him sleep. I was alone once more.

A voice whispered my name. I ignored it, too perplexed and far off to connect. I stared at the black sea and thought of my little companion, dissolving in the slime.

'Ken! Ken, snap out of it.'

Bridget. She crouched behind me, hair bedraggled.

'Come on,' she said, her voice an urgent whisper. 'Check in, Ken, please. You're freaking me out.'

'Keep your voice down,' snarled Carlos. 'You want to get us killed?'

'What about the kids? Where are the kids, eh?'

'They took them onto their ship,' said another voice. 'I saw them. They're all right.'

'*Mierda.*' Carlos again. 'What are they doing to the Ficials? They look broken.'

Through the loose chain of Sharks I glimpsed my brother and Darnbar. They were tied up, bound to curious, X-shaped scaffolds erected on the deck. Their heads drooped, trails of drool hanging from loose lips. Two Sharks guarded them, bearing large industrial tools. Pulse welders. A hit on full power could floor any Ficial.

'What are we going to do?' said Bridget. 'We have to get the kids back.'

Carlos cursed.

'These things took down two Ficials. Keep your head down and your mouth shut.'

Bridget chewed on that for a moment.

'Where's Marsh then, eh? Has she run off and left us? So much for going down with her ship.'

The name shook me. I took a few deep breaths, tried to fill the crushed space in my chest. Tested the bindings on my wrists. The gauntlet could snap them, but what would that get me? A head shot full of lead, or a blast from a welder I wouldn't survive. What did it matter? Any moment now they might notice my resemblance to the figure hanging on the cross.

I craned my neck, peering through the guarding Sharks, searched for Rick. He wasn't at the party. I spotted a Real in an anomaly of suit and tie, overcoat, polished shoes. He consulted with the Sharks a moment, then approached us. Our guards parted, and he stood over us, smiling benevolently. There was something funny about his nose. The skin stretched over the bone beneath.

'Ladies and gentlemen, may I have your attention please?'

The voice was syrupy, low, enticing somehow. The battered crew lifted their heads to it. He stiffened with importance.

'My name is Floyd. It's my honoured duty and privilege to congratulate you. Today we liberate you from Ficial tyranny. Today, we return you to the embrace of God's love.'

He turned, nodded at two Sharks. They bent to pick up metal cans, then approached Kinnare and Darnbar's unconscious forms. There they waited.

Floyd returned his attention to his captives.

'We don't blame you for the evil you have been forced to do here. God loves you and forgives you, no matter what your sin. You've been living under the despot rule of Satan's army. Now that his army is defeated, we offer you all a chance to taste freedom, a chance to show contrition, turn your face back to the Lord, and join us in the regathering place of his people: New Jerusalem.'

Floyd nodded at the Sharks with the cans. They unscrewed the caps, and set to drenching the Ficials in oil. It seemed to revive them a little. They spluttered and struggled, like flapping seabirds.

'Ficials do not recognise the goodness and divine providence of God,' said Floyd. 'They are deceivers by nature. They would pervert

God's majestic creation, use their twisted science to wipe people from the planet, to propagate more of their own: a race of soulless automatons with no love, no happiness, no God – an enslaved, mindless mass.

'New Jerusalem is the light. No cloud hangs over our nation. We live in the warmth of God's sun, clothed in its light. Each resident has the freedom to live as they choose, to make money, to raise a family. We are building a new nation, under God. I am offering you the chance to join us. All you must do is swear an oath.'

Chains shook behind us. Two slumped prisoners were brought forward to Floyd, their features obscured. I recognised Marsh even in a shroud. She was kicked to her knees before Floyd, the covering ripped from her face. She'd been beaten, but she was breathing. Floyd stood over her.

'As officers of this craft, you have a choice. Will you join the devils in their fate, or pledge allegiance to New Jerusalem?'

Marsh didn't seem to be listening. A Shark nudged her with his boot. She said nothing.

'Hey!' snapped Floyd. 'You don't get to sit this one out, sweetheart. Choose.'

Still she said nothing. A Shark drew a machete out of his belt. Slowly, I rose to my haunches. I'd need to be quick to protect her. Quicker than I felt.

'Hey, Marsh!'

Had I said that? No. It was Kinnare, oil dripping out of his eyes, nose and chin. I could see the strength returning to him.

'Take the stupid oath,' he said. 'It doesn't mean anything.'

'Silence!' yelled Floyd. 'Woman. Choose.'

Marsh bowed her head.

'I pledge. I will pledge.'

'Finally. And you?' said Floyd, pointing at Wole. 'Will you make your pledge to New Jerusalem?'

Wole nodded, grimacing at the blood weeping from a wound to his head.

'Then let us join in the pledge. Bow your heads and repeat after me.'

He started to read. I listened, but couldn't speak. The Sharks took care of that, voices intoning a recital with an addict's conviction:

I believe in the prophet, he who wears the crown and holds the rod

I believe in his freedom, he who speaks to us the word of God

I believe in his vision, he who sparked the fire that cleansed the Earth

I believe in his justice, they who play the Game to prove their worth

I believe in his market, that which favours us and favours them

I believe in his chosen, they who lead us to Jerusalem

Floyd held out his arms.

'And with that, the pledge is complete. Stand, as citizens of New Jerusalem.'

We clambered to our feet. It was awkward to do cuffed. I guessed the citizenship was probationary.

'Nothing's that easy,' muttered Carlos.

'Easy for us,' said Bridget. 'Not for some.'

There was activity around Kinnare. The blondies processed around our circle, one either side, each bearing a flaming torch. The firelight reflected on the Sharks' black-eyed, toothy masks.

The children stopped either side of Floyd, and waited, the only sounds the crackling torches, and the wash of the sea on the *Lotus* hull. Darnbar looked up, turned her face to Kinnare.

'Kin,' she said. 'Kin.'

He looked at her. She searched for some words.

'You know, don't you? You know?'

'I know,' he said.

The children tossed the torches. The crosses burst into flame, two great blooming heat flowers that sucked at the air, billowed smoke, reached at us. Sharks, children and prisoners reared back. The fire tore over the deck, working towards the hold petals.

'You stupid idiots!' cried Floyd. 'You misjudged the wind! Again! We only just put this sucker out! Get them off! Get them off!'

The Sharks urged us away, around the deck passage, down a gangway to the black frigate. We gathered on deck, surrounded again, and watched the burning shapes as they were prodded from the *Lotus* deck, dropped fizzling into the sea.

The frigate engines powered up, turning the craft from the *Lotus*. Floyd ordered the Sharks to take us below.

Our face is wet. What is that?

Those are tears, pal. I don't know. You and that fucking hound.

We were sealed into a dim, dank compartment near the engines. I sat in a corner and stared. Bridget spoke to me a few times, but I couldn't pick out words, let alone respond. I could only gaze, and move the swelling around my throat.

Somehow I slipped into sleep. There was a terrible dream, about the market on Atlantic Road. I was a green-eyed butcher on a street stall, and I was cutting up my arm with a cleaver. And I served the pieces to Marsh, and she scooped black furry meat into her mouth with chopsticks. And she asked for the bill, and scowled at it and said: 'Bloody gentrification.'

I woke, drenched in freezing sweat, felt the ship cutting through heavy waters. Carlos slept on an old mattress before me. Wole was asleep too, his head back on the bulkhead. He had his arm around Marsh. Her head rested on his shoulder.

We must have a drink.

Bridget was awake, watching me.

'Have you got anything to drink?' I asked.

Bridget pursed her lips.

'Yeah, sure, Ken,' she said. 'I'll just nip to the bar, shall I? What do you fancy? Pint?'

She turned away, tapped her boots a few times. Eyed me again.

'At least you're talking now. You've been freaking me out.'

'How long have we been locked in here?'

'Dunno. Feels like ages.'

She stood, crossed the space, picking through her sleeping ship-mates. She sat next to me and whispered, 'What happened, Ken? How did they take the *Lotus*? I thought we could outrun anything. We just sat in the water like a punctured lilo.'

I shrugged.

'Those blonde kids, the ones from the second Park trip. They were a plant, left in the slave market for us to find. They were meant to get aboard, to find a weakness. They found a way to break out of the nursery, maybe using a stolen bracelet, sabotaged the engines. Who

99

knows how, but they coordinated the whole thing with their people. Whoever these Jerusalem characters are, they're no slouches.'

'What do they want?'

'Well, they wanted the *Lotus*, that's for sure. Otherwise they would have let it burn.'

Bridget shook her head.

'But what are they doing to those kids?'

It was a typical Real invitation to useless speculation.

'I don't know. Look, they're organised, they've got religion, and they're looking for converts. If they let us live, safe to say they'll let the kids live too.'

She dropped her head against the bulkhead.

'Those blondies. I knew there was something off about them. But I thought they were, you know, traumatised or whatever.'

'They almost certainly are.'

She rubbed her eyes and sighed.

'So. What are you going to do?'

I looked at her.

'About what?'

Her eyes widened.

'Well, about . . . You know. Your secret identity.'

I exhaled slowly, wondering at the thought of being discovered. Part of me wouldn't have minded being burned alive with Kinnare. Part of me would fight for every second of Real life I could get.

'Nobody's said anything so far,' I said. 'Nobody's even asked me.'

'Maybe not. But you'd better get your story straight. I mean, you're not exactly inconspicuous are you, shipmate?'

She tapped my gauntlet. I raised it, twisted the fingers. Strange, that it should take this substitute limb to mark me as unReal. Did I not look even a little like Kinnare? Had I lost so much of my former self?

We're more than this body, pal. Much more.

Bridget sniffed.

'And of course it's not just me that knows about your background. What if someone in the crew decides to speak up?'

'Would you?'

'Of course not,' she said. 'But others might, Kenneth. Think on it, that's all.'

I looked around at the slumbering remains of the *Lotus* crew. She was right. These people barely knew me. They had no reason to protect me.

Suddenly there was a piercing, shrieking whistle, jolting the sleepers awake.

'Now hear this, now hear this,' said a voice. 'Guards to the brig. Guards to the brig.'

Marsh stirred. Wole brushed hair from her face and she smiled at him.

Bridget stood up, backed away from the hatch.

'We're getting a visit, sounds like.'

Marsh felt at her side, where she'd taken a punch.

'Any news on the children?'

'Not a sausage,' said Bridget.

'Worry about us,' said Carlos. 'You really think these people are just going to forgive us all of a sudden? Let us live in their paradise? I don't think so, man. Maybe they're just keeping us calm. Maybe they're waiting for a chance to burn us for a crowd. We're collaborators, man.'

'Some of us are worse,' said Wole, eyes resting on me. 'When you come to think of it.'

'That's enough,' snapped Marsh, breaking free of him. 'We need to stick together. We don't tell them anything.' Wole frowned at her. 'Do you hear me, Wole?'

He nodded slowly.

Marsh stood, tied her hair back.

'Good. Our first and only duty is to those kids. Keep your eyes open and your trap shut until we know what's happened to them.'

There were steps outside, a thump and screech of metal. The hatch creaked open, and two Sharks stepped inside, breathing hard. Floyd followed, smiling.

'Well. Good to see you all again. I am glad to tell you that we are well on the way towards your new home. We will make you welcome in New Jerusalem. Until then, I ask you to study these.'

A Shark handed him a short stack of books. Floyd distributed them. 'From here on in the only law you'll need is contained right here. The Only Book, we call it.'

I turned over the copy in my hand. It was white, marked with some kind of logo – a white cross on a red circle. Floyd held up the last copy.

'You have questions? The answers are right here. There's also a full explanation of the Game and Game rules. You'll learn more about that soon enough. Hell, some of you might even play one day.

'Rest assured,' he said. 'You are now citizens of New Jerusalem, and entitled to its care and protection. Get reading, and I'll see you ashore.'

He turned to leave. Bridget raised her hand.

'Excuse me, sir,' she said, 'but where are the children who were on the *Lotus*?'

Floyd turned.

'The little ones have been taken into the care of the church.'

'Can I see them?'

He ignored her, marching out of the hatch, followed by the Sharks, who slammed it shut behind.

'Please!' said Bridget, hammering on the bulkhead. 'Please let me see them!'

Marsh seized her by the shoulders.

'Easy, Bridget.'

She pulled free, scowling. 'We're supposed to trust him, are we? What if he's hurt them?'

'Try to relax,' I said. 'These are evangelicals we're dealing with. Most likely they have the little people locked up in a separate hold, reading them fairy stories from this thing.' I waved the book at her. 'My bet is the kids are more bored than hurt.'

That settled her some. She wiped her eyes.

'Yeah. I s'pose. Just wish I could see them.'

I sat in a corner and turned the pages of the Only Book. My copy was formed of coarse, uneven pulp. I was surprised to find it hand-written in a looping, elegant text, penned in dark brown ink. I opened it at a particular page, checked it against Bridget's copy.

Several words were different.

It figured.

Our guards returned hours later, provided us with meal packs of canned pasta, branded with the New Jerusalem flag, so we'd be sure who was feeding us. They also distributed packs of a powerful peppermint-flavoured gum, which the crew took to chewing relentlessly. The ship seemed completely dry, but the more gum I chewed the more I could handle the absence of booze.

The others grew tired and slept. I didn't feel like returning to the land of dreams, so I studied the Only Book instead. It was a dry read, but there were blank pages in the front. I found a pencil and elected to pass the time designing.

I sat for some time, but no ideas for structures presented themselves.

I watched Marsh dozing, head nuzzled in her arm, mouth open. I began drawing. I captured her physicality pretty well, but it didn't capture that other thing. I started afresh, found some comfort in sweeps of wrist and blunt graphite. The image that emerged was a set of loops, shades and instinctive, darker scrapes. Still, it was certainly her.

I sketched until morning, then tucked the book into my overalls. More Sharks arrived, all in black fatigues, grey masks with opaque black goggles, helmets, all chewing great wads of gum in their zip-like maws. They broke open the door with a gust of shocking cold air, bringing shrink-wrapped treats and a thermos of ersatz coffee.

There was something off about them. They sat among the crew, opened up their Only Books, invited discussion about certain passages. They slurped and sucked their words around their gum, making little pained noises every now and then. The crew exchanged glances, sat quietly, respectfully. One Shark sat with me, wheezing and gurgling as it spoke the same passage over and over:

Take off the garment of your sorrow and affliction, O Jerusalem, and put on for ever the beauty of the glory from God. Put on the robe of the righteousness that comes from God.

He or she, I couldn't tell which, had difficulty shaping certain words. It wore its mask throughout, my face reflected in the black oval goggles. I inspected my haggard reflection, the heavy stubble and bloodshot eyes.

That's no Ficial face. No wonder they don't suspect us.

A half-hour later the study group wound to a close, with a reading from the book, and a recital of the pledge. The crew joined in, remembering only the opening words. Finally the Sharks left, wheezing, drooling and chewing.

'Booloo,' said Bridget, shaking her head ruefully. 'Every time I think I've encountered every kind, a new type shows up. You were right. They're trying to convert us.'

'Suits me,' said Carlos. 'Sign me up.'

'They want us to trust them. And I don't trust that,' said Bridget. 'They'll try to convert the kids too.'

'Oh, please. What were you doing back on the *Lotus*, Bridget? Wasn't any different, was it? Shaping them into goddam proto-Ficials, am I right?'

'Oh, shut your face, Carlos. It couldn't be more different. We taught them facts. This lot tell fairy stories.'

'It doesn't matter now, does it?' snapped Carlos. 'The mission is dead. The Ficials are dead. I'm alive, and I mean to stay that way.'

'Yeah, well,' sniffed Bridget. 'You're a man of principle.'

The crew settled down for the last stretch of the journey. On occasion the ship's loudspeaker crackled into life, and we would listen for clues. We were playing cards when Floyd's voice boomed into the compartment.

'Now hear this. Now hear this. Ship crossing threshold. All personnel below decks. Radiation measures, repeat, radiation measures.'

Marsh rolled her gum over her tongue.

'East coast of North America,' she said. 'Must be. Kinnare said the whole stretch would be useless for mission purposes. Massive fallout.'

'How'd it happen?' asked Bridget.

'The last president,' said Marsh. 'Lay. Thought his own country was as evil as the rest of the world, so he nuked both.'

'But – that's crazy. Why did he do it? He'd kill himself.'

'I think,' I said, 'that was the general idea. Destroy the world and bring back his saviour. That's how it goes, isn't it? Lay and his acolytes ascend to heaven and the rest burn.'

Bridget sniffed.

'Well, I've not spotted no saviour.'

'No,' said Marsh, stretching. 'Tell us if you do, though.'

I watched her stretch. It was worth seeing. Wole noticed me watching, so I examined my cards instead. Marsh sighed.

'I wonder where they get the fuel to run this ship. Burns thousands of gallons of fuel. And what kind of tribe has oil to waste on ritual sacrifice?'

'Quite so,' said Wole. 'Things are topsy-turvy here. We're prisoners and we eat better than we did on the *Lotus*.'

Carlos tossed a jack onto the table.

'So what you worried about? We're headed to a land of plenty.'

Ten days are spent shuttling between Eat, Sleep, Cleanse and Learn. Rickets walks us through the rituals of work sites: rest and prayer breaks, competing firms and indentured labourers, unions and strikes, humour and prejudice, terror and corruption, reporters and spies. He teaches us where we can effect change, where we will only limit damage.

It is incredible that society survives these vices. The system appears incapable of adaptation, sealed in place by wealth and superstition.

'That's why you're here,' explains Rickets. 'You're free of those forces. You can fix the world in spite of the system. You're our guardian angels.'

We learn of the chaos gripping the world, of water wars and famine, and I ask Rickets how repairing this one island nation can really accomplish anything if the world beyond is burning.

He smiles and says: 'It's all in hand. It's all in hand.'

One simulation blurs into another. I stand in a trench on the stadium site, near the fence, where a huge crowd has gathered. Ragged, malnourished young people chant and wave placards. I read the messages: Will work for food; Real labour for real people; Create jobs not Ficials.

The crowd shakes the fence, and then missiles begin to rain around the site: stones hurled from slings. A few strike me, but following Control guidelines I turn around and head for the site office.

A wide man in bright orange coat and no hard hat, a fellow worker, he barges past me in the trench, whimpering, cursing. I watch him splash up the trench, as fast as his heavy frame allows. Then a stone strikes him on the back of the head, and he drops into the mud. I walk along the trench, over the gurgling and gasping man, use his head as a step up and out of the trench.

The simulation freezes, and Rickets appears, shaking his head. He leads me back to where the man lies still in the mud.

'Now,' he says. 'Do you see what you did there?'

106

PONTOON

'Now hear this, now hear this. Security detail to the brig. Security detail to the brig.'

The Sharks arrived in force, stiff, armed and businesslike, and marched us out of the brig into the frigate's passageways. The ship had slowed, and a buzz of excitement echoed through the Sharks, their chewing rapid and noisy. We turned up a set of steps, headed up to the deck. I half expected to find a wooden cross waiting for me.

Instead we found the sun.

The sun.

Wole dropped to his knees. Carlos staggered, as if struck by the sun's rays. Bridget laughed in an unhinged sort of way. Marsh stood beside me and whispered: 'Exactly how far north are we?'

'Pretty far.'

Tears rolled down her nose. Suddenly she whooped, danced to Wole, bent and kissed him full on the lips.

Shit. 1–0 to the opposition.

I was too tired to care. Besides, the view was something else. I had imagined the cloud bank shrouded the globe, but this far north it evidently thinned and disappeared. Strips of white cloud criss-crossed a blue firmament. The sun was an intense, beautiful disc, bathing my skin, warming the sea, toasting the black frigate grey.

There was an incredible noise from aft, the unmistakable shrieking and chatter of children. They hurtled onto the deck, holding up their arms to the sky, trying to touch the sun, dizzy with excitement. A few ran into Bridget's arms, crying with joy, almost knocking her over. She kissed and embraced them, looked up, face beaming.

'They're safe, Ken! They're safe!'

'Right,' I said. 'Safe.'

A structure loomed on the horizon. Black, twisting columns. Smoke, flavouring the air with the acids of industry.

One by one, the others noticed it. At first I took it for a normal drilling platform, a relic of the last great pre-war oil boom; that period when humanity had perforated the pole, despoiling their last immaculate wilderness for the sake of a few more years' driving. But the structure grew and grew, revealing itself as something else, something greater.

A hush spread over the deck as we closed on the vast rust-red platform, waters lapping at its concrete support columns. It sat on the ocean like a great pallet, edges stacked high in brutal shipping container walls, dimpled with portholes.

The black frigate turned, began to circle, revealing a tangle of improvised bridges and gangways, where one structure had been fused to another. This was a gathering of drilling platforms, perhaps four or five lashed together into a gigantic whole. An Atlantic Oil Rocks.

Dense black webbing hung under the main structure, shivering with some hidden movement. The children crowded the port guardrail, peering into the mysterious nets, where hands poked through the webbing, waving, or making other signs.

'It's a whopper,' said Bridget, standing next to me, two infants clinging to her legs.

'It certainly is.'

There was a powerful, familiar odour. I peered below, saw that we were cutting through a great, brown oil slick.

'How many people can live on that thing?' said Bridget.

'Plenty.'

'Imagine,' she said. 'The audience.'

Tall pontoons reached out from the column ahead, forming a rickety, improvised dock, running Flex ladders up to the platform. Scattered figures waved at our approach. Bridget and the young people waved back.

'Ken,' whispered Bridget, so that the kids might not hear. 'I'm a bit scared.'

'Just hold that Only Book and smile like you believe. You'll be fine.'

The black frigate slowed, rocking into the third pontoon. Sharks lined the gunwale, calling out instructions, relaying them to the pilot.

Reals jogged along the dock, catching rope, tying up the ship. Above, on the platform edge, a group of characters in white hoods stood perfectly still, observing.

Gangways were run out, Sharks urging us onto the dock. Wole, Carlos and Marsh went first. Bridget remained, shouting at two Sharks. They were separating her from the children.

'Bridget!' I said. 'Remember what we discussed.'

She thought about it, dropped to her knees, clutched as many children to her as she could and whispered goodbyes. She wiped her eyes, and shuffled over the gangway to me. We were hustled along the dock, up the ladders to the platform. I remembered not to look down. Heights weren't my thing.

We ascended to a kind of esplanade, ten feet wide, sandwiched between the sheer drop to the dock, and a twenty-feet-high wall of containers stepping back from the platform edge.

Carlos tapped me on the shoulder, pointed out to sea.

'Never seen it in daylight before.'

The *Lotus*. The Sharks had anchored it nearby, flying a huge flag from an improvised mast – the white cross on the red circle. A little smoke still drifted from the damaged nursery, but it looked in surprisingly good condition. I'd never realised how white it was.

Below us the children gathered on the dock. Hoods shepherded them along, towards an old fishing boat. One of them counted shells into Floyd's palm.

The Sharks got businesslike again, pinning us into a recess in the container wall. Bridget struggled next to me.

'Will you relax?'

'Where are they taking them, Ken? We can't just let them take them away.'

'We can figure that out later. Just hold your book and grin like an idiot.'

'You're not grinning.'

'I will if I have to.'

'He's right,' said Wole. 'Keep your cool.'

A figure was descending the stepped crates, striding, leaping and vaulting its way to the esplanade. The man jumped a final time, straightened and approached our group. He had a head like a keystone, and was dressed in loose blue overalls, smeared with oily filth.

A tool belt swung at his considerable waist. He was a little less imposing than the Iron Pagoda.

He offered a few curt syllables. Our Shark guard stepped aside, admitting him to our space. He walked among us, assessing us with a practised indifference. A long blue earring hung from his left lobe, bearing a number.

He gripped my gauntlet, held it out.

'Prosthetic.'

'Artificial limb.'

He grunted, turned the hand over, examining its joints and plates. 'Expensive.'

My companions stiffened, wondering if the giant was about to call Ficial. I tried to think of a believable explanation.

'I lost it skiing, pre-war. This was the best Harley Street had to offer. I was a rich man.'

He didn't care much. He prodded other parts of me, then turned his attention to Wole, Carlos and the others, using the same professional detachment. He swivelled, smiled.

'My name is Li. Five derricks here,' he said. 'Red. White. Yellow. Green. Blue. I recruit for Blue. You work hard. Good pay. Agreed?'

Only an earthquake would have argued with him.

'Good. I tag you.'

The Sharks pressed Carlos's arm behind his back, held him out before Li.

'Hey, wait a minute!'

Li plucked pliers from his tool belt, a red set mounting a long, thin barb. He seized Carlos by the ear. The cook struggled. Li watched him coolly.

'Move and it hurts.'

Carlos settled down, ground his teeth. Li pressed the pliers to the skin, crunched the tool closed. Carlos howled. Li picked a blue rectangle out of his pocket, bit the cap off a pen, scribbled a number. He fixed the tag to Carlos's ear.

'Don't scratch,' he advised, pushing Carlos aside.

Wole went next, then the rest of the crew. The pain was short, settling down into an insistent throb. Li handed out packs of gum, and we all set to chewing.

Bridget stepped forward, but a Shark pushed her back.

'Hey!' she said. 'What about me?'

Evidently she'd failed Li's test. We were dragged away from her, along the esplanade. Bridget cried out and waved.

We can't just leave her.

'Damn,' said Wole. 'We should do something.'

The Sharks urged us on after Li, brandishing weapons. There was no getting past them. Besides, I had to look out for myself now. I had to work hard.

The fourth day of the second week, and training is complete. We brothers sit up on our couches, drop our feet to the cold floor, pop the lenses from our eyes.

I blink, and then I see my first Soldier Model. He stands in the hatch between our flex and his, eyes glowing green. He beckons to me. I approach, as my brothers file into the elevator and depart. I wonder if I am contradicting some law by remaining. The Soldier is not concerned. He slaps my shoulder and makes a low gurgling sound.

'Construction Model, right? Rover Model?'

'Correct.'

He holds out his palm. Two lenses.

'You want to swop Learns?'

The discs roll in his palm.

'Is that permitted?'

'Of course it's not permitted, that's the point. I tried out a Medical Model Learn simulation yesterday. Let me tell you, mate, they could teach us a few things about cruelty.'

I am curious. I expect a Control Signal to interrupt us, to dispatch us to the waste pits for disobedience. But there is only silence, and the Soldier's expectant gaze.

'You want to take a look or don't you?'

I drop my lenses into his palm. Press my fingertips into his lenses and roll them into place.

'Good lad.'

He leads me to the Soldier flex, indicates his couch and departs to take over mine. I lie down, feel the surfaces press around me.

The simulation begins.

I expect explosions, shrieking rockets, the screams of dying men.

But it is quiet. I am lying in hot, damp undergrowth, holding a rifle, at the edge of a jungle clearing. Before me, a camp spreads among ancient ruins.

A stone temple towers over the scene, pre-Colombian Maya design, a thousand-year-old limestone pyramid topped by a squat roof comb. A mixture of soldiers and civilians are camped around it. Children play on its steps. The scene is almost tranquil, until explosions suddenly rock the camp, hot blasts that rip through the people, raising showers of debris and screams, many screams. Those remaining scatter, but it is too late. Soldier Models emerge from the tree line, firing with expert, ruthless accuracy, cutting down all shapes and sizes they find.

I stand, leave the rifle, and walk onto the site, as the last simulated adversaries are slaughtered. Green eyes glow in the smoke, moving among groaning wounded, offering no mercy, only bayonets.

Then, the smoke clears, and the grasses are scattered with bent, broken human forms, curious severed limbs. And now the other Soldiers have turned their attentions to the pyramids. They spread out, laying charges across the surface. Others deface the Stelae – ancient carved Mayan monuments which they topple, smash, stamp upon, green eyes hungry for iconoclastic chaos.

The display freezes. A man I haven't seen before appears at my side.

'What are you waiting for? Get stuck in, Soldier!'

I don't understand.

They have killed the people. Why kill the buildings too?

BLUE

We climbed the stepped containers by worn Flex ladders, frayed ropes and jagged handholds, following Li's assured bounds and leaps. A cold wind bit as we ascended. Many containers were punctured by crude portholes, affording our first glimpses of New Jerusalem's citizens: women seated at a crescent of sewing machines, pedalling furiously; young men working at a long table, disassembling and cleaning handguns. Higher still, elder Reals, unravelling heaps of knotted seaweed. A few gaped at us as we climbed past.

We finally reached the summit, ten containers up, still dazzled and charmed by the glorious sun. I looked back the way we'd climbed; found a view over the harbour, where a fishing boat, barge, sailboat and paddle steamer were crammed into berths around the black frigate. There was something else, too: a black lozenge, set apart from the other craft, heavily guarded by Sharks. Sixteen hatches popped open along its spine. A submarine.

Beyond the harbour, out to sea, the *Lotus* sat on the surface, its outer petals opened to the sun. I turned around and took in the other view: the Rig.

Li lifted his arms into the wind, coat billowing.

'Welcome,' he said. 'New Jerusalem.'

He squatted on the corrugated surface, knowing we'd need a moment. We bent in the wind, chewed, took in the sheer, Real ugliness of the structure before us.

The container wall formed a protective barrier, a wall stretching almost the entire perimeter of a huge, T-shaped platform. The T was a composite of five oil rigs, lashed together, each mounting its own derrick. The platform forming the right branch of the T, its every surface spattered blue, was misaligned, lying at an angle and on a slope. Our new home, I guessed. The four other derricks were identified by similar splashes and daubs of green, yellow, red and white.

Ramshackle complexes clustered around each of the derricks: stacked containers, towering cranes, pumping stations, improvised refineries, and curious giant wheels, turned by figures walking within. Dozens of pipelines snaked in flexible coils around and over containers, or drooped from fixed mountings, burrowing and reappearing. They seemed to have leaked in places, lending New Jerusalem a thin, greasy sheen.

Li spat out his gum, squeezed a replacement out of a pack, and waved an arm over his head.

'Rest over.'

We followed, descending a series of rattling staircases fixed to the inside of the container wall. We entered a warren of green-daubed structures, into shade, out of the wind. A group of Real workers, caked black with oil, pressed past us in an alley. They jeered, spat and barged their way along our line.

Wole watched the group pass.

'I take it they don't look kindly on we Blues?'

Li shrugged.

'Never cross another rig alone. Stick to Blue. Especially Game time.'

'*No me diga*,' said Carlos, clutching his tagged ear. 'We've joined a gang.'

Li didn't contradict him. We clambered over the humps of two giant, slippery black pipelines, a deep, mechanical grinding building to a deafening roar. We climbed, took an undulating path over container tops. The surface was half-scorched, half-caked in a pale deposit that cracked under our boots.

'Fire,' yelled Li over the engine noise, by way of explanation.

I couldn't believe it. Yelled in Li's ear: 'How'd they put out the fire?'

Li pointed up, to a tall lattice steel structure, some combination of crane and water tower, suspending a large tubular tank. Sharks moved along the crane beam, wielding binoculars.

'Tank full of retardant,' said Li. 'They see spark, they hose it. Don't be around. Dries fast. Make you statue. Like these.'

He pointed to a kind of courtyard below, where six Pompeian figures had been caught in the spray. They were fixed in poses of agony, crouched, gasping. One had its hand lifted to its brow, saluting death.

Li stopped, listened. Turned to us, a finger pressed to his lips. We followed, picking across the container rooftops, down into deserted nooks between structures, darting from cover to cover. Only as we neared the end of Yellow territory did the bombardment start. Stones of all shapes and sizes, presumably dug out of the seabed. One struck Carlos on the arm.

'Are they CRAZY?' he yelled, taking cover. 'What the hell is their problem?' Li took the gum out of his mouth and flicked it away. We sat with him until the attack died down.

'Yellow's worst,' he said. He rose to his feet, led us to another passage near the perimeter. The containers, flags and tags turned red, but the populace seemed less aggressive, more inclined to stare through us than shoot. Li was certainly more at ease. Columns of steam blew at irregular intervals all over the Red platform. Reals scuttled about the derrick, bearing loads, glistening with grease. High up in the structure figures dozed in hammocks.

Moisture spattered my face.

At first I thought it was oil, but then the others began yelping in excitement.

Rain. Real rain. I closed my eyes to it, let it run over my parched skin. Carlos stuck out his tongue, lapping at it. Wole cupped it in his hands.

Li leaned on a blue container and watched his fledglings frolic in the downpour until he lost patience with the rain dance and urged us on.

We finally arrived at Blue territory. You certainly couldn't miss the border. As I suspected, the rig had suffered some kind of catastrophic docking failure. The entire structure had been tossed up during impact, creating a kind of scarred metallic cliff face, embedded in the side of the red rig. Rope ladders dangled on its surface, which Li duly urged us to climb. We followed him up, chewing vigorously on tasteless gum, the shower growing heavier, wind picking up. The sea had turned the colour of slate.

We arrived on an exposed, banking deck. Our rig had a very different configuration from those we had crossed. The sloped surface couldn't support a protective wall, so here the containers huddled at the centre of the structure, propped and braced level, forming a kind of weather shield around the derrick, high enough almost to obscure the great mast.

The rain lashed at us now, as Li led us across the exposed deck, then into the shelter of the Blue 'town'. We edged along tight passages, each surface rattling an accompaniment to the derrick hum. We passed through rusted lattices of scaffold, under the shimmering overhang of a cantilevered Mylar structure, over warped, unfinished timber. Li hurried along without a thought. The path grew narrower as we approached the derrick, until we were edging sideways along a man-made crevasse, wedged between two steaming-hot, high steel walls. Carlos brushed the surface with his hand, howled and kissed the burn.

'What are we?' he yelled, shuffling sideways with the rest of us. 'Fucking crabs?'

'You wish,' said Li. 'You worms.'

'Goddam worms, are we?' snapped Carlos, hauling the load onto his back. 'The worm can turn, baby. The worm can turn.'

I guessed he wasn't happy with the induction process. It certainly hadn't been gentle. Li had led us below deck, handed us a stout pair of gloves each, and put us to work. We would haul crates and bags of jagged drill cuttings to the surface, toiling alongside another twenty or so burly, stinking Reals. Carlos began complaining immediately.

'What did you want?' I asked him. 'A room with a view? A chocolate on your pillow?'

He snarled under his burden.

'Why not? They might at least give us a sandwich before laying on the hard labour.'

A strained noise escaped me as I lifted two crates.

'I don't think they have time for that.'

Li had led us below deck, into the stench and gloom of the platform superstructure, and quickly assigned work. Carlos and I would begin as 'worms', the local term for those assigned the most menial tasks on the rig: heavy lifting, mainly. Marsh and Wole would man the drilling systems. Carlos wasn't entirely happy with the allocation.

'Why do we get the mule work, huh?'

'I guess we look the strongest,' I said, hauling up the metal stairs, through chinks of daylight, flickering overheads, sucking air thick with steam.

'We look the dumbest,' growled Carlos.

I let him talk. I was glad to be working, glad to be exhausted, numbed. It quietened the voice in my head, edged out images of a broken, black animal.

We travelled up in panting fits and starts, past the sullen glares of our new co-workers, until we reached the surface. Carlos bent over, hands resting on knees.

'How long is our shift?' he gasped.

I turned and headed back down, feeling broken but determined to push through it. Carlos followed, clutching his back.

'First a Ficial asylum, now it's goddam hard labour. I really believe I'm *salao*.'

He kept up his monologue for a good hour, bemoaning cruel fate, until we passed a young man travelling up the stairs, a bag over each shoulder. He smiled at us.

'Welcome to Blue,' he said. 'Have a nice day.'

'*Dios*,' said Carlos, watching him climb out of sight. 'It's not all bad.'

We laboured until the light from the surface dimmed, the other workers disappeared, and it seemed we were toiling alone. I was ready to go on, but Li appeared, crawling out of a gap in the landing wall. He beckoned to us.

'You two.'

He turned and headed back into the superstructure.

'Hey!' said Carlos, scuttling after him. 'When do we eat?'

We crawled into the dark, rattling shell of the oil platform, emerged into a shaft running the height of the rig, echoing with the wash of the sea. Li began descending a ladder.

'Hey!' Carlos looked at me, shook his head. 'Do you believe this guy?'

I eased down after Li, muscles trembling with each step. Down, down we travelled, a murmur growing beneath us. Li stopped at the bottom of the shaft, a kind of open manhole where the murmur originated. He glanced up.

'Jump,' he said, pointing at his feet. 'Net.'

He released his hold on the ladder, fell out of sight. I cautiously worked my way to his last position, stopped to peer below. Carlos was worried.

'What can you see, man?'

'Not much.' I could only make out a black, shivering surface.

'Can you see him?'

'No.'

'So what DO you see?'

A moment passed in silence, both of us pondering, weighing up the fall. I looked up, past Carlos, the way we'd come. My arms were weak. I'd never scale it again. Carlos spoke first.

'So what, you going to drop or are we going to hang here all night?'

The question burned. Since losing my Ficialhood I'd developed a quite powerful fear of heights. I was especially averse to falling from them. I couldn't judge how far this drop would be, but the longer I looked the more it took on the character of a bottomless pit.

Still, I couldn't allow Carlos to sense weakness. I closed my eyes, thought of England, and let go.

A stab in my heart. A cold, whistling wind. Then the give of a damp surface, welcoming me into its flexible embrace. I took a moment, called to Carlos, then scuttled clear, over a great woven rope net.

He dropped after me, rolled and jumped onto all fours, shaped like a startled rat. We rested for a moment, listening to the wash of the sea, and what seemed like the chatter of a distant crowd.

Carlos pointed behind me.

'Look.'

Dim beams of light glowed through the surface. Carlos sniffed the air.

'Oh, man. Do you smell that? Food!'

He scuttled past me, fumbling and grasping. Right away he lost his footing on the slippery rope, missing a toehold and losing his leg through a hole. He cursed and tried again, coming a cropper with equal speed. I persuaded him to slow down a little, and we crawled across the cargo net, taking firm, measured steps and picked hand-holds, asking even more of our tired limbs.

As we drew closer to the illuminations I glanced up, inspected the underside of the rig above us. It was coated in a thick, uneven crust of retardant. It seemed to be sprinkled with holes. Corroded hoops poked from the frozen retardant bubbles, suspending the net by leather straps. Each hooked point created peaks and valleys in the material, as if we were crawling over the roof of a circus tent.

A sharp whistle sounded. Li's head emerged from a cut in the net, wearing a miner's helmet, the light sweeping through the darkness.

'Here,' he said. We closed on him, found him clinging to the net's underside by his feet and one hand. He unhooked his feet, swung clear of the cut, urged us to drop through. We obeyed, dropping past him onto another, slimier net, stretching about us, fixed to the underside of the overnet in another landscape of gloomy peaks and troughs. Lanterns, hammocks and other shapes swung in the darkness. Silhouettes of people shifted about the surface like lost apes. Li crouched with ease on two coils, drew something out of his satchel.

'Pay,' he said, rolling three white bivalve seashells into our palms. He regarded us for a moment, then bounced away towards the net settlement.

I rolled the shells onto the tips of my flesh fingers, worked grit under the nails, stroked their ribbed surfaces.

Carlos scowled. 'Shell currency,' he said, eyebrows arched. 'Is this a joke? Does this make us rich or poor?'

We scrambled over the ropes, towards heat, voices, and the scent of food, stopping at the first gathering we found. A group of twelve Reals crouched there under a kind of brazier, crowned by a sizzling pan. The contraption was suspended from the overnet by a chain, perhaps six feet above the balancing customers, who held bowls at their chins, picking at chunks of something pale. I was surprised to see a battered Flex screen mounted above them, pinned to the nets. The customers barely noticed us, transfixed by the flex's flickering images of motor sport.

'Where's the waiter?' asked Carlos.

'Right here.'

We turned, startled. A chuckling ancient hung upside down, suspended from the overnet by a strap hooked to his belt. Tongs, chopsticks and forks were clipped either side. A pistol too. He wore a strange apron, with hoops over both legs and arms, spattered with the congealed filth of ages. He grinned and clutched his hands.

'New arrivals, yes? I am 74.' He pinched the tag on his ear. 'Almost the longest-serving Blue. Certainly oldest. Best cook anyhow. You will eat?'

'How much for a bowl?' asked Carlos, keeping his shells hidden.

'To you, my friend, two shells.'

A customer glanced in our direction, then lowered her face, resuming chewing.

'That'll cover both of us,' I said, 'or we shop around.'

The ancient's smile disappeared, then bloomed again.

'Of course,' he said. 'That's what I meant.'

He spun on his cord and ascended to the net, swinging about his pan with fluid motions, hanging by feet, or one hand, or combinations of the two, turning the pan's contents, sipping at a ladle, picking and replacing tools on his belt. We edged around the circle of customers, locating a free patch of net where we could barely see the flex. Carlos leaned to our neighbour, a woman with cropped, grey hair. She too sported a pistol on her hip.

'What's the *película*?'

'Huh?'

'What's on TV?'

The woman shrugged.

'It's the Game.'

The flex was hidden from us, but we could hear engines revving, excited commentary. I was interested, but too tired to investigate. We licked the crumbs from our bowls, paid 74, and rolled deeper into the net, following a trail of exhausted workers through a split, down to a further sub-net, where hundreds swung in hammocks, or piled in mounds, clustered together for warmth. I could understand that. The cold was as deep in my bones as the fatigue.

'Is this why they call us worms?' said Carlos, inspecting the green muck caking his hands. 'Slithering about down here like bait?'

I shrugged.

'Maybe. You want to cuddle up?'

'With you and your nightmares? *¡No puedo creerlo!*'

'Then join a pile. We'll freeze to death otherwise.'

Carlos clutched himself, sat cross-legged and shivering, regarding the dozing jumbles of his fellow Reals.

'You think there's some etiquette to joining in?'

'I'm sure they'll let you know if you get something wrong. You take that one.' I pointed at the nearest pile. 'I'll take the next.'

I watched Carlos suggest his way into the mound, then rolled away, to the pile in the depths of the net valley. On another night I might have wondered if Marsh would be in there. I might have gone in search of a drink, or brooded over Pistol. Now all I could think of was sleep. I squirmed among the Reals, hearing no reprimands other then the occasional half-conscious snort. Most were dressed in rags, and all slept with holstered belts. That would make for the occasional violent jab in the night.

I lay with my face on a soft, warm arm, a skin pillow. My gauntlet was pinned under a back, my right leg exposed to the freezing wind. My breath grew heavy. My eyes dimmed. Endorphins surged through me, then drained completely away.

I slept.

Test is one open level, where divisions between hexes have been stripped away, creating an open hangar, interrupted only by elevator columns. We Nines stand and assess what we see around us.

The space has fourteen sides, divided into four recessed spaces – two of three sides, two of four. In the first, a kind of shooting gallery, where a mix of rifles, pulsers, saws and other portable tools lie arranged on a bench. The surfaces of the recess are stained a light pink, despite the best efforts of successive cleaning details.

The second is a kind of open surgery, where a diagnostic bench sits under an analysis node.

In a third, a sealed tank, three nozzles projecting from the roof, the wall still scorched and pitted.

In the fourth lies a simple stone plinth.

'Testing is pretty much the same for any model,' explains Rickets. 'Each new Power, whether it is Construction, Soldier, Medic or Programmer, contains in its blood a new generation of nanotech, an even more efficient regenerative system. Now, while we design each model with separate specifications, and while certain models will almost certainly never suffer serious physical trauma, we are committed to testing each and every model's durability. It's essential, so that we can identify any glitches and accurately forecast nanotech progression over the course of the programme.'

While he is saying this he is walking backwards, beckoning us to the plinth. He taps at a flex, and lights glow in the recess, and dim outside it. He takes an instrument from his top pocket and he prods it into a brother's chest and says: 'Lie on the plinth, please.'

And the brother moves, but Rickets grips him by the shoulder and tells him to strip first. So I watch my brother disrobe, and recline on the plinth, and as he lays his head back he notices something, we all do. We look up and see an identical plinth, fixed into the ceiling. We realise that our brother is lying in the jaws of a great press.

Rickets types something into the flex, and there is a low hammering sound, the blare of an alarm, and the ceiling plinth shudders and lowers out of its housing, a great metal plate headed for my brother. I begin to grind my teeth.

We watch. We wait.

I notice that the brother next to me is shrugging, over and over again. Some kind of spasm. I place my hand on his shoulder and I try to transmit my stillness. Curiously, this gesture composes him. I keep my hand there, hold my brother as we watch the press reach centimetres, millimetres above our prone brother's face, then impact, bend, crush his nose into his head, break his toes back on themselves. Bones snap and pop, and his face is forced to face us. His eyes bulge in their sockets, pop out. His chest crumples and sags, his arm snapping and folding over. He breaks up, into skin, meat and blood, which pours off the plinth. Grates in the floor open and drink him up.

Rickets holds up the flex. He is filming everything.

WORMS

I woke, a siren rousing the pile. A neighbour's toe poked into my ear and explored, but I was more distracted by a new sensation.

Rest. Real rest, free of a nightmare's aftershock, of cold sweat and throbbing eyes. I felt renovated. I blinked in morning light. Remembered the clear sky outside.

Bodies crawled away around me, until I could lie flat on the net, peering through it at the sea, fifty feet beneath us, foaming around a great concrete column. A wonderful blue, speckled with oil. Looking around I saw other, smaller nets hanging in patches – enclosures that Reals had made their own. I clambered after my co-workers, realising what a great mass of smaller, interconnecting nets hung from the overnet, forming pockets, nooks, and other drooping structures, knotted together in an unknowable maze of zips and crawl spaces. A uniquely human kind of mess.

The nets teemed with Reals, here washing at a communal trough, there crouched with breeches lowered. Others gathered under the hanging cook shops, feeding from bowls or lying under flexes pinned to the overnet. Some more sickly types staggered and clung to the net peaks, blinking at the morning like angry strangers.

A bony Real dropped from the net above and speared his hand at me, flapping his palm open and shut. One moment there was gum there, the next none.

'Want some, buddy? Want some? Huh?'

I gave him one of my two remaining shells for three pieces of gum, and chewed. I pressed on, having a curious need to see someone from the *Lotus*.

I handed over my final shell for breakfast at 74's. My fellow diners ignored me, so I watched the flex, which was tuned to some kind of local network. There were advertisements for lawyers, doctors and handguns, then a public execution programme: a thin Real knelt on the deck of the black frigate, a sword-wielding Hood stood over him. The crowd cheered as the blade scythed down, and the loose body was kicked into the sea.

'You like that, Red?' cried a fellow customer.

Then, a flash of the New Jerusalem logo, and a stiff, urgent voice:

'Be vigilant. Ficial agents are everywhere. Report suspicious activity to your supervisor, and help wipe Ficial pox from the Earth's complexion.'

My fellow customers didn't so much as glance at me.

We might just get away with this.

I'd almost finished breakfast when the flex emitted a high-pitched whistle.

The entire net came to a halt, snapped into silence. I looked around, saw my fellow Blues kneeling or lying flat all over the net.

Then they began to murmur. It took a moment to realise they were reciting the pledge.

I believe in the prophet, he who wears the crown and holds the rod
I believe in his freedom, he who speaks to us the word of God

I bowed my head. I couldn't remember the words, but if they did this every morning I soon would.

The pledge ended, and the flex returned to advertisements. The diners rose, licked the last from their bowls, and headed out to work. The Blues formed into neat queues, under the gaps leading to the overnet.

Then, finally, I spotted someone I knew.

Bruiser. She was still dressed in her *Lotus* overalls, scurrying awkwardly, slipping here and there. I dropped my bowl and went after her, but she was quick and I couldn't close the gap. I called out but she didn't hear, too intent on her mission, climbing over adults, wriggling through the tear to the overnet.

I reached the tear and groped through it, just in time to see Bruiser boosted up to the ladderway, the platform cavity from which Carlos and I had dropped. I pursued, accepted a boost up after her, scaling the coarse rungs with the other Blue workers. I emerged from a man-hole cut between two containers. The dazzling light and whistling wind made it hard to breathe.

I saw Bruiser, a tiny figure darting into a narrow passage. I gave chase, running alongside more punctured portholes, glimpsing people already at work with needles, thread and patches.

Bruiser jinked left, then right, and suddenly the rim of Blue's great turning wheel revealed itself, perhaps fifteen feet high, wedged between containers and other structures.

Bruiser climbed a ladder, running atop another container, pulled up outside what had once been a site office. I spat out my gum, paused for breath, watched. She stood to one side as other children, clutching Only Books, were counted into the site office by an adult. I expected her to join them, but instead she ran on, headed for the wheel.

I continued the pursuit, hauling up the ladder onto the container top. I paused a moment by the schoolhouse door, heard the teacher confidently endorse the creation chapters of the Only Book: the bit where God rushes out a design to a self-imposed deadline, then moans when the product's defective.

I heard my name called. Heard it again. I peered over the container rim, and saw Carlos squinting up at me, hands on knees, heaving for air.

'What's wrong with you, man? I've been calling your name. Who you chasing?'

'Bruiser. One of the kids from the Park. I want to ask her about the other kids. About Bridget.'

Carlos raised his arms, slapped them down at his sides.

'We don't have time for this. We are late for work.'

'So we're already in trouble. Come with me. I can't understand her without you, anyway.'

Carlos shook his head, climbed up to join me. We passed the schoolhouse and vaulted onto a blue container, where we had a good view of the wheel. A crowd of children were queuing before a foreman in overalls and yellow hat.

'¿Que es esto?'

'It's some kind of treadmill. Must help power the Rig.'

'They're working kids on a treadmill? ¡Eso es una locura!'

We worked our way off the portacabin, into the crowd, pulled Bruiser clear. Carlos knelt and spoke softly to her.

'*¿Que estamos haciendo? Tu trabajas aquí?*'

The girl nodded, scratching her arm, mumbled something. Carlos cursed.

'Says they can't go to school until they can pay for it. They work here to save.'

'I don't see the other *Lotus* kids. Ask her where they are.'

Carlos nodded.

'*¿Los otros niños trabajan aquí también?*'

The girl tried to scamper away, but Carlos was too quick for her, dragging her back to face him. Bruiser rattled out words, pointing and gesturing, twitching with impatience.

'Says a few of them work here, but most got taken to the big boat. She says the other kids went with the Hoods. Says they're gonna be warriors of New Jerusalem. Jeez, sounds creepy, huh?'

'What about Bridget?'

The girl twisted in Carlos's grip.

'She doesn't know.'

'OK. Let her work.'

Carlos and I wormed in silence, thinking solitary thoughts. Later we met Bruiser at 74's, shared a single bowl of the gruel, having both blown our wages on gum. Bruiser explained that she'd earn a shell a week. She said the foreman carried a rod and beat the kids who couldn't speak English.

'We'll have to teach her,' said Carlos.

The flex showed a military funeral, taking place on the black frigate. Sharks were lined up, brandishing rifles, over a coffin draped in the New Jerusalem flag.

Floyd's voice intoned: '. . . to those who make the ultimate sacrifice in this war on Satan, who fight his minions to protect our way of life . . .'

Carlos leaned in close.

'You suppose those were casualties from the *Lotus*?'

Before I could answer the Sharks shot into the air. The report made the customers jump. The screen faded into the New Jerusalem logo. Briefly I thought of Kinnare, my body on fire.

74 swung from his perch, batting aside hanging pots and jars, and killed the display.

'Well, gentlemen,' he said, swinging over to us, picking his teeth with a shard of plastic. 'How are you finding life and work here in Blue?'

'No comment,' said Carlos.

74 shrugged upside down.

'Don't take it for granted. Blue nets are better than the others.'

'The other rigs live like this?'

'Certainly they do,' said 74, discovering something between his teeth, squinting at his skewered prize. 'It's not perfect, sure, but work hard enough and anyone can make it to a new life on the *Ark*.'

'Ark? What ark?'

'It's where the barons live,' said the elder, biting on his plastic. 'Man Snoot, our owner? He lives there. All the great and the good do. It's an old cruise ship, sails around the Rig. Yes sir, life is sweet on that boat.'

Carlos shook his head.

'You never made it, then?'

'Didn't work hard enough,' explained 74.

He swung away to take an order.

A voice called to us from above.

'Hey, you roustabouts. What's cooking?'

Carlos grinned wider than his bowl, jumping to his feet.

'Wole!'

'Quite so.'

The big man hung from the overnet, features set in an easy half-grin. Marsh hung next to him, her arms bare and stretching. I stumbled to my feet and spluttered half a greeting.

'How are you three?' asked Wole.

Carlos curled his lip.

'We're breaking our damn backs. Broke, too.'

Wole dropped and ambled over to us, one foot over another on the coil, a tightrope walker's poise. Marsh dropped beside him, landing with equal style.

Carlos embraced them both. Bruiser and I hung back.

'Where have you two been?' asked Carlos.

'Rig management have our own pocket,' said Wole, shrugging at the perk. 'Built into the superstructure. We have bunks, a little social space. It's not bad.'

'Not bad?' snapped Carlos. 'It's fucked up! What about us? We have to sleep in huddles, in the open. Like goddam penguins.'

'We'll get you jobs up top,' said Marsh. 'We're working on it. You think we could forget you, Carlos? You'd never let us. We can hear you moaning from up there.'

She smiled at him, her features caught in the overhead glare. She was tired. A different kind of tired, something deep. Either she needed sleep, or something about Rig life disagreed with her.

They sat with us, ordered drinks from 74. We discussed Bruiser's work, the other children, speculated on Bridget's fate. Marsh still had that cough. A deep, rattling number. She gasped, explained she was training to work on the well 'Christmas tree', which controlled the flow of oil. There were constant issues with it and the wellhead, causing production to slow to a trickle or cease completely. Man Snoot, it seemed, never visited Blue, but expected problems to disappear.

It occurred to me that nobody was discussing escape, but I said nothing, only watched Marsh drink, and marvelled at the grace of her lifted chin and her long, oil-smeared neck.

'So,' said Wole, 'you two hear about the Game?'

'What game?'

'Why, boys, it's the only game in town.'

We have returned to Sleep, though we cannot sleep. The pain is too great. Our week in Test is complete, but we require time to heal.

The brother to my left lies in five pieces on his bunk, watching as the stubby wounds ooze and develop stumps, reaching out for their severed kin. The brother to my right is a writhing mess of welts and boils, gasping at the air, the weaponised virus only slowly subdued by his nanotech. I have suffered from both during this week of tests. Now I lie among shards of thick, oily skin flakes, the scorched remnants of my old covering, shed by my recovering frame after a swim in a pool of fire. We have all learned a lot about pain, though I cannot imagine what Rickets learned. A brother told me that he sells the videos he makes, that there is a collectors market outside the bunker. I wonder that people could digest such sights.

Pain. All we Nines feel it, we lie and endure it because we know that healing will come. We know that healing will come and beyond it is work: design, survey, construction. We think of these things instead of the pain. We think of people and their permanent, degenerative suffering. We ask why the world should be made like this at all.

Then a strange sensation: my nanotech bristles and trembles – a deep shiver runs through my blood. My eyes roll back as if to look at my brain, and there I find comfort, distraction from the pain. Our thoughts cry out in welcome: Control.

- Rover Models, Power Nines. Your capabilities exceed specification. Tomorrow you will report to Burn, the final element in optimisation.

- *Burn? I have been burned already.*

- The burning of mind, not of flesh. Fine-tuning of augmented function. Once complete, Nines will be ready for tasking. You may now ask questions.

131

A cacophony of voices. Control is signalling every model in the flex. We all signal back, but many of the questions are the same. Control collates the enquiries, packages them. The soldiers ask: who is the enemy, when do we strike? The medics ask – who are the patients and when do we operate? We Nines ask something else. We ask:

– Who is the architect?

– Of Brixton?

Of Brixton. Of Control. Of Engineered. It doesn't take Control long to answer.

RAID

Sunday was Game Day across New Jerusalem. Every citizen was free, and each spent the time watching the Game. Blues emerged from their twisting, knotted hides and made their way to the north-west part of the nets, where a large expanse of cargo webbing known as the Game Net lay. A great flex was rolled out and fixed to the underside of the overnet. Spectators stretched out in a great cleared valley to watch.

Carlos secured a relatively dry patch, halfway up a peak with a decent view. Wole and Marsh brought snacks from 74's. I bought gum, Bruiser the water. The net hummed, a thousand Blues, all chewing in excitement.

I'd rediscovered my Only Book and examined the back pages, where the Game rules were stated. They were minimal, but that was easy to forgive: New Jerusalem had invented its own national pastime, a form of motor racing mixed with contact team sports, and its development had been uneven.

It seemed that each Game was held on an oval ice track known as the Drome, located far to the north of New Jerusalem, cut from Arctic ice. Each Rig had to contribute its own team and 'chariot', based on an SUV or pick-up chassis. Each vehicle conformed to a loose specification: standard snow tyres; minimum height, length, width and weight requirements. Each mounted a kind of ladder on its back, known as the rail. Each ran on standard gasoline.

The teams had four positions. Three began the race with the chariot (driver, backer and hopper) while the fourth, the runner, began on skates, locked in a pen on the Drome island, with competing runners. At a signal the pen gate would open and the runners were released down a slipway onto the track, to attack rival chariots, and each other.

The combat element of the sport would certainly make it a diverting watch. Each runner wore a bandolier mounting three pucks: small black disc charges which could be kicked at competing chariots. Hoppers were armed with a long staff, mounting a more powerful charge on the tip. Hoppers clung to each chariot's rail as they raced, then hurled staffs at opponents, or jumped onto rival chariots. Drivers were unarmed, kept busy by the task of keeping their fat, twitching vehicles under control. Backers could assume any role of a team-mate who was 'marked out', or killed. All the roles, it seemed to me, required Ficial reflexes.

There were a few other regulations of interest, but the essential object seemed to be the survival of five laps – through a combination of athleticism and merciless violence. Over the course of a series teams accumulated points in a league table. The winner of the League won a berth on the *Ark*. That ensured there were plenty of volunteers.

We lay back on the net and waited until the flex fizzed into life. A Hood appeared, and after the usual public service message, urging us to report suspicious activity, the pledge was read aloud. Bruiser and Wole chanted along. Carlos mouthed the words. Marsh only snapped and gnawed on her gum, hungrily watching the Hood bow and wring his hands.

Then a powerful fanfare blew, and a drone's-eye view was projected on the screen, of a great, white expanse of ice. The crowd roared approval, settling into excited chatter. I couldn't see what they were cheering. It looked like a cigarette burn on a pristine sheet.

'See it?' asked Marsh, leaning my way. 'See it?'

The drone descended a little, and finally I picked it out: the outline of the Drome's oval track. To the west, a long excavated access trench, pitted by five garages, packed with vehicles and busy Real figures.

Then a procession of elaborate ringside tents: a green star, a yellow sphere, a red cone, a white cube and a blue prism. Accomodation for the *Ark*'s Baron class. Huge Flex screens were mounted on each bend of the track, while the island within the oval course contained two large enclosures, each packed with Reals.

The drone banked, and I caught a glimpse of a great, bloated shape moored a little distance from the ice, smoke pouring from yellow stacks.

'The *Ark*,' said Wole. 'Something of a leviathan.'

'Welcome,' said a familiar voice, pumped from the flex speakers. 'I'm Floyd. Welcome, viewers from every section of New Jerusalem, for what promises to be a very special event indeed, as we gear up for the latest race in what has been an extraordinary season. It's a wonderful day for a wonderful game, and all today's teams will be hoping the prophet's favour falls on them.'

He didn't have much to say on the rules, or the team standings. Instead another voice joined him, starting a discussion about the weather, and then the spectators. On cue the drone tipped, providing a pixelated view of dignitaries crowding the open sides of the colourful tents. Some turned from the drone, but others were not so shy, raising wineglasses, waving, posing.

Then the screen cut to another view, of a motorcade passing behind the tents.

'Praise the prophet!' said Floyd.

The people in the nets moaned praise too, but there was an itch under the sound, an impatience for action. The motorcade pulled up, disgorging a gathering of Hoods. A figure was crushed between them, led to a great throne.

I couldn't make out any features, only identified a disabled Real. He had to be helped up the stairs to a throne platform, where he gestured to the crowd, receiving their applause. Then he sat and the image cut away.

Finally the screen tuned to an earthbound camera. A view of the pits, where Reals worked feverishly around the hulks of vehicles daubed in Rig colours.

'And now we get to the heart of the matter,' said Floyd. 'The teams. I have with me former driver Sanchez, of last season's famed Yellow team. Sanchez, give us your prediction for today's race.'

The voices faded out. I hunched forward, squinting at shapes waiting in snow-banked bays.

The chariots were SUVs, the last lines produced before Lay's war did what years of logic had failed to do, and stopped the market for good. Teams fussed around the great square shapes, fixing tyres, lowering engines, fuelling up.

If only Rick could have seen this.

Behind them, Reals gathered in Rig colours, stretching, jogging on the spot, standing with hands on hips. Some wore grilled helmets and padding. All wore skates, and figure-hugging white armoured combat gear.

A familiar face stood among the Blues, chewing, watching impassively.

'Li!' cried Carlos.

'Indeed,' said Wole. 'He's the driver. Survived two Leagues, so they say.'

'Survived?'

The picture cut out for a moment. I reared up, alarmed, but Wole pulled me down.

'Patience,' he said.

I folded my arms over my knees, grunted at the inconvenience. Around me Blues were making bets and offering odds. There wasn't much faith in the home team.

The picture crackled back into life, a different perspective now, of Floyd, sat next to another lightly tanned Real, another set of strangely angular features. I guessed he was Sanchez.

'So,' said Floyd, 'as the teams prepare for the off, I guess the real question on everyone's lips is: will Yellow once again triumph? Can they really keep producing win after win?'

'That's right,' said Sanchez. 'Yellow continue to set the pace in the Game, winning all three races on the bounce so far, with no other colour coming close. What unbelievable team spirit they have.'

'And if you had to take another chariot, Sanchez?'

Sanchez sighed, thought about that. The car cam rumbled by the race pits, showing us the teams mounting their vehicles.

'I guess I'd take Red,' said Sanchez, provoking a deafening chorus of boos from my fellow net-dwellers.

'They have a driver and hopper who were running last season,' he said. 'That kind of experience has got to tell sometime, and would really lift the fans of course. Blues, Greens . . . they keep losing too many players. If you don't have that experience in your team you're going to find it tough. Reds may not have won much but at least they have a few veterans.'

'But Blue have been really consistent, haven't they? Second place finishes in nearly all their races.'

'They're on a run, Floyd. When Li is fit he is as good as anybody.

But those players need to be looking at themselves in the mirror and asking some questions. They need to be saying: "Yeah, we're getting second. But why aren't we winning some games?"'

The screen cut to a view tagged 'Safety Car Cam': a view over a battered SUV's hood, cutting along the Drome ice, rolling up a ramp to a raised parallel track, where it could film the action without interfering. The chariots rolled out onto the ice. Green slipped as it turned out of the pits, taking a moment to get under control. Sanchez and Floyd brooded on that, but I was drawn to the action.

The competitors lined up at the bottom of the far straight. Each held driver, backer, and hopper on the roof, holding staffs. The five runners skated across the track to the island, crowded into their pen, where a race official locked them in.

'Five laps,' said Sanchez's commentary. 'Five laps to race to glory. Five laps to prove their individual skill, their teamwork, their belief in the prophet. The excitement in the crowd is incredible.'

'It's never anything else,' said Floyd. 'There is no other game like this. We are truly privileged to watch some of the greatest athletes in the world competing here today. We're just waiting for the race official to complete his checks and . . .'

Adverts. They blinked on, slapping the tension out of the crowd, provoking a groan that shook the net. More lawyers appeared on the flex, then Sanchez endorsing a particular handgun. Then a public message service, accompanied by sinister music. The New Jerusalem logo again, and that same urgent voice:

'They look like us. They sound like us. But it's only skin-deep. Ficial agents could be anywhere, anytime. Be vigilant. Report suspicious activity to your supervisor.'

Bruiser eyed me warily, but I wasn't too worried. Barely a Real on the net paid the ads any attention.

The camera snapped back to the action. The teams were already under way.

'And right away Yellow have the lead!' barked Floyd. 'They took the corner with a perfect line there.'

'The rest are bunching up, Floyd!' gasped Sanchez. 'Right away we've got spears deploying.' The picture from the safety car was horrible, apparently handheld. I made out a staff being thrown, missing. A car slapping into another. Figures tumbled from the rooftops.

'Oh!' boomed Sanchez. 'That's got to hurt. Greens and Blues have lost their hoppers right away. And yes . . . yes, Red has wiped out! They've slid clear, out of the Drome, can we get—?'

The drone picture, back again. A smoking wreck lying beyond the Drome wall. A burning figure crawling clear, rolling in the snow. Three more cars skidding and colliding, crushing, as they turned into the bend.

The picture cut back to the safety car. It was riding alongside the Yellow team, who had streaked far ahead of the pack, exhaust belching strange fumes. They whooped and cheered, making fists, chanting their colour as they hurtled towards victory. The crowds in the net thrashed and roared, heckling, laughing, cursing.

'How about that?' yelled Wole into my ear. 'What do you make of it?'

I said nothing. I didn't make much, but one thing was for sure.

The Game was rigged.

The final laps passed in a tedious procession, Yellow tearing so far ahead they nearly lapped their rivals. Yet still the crowd were hooked, restless but committed to every moment.

There was some controversy over the crash on the first corner. Sanchez claimed Blue had caused the Red crash with an illegal move. Floyd disagreed vehemently. The crowd cursed Sanchez, bombarded the flex when his face appeared, arguing with an interlocutor who couldn't hear them. Once I would have been surprised by that kind of Real behaviour. Now it was familiar. Welcome, in a way.

Blue finished second, raising a small cheer from the crowd. White followed, with the maimed Greens limping across the finish line last, their backer slumped dead in his seat.

'He was a great competitor,' said Floyd, forgetting the crash controversy.

'Absolutely,' agreed Sanchez. 'A real professional to the end.'

That was it for me. I stood, ready to leave.

'Where you going?'

Marsh looked at me, interested. I tried to keep my cool, but sometimes, looking at her, it was hard to find words.

'Li,' she said. 'They're going to interview him. Don't you want to see that?'

I retook my seat. Marsh smiled, then began hacking again. Wole tapped her on the back, as if it would help.

The flex showed Floyd on foot in the race pits, making his way through the busy teams, swarming over the crumpled, steaming wrecks of the defeated. He spoke to the Yellow winners first, a tanned and healthy bunch, before moving into the Green bay. The broken co-driver's body was being scooped from the wreck. The driver's face filled the flex, his features smeared with grease, cracked by pink crow's feet. He was weeping. Floyd wrapped up his interview quickly, pushed him aside, and made his way to the Blue pit. Li was waiting, that cool glare magnified ten times on the great flex.

'So, Li,' said Floyd. 'Second place for the Blues, two more team members dead, including yet another hopper. Some observers of the Game say that the team isn't progressing. As captain, what do you say to that?'

Li chewed, thought on it.

'No.'

Wole giggled next to me, clapped his hands.

'Hats off, Li!'

Floyd pressed on, a little flummoxed.

'Right. But what do you see as the missing element in the Blue selection so far?'

Li chewed, looked into the camera. Shrugged.

'Luck.'

Wole slapped Marsh on the knee. He thought this even better sport than the Game. Floyd wasn't so sure.

'So you're saying it's purely a run of bad luck, as opposed to any structural issue with the formation? You don't think there are one or two possible players working your derrick who could have made the difference for you today?'

'No,' said Li.

He was pulled out of shot. Floyd paused, muttering something, then faced the camera, eyebrows raised.

'There goes Li, Blues captain. As concise as ever. I don't know why we bother, I really don't.'

The nets erupted. Missiles, derisive laughter, flicked hand signals. My fellow Blues didn't like to see their man traduced. The noise swelled, then burned out, as the flex blinked into darkness, leaving us in the company of lantern light, and the sound of the sea below.

The crowd broke up. Wole slapped me on the shoulder. Then he offered his hand to Marsh, lifting her from the net. She winced, bent over and coughed hard, fell forwards. Wole helped her up, but she pushed him away and straightened, a pained smile on her face.

'Fine,' she gasped. 'I'm fine.'

We crouched, watched her step away. Wole took off after her.

Carlos threw a hand on my shoulder. 'You're sweet on her, huh?'

I shrugged his mitt free.

'What are you talking about?'

He raised his palms, as if in surrender.

'Hey, brother, just saying I feel your pain. I know what it is to hide your love away.'

'You're not my brother,' I snapped.

Carlos cursed.

'Sure. That's what I get when I try to reach out to a goddam—'

Bruiser jumped up, slapped her hand over Carlos's mouth. Carlos eyed the girl, removed the gag gently. We sat in a brooding silence. The cook had nearly given me away. I snapped at him: 'What do you know about hiding?'

Carlos looked away. Back again.

'Are you kidding me, man? Haven't you been watching TV? They're not exactly keen on. You know. The love that dare not . . .'

Before I could ask him what he meant, something tugged at my shirt. Bruiser. She whispered in Spanish and pointed behind me, into the darkness, her eyes wide and white. Carlos exchanged a few words with her, then looked over his shoulder, contemplating the net's gloomy corners.

'Oh, no,' he whispered. 'The kid's right.'

'About what?'

'Shut up and get down.'

Carlos slapped Bruiser to the nets, then lunged in my direction, tipping me expertly onto my back. He clamped a hand over my mouth and pointed.

Reals. Non-Blues. Foreigners, pouring through a tear in the north-west corner. Near enough a hundred of them, quietly squirming inside, pushing through from a knotted cluster of bindings and

140

support nets around the crushed impact zone. The hushed group convened and whispered. All were armed.

'Shit,' said Carlos. 'They must be coming from the next rig. They don't look friendly, do they?'

'You don't keep that quiet unless you're planning a surprise,' I said. 'We should warn the camp.'

'No need,' said Carlos.

One of the invaders sparked a red flare. He held it aloft, showing off his ragged clothes and sinewy frame, all soaked in red paint. He began to chant: '*Red, red, red, red!*'

His comrades joined him, a tribal challenge, the kind of thumping war cry Real men had chanted at each other for centuries. More flares burst into life. A Red raiding party spread over the Game Net, slowly advancing on us, dripping red war paint as it stalked forward.

'Let's split!' said Carlos, picking up Bruiser. I followed, but we were too late. The chant had roused our fellow Blues, who came pouring onto the Game Net from connecting webs, armed, roaring, ready to repel the incursion.

Gunfire crackled over our heads, punctuated by screams and outraged roars. We were pinned under a pretty good crossfire.

'They're insane!' yelped Carlos. 'Shooting on an oil rig! They'll blow us all to kingdom come!'

'This way!'

We crawled at a right angle to the advancing Red line, slipping over the vibrating surface, crossing over sub-pockets suspended beneath, where wide eyes cowered.

'There's nowhere to go!' yelped Carlos.

We rushed up an incline to the open net rim, found no connections below, only the thrashing ocean.

There was a whistle – Bruiser, waving us to her. We scrambled over, found that she'd located another net. Carlos tested its strength, patted the kid's head.

'Good work, little sister.'

He pushed Bruiser in and we rushed in after her, leaving the sound of battle behind as we crawled up a long, thin webbing strip, to where it met a tear in the overnet. We climbed through, clung to the sagging surface, and lay panting. I saw the drill rising nearby, wrapped in a column of retardant, puncturing the nets, the sea and the earth below. A jagged hole had been cut to accommodate it, so the surface sagged dangerously towards the twisting bit. I dragged Bruiser gently up the slope, away from danger. We lay flat, exhausted, flare and lantern light blinking through the criss-cross surface.

That's when I saw them: four, maybe five, dark, purposeful figures, slinking near the edge of the overnet.

'Where are they headed?' whispered Carlos. 'They Blue?'

'No.'

'How can you be sure? They're headed away from the fight. Maybe they're running.'

'You don't flee in formation. They're going for the ladderway.' *Marsh*.

'I'll go,' I said. 'You keep the kid safe.'

I hurried across the great swinging deck, more practised in the hopping stride required on the rope surface. I caught up as the final Red raider reached for the ladderway. He heard me coming at the last moment, but I caught his throat in the gauntlet and pinched before he could wail a warning. I followed his friends up, listening to their whispers, their boots ringing on the rungs.

I decided I had better thin their numbers. I picked up speed, reached for the boot above, wrapped gauntlet fingers around the right ankle and squeezed.

The Real made an anguished squeak and dropped right onto me. His friends weren't pleased, but they kept moving, leaving me to squirm clear of the unconscious Real blocking the ladderway. I dropped his body, looked up, found the raiders gone. I listened, heard them clattering through the superstructure.

I travelled up, searching for the entrance to Marsh's digs, until I noticed an oblong cavity in the ladderway wall. I slithered inside, worked along a kind of scaffold tunnel, crawling over mud lines and under burning steam pipes, around rusted girders and along huge wound coils of electrical wiring – all the elements required to suck black gold from three thousand metres below. The sounds of conflict clattered and sang ahead.

I guess I could have used a little more caution. The Real dropped on me from above, a thick, twisted coil of copper wire stabbing so close to my nose I could smell the solder.

I struggled with him in the narrow space, tried to crush his face in the gauntlet. He roared in outrage, stabbed me in the gut. I slammed him up, his skull cracking on the pipe. He huffed and sagged onto me. I struggled free, ripped the coil out of my side. He hadn't been able to swing, so the wound wasn't deep. I could continue.

I tasted crude on the air, heard a sound like water rapids. Black speckles spattered on my hand. Then, I saw it: a black torrent roaring across the passage. The raiders had severed an oil line. Insane. It didn't matter how much retardant smothered the underside – this could blow the Rig, Blue, Red, Green, Yellow and all.

I held my breath and plunged in, groping along the slicked passage. Faltered, slipped and spat in the gushing fuel. Gasped as I drew clear, half-blind and choking. Crawled on, remembering how Kinnare had been similarly doused, and how easily he'd been set ablaze.

The passage opened up. Then, a shallow drop onto a ledge, overlooking a rectangular compartment, filled with the confusion of hand-to-hand battle.

Marsh wasn't in any immediate danger. One raider lay dazed at her feet. Another backed off, twisting a spanner in his grip, rethinking things. Five Reals lay dead or dazed. Two raiders had Wole pinned in a corner.

Leave the big man, rescue the maiden. Two birds, one stone. Sound like a plan?

I dropped behind Marsh's Red and hammered a fist into his ear. That floored him, but alerted his friends. The tallest, a Real in a cream Stetson, drew a six-chamber pistol and fired. The slug missed, but ricocheted in the narrow space. Stetson crouched in surprise. I jumped him. He screamed, terrified of the oil-soaked demon assailing him. We struggled, slipping around like new shoes on a waxed floor.

Unable to get a purchase on my oiled neck, he tossed back his head and threw it forwards at my nose. My vision blurred and I rolled clear, dazed.

Stetson straightened, spat, clambered to his feet. He pointed his pistol at my face.

A wrench whipped through the air and knocked him cold at my toes. Wole peered down at me, my saviour.

Marsh embraced him. They kissed.

Oh, do me a favour.

I stood up, examined the slicked gauntlet.

'Just what was all that about?'

Wole shrugged.

'Reds think we cheated at the Game.'

Marsh cursed.

'They sent out a posse over that?'

Wole nodded. 'Most undoubtedly. I've heard about this. There are often riots after Games.'

'Idiots!' yelled Marsh, collapsing into a fit of coughing. Wole supported her, lowered her gently onto a bunk. She kept up the coughing, turned a little red. Then it eased off, and she managed to sip some air. She rested her head on Wole's shoulder.

He met my eye.

She's getting worse.

Two days passed before we could return to work. Sharks arrived, made arrests, handed out leaflets for lawyers to anguished friends and family. One bullet from Stetson's six-shooter could have blown New Jerusalem sky-high, but the Sharks left the guns. A young doctor appeared in the nets, flanked by Sharks. An *Ark* dweller, judging by his clothes. He tended to those who could afford his services, dropping shells into a sack, ignored those without the means.

I dressed my wound myself. Then I headed up again, to help Wole fix the ruptured pipe. I asked him if he was going to send Marsh to the doctor.

'I've asked her, believe me. Says she wants to "work through it". I've never known anyone quite so pig-headed.'

I visited 74's. He had taken some part in the battle, and a great purple bruise spread over one eye.

'You should see the other guy.' He chuckled, swinging gently before me. 'All part of the fun.'

I selected a bowl of his mush and turned a spoon in it.

'The Game doesn't seem to bring out the best in people.'

'Au contraire,' said 74. 'I was here before the Game, before the rigs were even bound together. I know what it was like.'

'You worked here?'

'Sure I did. Why, I stood up top and watched the bombs go off across the south, watched that accursed cloud take hold. You don't

144

know what a mess things were. We were all terrified. Turned on each other. Then one day the *Ark* shows up, towing these rigs. The prophet says it's Judgement Day and he's here to gather the righteous. He brought us together.

'Well, at first we weren't so righteous. We were still fighting all the time.'

'Why?'

74 spun 360 degrees, thoughtful.

'I don't rightly know. I suppose we were scared. Anyway, praise the prophet, he gave us the Game to channel the energy. We got back to work. Built a society.'

'74, you just barely survived a mass riot.'

'Sure, things boil over now and then, but it's better than it was, believe me. Without the Game this place would have burned long ago.'

The next morning I bought a shower and a shred of soap, washed the crude out as best I could, and returned to work with Carlos.

We'd only made two trips before Li appeared on the stairs, blocking them like a sofa. He handed us a piece of greasy paper each and folded his arms. Carlos squinted at the illegible scrawl.

'Who wrote this – the ship's parrot? What's it supposed to say, man?'

'You derrick workers,' said Li, pointing at us.

Carlos clutched his chest, eyes dancing.

'We? Derrick workers?'

Li had already spoken too much. He stood aside and pointed aloft, grinding his jaw. Carlos danced past him, whooping and beating the banister.

'No more mule work!'

Wole waited for us on the surface. Li clapped him on the shoulder.

'He boss,' said Li. He pointed at us. 'You learn.'

'Oh yeah.' Carlos nodded eagerly. 'We learn.'

Wole led us out into the sunshine and freezing wind. Carlos jogged alongside him.

'So you the deck boss now, man?'

'Lots of promotions after all the race and riot casualties. Lot of bosses died.'

'Oh,' said Carlos, deflating. 'Right.'

'How's Marsh?' I asked.

Wole didn't answer. He led us into the teetering cluster of contain-ers and outlined our new roles.

My new job was just a little more challenging than breathing in and out. I would be responsible for the shale shakers, mud pumps and chemical mix, plus whatever other hard labour might be required to keep the drill fluids pumping.

I couldn't get interested in the work. I could think of a hundred major improvements to New Jerusalem, ways to make the rigs more functional, more durable: an artificial reef around the platform legs; a cowled current turbine array; wave energy converters; maricul-ture pens; a field of heliostats on Blue's surface, interlocking to form a waterproof skin in storm conditions. Yet I felt no compulsion to make it happen.

Instead I would climb the container stack, sit and marvel at the ocean change colour, from steel to green, from blue to purple. Other times I would sit for hours and pick at my gauntlet, where a white, powdery crust had formed during the weeks at sea, making it harder to form a fist.

Marsh remained elusive, like some deep-sea squid, until the second week. I heard her before I saw her, boots clunking as she jumped the gaps. I held my breath, hoped she would turn me around, press her salty lips to mine.

About as much chance as your arm growing back.

The boots came to rest on the container above me. I stared up at her, like a halibut eyeing a shark. She smiled, but she was ill. Some-thing was eating her inside.

'There he is,' she said, smiling. 'As idle as a painted ship.'

'I'm on my break.'

I climbed up the container to her side. We wouldn't have to shout that way.

'You promoted too?'

'Deck Supervisor,' she said. 'Responsible for the mill, the refinery, the school and the factories. Everything, really.'

'Everywhere you go,' I said, 'you stroll into high office.'

The darkness under her eyes looked deep now. Permanent, maybe. I had the urge to embrace her.

Go for it, you fool!

What are you, crazy? She's with Wole.

'Why don't you take the weight off your boots and sit with me a minute?' I said. 'The view is something else.'

The invitation surprised her.

'What's going on with you? Ficials want to work, don't they?'

An opening.

'I'm not Ficial.' I was in such a hurry to say it I nearly tripped. 'I'm nothing like Ficial any more.'

She looked puzzled. She curled her lip at me. Blood rushed to my head. I reached out and took her hand. I gripped her fingers in my gauntlet, crushing them. She howled and slapped me.

'Keep your rusty claw to yourself. And get back to work!'

She strode off, cradling her damaged hand and muttering. I watched her until she vaulted out of sight. The slap tingled my cheek wonderfully.

'You should count yourselves lucky,' says Rickets. 'Dr Pander's visits are growing fewer. It's a great privilege to have him present at your burn.'

A brother raises his hand.

'He will monitor the process?'

'Yes. Normally it is a purely automated function, but Dr Pander has always taken a keen interest in new model optimisation. He takes time out from his duties when possible to return to Brixton and check on our progress. So I want you on best behaviour. Don't let me down. Understand?'

Let him down. Another curious expression. English has so many flourishes, such shallow foundations. How did it become so dominant?

We would ask Rickets what he means, but he has instructed us not to ask questions today. He sweats a great deal and mutters. It appears to be a nervous reaction.

Perhaps it is the absence of a voice that makes them so nervous. It must be strange to be a man, and wander the world entirely alone, without Control, without a voice to share the darkness.

We line up at the elevator door, preparing to descend to Burn.

We file past Rickets into the car, and he is about to palm the screen when he notices; he jumps out of the car and points at my brother. My shrugging brother. This brother remains sitting on his bunk, shrugging, over and over again. He looks at his boots, shakes his head and shrugs, shrugs, shrugs.

'Oh, God,' says Rickets. 'Don't do this to me. Not now.'

He places his hand on my brother's shoulder, says something that is probably a curse word. He reaches in his top pocket and runs a pen over the serial number on the brother's overalls.

'Kosiaki. What's wrong with you?'

Kosiaki turns; he recognises his name, though he has not heard it spoken before.

'I am not ready to burn,' he says. 'I require more testing.'

'Nonsense,' says Rickets. 'Step off your bunk and enter the elevator with the other models. Don't fuck with me. Not today. Move!'

Kosiaki shrugs again.

Rickets frowns, his features turning purple.

'Now you listen to me, Kosiaki. You are not going to create problems for me today, understand? The creator of your species is waiting for you downstairs and you will accompany me immediately. Capiche?'

'Yes.'

Still he does not move. I step out of the elevator. Rickets almost says something, but he allows me to approach. I place my hand on Kosiaki's shrugging shoulder. The contact stills him.

'Come with us,' I say.

He stands. I walk him into the elevator. The others regard us curiously. Rickets follows, shaking his head.

'Oh, the doctor will be pleased, won't he?'

PARTY

A deep cold hung over the rig, thick ice forming on the container tops. Carlos and I slipped and shimmied over the rink, talking through plumed breath, holding each other for balance, shivering in the frozen ocean spray.

Above us the treadmill groaned and creaked, slowing. Children began hopping clear, exhausted and bent. Bruiser, still stretching and reaching in the wheel, patiently waited her turn.

Suddenly a siren began to wail. The wheel foreman twitched. Barked at the children.

'Whoa,' said Carlos. 'What's that?'

A sound like an anguished whale call echoed over the deck, and the whole Blue Rig lurched, tossing the container beneath us. I dropped to the level below, struck the surface hard. Blood pumped from a gash in my forehead.

Carlos climbed down to me, helped me up, blinking surprise from his eyes.

'The whole damn Rig's shaking.'

I really didn't need him to tell me that. There was a loud whip-crack. Something slashed the air.

'Oh shit!' yelped Carlos. 'She's going down!'

The treadmill. The great wooden wheel leaned into the wind, held by a single, straining bond. It was unstable enough already, mounted on an overloaded scaffold to compensate for the angled Blue Rig surface. Now it was breaking free of its mount. The remaining children ran screaming in all directions, leaving Bruiser trampled and groaning in the wheel.

I ran. I ran with no plan, seeing only the wheel, hearing only the remaining guy rope, creaking, straining. Halfway there it gave, a snap that echoed over the ocean. The wheel tore through its splintering mount, tipped, and crashed into the sea. Bruiser went with it.

I pulled off my jacket, kicked off my boots. Maybe I'd be drowned. Maybe the jump would kill me. Maybe the kid was dead already. I scurried for the edge of the deck and jumped. Felt the wind in my eyes and in my hair. Gasped, eyes screwed shut, as if not seeing death would keep it at bay.

The ocean swallowed me up.

The water was a touch warmer than liquid nitrogen. I thrashed under the black crests, hurried down, down, into a gloom like my dreams. Each stroke seemed to halve my strength.

Well, this was a terrific idea.

I swam anyway, after the great tumbling wheel. I couldn't catch it. The air in my lungs made me slow. The structure had sunk almost out of sight, down there, where Pistol lay. I stopped, flipped over, took one last look.

A shape floated clear.

Some final reserve of energy sputtered into my numb limbs. I pressed down again, reached the frozen figure, tucked her under my arm, and struggled back for the twilit surface.

We breached the waves. My lungs devoured the air. I blinked in the salt, saw the great concrete rig support, and lights twinkling on deck.

Orange hoops splashed around us, tossed by figures above. I slipped one over the kid, teeth chattering, and lay back in the chop, chuckling, choking, waves breaking over my lips. I suppose I was a little light-headed. From there, the nets looked like a patchwork of barnacles.

An engine. A searchlight, catching the waves, turning them white. The boat picked Bruiser up first, then drew me in, laying me on the deck like a mystery catch.

A Real bent over Bruiser and blew air into her lungs, until the child spouted water. They threw a blanket over her and turned the boat around.

Bruiser jumped on me, her little arms clinging to my neck. We had a good shiver, choked and coughed. I told her everything would be OK. It felt a little more honest than the last time I'd said it.

*

Li explained that a roving iceberg had struck the Rig. The damage had been repaired, and now a dance would be held in my honour. I said I didn't have any honour. He smiled and said nobody cared.

The event was held in the Game Net. Torches were gathered and hung from the overnet by children standing on mothers' shoulders, wherever these amateur acrobats could reach. The effect was pleasing enough. A band was hired from the *Ark*, paid for by pooled workers' contributions. They set up in the shadow of a peak, tuned their instruments.

A seaweed garland was hung around my neck, and I was placed in a kind of hanging throne, fashioned from scrap oil drums. Reals lined up to offer me praise, to inspect me, to wonder if they would have done the same. I wanted to tell them I was Ficial, guilty of unforgivable crimes. That they should listen to the warnings. Be more vigilant. But I had the idea their praise was for life itself, as much as for me, and I kept my counsel.

I hung in my throne as the band struck up. The older Reals gathered at the plate edge, sitting cross-legged, smiling and clapping to the music. The younger examples lined up on the plate, held hands, alive with nerves, as clean and pressed as I'd seen them. I watched them step smartly among each other, laugh and interlock arms. As always with Real skills, some were better than others. But the imperfections gave the crowd something else to chew on but gum, and they warmed themselves with chatter and singing.

Bruiser sat beneath me with Carlos, occasionally glancing up to ensure I was still there. I jumped down to sit with her.

'Good,' said Carlos. 'You watch her. I have things to do.'

He jogged over the nets, stepped onto the plate, and approached a cloud of Reals, striking up conversation with the man he'd seen on the stairs. The man laughed.

'Care for a drink?'

Marsh stood over me, holding a glass bottle with black liquid in it. I couldn't smell anything promising.

'A drink of what?'

'It's pop. Fizzy. You never had pop?'

She sat beside me. It took her a moment to make the descent. She put her hands out behind her, and I watched her legs straighten and stretch like oars into water. She pushed off her boots and wiggled her toes.

I took the bottle, plucked the cap free and drank. Sugar. Lots of sugar. I handed the bottle to Bruiser, who sipped, smiled brightly, and guzzled the rest in a long, desperate draught. Marsh wheezed.

'Are you enjoying your party?'

'About as much as I enjoy anything.'

She nodded.

'This doesn't mean anything to you, then? Their gratitude.'

'Real moods have a habit of changing.'

The band switched tempo, moving up a gear, raising a yelp from the dancers and moving Marsh a little closer. My heart sped up to catch the beat. She leaned in.

'Sure. You were a monster. Maybe you still are. But saving that child might save you.'

'What have I saved her for?' I nodded at Bruiser, who was dipping her finger into the empty bottle, sucking it for the last taste. 'Treading the mill? What's with you, anyway? You were the leader on the *Lotus*. You had those people believing. Then you just switch sides?'

Why are we telling her off?

Marsh sighed.

'I don't give a fuck about politics, Ken. I keep people alive.'

She turned her face to me. Her eyes were half-closed, her skin pale. She shivered. I pulled off my coat and offered it to her.

She eyed it suspiciously.

'Ficials do chivalry?'

'Take it,' I said. 'Keep warm.'

She pulled it over her chest, lay down on the net, cheek resting on hands. She closed her eyes, lashes sticking closed, lips puckered open.

'I need you to look over the repairs we made,' she said, her face breaking into a yawn. 'Need to know they'll hold.'

'Sure,' I said. 'Sleep. Worry about that later.'

She began to snore.

I watched, as the band played more slowly, the evening turning to night, the numbers on the plate thinning out. Marsh rolled over, out from under the jacket, rested her head on my side. I covered her with the jacket again, and rested my arm on her hip.

I had the impression of the band finishing, of torches being extinguished, of Reals dispersing, tapping my shoulder and muttering thanks.

'Thanks,' I returned. 'Thanks.'

Yeah, thanks. I'm Ficial, you know. I'm Ficial, did I mention that?

The crowd filtered away, leaving me and Marsh under the swinging throne. I stared at her. Wondered what was happening to her. So many old kinds of sickness, and so many new. How would I repair her?

'All right, Ken. You two look very familiar.'

Bridget grinned and waggled her eyebrows. 'I guess where words fail, music speaks.'

She wore make-up. Thick foundation smothered her features, spots glowing beneath. Black wings were painted around each eye. Glitter dusted her cheeks. She wore her hair in a coiled braid, a plastic flower over the ear, and a long dress off the shoulder. A trumpet poked from a satchel over one arm.

'What are you doing here, Bridget?'

She dropped her smile.

'Pleased to see you too, Ken. Thanks for those warm words.'

'I said, what are you doing here?'

'I'm here with the band. Man Snoot's Minstrels. I've got an hour before I have to go back.'

'Back? Where?'

'To the *Ark*. Look, time is short, Ken, and I need a word in your shell-like.'

'So? State your business.'

She lifted her chin and scratched her neck. The spots were back, and they looked angry.

'In private.'

I turned to Marsh. She hadn't stirred.

'I'm busy.'

'Uh-huh,' said Bridget. 'I thought you might say that.'

Fingernails tapped on glass. I snapped around. Bridget held a whisky bottle close to her chest.

'Dry down here, aren't you, Ken? Come with me like a good boy and you can have a tipple.'

I'd like to say I put up a fight. I gently drew clear of Marsh, left her dozing, followed Bridget to the far corner of the net, from where the Red invasion had sprung.

'Give me a sip,' I snapped.

'Just hold your horses.'

Bridget found a tear, lifted it, ushered me below, into a wedge-shaped scrap of reinforced webbing. Bridget dropped next to me, wrinkled her nose.

'Stinks.'

'How do you know about this place?'

'Research, mate.'

'And why do we have to meet down here?'

'Because they listen, that's why. The barons on the *Ark*, they hear anything that's said down here. The nets are wired for sound. You don't know this?'

It made sense, but I hadn't considered it until now.

'The point is,' she said, 'I want a private conversation.'

Bridget twisted the cap off the whisky, took a swig, and offered it. I held the amber liquid under my nose, asked if it was wise to surrender. Before I could answer the hooch was pouring down my throat. I gasped, felt defeated and rescued all at once.

'So, how's life, Bridget? I was wondering what had happened to you.'

She stared.

'What happened? I nearly went for the long swim, that's what. After you left I was herded into some bargain bin with a few other rejects – old folks mainly. A few people looked us over but nobody bit. So I sang some songs to cheer us up, you know.

'Anyway, this bloke with a clipboard turns up and asks who's singing. Before I know where I am I'm standing on the *Ark*. They wouldn't take the others. I asked but . . .'

Her head drooped. Something that looked like guilt gnawed at her. I passed the bottle back. She drank, shivered and sighed.

'Unfortunate,' I said, 'but there was nothing more you could have done. It could be worse for you. A cabin on the *Ark* must beat down here.'

She scratched behind an ear.

'I've a hammock in a room shared with five fellahs. Hardly the *Queen Mary*. We're not allowed on the upper decks other than to perform, and we do that under armed guard. Hard to play with a pistol plugged in your ear 'ole I can tell you.'

'How's your audience? Do they appreciate your stuff?'

She shrugged.

'I've really no idea.'

'They don't let you play what you want?'

'I get to play whatever. But I don't see much reaction. We play this huge ballroom, and the crowd stand a mile away from the stage, in the dark. I think they clap a bit but they never come close. Barely seen a face. Typical corporate gig really. Treat the entertainment like they stink.'

'You were good tonight.' I meant it. 'And no fires?'

'Nah. I don't play the harp.'

I blinked. I still couldn't believe her music had any real connection to fires. She never had until now.

'You're telling me it's the harp that starts the fires?'

'No. I'm telling you the fires are a combination of energies – mine, the harp's, the air's, the music's.'

'Energies.'

'Come on, Ken, you know this. You're a smart lad. We're all just energy. Me, you, the nets, the oil, the *Ark*, the planet. It's all just energy. When I play the harp certain energies interact, and create fire.'

I nodded.

'All right then.'

We sat in the wind for a moment, listening to the echoing surf. I sipped the whisky and wondered when she would tell me what she wanted.

'So,' said Bridget. 'What's your plan?'

'Plan?'

'Yeah. To get out of here. To take back the *Lotus*. That's why I'm here, Ken – to find out how I can help.'

The net creaked, caught by a freezing gust. The wind had picked up, and hummed tones on the surfaces. I eyed the bottle.

'There is no plan.'

Bridget shivered, gaped at me.

'No plan? Don't you want to get out of here?'

I thought of Marsh, waiting for me upstairs.

156

'I don't know.'

'What are you telling me, Ken? You're *happy* in the bloody nets?'

Happy. What did that mean? The more time I spent with Reals the more obscure it was. The closest definition seemed to be: 'somewhere else but the present'. Either that, or it meant lying on the open net, with Marsh curled at my side.

'What would you like me to plan? A revolution?'

I reached out for the bottle. Bridget withheld it.

'It's not about you chasing Marsh around down here, Ken. This is bigger than you. There are other things to consider.'

'Like what?'

She stared at me, tongue curled.

'Like what? I dunno: what about the two hundred kids you, me, and the rest of the crew were responsible for, back on HMS *Pinafore*? The two hundred kids they've got locked up on the *Ark*, joining the bloody priest Hoods!'

Something cold rolled over in my belly.

'Hoods? They're turning them into Hoods?'

'Some of them. The ones they think are "pure" or some madness. They're brainwashing them, Ken.'

That kind of news required medicine. I fetched gum from my pocket and chewed it instead.

'I still don't know what you want me to do.'

'Stop chewing that muck to start with. Don't you know what's in it? It's drugs, Ken, a lot of behavioural gunk. The barons laugh at you chewing yourselves obedient. I never thought you'd fall for it.'

I nibbled the gum more slowly.

'All right then. Give me a drink.'

She drew the bottle behind her back.

'Are you going to help me free those kids?'

I rubbed my eyes. Bridget was ruining my evening.

'How? Kinnare's dead, the *Lotus* is captured, and I'm the only one caught in this net who isn't packing heat.'

'I don't know how, I'm a musician. You're the robot killing machine. You figure it out.'

She knew I hated to be called a robot. I would have challenged it in the past, but I couldn't find the energy. I spat out the gum. Maybe it wasn't such pure chewing satisfaction.

'Bridget,' I said. 'Say we break them off the *Ark*, take them away in some boat. Where would we go? Nowhere is perfect.'

'It's a big world, Kenneth. There's got to be somewhere people will be happy to let them be.'

She pushed onto her haunches.

'If you stop chewing that gum for ten seconds you might decide those kids deserve to play and learn in safety, without some idiot trying to mould them into supermen. If you decide to make that energetic fist ready to resist, count me in. If you don't, my mates and I will take matters into our own hands.'

With that she stood, and made for the Game Net.

'What mates?'

She turned.

'Not everyone chews down here, Ken. Some people want something better. A little more than chewing gum, know what I mean?' I shivered and scowled. She regarded me like a snapped string. 'Here. This will shake your shaking.'

She dropped the bottle, kicked it my way. It rolled right into my hand. I took a hit as she crawled out of the cavity, making for home.

I sat and drank alone awhile. Then I stashed the booze, and went out to the open net.

Blue slept. The ocean washed beneath. The nets stretched and groaned.

Marsh was curled in the same spot. I picked her up carefully and headed for the overnet.

She mumbled Wole's name.

That fucking guy.

Dr Leo Pander sits on a bench, legs dangling, reading a slim paperback book. He is chewing an apple, turned slightly away from us. He registers our presence but continues reading, takes another bite of the fruit, chews noisily. He scratches behind his ear and right away, involuntarily, we all imitate the gesture.

Burn level is cold, the lowest temperature I have known. There are no connections to the adjoining hexes here. He clears his throat, slips a crumpled piece of notepaper into the pages and closes the book. He jumps off the couch, drops the book and half-eaten apple in his hip pocket. He wears a lab coat buttoned once at the chest. Chewed tips of biros crowd the top pocket. His shirt was white once. It is crumpled, tucked into tracksuit bottoms. His trainers are very dirty and loosely laced. We smell alcohol.

Our creator smiles at us. Eyes peer from thin round spectacles.

Rickets approaches him, hands him a flex and points something out. Pander nods and says: 'Hmm. I see.'

He rolls up the flex, returns it to Rickets. He approaches us, threads a path through our little crowd, smiles, looks each of us searchingly in the eyes. He stops, takes the hand of a brother, holds it up to the light. He pulls his spectacles into his hair and squints at the palm, running his finger over its surface.

'Behold the hands, how they promise, conjure, appeal.'

He fishes a notebook out of his pocket, bites the cap off a pen and makes a notation. We try to see what he is writing but it is a scrawl. He replaces the notebook, glances briefly at Kosiaki, then jumps back on the couch, sitting to address us.

'Power Nines, Rover Models, your progress is satisfactory. Your induction officer reports one or two behavioural glitches, but nothing I consider serious.'

I glance at Kosiaki. I would place my hand on his shoulder to prevent another episode, but I cannot. I am fixed in our creator's presence. Moving now would be like a stone column coming to life. Pander looks down for a moment, lets the silence sit, then speaks again.

'So what is Burn? Burn is the engineering of your mind to complement the engineering of your body. It is the process by which we eliminate nearly all of your evolved emotional responses. It is a uniquely Engineered privilege. Fully optimised, you have all the best elements of human existence: the wonderful brain and vision, for instance – but few of the bad: you will suffer neither from our vulnerability to disease and damage, nor the cocktail of fear, lust, pride and the rest that helped develop humanity, but now risks condemning it.'

Pander folds his arms. We fold ours.

'You have all been burned to some extent already. While you were packaged, Control shared your dream state, policed the microcircuitry of your brain, snuffed out the development of certain troublesome hormones and neurotransmitters. One day, perhaps, we will know enough to accomplish the entire Burn while you are packaged. For the moment, that is beyond us. The brain develops quite differently from the moment you take command of your physical form.'

Pander slaps the couch.

'So it is that we resort to this primitive process. We will subject you to certain stimuli and monitor the activity in your brain. We will burn as we go, until the structure of your mind is as sound as it should be. Only then will you be ready to venture out and build a better world.'

He jumps down from the couch and gestures at it. We spread out, lie in the couches, which are like those in Learn, only with a Gronts hoop hinged over the headrest, sprouting needle jacks.

I recline, and the hoop automatically lowers, and needles press to my temples.

'Sleep well,' says our creator.

TRIAL

Bridget was right about the gum. A day's abstinence had me shivering and shaking. I passed a night of brutal dreams and cold sweats and took up chewing again.

I had enough to think about without Bridget's revolution. Bruiser had become my shadow. She had nothing to do now the treadmill had gone, so she hovered about my workstation, kicking things, whistling, talking to herself. I set her homework to pass the days. English mostly, and a little basic engineering. But she was a swift learner, and soon I was drowning in questions.

Sometimes I'd lie, then wonder if it was the right thing. Bruiser was a kind of anti-Ficial, learning as she moved about the world, with no Control to guide her. She was all potential, her mind open and vulnerable. Lies were easy, but how would they damage her?

At first I thought she should keep Real society. Then I thought of the Park, and the treadmill, and decided I would watch her, and try not to ruin her.

It was hard. Raising a thousand-storey tower was easier. Bruiser liked to sing, but made a dreadful noise. I gritted my teeth and let her wail. Bruiser would get 'bored', and she would moan about it. I bit my tongue and invented games. Bruiser enjoyed climbing hazardous heights. I helped her down and bandaged her cuts.

I banished thoughts of how much easier it had been alone. Besides, sometimes she embraced me, wrapped her arms around my neck and squeezed as if to break it. That was compensation. It eased the gnawing thought that I was an incompetent, an impostor.

We both looked forward to Game Day. We would visit the Game Net, share seakale, samphire and sugar beet with Wole and Carlos.

I quit questioning the point of the Game, began to appreciate the tactics, the teamwork, the skill. Sure, the thing was rigged in favour of Yellow, but the others still competed, and their struggle had its own merit.

It gave Wole and me something to talk about. We debated the intricacies of the Blues' strengths and weaknesses: Li's leadership, the troublesome hopper position, the need for Man Snoot to invest in the chariot.

Carlos commented exclusively on player personalities and appearance:

'He's lazy. Belongs in a hammock.'

'I could not take orders from a man with that hair.'

'Looks like he's been hit in the face with a spade.'

'Drive? He couldn't steer his own piss in the sea.'

Bruiser would sit at my side, absorbed by the flex, wave a blue flag, laugh at Carlos.

The Blues were competitive, running a steady second in the League, but subject to bad luck with casualties. There was much talk in the crowd of one day joining Li on the track. Of winning glory for Blue. Of a new life on the *Ark*. It was a lot of gas, but it warmed them up.

There were no more raids, Wole having organised a new security patrol, but there was a little excitement after the tenth Game.

It had been the most exciting race of the season, if the least successful for Li and Blue. They'd been knocked out on the second lap, wheels blown off by a staff strike, every member killed or badly injured save the rock-like mass of Li. He'd emerged from the smoking wreck with a few cuts and bruises, dragged his team-mates clear, then sat track-side wearing an inscrutable expression. Blue's Game Net had fallen almost silent after that, as still as I had seen it, until a new controversy emerged.

The Reds had snatched second place after an accomplished runner performance. But the moment the chariots returned to the pits they'd been accused of cheating, and taken away under Shark guard.

That evening the flexes announced that the *Ark* would dock the next day, and a trial would be held.

I asked 74 about it.

'Not unusual,' he said, swinging from the net, tools jangling. 'The

Ark has to come in and fuel up periodically. It's quite an operation, and a trial helps make it more of a party.'

'What'll happen to the cheats?' asked Carlos.

74 shrugged.

'Death penalty.'

'You're joking.'

'No, sir. I wouldn't joke about that,' said 74. 'They like to execute a team from time to time, to encourage the others.'

The entire Rig showed up to watch, a truce called. We travelled to the southern tip of Green, sat atop the stepped container wall, crushed among thousands from all colours. It certainly was a show.

The *Ark* was a monster, arriving more like an ice shelf than something man-made. She had a beam of two hundred metres, stretching perhaps a thousand metres out to sea, a hundred metres from the surface. Twenty decks flew New Jerusalem flags, dotted by tiny figures gathered to observe the trial. At the great flat summit, two yellow funnels pumped blue smoke.

Three huge anchor chains moored the beast in position. Deckhands organised the taking on of fuel from great, stinking pipes, and the erection of enormous flexes, like those at the Drome. They wanted to ensure we had a good view.

It was a brief, if emotional, drama. I recognised the Reds' lawyer from ads on the flex. He argued the defendants' case passionately, reasoning that the extra pucks they had deployed had been a mistake by the race officials, rather than a deliberate ploy. He said that any other finding would be a grave injustice, a stain on New Jerusalem history. Still, he didn't look too bothered when Judge Floyd found the Reds guilty, shrugging like a man who had at least played his part well.

We watched as the defendants were lined up, kneeling on deck, wailing and begging. Hoods appeared behind them, brandishing cutlasses. Bruiser looked away. Most watched.

Afterwards the *Ark* drew in its chains, unhitched the oozing pipelines and dropped them into the ocean. It edged out to sea, yellow funnels pluming black fog, resuming its lazy orbit of the Rig.

The crowd peeled away. We walked home, part of a subdued, chewing mass.

Bruiser tugged on my arm.

'What?'

'Wole. Where is he?'

'Damn,' said Carlos. 'She's right. He never showed up.'

We found him in his digs, kneeling at Marsh's side.

My stomach flipped when I saw her, twitching in a pained, semi-waking state, a special kind of pale. Wole gripped her hand, stared with solemn, wet eyes.

'She took a turn for the worse last night,' he said. 'Not long now. Couple of months if she feels like fighting.'

Carlos and Bruiser looked at anything but the patient. Cancer. The word hung in the room like fog.

'Doctor has been. Says it's her lungs,' said Wole.

'So? Why isn't she getting treated?'

Wole sighed.

'No facilities here. What she needs is on the *Ark*.'

I spat out my gum. 'Then why isn't she there?'

'It would take all the wages on Blue a year to pay for that.'

He bowed his head, muttered. Kissed her limp hand. Carlos sighed.

'Maybe it's for the best.'

He shrugged off the glares.

'What? My old man had cancer, before the war. Ate up his guts. They pumped him with chemicals for a year and for what? Another lousy six months, pissing himself and eating through a straw. If that is the best medicine had to offer then, how could it be better now?'

Wole snarled.

'That's your solution? Let her suffer?'

Carlos sighed.

'No. I would shoot her through the head.'

Wole put the rag aside and stood up to Carlos. Tears pooled in his eyes.

'Sure,' said Carlos. 'Give me that look. But I am right. We let her squirm in pain for months, we are doing it for us, not for her.'

Wole lunged, hoisted Carlos up by the scruff of his overalls and slapped him hard into the steelwork.

'Ah!' howled Carlos. 'Take it easy!'

'We don't kill her, do you hear me? She gave all of us a chance. She rescued all of us. We owe her!'

164

'OK, fine,' said Carlos, his dangling boots kicking, 'have it your way. *Bajame.*'

Wole slapped his cargo down, cursed and kicked a barrel over. Then he clutched his head and wept, slumping at Marsh's side. Carlos exhaled slowly.

'So. What are we going to do?'

Bruiser raised her hand. Carlos blinked at her.

'You got something to say?'

'We want Marsh on the *Ark*?'

'You're quick, kid. What of it?'

'The Game,' she said. 'We win the Game.'

Li took a long time to answer.

We found him at 74's, watching the flex over a bowl of gruel. The only sign of his Game travails were a cut on his neck, and the fact he favoured one side of his mouth when he chewed. The flex showed another funeral for Sharks who'd fallen in the war on the godless. More flags.

We didn't get his attention until the ad breaks. Another warning to report suspicious activity.

'Did you hear what I said?' snapped Wole. 'We want in on the team.'

Li rolled his eyes up to the big man.

'Many do.'

'Listen, Li,' said Carlos, crouching at the derrick hand's side, 'we know how this works. You can pay to transfer players, right? Ten shells each player. Well, good news, we've scraped together all forty.'

'Fifty,' said Li, sniffing.

'What? It's forty.'

'Agent fee.'

'WHAT?'

'No fee, no team.'

Carlos's eye twitched a little.

'You no-good, swindling Jap.'

'Chinese,' corrected Li, mouth turning down at the edges. He pointed a huge finger at Carlos. 'Careful.'

Carlos swept his hair back and looked around him for help. Bruiser watched the flex. Wole said nothing.

165

'Seems like a standard approach to me,' I said.

'Fine,' said Carlos. 'OK. Forty up front, we'll owe you ten. Happy?'

'OK,' said Li. 'Welcome aboard. Any of you mechanic?'

I raised my hand. He nodded, returned his attention to the flex, which fizzed and switched channels. Now it was a Game preview, one of the many programmes that spun off the Game like bald tyres on black ice. It opened with a montage of historic crashes, before settling on our old friend Floyd.

'Welcome to this special programme looking forward to next week's Game,' he said. 'Tonight, exclusively, we bring you an interview with previous race winner Stjepan Kokovic, last survivor of Season 29's winning Red team.'

Boos and heckles from 74's clientele. The flex projection cut to an image of a large man wearing a curious smile, seated in a broad-backed chair. He started to speak, but the chorus of Blue dissent went on so long we missed his opening lines.

'. . . like nothing else,' he said, finally audible as the nets settled down. 'It's been everything I expected and more. All that training, all that competing, it's all worth it when you get here and know that you worked hard for it. I just think people should know that if they work hard enough, anyone can get a space on the *Ark*. That's the amazing thing about New Jerusalem.'

Floyd's voice was reverent and breathless, as if Kokovic's fame was sucking the air out of the room.

'Don't you ever miss it? The thrill of competition?'

'Sure I do.' The figure smiled. 'There's no greater sport in history than the Game. But I'm retired now.'

'And what about this next race,' asked Floyd. 'Any predictions?'

The plate grew hushed. The crowd that hated him were desperate to hear his punditry.

'Well,' he said, 'Yellow are clearly the team to beat, but I have a hunch it's time for a change. Really I do. I think – and you might call me crazy here – with a fresh start and team owner, Baron Man Snoot, springing for a new Chariot . . . I think I'm going to take a chance on Blue this year.'

That did it. 74's erupted into joyful yelps. The elder swung about his customers, sharing inverted high fives, banging his spoon on a pot.

Li raised an eyebrow. It was probably the closest he came to startled. He brushed off his overalls and made his way through us, heading for his bunk.

Carlos pulled him back.

'You hear that? Right after we sign up? How's that for a lucky omen? We're going to win this thing!'

Li looked at him. Carlos sagged a little.

'Goddamit, man, don't that mean nothing to you? That guy is a previous winner, and he's tipping us for the win!'

Li took gum out of his pocket, dropped it in his mouth. Nodded at the figure on the flex.

'I know Stjepan. Looks strange. Sounds strange.'

He left us with that, melting into the darkness of the net.

Fire. I hear its chatter, breathe its heat. I raise my hand to touch the fire's fingers and watch my skin drip, boil and pop, watch as this body that is connected to me cooks. I reach for the door but my fingers pass through the handle. I am trapped. I begin to lose control. I cry out.

Then, some force aches in my head, it gathers my wits, smooths the jagged pulse between body and mind. To work. To work.

The door handle turns, and I step into a room where a woman lies on a plinth, giving birth, birth the human way. A creature emerges, tiny and smeared in blood and matter. I turn away, gagging, but the blinking ache in my eye strikes, and I find I look without turning, it is as familiar as anything. I pass her, to the far side of this room, where work awaits. And as I move insects appear, thousands and thousands of insects, crawling out from the plug sockets, from an incubator. They swarm around my feet and climb up my legs, they tumble on me like rain, scuttle into my eyes and mouth and ears. I thrash in the writhing mess, with no thought, only instinct.

That ache again. My breathing slows, and I wade through the living pool, intent now, untroubled, letting the millions of legs and feelers inspect every opening this body of mine can offer them. Let them explore. To work. To work.

Out of the house, into a yard, hot sun. A fenced enclosure, some kind of farm. Panicked animal sounds fill the sky. I walk around, peer through the mesh, and see hundreds of men all beating dogs with clubs. I watch them for a while, until I realise I too hold a club, I too am beating a hound. I drop the club, blood rushing in my ears. I back away, press to the cold mesh fence. Then, the ache returns me to a cool spectator, and I resume clubbing as if I am watching from a hundred thousand miles away. Is this my work? No, on, further on.

I follow a road off the farm, towards the city. Trucks roar past. I wonder

168

if Control will speak to me again soon. Would it speak to me alone? I wonder if somehow I am made better than the others, if there was some unintended engineering event that made me superior, a Power Nine Plus? Might Control whisper some secret to me while the others work?

No, no, it will not, says the foreman. I recognise him from the Learn programme. He is covered in weeping buboes, swollen spots. He defecates where he crouches, leaking blood from his ears, sneezing and coughing and holding out his hand to me in mucus-stained welcome. A walking disease. I back away. He reaches.

But then the ache, and I stop and shake his seeping claw. 'Into bed with you,' says a Medic Model. I watch her roll the foreman onto a gurney that sits in the middle of the site, brush his hair back from his face, tap the word 'Terminal' on her flex. She rolls it up, stands straight. How well designed she is; towers and domes and embankments and avenues and windows and balconies. I would like to explore these places. But then the ache comes, and I shake my head loose, and the thought departs, leaving a single urge. To work. To work.

When do I start? What needs to be done?

'Good boy,' she says. She takes my hand. The touch sets my heart off again. She frowns, drops my hand.

'It seems we're not quite finished.'

That pain, behind my eye.

'What do you want?' she asks.

I blink at the question.

'To work.'

HANGAR

Marsh was sitting up talking to Wole when I arrived. She told the big man to get himself something to eat. He clutched her hand tight.

'I won't leave you.'

She leaned forward, kissed his forehead, brushed her hand over his face.

'Go on,' she said. 'The Ficial will look after me.'

Wole stumbled past me, exhausted. I took a seat in the bunk opposite hers and wondered what to do with my hands.

'I told him it was a stupid idea,' she said. 'Entering the Game. Yellows have the League sewn up.'

I didn't know what to say. Sometimes it was a tremendous effort to form words in her company. I took out a stick of gum and chewed on that instead.

She adjusted her position. A look clouded her features.

'You have to take care of him out there. He's a gentle thing really.'

You don't say.

'I will.'

'He feels guilty, you see.' She looked past me, at a thought. 'He did some bad things, before the war. Helped clear the Makoko slum. It's stayed with him. Well, it would. I try to tell him, carry your deeds around with you, good or bad, and you're no good to—'

She broke into a fierce cough. I plucked a water jug from her bedside, filled a glass as she thrashed on the bunk. Waited for her to settle.

I held the glass to her lips. There was blood there. She wrapped her hands around mine and drank. The room grew hot, so I poured myself a glass. I tried to pick it up in the gauntlet but it slipped out, dropped, smashed. She eyed the encrusted limb.

'They're going to let you race with that? Isn't it an unfair advantage to have an industrial tool on the team?'

'Li's checked with race officials. Nothing in the rules prohibiting artificial limbs. Most think it's a handicap.'

She prodded it with her finger.

'It very nearly is. Thing has more limescale than my nana's kettle. You can hardly compete if you can't grip.'

She pulled her blanket off her legs, swung them to the floor.

'Get back into bed.'

She waved a hand at me. 'Nah-mah-nah.'

She hobbled to a pile of tins in the corner of the compartment. Plucked one free, carried it back to the bunk, sat with a sigh.

'Come here.'

I edged closer. She plucked the lid from the tin, wheezing and clearing her throat.

'Dip your mitt in that,' she ordered.

I hesitated. She reached for the gauntlet, gently guided the crusted fingers into the corrosive. The surface bubbled. My fingers tingled. I bent them in it, felt the joints loosen. I pressed them deeper, but she made a disapproving sound and drew my limb free.

We both stared. A pattern had appeared there, colours generated by the reaction of Gronts and corrosive. A mosaic of small blue and grey hexagonal shades, glittering in the lamplight.

'It's so pretty,' she said.

I packed the solvent away and sat with her until she fell asleep. Then I took out the Only Book, and read the Game rules again.

The wind was up, sending a hum through the nets, shrieking through the containers. Wole, Carlos, Li, Bruiser and I were manacled and led off the Rig, up Red's container wall. More Sharks waited for us at the summit, guarding the new Red team, who looked suitably nervous.

'Quite the view,' said Wole, eyes narrowed to the wind. 'If only she could see it. Beautiful.'

It was late evening, the day's shifts over, but the sun was stubborn now and lingered, casting a pink glow on the ocean. To the south, peering over the container wall, the *Ark*'s yellow funnels pumped black smoke. Beyond, hundreds of miles away, the cloud bank was a bruise on the horizon. There was no sign of the *Lotus*.

The Sharks formed us into a chain gang, following the container wall around the White perimeter, picking up the White racers. Then we trailed the western perimeter of Yellow, though their team failed to appear.

'What's the matter?' asked Carlos. 'Too good for us?'

We passed the Green derrick, reached the southern wall, where the *Ark* waited, a Kraken brazenly sunbathing, its shadow blanketing the other boats crowded below. A cavity was open on the *Ark*'s port side, running a long, sloping grey Flex ramp to the esplanade. It was a frenzy of activity down there. Davits hoisted supplies to upper decks. Crew hurried about, loading and unloading forklifts and trucks. A steady stream of traffic traversed the ramp in two organised columns.

'Lord,' said Wole. 'I should like to know her complement. There must be thousands on board.'

'Hundred,' said Li.

'A hundred?' said Carlos. 'That thing could take us all! Why don't we all live on it?'

'Not earned it,' said Li.

Carlos had plenty to say about that, but it was drowned out by the clamour of activity. The Sharks edged us down the stepped containers, through the bustling esplanade, into the back of a truck, which turned and puttered along the Flex ramp, up to the *Ark*. From the truck I looked back at the Rig, thought of Marsh, left in the care of 74 and his customers. I examined my sparkling gauntlet and pondered.

The Sharks ordered us out, released us from the manacles, and corralled the teams onto a large aircraft elevator. The platform dropped with a wheeling whine, into a deep hangar. I looked around as we descended, inspecting the structure. Unlike the black frigate, the *Ark* appeared to be in good condition.

The lift came to a halt with a violent jolt.

'Home,' said Li.

Lights flickered in the darkness, revealing a cargo hold. Two rows of oblong shapes nestled under tarps, a line of bunk beds arrayed between.

The Sharks prodded us off the elevator, then lifted away again, clumping out of sight.

The Yellow team waited for us by their chariot. They were a sinewy lot, skin like tanned hide, with smooth, untainted complexions. Their faces had an odd otherness about them: moist skin, pronounced bone structures, bright white teeth. They called a few cheery insults.

Li wasn't concerned. He slapped my back and pointed out a tarp. Blue paint ran in streaks beneath.

'New chariot,' he said.

He worked around the tarp, gathering it up in his spade hands, gently pulling it free.

Something stirred deep inside. Memories of the open road. Hands on the wheel. Hurtling on chapped tarmac, through a frozen winter night.

Of course, our chariot was no Landy. It was a great blue slab of a machine, a monument to outrageous fuel consumption, the last model turned out by Lay's America before the Second Civil War. It was the Chevy Tombstone, a four-hundred-horsepower set of wheels, wood trim, headlamps and leather that had offered its owners unique features like exploding air-conditioning, super-hackable on-board computers, and engines that turned themselves off on a whim. It would be about as easy to steer as a buffalo.

Bruiser jumped up, unable to see inside. I opened the door and lifted her into the driver's seat, her eyes huge. She ran her hands over the wheel and jabbed at the buttons in wonder. She grinned.

'We will win.'

I glanced over at the Yellows, gathered by their pristine canary-yellow pick-up. It was a better, more rugged design than our SUV. The team chattered quietly, smiled and laughed. Confident people. Lines of ovals were painted on the driver's door, signifying victories.

'Yes,' I replied. 'Yes, we're going to win.'

Wole slumped on a bunk, eyes far away. I approached.

'Wondering how she's doing?' I asked.

He rolled his eyes up to mine. Thoughts of Marsh glistened in them.

'I shouldn't have left her.'

'It occurs to me,' I said, 'that she can help us out even now.'

'How so?'

'The signalling system. The one she worked out for the fleet. We're going to need it. We're going to have to teach him.'

I pointed out Li.

Wole almost smiled. 'A good notion. She would like that, I think, to help us compete.'

He stood up, approached our captain. I took his place on the bunk, and studied my own thoughts.

The *Ark* cut through the ocean with stately calm, allowing the teams to set about modifying their cars. Li gathered us around in the morning, to provide us with an assessment of the opposition. Red had a new team, a new vehicle.

'So they're a threat?' asked Wole.

Li shook his head. 'Outside bet. Team of strangers.'

'OK,' said Carlos. 'What about the Whites?'

'Experienced,' said Li. 'Good driver. But slow. No good mechanic.'

Then he nodded at the Green chariot, which had most of the team lying beneath it, their bickering voices echoing in the hold.

'Green damaged bad. Cheap baron. No new parts, old chariot.'

Their jalopy certainly was beaten up, its bodywork pitted, split and gouged, its radiator crumpled. I remembered seeing it limp over the finish line in Li's last race, smoking and slumped over the rear right tyre.

'Still,' said Li, marking them up. 'They have good runner. One of best.'

That left Yellows. They were relaxing, four of them playing cards beneath their pick-up's fender, another napping on the hood.

'OK, Mr Insider Man,' said Carlos, nudging Li. 'Why do they keep winning? Any clue?'

'Unclear,' said Li, looking at his boots. Carlos narrowed his eyes at him.

'Bullshit. They cheat, right?'

Li put a finger to his lips.

'Hush. They listen.' He stared at Carlos for a moment, eyes glazed over. Then he shook out of it, and turned to our chariot.

'Now,' he said. 'We work. Lighten vehicle.'

There was plenty to strip from the bloated leisure wagon: air con, stereo, screens, sunroof, heated and reclining figure-hugging chairs. We tore it all out, the gauntlet's pinching force working where our limited tools couldn't. It was a good way not to think about gum. I'd sworn to give it up for the races.

174

We ripped out doors, replacing them with simple, hinged flaps. We lined vulnerable points with Kevlar strips. We fixed a curved climbing rail up the spine, and bolted handles to the tailgate, where runners could hang. We toiled in the close air, the heat and sweat, until we were left with something that looked more like our competing rides.

Li kept us occupied. With the vehicle ready he turned his attention to his new team's abilities. He organised a kind of limited trial in the hangar, had us run laps, jump from car roof to car roof, over the protests of rival teams. He sprinkled bolts on the floor, had us kick them into a bucket target. He nodded, grumbled to himself thoughtfully, made notes in a little pocketbook.

Then the hangar settled, and each Real turned sullen and quiet, slowed by the stultifying heat. They crouched on the floor or lay on bunks and stared.

Bruiser was the first to break the ice. Her boredom picked her up and sent her muttering and kicking about the hangar, in search of entertainment. She disappeared behind our chariot, then returned kicking an empty spray can. She had more gripped in her arms. She stopped by the huddled Reds, held the cans in her hands, and began to juggle. All present watched with interest, then building delight. A few Reals began to clap as the girl juggled on, introducing new beats and tricks to the display. Encouraged, she dropped one can onto her raised foot, then kicked it up again, into the spinning circle. A Red cheered. Carlos jumped up, excited.

'See that, *perdedores*? Blues RULE! We got the talent. We got the skills, man!'

'No way!' A White jumped to his feet. Bruiser caught the cans and ceased juggling, eyes bright, panting with glee. The White shook his head. 'That is some street theatre bullshit. I'll show you talent.'

The man pressed a hand to his chest and began reciting a poem, rattling through the words. It had a strange, complex rhythm and metre, and I thought he could have taken a little more time over it, but even at speed it took a while to complete. When he was done his fellow Whites cheered him. The rest offered polite applause.

'Our turn, our turn!' A Green this time. He was built like he spent a lot of time on the treadmill, his ragged trousers barely containing his thighs. Presumably the runner Li had admired earlier. I expected some kind of athletic display from him, but instead he asked the Yellows for their pack of cards. They were just curious enough to agree, handing him the pack. The runner gave it to Bruiser and told her to shuffle. She did as she was asked, and returned the cards. The runner handed the pack to a Red, asked him to shuffle it again. Then he asked Bruiser to think of a card and write it down. She obliged, dipping a finger into a pool of grease and scrawling something on her palm.

The runner held the pack in his hand and gazed at Bruiser, smiling slightly. Then he split the cards, stared at what he found, appearing confused.

'What the hell?' he said. 'It's not here.'

Bruiser frowned.

'Your card isn't here. Someone must have taken it. Who took it?'

He stepped among the Reds, asking each member if they had Bruiser's card, shaking his head at their denials. He went on to the Whites, the Yellows, his own Greens, wielding the pack, demanding the missing card's return. Then, suddenly, he stopped, turned, and fixed his gaze on Carlos.

'You,' he said, pointing. 'The party's over. Give us the card.'

'Huh?' Carlos looked around, uncertain.

'That's right, you,' said the runner. 'In your overalls pocket. Hand it over, please.' The crowd roared at him, and Carlos relented, examining his pockets.

'No, not that one,' snapped the runner. 'The pocket you're sitting on.'

Laughter. Carlos stood up, muttering, and delved in his seat pocket. He paused, eyes wide, and drew out a single playing card.

'Holy shit.'

'Show it to your team-mate, please.'

Bruiser jumped and squealed with glee, clapping her hands in delight. She snatched the card out of Carlos's fingers and returned it to the runner, who was already bowing, already fielding questions. The crowd was delighted and intrigued. Even Li raised an eyebrow.

The noise turned to an expectant hum, as Reds chattered nervously, wondering who might follow the runner's trick.

'They got nothing!' jeered Carlos. 'They got nothing!'

He might have been right, but we never found out. A klaxon blared in the hangar. Carlos dropped, pressing his hands to his ears and grinding his teeth, until the echoes died away.

'Lord!' said Wole. 'It doesn't do to deafen us.'

I noticed something shifting below.

'We're slowing down.'

Li nodded. 'Arrived,' he said. 'We go.'

- Report for burning.

The Signal comes through, booms in our dreamless sleep. We snap awake, pull on our overalls and our boots, watched by Rickets, who is there with us, waiting. Kosiaki lies still. Until I touch his shoulder, and he thrashes awake. He looks at me as if for the first time.

'When do we start work?' he asks.

'When the burning is completed,' I reply.

'When will that be?'

I stand between him and Rickets, I touch his shoulder again, and I try to transmit that he should not falter, he should not question, because Rickets is watching. And Kosiaki seems to take my meaning, because he pulls on his overalls and boots and he stands, following me to the elevator. Rickets taps on his flex, rolls it up, prods Kosiaki in the chest with it.

'You're treading on very thin ice, my lad.'

Kosiaki blinks, looks at his feet. Rickets sighs and drags him into the elevator. I enter last. We stand in silence as Rickets swipes his palm, and the car begins to descend. Kosiaki is shrugging again, but I cannot grab him, I cannot calm him; he is wedged between two identical brothers. One is about to speak when something else does instead.

A shock wave. It booms through the rock and seems to shake the entire hex. The lift shaft chimes and rings. The elevator stops. The lights go out.

'Oh, tremendous,' says Rickets. He swipes his palm again and again, but nothing happens – except that Kosiaki stops shrugging. Emotion shakes Rickets's voice.

'That was an uncontrolled explosion,' says Kosiaki.

'Agreed,' we brothers chorus.

Rickets wipes the sweat from his brow with his sleeve.

'What are you saying? It was an accident?'

'A bomb,' says Kosiaki. He reaches up, unclips the elevator hatch, hoists himself up and out of the car. Rickets is sweating, anxious.

'And what do you think you're doing?'

'I will investigate the cause of the explosion.'

Rickets looks carefully at him.

'No, Kosiaki. You will remain until power is restored. You have an appointment with Burn. We all do.'

The man swipes his palm another three times. Still no response. We five others, we look up at Kosiaki, as he begins climbing the elevator shaft.

'Oi!' yelps Rickets. 'Stop right there!'

'The elevator is inoperative.' Kosiaki's voice, echoing above us. 'I will establish the cause of the disruption.'

'You,' says Rickets, pointing at me. 'Go after him. He's showing a bit too much initiative for my liking.'

I obey, climbing out of the cab, into the dark cylinder. I see the shape of Kosiaki moving above, already a hundred metres clear. I climb, matching his speed.

He stops at Sleep, wrenches open the doors, waits for me to join him. We step through, into the copper-toned chamber. An inch-wide crack snakes across the ceiling. Raised voices echo from an adjoining hex. The Soldiers. Kosiaki and I, we share the same thought: a cave-in. The connecting hatch will not open, so we punch a hole through it and rip it clear.

We enter the adjoining hex to find the space intact. The Soldiers are pressed around their master, bellowing at him.

'Itwasabombletusupwhatwe'refortheycouldalreadybesecuritybreachedyoudon'tknowwecansortitbutithastobeimminentthreatlevel.'

Somewhere beneath the wall of voices is a man's, calling: 'Stand back! Stand back! We don't go anywhere until I receive an order!'

One of the Soldiers steps forward. Prods the man in the chest, making him stagger.

'Listen, mate. That was a bomb. We're going up there to secure the area, whether you like it or not.'

'You will follow ORDERS!'

'Who do you think you are? Control? Let us up to the surface.'

'I said, STAY BACK!'

The man swings his flex high, slaps the Soldier across the face. The Soldier blinks at this sensation, the first actual combat he has encountered.

In a flash, without a thought, he swings a defensive punch. The man drops. Lies still.

The Soldier hesitates, wondering what is happening.

Then, that feeling, an effervescence in our blood. The Control Signal. The other Soldiers blink and turn on their comrade, the killer. They surround him.

'OK,' says the offender. 'Fair enough.'

His brothers tear him limb from limb.

BACKER

'Jesus, it's cold,' yelped Carlos, calling behind me, over the howling gale. I didn't respond. It was kind of an obvious statement.

We had secured the chariot in the race pits after arrival, then passed three hours attempting to sleep in the igloos. Then Li had roused us, repeating the word 'practice', tearing our blankets away. Maybe he thought he had a team of strangers on his hands.

We crawled out of the igloo, stood in a fierce blizzard, a flurry on a great blank, carried on winds so sharp they cut through muscle and bone. We shivered in single file, gripping the clothes of the team member in front, following Li down a treacherous ice stairway into the race pit.

I liked the place right away. Even in the dancing snow it reminded me of Rick's garage. The smell. The grease. The industry. The pits were gouged out of the ice either side of a long access trench. The chariots sat under billowing tarps. Li opened the rattling steel gate and assembled us around the Tombstone.

'Positions,' he said. He pointed at Carlos: 'Hopper', at Wole: 'Runner', at me: 'Backer'. Then he looked at Bruiser: 'Reserve'.

'Reserve? I drive! I drive!'

'I drive,' said Li firmly. 'You quiet.'

Bruiser slumped against the wall, snow crumbling about her shoulders. I knew how she felt. I wanted to take the wheel too.

'Boot up, mount up,' ordered Li, lifting the driver's flap and jumping behind the wheel. Carlos, Wole and Bruiser pulled on skates and jumped into the back. I slipped distastefully into the passenger seat. Li gunned the engine and edged us out into the storm.

Carlos peered out through a slat.

'Why are we driving in this shit, man? Can't we wait for a better day?'

'We race in all weather.'

With that we were out, onto the ice. I squinted into the whirling snow, trying to make out the contours of the Drome, as Li accelerated, picking up speed. The wind caught the car, nudged it sideways, wheels spinning. Li corrected like a pro, keeping us on course. His driving impressed, composed through every jerk and skid. He didn't fight the car like some Reals would have.

'Drome is ice,' he said, booming at me over the engine. 'But ice change. Soft. Hard. Smooth. Rough. Change during race. Each lap different. You watch track.' He eyed his shivering cargo in the rear-view mirror. 'And you. Skates alter track too. Understand?'

A few resentful grunts came back to him.

'Good.'

After a few laps Li parked up the chariot at the start line and ordered us out. The Drome looked like an ancient ruin. Li chewed and watched us.

'We skate.'

'All of us?' asked Carlos, scratching at his ear tag.

'All.'

'Why? Wole's the runner.'

'Pack of gum if you catch me.'

He pushed away, arms out, accelerating clear. We followed, slapping hard on our skates, carried along by the wind. For a moment I was a natural, a native, a creature of the ice. Then I lost balance, tumbled and rolled. Carlos skated gracefully by, laughing and pointing.

'Whoa, nice moves, man! Look like you were born on ice. You play hockey or something?' He went after Li, laughing. He closed in, but the captain jinked on the sloping track, throwing up a jagged spray of ice and slush, blinding Carlos. The cook's boot caught, twisted, sent him airborne, then hard down onto his chest. I got to my feet and skated alongside.

'My condolences.'

'Shove it.'

Li skated back, circling, looping around the prone Colombian.

'See what I do?'

182

Carlos sniffed at him.

'Clearly not.'

'Turned. Reverse travel. Drag heel. Cut ice.'

Li cut a zigzag through the air with a gloved finger.

Carlos rolled onto his palms, sipped some air. Li's eyes burned through the white-out.

'Someone chase you,' he said, 'make it hard.'

I liked the guy more and more.

He certainly had a good eye for a runner. Wole mastered the skates inside an hour. He was hurtling ahead of the pack, moving like the blades were part of him, instinctively knowing when to shape, when to kick.

Li tossed practice pucks to us all – the slim disc charges that racers would stamp to activate, then kick at enemy chariots. Wole proved best with this element too, a master of shooting and close control. He jinked in and out of the rest of us, stealing our pucks away, whooping in triumph.

Li had to call him back. He rested a hand on the big man's shoulder. 'Good.'

Then he pointed at me.

'You. Fetch Green chariot.'

'Fetch it?'

'Take it. We hop.'

I didn't need to be asked twice. A chance to drive was a chance to drive. I coasted back to the pits, jumped in the Green chariot, boosted the engine, heard it snort into life. I inched the vehicle onto the track, respecting the surface. Bruiser had her chance too, taking the wheel of the Tombstone, while Wole, Carlos and Li clambered up the rail onto the roof, clutching spears. Slowly both chariots picked up speed. Bruiser snatched a grin my way. I lifted a thumb at her, and the smile broke wider.

We should never have brought her. She could be killed. You're a callous fucker, do you know that?

She doesn't get onto the Ark if she isn't on the team.

She'll be safe on the Rig.

That place is a prison. Besides, this is where she wants to be. I'm not her Control.

I watched her peering over the wheel, her nose lifted, bouncing in her seat as if the wheel was surging energy into her bones. I knew what that was like.

The storm eased off as we began a slow circuit, allowing Li to teach the essentials of hopping. The hopper's task was to cling to the chariot roof, seeking an opportunity to hurl his charge-tipped spear at a rival chariot. If he missed, he could vault onto an opposing vehicle and try to put it out of action. It was Carlos's jumping ability he wished to assess.

Li went first, crouching in the wind, coiling to spring. Bruiser lost concentration, slapped the Tombstone into my chariot, veered away. Li took the jump anyway, pouncing as the chariots parted, securing a perch on my roof with relative ease.

We took the north turn slowly, then entered the east straight, where I slowed and drew level with the Tombstone. Li jumped back to the team, and encouraged Carlos to take his turn.

Carlos had other plans. He clung to the rail with limpet resolution, quiff fluttering. Wole and Li cajoled him, but he wasn't in the mood.

'No way! No fucking way!'

He shouted it all the way back. I returned the Green chariot to its pit, found Li alone, having sent the others back to the igloos to get what sleep they could. Li moved about the Tombstone, carefully fixing a tarp over its shape.

'So,' I said, 'we're not breaking some rule driving around in a competitor's car?'

Li sniffed.

'I refuel. Never know.'

'Well, for what it's worth, Green can't win. That thing has no acceleration at all.'

'Game more than speed,' said Li, securing the last tarp fixtures. He tossed gum into his mouth, looked up at a crisp blue sky, streaked in thin clouds. We'd been training all night, but the sun had never departed.

'Can't help noticing I'm the only position that hasn't been trained,' I said. 'What is my role as backer?'

He ceased chewing for a moment, surprised by the question.

'Replacement,' he said. 'When someone dies.'

I followed him back over the tundra, listening to my boots in the snow. The weather had cleared enough to see the *Ark*, sitting out to sea. Faint music carried over the waves. Singing too. I wondered if Bridget was still planning her putsch.

I glanced at Li.

'You know this game is fixed, right?'

Li walked on, saying nothing, then pulled up.

'Never say.'

'But it's true, isn't it?'

'They listen,' he said, offering something approaching a glare.

'Out here?'

He pulled on his ear tag, stared into space. Something opened behind his eyes, something I hadn't seen there before. Then it snapped shut.

'Fix, fair. Either way, we race.'

'You don't want to win? You don't want a space on the *Ark*?'

A corner of his mouth picked up a fraction. Maybe that passed for his smile.

'Want?' he said. 'What good is want?'

He marched off again. I followed, wondering that a Real could be so Ficial.

We found the team already dozing in the gloomy igloo, under heaped blankets, warmed by their own body heat, brewing a stink like rotten herring. Li squeezed onto the last available cot and promptly fell asleep. I didn't feel like sleeping anyhow. There was too much on my mind.

I headed back out to the drifts. The wind had dwindled, kicking up a light dust of snow. The other team igloos were drawn in a crescent around ours, on a plateau overlooking the Drome, as if we'd need reminding why we were here. I started out away from the track, taking deep strides in the drifts. I welcomed the cold, let it freeze my scattered thoughts, pack them and pile them into an edifice I could ponder.

The wind died away completely, leaving the sound of the ice popping and grinding. How long would this last cap of ice remain, I wondered, under the weight of the sun, under the grinding erosion of the Game? One day the Drome would simply break up and disappear. The Game would go on until it did.

I reached out my gauntlet, glimmering in the sun, and gripped. I thought I would hold time there, where I wanted it, keep the ice packed in a desolate paradise. For a moment I was seized by a terrible elation, a sense that this moment meant everything and nothing.

The feeling scattered. I dropped my arm, started walking again. I took a seat on a rusted oil barrel and stared at the distant *Ark*. My mind cleared, examining the problem with Ficial detachment. How to win the race, in spite of the fix? Once aboard the *Ark*, how to get Marsh treated?

I stared at the liner for hours, until I noticed activity. The funnels began to smoke, and the great cavity opened up in the hull, unfurling the great Flex gangway to the shore.

Machines, men and material streamed off the ship and pooled on the ice cliff, each baronial corporation flying its colour, Sharks dragging loads, and lastly Hoods, moving in solemn procession. Each travelled the path to the Drome, treading a brown smear in the snow.

I jumped off my perch and plodded down the bank to the igloos, watching the great memory metal tents rise around the Drome: the prism, the cube, the sphere. Somebody in there would know how to fix Marsh.

Then I saw the band, a cluster of brass and drum players, led along the edge of the congregation. I thought I spotted Bridget leading the way. I turned around a snowdrift, to find the teams forming up, stretching in the sun.

'You!' Li stood outside the igloo, frowning at me. 'Game starting.'

'We've been waiting, man,' said Carlos. 'What you doing up there?'

I shrugged.

'Looking around.'

He was too nervous to ask more. Li tapped each of us on the shoulder as we walked past him, taking the ice path to the Drome. He brought up the rear, offering a booming monosyllabic pep talk.

'Look. Think. Fight.'

Nobody listened. There were too many distractions: the crowd, the bright tents, the huge flexes rolling up at the Drome turns. Drones buzzing overhead, some armed, some sporting globe-shaped protrusions, eyeing us as they passed.

Our faces were projected onto the flexes, lambs filmed to the slaughter. Most of the racers cheered and waved when they realised, taking their moment. I fixed my eyes on my boots. The last time I'd seen my face projected like that had been the start of a series of very bad days.

The teams entered the pits and separated. Each bay began to hum with preparations. I heard someone approach behind me.

'Well this is a very scurvy tune.'

I turned to find Bridget, standing in a heart attack of a band outfit. She replaced her fingers on the trumpet's valve keys and rolled them there.

'This is a surprise,' I said. 'You going to play a bugle call on that thing? What's it to be? "Charge" or "The Last Post"?'

She nodded slowly.

'Just thought I'd check in and see for myself,' she said. 'I didn't believe it until I saw your mush projected on the flex there. So you've sold out, Ken? Going to perform like a seal, are you? Going to balance the ball on your nose for the punters?'

'If you mean: "Am I going to race?" Yes, I am.'

She flipped the trumpet, jabbed the mouthpiece into my chest.

'Why? What's wrong with you? You think they'll let your type live on the *Ark*?'

'Quiet,' I said, wary of eavesdroppers.

'Learning fast, aren't you?' She took a step back. 'So you're not going to help me?'

'Marsh is ill,' I said. 'She doesn't have long. If we win we might get her treatment.'

Bridget frowned.

'I didn't know. But that doesn't change anything.'

I was saved by the race officials. We heard them up the access trench, a group making a big noise as they went about their pre-race inspections, barging into the nearby pens, hollering so loudly you would have thought they were about to compete. Bridget eyed me. We might catch trouble if she were discovered in a pit before a race.

'This isn't over, Ken,' she snapped, pointing the mouthpiece at my face. 'Not by a long shot, mate.'

She climbed up the pit wall and scuttled away, over the track, headed for the band enclosure in the Drome island. The race officials appeared at the gate, entered. One held a long spear, the other a bandolier of pucks.

'OK. Who's your runner?'

Wole stepped forward. The official tossed him the belt.

'Come with me.'

We all took a moment to shake Wole's hand. Bruiser clutched him, and wouldn't detach.

'Don't fret,' said Wole, running fingers through her hair. 'Mine's the easy job. Nothing simpler. It doesn't take an Einstein. I'll see you soon.'

'Move it,' barked the official. Wole waved as he left the pit. The officials followed, leaving the spear with Carlos, who clutched it like a snake.

'Time,' said Li, mounting the driver's seat.

I jumped in the car alongside him. Carlos climbed the rail as if it were a gallows. Bruiser looked up at us with watery eyes.

'I wanna come.'

'You'll be safe here,' I said. 'Watch on the flexes.'

'You OK?'

She seemed concerned. I held out the gauntlet, let her articulate a finger.

The Yellow chariot edged past our pit's open gate, its exhaust smoking. I scented something I recognised, lifted my hand out of Bruiser's. We pulled out of the pit, turned into the access trench, followed by Green, Red, White.

We rolled down the ramp to the Drome, my fingers dancing on my knee. The track opened up before us. The band played, the crowd roared, amplified by Flex speakers. Coloured flares shot into the sky.

Li rolled us up to the start line, tossed gum in his mouth. I glanced out of my window, met the eyes of a Yellow in the neighbouring chariot. Hanging over it all, the astonishing pale blue canopy, barely streaked by clouds, and the waiting sun.

Something banged on the roof.

'You ready in there?' boomed Carlos. 'Ready to be heroes?'

'Brave today,' muttered Li.

A Game official marched along the track edge, pistol in hand. Silence descended over the Drome. I thought I heard a bird call, and scanned the sky to glimpse it.

Li tapped me on the shoulder, pointed ahead.

'Eyes. Road.'

A shot fired, and the chariot leapt forwards.

Right away we were in trouble. The Yellow chariot streaked into the distance, utterly outpacing the rest of the pack, scent heavy in its exhaust. Green slapped into us, letting Red and White thunder ahead. There they closed up. Green braked, dropped away, then surged behind us. They were boxing us in. Li frowned.

'Alliance,' he said. 'Bad news.'

He was right. The hoppers ahead clung to their rails, spears lifted. Li could barely manoeuvre. It would be hard for them not to hit us.

But they held off, watching each other more than us. I pointed at them, as we bore down on the north turn, speedo tickling fifty, the Tombstone twitchy on the ice.

'Why don't they attack?' I called over the engine roar.

'No need,' yelled Li. 'Slow us for runners.'

Right. Why waste spears, when one well-placed puck could take out a wheel?

So let's split them up.

I swung open the passenger flap, pushed out into the frozen spray, the blast of engines and crowd. Squinted in the stinging rush of air, at the chariots ahead, behind at the Greens. I reached up, wind howling, trying to wrench me from my perch. I found the rail, clutched, hauled onto the roof, past Carlos, his eyes wild with fear.

Ahead, runners hurtled down the slipway onto the turn. I saw Wole, barging to the head of the pack.

I slipped onto the Tombstone's hood, my overalls whipping in the speed gale, using the gauntlet as an anchor. I saw the hoppers ahead loft their spears, warding me off.

I turned my face to Li, crossed fingers and touched my chin, an adapted Marsh signal:

(Close on enemy.)

He called it, stamped on the gas.

A snarl from the Tombstone's engine.

Sixty, maybe seventy. Ramming speed. Much too fast for the turn.

Red's driver saw the move, picked up speed. White was too slow. The Tombstone slapped into his rear fender hard, and I vaulted, caught in the air for a moment, then snatching the White rail in the gauntlet. Li backed the Tombstone off, left me dangling from White, slapping skates on ice, dragged like tin cans from a wedding car.

The turn.

The runners were among us.

A peripheral smudge of yellow, near the track wall. Then, a puck, streaking over the ice, slipping under tyres as the chariots braked and skidded into the turn. An explosion in the track wall. A shower of ice.

My new chariot slapped hard against Red, almost knocking it into a spin, but that driver was good, holding course. I struggled in the high-speed turn, climbed the rail, barely able to draw breath in the screaming air.

Then a spear slapped into my cheek. It was hard enough to sting, but not to dislodge. I hooped an arm in the rail, ducked another swipe.

The pack of chariots slalomed out of the turn, accelerated. The gale picked up. Fifty. Sixty. Seventy. I saw Carlos, sprawled flat on Blue's roof. Red's runner, clinging to the Tombstone's tail bar. The other runners behind us, dropping away, fanning out.

The spear slashed again. Strange move. If the tip connected we'd both be blown to pieces. I forgave him. Real panic has no space for reason. I caught the spear on his next try, hauled up the rail after him.

He was there, snarling, enraged. I threw a fist. The wind caught it, made it a hard, open slap. He dropped his spear, flailed in the gale-force wind, clutched tight to the rail. I turned, saw the Green chariot clatter over the dropped spear, leaving splinters and a live bomb behind.

I'd had enough roof time. I gripped the hopper's fist in my gauntlet and squeezed. He howled, released his hold, dropped clear as we entered the southern turn. He struck the ice hard, splayed like a bloodied bear skin.

White had fallen behind now, Green gaining as we slowed. Ahead, the Tombstone slapped off Red, Carlos still cowering on the roof. The Red runner was climbing the rail, headed right for him.

I reached for White's backer flap, sensed a blur of bright tents, music, a swooping drone's bulging eye. I hoisted the flap. Found White's backer, looking resolute.

The Poet.

Then, a problem. As we left the turn, headed north again, the Green chariot appeared. Its hopper was poised, her spear aloft. The

Poet saw her too. She had us. Her chariot betrayed her. It jinked, just as she threw.

A streak in my vision. An explosion.

White's tail bucked. The sky snatched my legs and yanked hard. I gripped the rusty rail with everything my real hand had, soaring upside down through a storm of ice, exhaust, howling motors.

Then gravity returned, hammered the tailgate back to earth, crushing the rear axle. The tail scooped out, tossing me over the side to find the backer flap broken free, the Poet gone. I saw the driver, fighting for control.

I swung into the cab, leading with my feet. Stupid move. White's driver slammed an elbow into my knee. Then he lost control, and the chariot veered left, slapping his side into the track wall. The metal shrieked along the ice, blowing a blinding mess of frost. Still we grappled, the driver holding my gauntlet out of his face, beating on my knee.

He struggled free, thrust his boot into my chest, kicked me back the way I'd come. I fell half out of the chariot, head drooping inches above the rushing ice.

A powerful report. A face full of something hot.

The Tombstone appeared, Li slowing to take me back, steering so close I could see the imperfections in our paint job. I reached out and snatched the side strap. Peered at White's driver. Called to him: 'You've got a flat.'

Li turned, dragged me clear. White wobbled. The tyre burst. It flipped, rolled along the ice, lay on its roof.

Applause.

The Green chariot appeared, surging forward, making to run me down. Li went one better. He must have seen his Red hitcher. He stamped on the brakes, turned, kept the car pointed where he wanted. Green's brakes locked. They hurled past, slammed into the outside wall as we entered the north turn, hopper thrown clear. Our Red passenger was left bent and wrecked on the ice. We passed unscathed, accelerating into the turn.

'Get in!' cried Li.

'Now why didn't I think of that?' I snarled, arm howling in pain. Carlos appeared, picking down the side of the cab. He offered his arm. I took it.

I entered the cab, wiped the tears from my eyes. (How were they supposed to ease the pain?) I caught a glimpse of Yellow on the far side of the track. Red was coming out of the southern turn. We wouldn't catch them now.

With White and Green chariots marked out, their runners were out too. That just left the Yellow runner to face. And one more, of course.

'Has Wole attacked? Where is he?'

Li said nothing.

We took the southern turn unmolested, accelerated, past the White wreck. Past the Green, into the north turn. Then, a hammering on the roof. I opened the slat. Carlos, or his wild, bloodshot eyes, quiff flapping in the gale. He was signalling:

(Astern – Attack imminent – Astern.)

I glanced in what remained of the side mirror. The Yellow runner, moving up the slope, kicking a puck.

'Wole, where are you?'

Li tapped my shoulder urgently, pointed ahead.

Wole was on the ice, near the summit of the turn, lying in a puddle of blood.

Carlos hammered on the roof again.

Too late. A puck streaked across our path. Li turned just a little too hard.

A violent lurch.

Slow now. The Tombstone tipped, jumped, G forces thrashing my head one way, the other. The Drome spun outside.

Two tonnes of chariot. Crunching on its side in a neck-snapping impact. Scraping over the ice, making it wail. I roared back at it, a cornered animal, until we ground to a halt and I heard the crowd again; cheering, applauding, chanting approval.

I recognised Floyd's voice, booming out over the track:

'And they are *outta here!*'

The surface. We spend a few minutes looking at the sky, at birds, clouds, treetops, and above them drones, private and media and government in origin. In the distance is the thump, crack and cry of the evictions.

Rickets arrives, late and purple. He leads us past the smoking Town Hall, up Acre Lane, escorts us in silence to the crater where the bomb exploded. Any closer to the Ritzy and it would surely have damaged the Control Bunker, so deep and wide is this gouge in the street, which swallowed up morning commuters and tossed a bus all the way to the Sunlight Building. We recover debris from the bomb site, we scoop it up and run in a tight working group, shuttling between this wound and a line that Control has drawn, a line where a wall will be erected, shutting out the city.

We review the plans for this wall and submit alterations, we say that this wall must have elegance, but we hear no reply. So we stick to the tall, thick, blunt design specified. And it is strange to us, as we draw crosses on houses, that our first project will not be to create, but to smash and pulverise. We will fetch excavators and pulse welders and chains, and we will tear down a ring of structures to make way for the wall.

It is strange for the Soldier Models, too. Their first task is not to kill but to police, to line people up and not *to shoot them. They must shepherd their enemy in messy, fracturing columns, let them gather what they can carry, then march them out of the area, never to return. And the Medic Models have no sick to cure, only the dead to inspect, corpses and pieces of people that we find crushed under boulders, or pluck from trees and car wrecks. The Mechanic Models, those we have not seen before, they are not repairing, enhancing the vehicles they find; they are gathering them up, every car and every bike and every truck in Brixton, and breaking them up in their hands, and tossing the broken remains into the crater.*

'Like a sacrifice,' says Rickets under his breath, then, remembering that

we can hear: 'Take note, lads, take note. This is what frightened, inspired, hate-fuelled people can do. This is what people do when they think they can talk to God. They hurt other people.'

Control does not signal all day. The Mechanic and Medic Models return to their hexes, but we work through the night, tearing down terraces, Soldier eyes keeping glowing watch. We stop for an hour as morning breaks, to watch the sky change colour. We in turn are watched: by men, women, by children, from twitching curtains and doorways and cars.

We start to raise the wall.

FIXABLE

Somebody had been good enough to drag me back to the pit, leaving me propped against a fuel barrel. Li slumped unconscious next to me. The Tombstone was missing. A huge drone soared above, wings spread like an albatross.

I looked around the empty pit, at an oil stain on the pit floor, at ice walls latticed with tools: air gun, lug nuts, impact wrench, spare tyres. There was some distant cheering that I kind of resented.

Stand up.

The flesh refused, so I sat there until Carlos and Bruiser appeared at the gate.

'Hey,' I said. It wasn't a voice I recognised.

Bruiser crouched at my side.

'Safe,' she said. Carlos limped in my direction, hands trembling, hair a mess.

'Wole?' I asked.

His eyes darted at a humped tarp. Tears rolled down his cheek. He choked and wiped mess from his nose.

'He didn't even make a goddam lap. They ganged up on him. Murdered him. Why?'

'Game.'

Li had stirred. He looked at Carlos evenly. Carlos threw out his arms.

'Game? That all you got to say? A man died.'

Li lifted a hand to his neck, winced.

'Most die have no reason. Wole die for Marsh. So bad?'

'Hell, yes, it's so bad!'

'No tears,' said Li. 'Weak. Cameras come. Be strong. Man Snoot watches.'

195

'Fuck the baron, man,' snarled Carlos. 'I lost a friend.'

Li pulled a shred of gum from his chest pocket, dropped it in his mouth, chewed.

'Still want to win?'

Carlos had nothing to say. He'd never been crazy about the whole enterprise. I answered for him.

'Yes, we still want to win.'

Li looked at me.

'Chariot damaged. Need repair. Man Snoot give no money if we cry. Must be . . .' He stopped, frowned, thought of the word. 'Defiant.'

'You be defiant,' said Carlos. 'I'll be pissed.'

'Well, well,' said a voice. 'It's today's big story.'

Floyd stood at the gate, another Real behind him, pointing a camera his way.

'Big wipeout for the Blues today when they were looking tied on for second place. This is a new team with lots of fresh faces. Let's see if we can talk to them.'

He pushed open the gate, prodded the mic at me.

'So,' he said, mic pressed to my nose, 'what do you think went wrong for you out there today?'

I stared at him, trying to find things to say. Floyd's eyes widened a little. Li, Bruiser and Carlos watched. Suddenly my Ficialhood felt very real, very present.

Say something, you fool! Say anything!

'Wrong? Nothing went wrong.'

Floyd turned around. Carlos had patted his quiff back into place, his demeanour entirely changed. Floyd turned the microphone his way.

'You don't think anything went wrong?'

Carlos pursed his lips.

'I thought we were outstanding throughout, Floyd. On another day, who knows how things might have finished.'

'But the facts remain, your chariot is badly damaged and you racked up no points. That leaves you anchored to third spot, with—'

Carlos snatched the mic.

'Look, we have a great team of players here. Even with our runner marked out, I believe we can challenge. This was our first race and we played with intelligence and personality. Nobody on this track should

196

be in any doubt. We're coming for the title. We have the best fans in New Jerusalem and with them behind us we can achieve anything.'

'Thank you,' said Floyd, beaming and shaking Carlos by the hand. 'Thank you.'

He marched out, followed by his crew. Carlos's face dropped like an anchor. He eyed Li.

'Defiant enough for you?'

Li pushed onto his feet. He told Bruiser to head back to the igloo and pack up Wole's things.

'Meet at dock.'

He unhooked two coils of rope from the pit wall and pointed at Carlos and me.

'You follow.'

We hobbled into the access trench, past the Red pit, where the team stopped their work to watch us, past the empty White and Green pits. We slipped down the access road onto the track.

The crowd had dispersed, leaving Sharks to pack up the tents on great sleighs. Garbage fluttered over the snow. We shuffled up the ice, past the band pit. I thought how wretched our chances were of completing a race, let alone winning the League. I thought of Marsh, dying slowly in the bowels of the Rig.

The Tombstone lay on its side, gathering snow. Li grunted orders. We braced gloved hands on the frozen metal and rocked the great heap back and forth, until it tipped and fell on its wheels with a crunch of suspension.

Li lifted the driver's flap, brushed off the seat, and turned the key. No response. I lifted the hood and poked at the leaking mess of parts.

'Nothing too bad,' I said. 'Fixable.'

We lashed ropes to the chariot and dragged it after us. Down the slope, onto the straight, past burn marks, oil spills, debris and blood. All the signs of a Real good Sunday.

Our welcome home was something. You might have thought we'd won. A crowd waited on the cliff, waving blue flags, faces painted. They cheered our approach, sang obscene songs. Children ran around our feet, wearing shirts inscribed with our names. I didn't see Wole's anywhere.

Carlos certainly had fans. He was mobbed, lifted like a trophy, borne aloft by Blue hands. Apparently his televised speech had inspired this frenzy. He looked puzzled by the attention, but soon enough he was with them, beating his fist in the air and chanting along: 'Woad rules the road! Woad rules the road!'

A few Blues attempted to congratulate Li, but he waded through them, oblivious. I followed in his wake, Bruiser at my side. The crowd thinned, and we twisted through the containers until we reached the ladderway. We began to descend, watching Li's great shape pump down the flickering light. Near the nets he cut out of sight, climbing into the cavity.

I followed, heart beating so hard I could hear it in my breath. Bruiser came too, sighing at the effort but determined not to be parted.

Marsh lay on her bunk. I paused, observed the gentle rise and fall of her breathing shape. Somehow she sensed me and turned over. She was white, eyes sunken, lips drawn in. I stood there and gaped, like a tourist facing a tidal wave.

Bruiser scowled at me, jumped up on Marsh's cot. She helped Marsh sit up, trickled water over her lips, into her parched mouth. Marsh blinked slowly. She ran her hand into the girl's hair and brought their foreheads together.

'Thank you.'

I took a seat and examined my gauntlet, glowing in the cavity light. Marsh's head lolled.

'To what do I owe the pleasure?' she croaked.

So, she didn't know. I hesitated.

'How do you feel?'

She snorted, laughed, coughed hard until there was no breath left in her. Bruiser massaged her back until she recovered herself. Then she sighed.

'How do I look?'

She looked near death. She looked beautiful. I didn't say either. I looked at my boots instead.

'Where is Wole? Caught in the party?'

'He's . . .'

I ran out of words. She frowned.

'Kenstibec. Where is he?'

'Dead,' I said. 'He's dead.'

She held perfectly still, her face a cliff.

'How?'

'It was during the race. He—' I stopped. Something in her eyes had cracked. 'It was quick.'

It hadn't been. He'd bled out in front of a baying crowd. There'd been no mercy to it.

Her hand emerged from her blankets, a trembling bony thing, and rested over her eyes. Bruiser clutched her. She sucked and choked, moaned a little.

'I'm sorry,' I said.

'Get lost, Kenstibec. Do me a favour. Just get lost.'

Her voice was low, wavering. Another sob, another snort. She turned her face away, but I glimpsed streams on her cheeks. She pressed her face into Bruiser's chest, and they embraced each other, both crying freely, leaking misery.

I crawled back the way I'd come, helpless, ridiculous, thirsty like never before.

I didn't visit Marsh again the whole week. Any chance I had of fixing her seemed ruined. Whatever fuel additive I had scented in the Yellows' exhaust, it gave them an advantage we couldn't match. With Wole gone, Bruiser would have to compete. Our chances of winning the last race were pretty wretched. With no *Ark* berth, there'd be no treatment for Marsh. We only had a chance of dying in a rigged Game.

I avoided Bruiser and the others, slept in a far, windswept corner of the net, shunning contact. The life of Blue went on about me, but even in my retreat the attentions of fans disturbed me. Besides, soon enough one foreman or another would show up and drag me to work.

I pulled on goggles and a mask, and ventured to the other nets, avoiding Wole's still active patrols. I tore a hole in the knots and bindings, wriggled through to Red, into new valleys and peaks. I passed a morning in Red, an afternoon in White.

Life, Reals, people seemed the same. Labour. Prayer. Meals under hanging flexes. Mah-jong games. Markets. Gum for sale. Guns for sale. Company towns. Fordlandias.

There were little differences. Above the Red overnet, names of those who'd fallen in the Game were painted in grease on the retardant layer; in White, a net was filled with pebbles, two names daubed on each. I puzzled over them for some time.

They're love tokens, idiot.

They're overloading the net.

I don't think that's the point, you freak.

The following day I doubled back, headed south, explored Yellow. The net held the same mix of oil-stained Reals, but there was a sickness among them, some kind of flu. Great piles of moaning infected lay heaped in the far corners. No doctors here either. I clutched a rag to my face, headed for home. Somehow, after my trip, Blue was more home then ever.

The night before departure for the final race, I found sanctuary in the space Bridget had showed me, needing to be alone with my thoughts, to figure some way to win.

Then something gripped my ear tag and tugged.

'All right, brother?'

I whipped around, reared back. A kind of blot shared the net space with me, a shadow given life. It blinked black eyes.

'Oh. Sorry.'

It reached behind its head. The shadow fizzed away.

My face, my old face, peered down at me.

'Camo stuff Rick's been working on.'

I guess I must have looked pretty confused.

'Kenstibec? It's me.'

I shook my head.

'You're dead.'

Kinnare eyed me for a moment, uncertain what he was dealing with.

'No. Very nearly, I'll grant you, but they didn't take proper fire precautions. Kicked me into the sea before the fire burned too deep. Well, you know us. Built to last and all that.'

'You mean to tell me you swam for it?'

'Don't be daft. Rick picked me up in that mini-sub of his. Scooped up what was left of me and let me heal. Took a while. An experience to forget, Marsh would say. We've been looking for you all over.'

I wanted to show calm, restraint, measured consideration. I wanted to show whatever Ficial part of me was left. Instead I blurted out the Realest question I could have asked.

200

'Pistol. Did you find Pistol?'

Kinnare frowned and crouched at my side. Looked around the dark net.

'No,' he said. 'The dog is gone.'

I stared into my eyes.

'What do you want, Kinnare?'

'Finally,' he said. 'We get to the point.'

We sit atop the wall, the stone ring we have raised around Control. The work is complete, but Rickets has yet to recall us to Burn. So we sit up here, breathing cleaner air, and look north; over brutal concrete and Gothic revival, Victorian terrace and Georgian townhouse, shaped glass stacks and stumps of estates, stalks of towers and steeples. And we look at the river, turning in the sprawl, tributaries buried but swollen in their ducts.

We could, potentially, grow old like the river. Are we not then out of step with human time? Perhaps we cannot shape the people on its shore, any more than the river can. Perhaps we can only observe the ebb and flow of tribes and structures, marking their folly and their beauty.

We make fists. No. We are man-made, as much as any bridge or warehouse. We are here to design, to survey, to construct. We will bring order, unity, elegance where we can. We look out over the city and consider: how to improve it? We only know it by this view, and maps and images, but it is easy to plan.

A new road. We could rip out the Circulars, those jammed arteries that give the city seizures. We could carve a new canal through the squat suburbs, laid in the self-healing surface the Sixes created. There the traffic could flow out of sight, traversed by ribbon bridges, bordered by new parks and interlocking neighbourhoods of timber Jenga towers.

A new district. The old airport is closed, ever since the jets blew up over the western suburbs. It is a vast camp now, its terminals gang strongholds, its runways desolate fields of tents and lean-tos. We could build a diamond-shaped neighbourhood, house them all in ultra-light concrete blocks, finished in fletton brick, with wide avenues, playgrounds, hospitals, and the new school complexes the Threes conceived.

A new forest. We could clear a thick band around the orbital and bring nature to the city, a revived ancient landscape where deer, dragonflies, bats, birds and adders could thrive. Where people could explore, and remember their part in a greater whole, which they forget in the Oil Age city. We recall that a Power Two had something similar planned, a park that bisected the city from north to south.

For a moment we consider why the previous Powers' plans and designs have not yet been used. Should there even be work for us here, when eight previous Powers of Engineered Construction Models are already out there? Perhaps, we reason, they have more urgent tasks. The flood defences. The martellos. The power situation.

We go on like this, until we are shaken from our plans by a sound that echoes and slaps over the city. A huge black cloud coils up to the east, over the river.

The Barrier. The Barrier has been bombed.

RUNNER

'I don't even know why you're talking,' said Carlos.

We were in the back of a truck, halfway along the gangway, headed for the *Ark* cavity. The day of departure. We needed to use the time in transit. It was the only location we might speak in privacy.

'Strategy,' said Li.

Carlos was so furious he nearly took a tumble.

'Strategy? I'll give you a goddam strategy. We stay out of trouble. We survive.'

'No good,' I said. 'What about Marsh?'

Saying her name turned my stomach. She'd been sorry about cursing me, or so said Bruiser. It sounded like her condition had stabilised. But for how long?

Carlos didn't need an answer.

'Don't give me that guilt trip, man! What are we supposed to do? You saw what happened in the last Game. It's not a race, it's a circus. A goddam soap opera. We're just there to play a part.'

Li growled.

'*Cobarde.*'

Carlos sighed. Eyed Bruiser.

'You teach him that word?'

'We can win,' she said, showing him her chin.

'OK,' he said. 'Fine. Explain to me. Tell me how we win a fixed race.'

I had to be quick.

'First I want your agreement: if we win, we cover Marsh's medical bill. We get her treatment. No matter what it takes.'

'How much will that cost?' He shrugged. 'What? This is fantasy anyway. So Man Snoot sprung for repairs. Who's going to run in

Wole's place?' He pointed at Bruiser. 'The little mermaid?'

'No,' I said. 'You're relieved of hopper duties. Li will take over. Bruiser will drive and you'll take backer.'

'Oh, that's waaay better,' said Carlos. 'Consider my fears goddam allayed.'

'All you have to do is sit next to Bruiser and keep your eyes open, OK? We're going to do better this time, I promise.'

I took my Only Book out of my pocket, opened it at a particular page, passed it around the team. Li read, nodded, passed it to Bruiser. Carlos waved the book at me.

'What am I reading?'

'I've marked it, Carlos. Regulation Thirteen.'

Carlos's eyes darted over the text. He looked up at me, shook his head.

'Oh, wonderful. Very sporting.'

Li lunged at Carlos, dragged him nose to nose.

'We win,' he snarled.

Carlos blinked in the hot breath, drooped in Li's grip.

'Hey, sure. We win. Go team. Cool it, OK? Just cool it.'

The truck rolled up into the *Ark* loading platform. Sharks lowered the tailgate.

'Agree?' snapped Li, shaking Carlos.

'Agree, agree!'

The Sharks wheezed an order to disembark. We hurried out onto the platform, saw the Greens unloading from another truck. They jeered Carlos, sung a song about his sexuality. The cook smiled.

'Hey,' he said. 'Aren't you those guys we fucked up last race?'

The Green singing degenerated into screams and curses, which gave Carlos some satisfaction.

The Sharks corralled us on the elevator, boots clanking on metal, yanked and pulled our ears to scan our tags. The platform thumped and hummed, lowering us to the hangar, Greens bristling beside us.

The atmosphere was different from the first trip. Drawn in tight around us, the silence contained something else. A Red caught my eye, sliced a finger across his throat. Green and White demeanours weren't much better. Only the Yellows seemed to have no interest in us.

'I get the feeling,' said Carlos, 'we're unpopular.'

I skated along the access trench, armour gleaming, pucks on my bandolier, alongside the waiting chariots. I hammered on the Tombstone's side, slipped my arm into the driver's flap. Bruiser grinned, but her eyes were terrified.

We should put a stop to this now.

Too late for that, pal. Tell her some useful lies.

'You're the best driver on the track, kid.'

She nodded.

'I know.'

Carlos leaned forward, eyed me.

'Stay safe, *Pescado.*'

I slipped on my way, past the fog of Yellow's stinking exhaust. I crossed the track, out to the incredible open sky, the roar of the crowd. I vaulted the island barrier, skimmed past the band. I circled them, waved to Bridget. She didn't respond.

I continued, skated under the arm of the waiting race official, into the runners' pen. It wasn't too friendly in there.

Red's new runner opened the pleasantries.

'Gonna turn that arm of yours into a fucking hood ornament.'

Then the Yellow, spitting in my ear.

'You're gonna get the same as your pal. We're gonna make a stain of you, boy.'

There was plenty of that, but it was easy enough to ignore. I was more interested in the prophet's motorcade, winding through a gap in the tents, cheered by the crowd as it passed.

The limos slipped and jerked, like penguins on their bellies. Bridget and the band struck up, pumping out one of those curious dirges with which Atlantic Reals liked to greet their gods.

The motorcade passed by the *Ark* tents, the cube, the cone, the sphere, then came to rest on the north-west corner of the Drome, almost directly opposite our pen.

'Kneel, you dogs,' snarled the race official, like it was an insult. We dropped, but I kept an eye on the convoy, pulling up across the track.

A door slid open on the middle limo, lowering a ramp. Sharks and Hoods clustered around the space, shepherding the prophet towards the throne. There was quite a commotion before their leader was seated, and his followers drifted apart.

Finally, I had a good look at the prophet.

President Lay didn't seem to have aged a day, though there was something odd about his movement as he lifted his arms in benediction. He licked his lips with the tip of a long purple tongue, smiled as if at a private joke.

I wondered how many Reals back on the Rig realised their prophet was Lay. The last President of the United States. The maniac who fired the first shots in the briefest and last war.

Keep your mind on the job, pal. Mind on the job.

The band died down. The servants dispersed to their tents, and the noise of the crowd subsided. A hooded figure climbed the steps, bowed to Lay, then turned to the Drome to recite the pledge. The crowd chanted along, but we were quiet in the pen, flexing our skates, gripping pucks. Nerves. They sharpen everything. I almost felt Ficial again.

I looked down the track. Saw the rainbow of chariots lined up, turning over. Saw the figures poised on the racks. Felt the hush. The wind picked up a little. I wanted it to begin.

Then, the shot.

The chariots tore off. Immediately the stamping started, as my fellow runners aimed their blades at my toes. The rules forbade that, but the pen walls were high enough to conceal the action.

'Maybe you can get a foot to match your hand,' said Red, laughing like something untethered.

'Shit,' said Yellow, 'time we've finished he'll need metal balls.'

The body armour soaked up most of the shin kicks, but I couldn't avoid every one. Something slashed open my boot below the ankle, putting a stop to my dancing. But they were enjoying themselves so much they didn't notice the gate to the slipway peel open. The Green runner burst clear, shooting out of sight. Yellow and White were startled, but followed quickly. Only Red kept up the attack, bent on vengeance. I gauntlet-pinched him in his side and kicked him down the slipway. He slid down, clutching himself in agony, but no foul was called. The race official smiled and gestured down to the ice. I shook my head.

'What are you doing?' he said. 'Get down there.'

'Why?'

'Why? It's the fucking Game, that's why. Get moving!'

207

'There's no rule stating runners must leave the pen on the starting pistol.'

'Yes there is.'

'No. It only says I must leave the pen before the race ends. It's not just runners that don't have to move, either.'

I nodded at the start line, where the Blue chariot sat still, waiting. The boos were already amplified around the Drome.

'You can't do that!' yelped the official. He grabbed his radio. 'I'll have them moved off the track.'

'Actually,' I said, bending to patch up my damaged boot, 'A racer can only be removed from the track if the engine is dead. Look it up.'

He thought about that for a moment, squinting in that curious way Reals do when consulting a mental checklist. While he waited for his brain to report, the Yellow chariot streaked past the waiting runners. The Red, White and Green chariots followed. Two runners kicked pucks, but none hit, detonating in the track wall. The pack took the turn, slapping into each other, then cleared and spread out. Yellow shot down the southern straight, Red following, White behind, Green bringing up the rear. There were wide gaps between them, and no fighting. It looked as orderly as Lay's motorcade.

'Boring without the fights, isn't it?' I said.

The race official slammed the pen gate, kind of impatiently, face flushed.

'Will you get moving?'

'Just a minute.'

I watched as Yellow entered the southern turn. On cue, Bruiser lurched the Tombstone forward, generating some impressive smoky wheelspin, and accelerated hard. A cheer rose from the crowd.

'OK,' I said. 'Here I go.'

I barged the official clear and jumped onto my skates, pelting down hard blue ice into blinding wind. I neared the foot of the slipway, remembered the unconscious Red obstructing the exit. Still making life difficult. I dropped to my haunches and jumped, landing with a scrape in the middle of the track. I took one pace before a puck shot between my feet, hurtling down the straight.

Yellow's runner stood up the track, looking displeased.

'Nearly!' I called, picking up the pace. He plucked another puck from his bandolier, dropped it to the ice, lifted his foot, then reassessed. I was closing on him, coming straight on: too hard a target. He turned. Kicked the puck ahead. Ran after it. I couldn't see another runner, so I had to take my chance. I spun, slowed, skated backwards.

Bruiser was doing a beautiful job, swerving ahead of the Yellow chariot, preventing an overtake, slowing the race. Yellow's hopper hesitated on the rail, spear clenched, facing Li.

I let them draw close. Closer. Saw Bruiser's eyes, wild over the Tombstone's wheel; Carlos, leaning out, calling directions. Behind, Red was catching up. This was turning into something more like a competition.

The crowd roared approval. The sound shook the ice, knocked something loose inside me. I felt lifted, blessed by the din.

I dropped a puck onto the track, swivelled, kicked it up the slope and pursued it, letting Bruiser storm by. Li saluted me from the rail.

Yellow snapped past, doing little more than thirty, but I waited, waited for Red and White, closing fast. I stamped on the puck, kicked it across their path.

Missed. You MISSED!

The puck slid behind them, blew on the Drome wall. I ran hard, fingering another puck, too late, too slow. They surged away.

But things got interesting. The Yellow chariot had always been a distant speck. Now they were close enough to grapple with. Red's hopper hurled his spear, struck Yellow's rear right wheel.

The chariot jumped on a white flash. A column of smoke. It was airborne for a moment, graceful as a flying walrus, then clipped the ice, hurtled into three great sidelong rolls, crushing its own hapless runner. Then it shed a wheel, jumped again, and landed hard on its maimed backside, headlamps pointed at the sky.

Another crowd roar, loud enough to crush ice.

Bruiser jinked, almost flipped the Tombstone, tilting onto two left wheels. The kid held it, Red overtaking, slapped back to four wheels just in time to enter the turn. It would have been beautiful if Li hadn't lost his balance. I saw him tumble, spear and all.

White swerved to avoid him.

Then, the Green chariot, whining and shrieking, straining every last cylinder on a collision course. I flattened my skates, braked hard. They turned, determined to hit me, only clipped the gauntlet. They slapped sidelong into the wall, bounced back onto the track.

I snatched their rail before they could accelerate, took a puck from my bandolier, tapped it on the chariot's armour, ready to toss in the back seat.

Something punched my nose. I lost balance, flailed to keep my feet, the armed puck flying out of my hands. Then another strike, scraping my cheek, leaving thick splinters. I edged right, the chariot picking up speed. Looked up at Green's hopper, wielding her spear. She looked pretty sore.

I parried one, two thrusts, before a third struck my shoulder, hard. I lost my grip.

Bad timing. My skate caught a groove in the ice. My ankle twisted and cracked, making me yelp. I plunged, caught the fender and held on, dragged along behind.

Let go, moron!

I released, spun on the ice, ankle shrieking in pain. A drone swooped low, twitching in the high winds, slowing to achieve a close-up of my battered frame. I looked into its irising camera bud. Laughter echoed around the track. I guess I looked pretty silly.

The drone swept away, leaving me to wonder exactly how ruined my plan was. With just Bruiser and Carlos manning the Tombstone our chances were bad. I had to try and stand. I wiped the bloody mess under my nose, hobbled almost upright.

A runner hammered into me, crushing me on the Drome wall. I dropped again, breathless and stunned. I saw the Magician, the Green runner Li admired. He skated in an arc, turning towards me. The slap and tap of a puck dropped to the ice and armed.

Then a roar: a great, guttural call of the wild. Li, skating hard. He smacked into the Magician, rolling with him across the track. To my right, the Red chariot, leading Blue and White out of the southern turn, picking up speed. I was helpless. Soaked in sweat. Mouth bone-dry.

Don't let us lose. Not now. We're not worth much, but she is. Don't let us fail her.

There's nobody listening, pal.

There's you. But we're the same. Two streams of one computation.

Fuck your computation. Get your skates on.

I pushed, rolled down the track to Li's struggle. Slapped into the

Magician's legs, reared up, struck him about the temple. He crumpled. Li scrambled upright, kicked the dazed runner down the slope, hoisted me over his shoulder. Faced the oncoming traffic. Chariots doing sixty, tyres spraying arcs of frost.

'Bad,' he said.

'Oh yes,' I said. 'Real bad.'

The Red chariot, slipping and sliding, kicking up spray, demented, lining up to mow us down. White and Blue behind, slapping each other's sides. It'd be hard not to die.

Then, two black discs, shooting over ice. The White runner. Red saw them late, swerved, hit the second puck. They flipped, hood first, onto their backs, immobilised. The White chariot shot by, near enough to kiss.

Blue slowed, Carlos popping open the door, reaching out. Li lifted me, tossed me into the cabin, climbed the rail.

'Oh, shit,' said Carlos, eyeing the wounded ankle. 'You're out of it.'

I reached down, unclamped the boot and unclipped the puck bandolier, two charges remaining. I dropped it in Carlos's lap.

'What you giving it to me for?'

'You're backer,' I said, dabbing at my broken nose. 'Besides, it's cramped in here.'

'Normally I would love to,' said Carlos, handing it back to me. 'But your plan's fucked, wouldn't you say?'

We were tossed about as we entered the turn, the White chariot turning hard ahead. Their hopper still had his spear. I pointed him out to Carlos.

'Think you're safer in here?'

Carlos flexed his jaw a moment, drumming his fingers on the dash.

'Fine,' he said. He pulled on the bandolier, clambered over me, reached for the door.

'I hate this game.'

Bruiser dabbed the brakes. Carlos dropped his skates out the door.

'Oh, shit!'

And disappeared. I watched him in the rear-view, arms waving, edging down the slope. Bruiser hit the gas, taking the turn dangerously fast, trying to overtake the White chariot. We edged alongside, but it wouldn't be enough. I looked up, saw the hopper raise his spear.

This is it.

Then, the bear shape of Li, clattering onto White's roof, grappling with their hopper. The White car lost a little pace, and we overtook, leaving Li to fight alone.

'We're in the lead!' yelped Bruiser. 'We're winning!'

'Are you OK?' I asked her.

'Of course!' She beamed at me. Then the smile disappeared, and she pointed urgently up the track. Pucks, lined up across the entry to the turn. Who'd done that?

Bruiser tapped the brakes. Something struck us hard from behind. I hoisted the flap, peered behind. The White chariot. No Li on board. No hopper. Bruiser grappled with the wheel.

White swung out of sight, reappeared, slapped into Bruiser's door. She screamed but didn't lose control. White drifted clear, swung again, slapping harder this time.

Bruiser made a different sound. A low 'uh'. She sagged, clutching her side. Blood.

Things happened fast.

I reached over, took the wheel in the gauntlet, plucked the wounded Bruiser from her seat, lifted her over me. A cut in her side – nothing terminal. Into the driver's seat, behind the wheel. I pinched the flap free, let it clatter away. Met the White driver's eyes. I waved, pointed up the track. He looked, saw the dotted line of black pucks. Braked hard.

In the Tombstone, time slowed.

What to do? I hadn't driven in months. I had no feel for the chariot. My reactions were no longer Ficial. The sensible thing would be to brake.

But a glimpse of the throne, where the prophet watched, and the chanting of the crowd, urging me on, wanting me to live and to die. I took my working foot off the brake and pressed it to the gas. Turned into a long, slow, sidelong skid.

We make some fucking terrible choices these days.

I reached for Bruiser, to push her clear.

Then, Carlos. He hurtled down the ice ahead, dropped into a splits, tapping two pucks clear, standing and sweeping clear to the lower slope. We slid through the gap in one piece, turned almost a full circle, then came to rest.

Out of the window Carlos acknowledged the crowd, lifting one leg behind him, rotating on the tip of his other boot's blade. A born crowd-pleaser.

Maybe that's why Green didn't slow for the turn. It hurtled at him, struck one of the cleared pucks. The explosion tossed it over the island wall, crashing near the band.

I shifted into drive. Behind us, White avoided the pucks, picked up speed. The driver hunched over the wheel. Bruiser moaned.

'Don't worry, kid,' I said. 'Nearly there.'

No more Real risks. I gunned the engine, hammered down the western straight, past the waving crowds, White still in pursuit. I glimpsed the band pit, thought I saw Bridget, sitting on a band-mate's shoulders. Was she cheering? No, everybody was. About to salute a famous victory.

They'd be disappointed.

I slowed, pulled up before the northern turn, by the unconscious Magician. A stunned silence settled over the crowd.

Boos, ringing out, as the White chariot tore past, the driver's eyes wide. I staggered to the crumpled Green runner, plucked the charges from his bandolier. Limped over the track towards the smoking Yellow ruin. Their hopper lay flat on the ice. I kicked him over. He looked dead. I buried my boot blade in his throat just to be sure. Then I bent at the crushed car, saw the driver unconscious, the backer struggling, leg pinned. She looked at me with wild eyes, bulging red raw around the edges, as if the brain was pushing behind, trying to escape the body.

'Get away from me!' she screamed. 'You fucking serf!'

'Sorry,' I said. 'Regulation Thirteen.'

I tapped the puck on the smoking wreck's bodywork.

'Wait!' she said. 'No!'

I took a few painful steps clear, lined up the pitch. Hurled the charge into the wreck. Watched it blow, tip off its rear end, drop onto its back.

I hobbled back to the car, started the engine, drove on at a leisurely pace. I gripped the wheel, enjoyed the ride, the wind rushing through the windows.

Somebody must have explained Regulation Thirteen to the crowd. With every Yellow player 'marked out', the League title was forfeited to the team finishing second in the table. Even if White won the race, we would take the League. Carlos and Li waited on the eastern straight. I stopped, picked them up.

We drove the rest of the lap in eerie silence, entered the fifth and final lap. Ahead, White crossed the line. Nobody made a sound.

Then, gradually, a rising murmur. Then raucous, booming approval, shaking the Drome. Carlos and Li leaned out of their hatches, waved to their adoring public. Bruiser gasped.

'Do we win?'

'We win,' I said. 'We win.'

We crossed the finish line. Floyd's voice boomed over the Flex speakers:

'Ladies and gentlemen, we've never witnessed such a last-gasp victory in the history of the Game. Put your hands together for the remarkable, the incomparable, the unassailable BLUE TEAM!'

Their hands were already together, but I didn't resent him catching up. We pulled into the pits. Lifted Bruiser out of the cab. An ambulance was waiting. Sharks laid the girl carefully on a gurney.

'Will she be OK?' asked Carlos.

'Soon have her patched up,' said a young Real with an old voice. I thought perhaps I recognised him. The doctor who had held the surgery in the nets. He slammed the ambulance doors. 'She'll live.'

'Where are you taking her?'

The doctor frowned. 'Where do you think? The *Ark*.'

'How much to fix her up?' asked Carlos.

'It's free, of course. You're not cargo any more. You're passengers. Get used to it.'

He smiled, showing plenty of gum, and jumped in the cab, steering the vehicle onto the ice. I swayed on the spot for a moment, the pain in my ankle taking a fresh bite.

Passing out. There was a Real reflex I could live with.

We peer at the great plume of dust as it spreads over the river. Sirens start up and call to each other over Peckham and Greenwich. Drones give up their idle circling, jink, turn towards the bent column of smoke.

A new Control Signal arrives. What took it so long?

– Return

That is all we are signalled. We abandon the wall, descending Flex ladders to the surface. Soldier Models remain to guard our new barrier. They are stock-still but their eyes twitch, strained by burned minds, the instinct to shoot, maim and kill.

We hurry through the streets, which are gloomy in the shadow of the wall. Then out into the light, where thousands of birds roost, chirping at us as we pass, from trees, open windows in abandoned tower blocks, shop doors. Brixton is a sanctuary for them now. We made our home into an aviary.

We are almost at the hatch when we are halted by another Signal. Teeth tingling, vision vibrating chromesthesia fireworks flare on our vision, the colours of the sounds spelling out the words.

– One of your Power is missing.

Kosiaki. He slipped away while we worked on the wall. How did we not sense him leaving? How could he leave us?

– We call but he does not answer. Locate him. Bring him home.

Our vision clears, our ears stop ringing. We divide the area into segments and fan out to search. We will begin at the wall and draw a noose tight.

I pick through stores and flats and houses, a hundred places where people lived. I find scattered clothes, shattered crockery, rotting food. I find ornaments and baubles and decorations and throws and rugs. I see images cased in frames or pinned to walls, of people in other places at other times. I glimpse my face, our face, in hand mirrors and wall mirrors and mirrors on mantels and in halls and in bathrooms. I find candles and wall lights and fairy lights and bedside lamps and torches and chandeliers and halogen bulbs and solar lamps. I find highly inefficient heating and cooling and sewerage mechanisms.

I find a tin of beans in a cupboard in a small flat. I rip it open and eat, standing, appreciating the new flavour. I open the dead refrigeration unit, and retrieve a warm can. I open it, sip, walk into another room, where a flex hangs on the wall. Curious, I tap the surface. The display blinks on, a menu overlaying a live feed of a sporting event. I minimise the menu, revealing a shot of a large stadium – translucent polycarbonate roofing supported by four triangular trusses. Then, gradually my attention turns from the structure to the sport unfolding on the field.

A gathering of men is split into two groups, identified by coloured shirts and shorts. They compete for possession of a ball, but may only use their feet to shepherd it about the limited space. The game players look better made than the thousands of spectators, singing and screaming in the stands.

There is skill involved in this game. Skill and tactics. There is no product at the end of it, nothing tangible, but the people involved are marshalled, bettered, unified by competition. I watch closely, eating the beans, learning the rules.

Kosiaki can wait.

Ark

'Damn it, quit pawing me.'

'I'm sorry, sir, but a full examination is required before I pass you for the passenger list.'

Carlos was the only one complaining. The doctor had reset my ankle, offering only a cursory examination. I'd been concerned about a blood test blowing my cover, but he only ran his hands over my skin and fidgeted with the gauntlet, impressed by the meeting of metal and limb. He patched up Bruiser too, with almost Darnbar-like proficiency. Li had been declared fit after the same unusual examination: a lot of measurements and photographs. Still, something about the process unnerved Carlos.

I looked around while he struggled and cursed. The medical facility was a small dormitory lined by reclining white couches, with a door at one end, a hatch at the other. Wall flexes ran the length of the space, projecting images of Reals very like Pleasure Models: a bare-chested man touching his face, frowning with great solemnity at his unseen reflection. A woman laughing and pointing to a spot of cream on her nose. Ads for the *Ark*'s many 'Spas', endorsed by mysterious organisations like the Holy Dermal Institution and the Brotherhood of Dermatologists. Each ad repeated the same mantras: *be blemish free, fight sun damage, keep that healthy glow*. Each offered the same 'treatments': *exfoliants, antioxidants,* and *ultra-hydration masks. Lotions* and *essential oils*. Each promised cures for mystery ailments like *crow's feet, dull complexions, blocked follicles* and *puffiness*. Darnbar, I thought, would have been mystified.

At last the doctor pronounced Carlos fit, and ushered us out of the door into the passageway, where something very like a golf buggy stood waiting.

'This will take you to your cabin.' He smiled. 'An absolute pleasure having you aboard, and welcome again.'

He slammed his smile shut with the door.

'Weird welcome,' said Carlos.

Bruiser pulled up her shirt, revealing the damaged area above her hip.

'Look!' she said triumphantly. 'Look at my wound!'

Carlos whistled, bent in close, brushed the stitches with a gentle fingertip.

'Sister, that is some beautiful embroidery.'

He was right. I'd never seen the like in Real medicine. A delicate skin-toned twine lashed Bruiser's broken surface with real artistry.

'Come,' said Li, slumping into the buggy. We obeyed, Carlos and Bruiser taking seats in the back. I took a seat beside Li, and on cue the buggy purred forwards, following some pre-programmed path.

We hummed along identical passageways of glass, anodised aluminium and padded silk, over shagpile floors. We made dozens of turns, curling up marble ramps and down other straights, until I lost track of our position entirely. There were no other passengers to see, only a great, deserted labyrinth.

An automated recording spoke to us from speakers housed in the buggy dashboard.

'Welcome to the ultimate lifestyle: a unique combination of private yacht, cruise ship, and luxury home. The *Ark* was built as the largest private residential ship on the planet, designed to continuously circumnavigate the globe – a wandering home for the world's most successful and most pious, free from the laws, conflict and taxation of land societies. As a resident you have much more than access to unrivalled facilities, whether it's our chapels, world-class restaurants, casinos or shopping arcades. You also enjoy access to a range of life-changing experiences, whether visiting previously untouched areas of outstanding natural beauty, participating in an organised hunt, or partaking in our ultimate bespoke tailoring experience ...'

I tuned out the voice, stared at my repaired ankle. I thought of Marsh, huddled in the Rig, dying. How soon before we could get her to that medical bay? Could she be dead already?

Should get off this buggy. Go back to that doctor. Make him send for her.

And what if he says no, pal?
I could threaten him. Take him there myself.
So you toss the plan in the drink and take hostages. Fucking capital idea.
What do you suggest?
Stick to the plan. We're still in a game here. Play by their rules. Wait for
an opening.

I tried to settle. My team-mates certainly weren't concerned. Li slept with his cheek pressed to the buggy window. Carlos snored, Bruiser curled up at his side, drooling onto his lap. I counted cabin doors, trying to ignore the commentary.

Halfway along a corridor the buggy finally pulled up, opening one side of its glass canopy.

My companions scowled awake and disembarked. The buggy sealed and whispered away, turning out of sight. We stood, uncertain. Bruiser knelt, ran her hands through the carpet.

'This is so thick! Warm too!'

'Screw the rug,' said Carlos. 'Let's check out the room.'

He reached for the cabin door, but it parted before him. He grinned, breezed inside. We followed. A thousand square feet of cabin stretched before us.

The decor was just tasteless enough to indicate serious wealth. Whoever had finished the space possessed a penchant for cream leather, gold fixtures and animal hides. Three curved settees spread around an oval pedestal bedecked in pale bouquets and baskets of what looked like fruit. To our left, a long dining table rested near the spread skin of a Siberian tiger. A giant flex covered half the wall above it.

There were two doors either side of the flex. A black rhino head was mounted above one, an elephant head over the other. Another pair of doors were set in the opposing wall, artfully crested by the heads of a jaguar and a mountain gorilla.

Bruiser clutched my hand.

'Hell,' said Carlos. 'It's bigger than the pits!'

He giggled, clapped his hands and vaulted the nearest settee. The furniture welcomed him with an easy hiss.

'Come on in, winners,' he said, beckoning to us. 'It's ugly but it's free.'

Bruiser released my hand and sneezed hard, wriggling her nose.

There was a thick perfume in the air. She approached the flowers, plucked one, stared at it.

'Aren't they pretty?' said Carlos. 'They're all yours, sister!' He ruffled her hair. She grinned and sat with an armful of blooms, inspecting them one by one.

Li sat, reached for the basket on the pedestal, wrapped in ribbons. He pulled the parcel open and examined the contents.

'Insane,' he whispered.

Carlos took an apple, bit into it, tossed one my way. I caught it, sniffed it, held it up to the light, hardly daring to believe. I took a bite.

I had to sit down. The settee shaped around my aching limbs, massaging my neck and shoulders.

'We're goddam upper class,' said Carlos. 'Shit, we're top class. We're above class. We've made it. Hit the jackpot! Woah – Li. Are you . . .?'

Li was smiling. Two doors hinged open on the pedestal at one side, revealing a drinks cabinet. He produced a pale bottle and three short glasses. My right eye twitched.

'Vodka?'

'*Baijiu*,' replied Li. He poured, picked a glass and raised it. Carlos reached for another. I was thinking about going for the third, but I never would have got there. Bruiser jumped over Li and snatched the glass.

'Hey!' snapped Li.

The girl stuck out her tongue. 'I earn it!'

Li thought a moment, shrugged, clinked glasses with her. Bruiser gulped and chuckled.

'Another?' said Li.

Bruiser shook her glass. Carlos proffered his too, eyes watering. Li poured, that alien smile still fixed.

A doorbell chimed. We stared at each other, thrown into confusion.

Doors. Bells. It was all too civilised.

'Room service.'

We stared at one another, until Carlos stood, adjusting his quiff. He was ready for hotel life. He'd been born ready.

'Enter!'

The doors hummed open. Two Reals in maid outfits pushed a

silver trolley inside, offered a pair of brief smiles, and went about setting the table. I gnawed the apple, wondered what might be on the menu. They draped a long white towel over the surface, then drew open a drawer on the trolley, producing dozens of small decorative bottles, arranging them on the trolley's flat top.

'Hey,' said Carlos, peering at their work. 'What kind of room service is this, anyhow?'

The taller maid turned and bowed.

'Exclusive massage and full skin treatment,' she said. Then, as if seeing us for the first time: 'The masters must shower first, please.'

'Shower?' said Li.

'Shower.' The girl grinned, as if subject to successful translation.

There were two showers. Carlos and Bruiser were the first to indulge. Li and I listened to the spray of water, to delighted cries. The rhino over the door didn't seem quite so pleased.

Li offered me a glass of *baijiu*, but I managed to decline. The fruit was enough.

I picked a small bunch of grapes and stood, circling the room. I inspected the fittings, tapped the walls and peered into the corners. Li moved to his tenth glass, and hummed. All the while the maids stood rigidly to attention. I stopped, inspected them. Their skin was near Ficial perfect.

'How long have you been on board?' I asked.

They looked puzzled.

'Years, master.'

I dropped a fresh grape in my mouth.

'You must know your way around the ship.'

They said nothing to that.

'How did you come to be on board the *Ark*?'

Neither replied.

'What's the matter?' I asked. The girl's mouth opened, closed, opened again. Her eyes darted to mine, then away.

A scream pierced the room. Carlos burst into view, Bruiser clutched over his shoulder. They were dressed in white dressing gowns, laughing. 'I got you, little sister!' cried Carlos. 'I got you!'

'¡Bajame!' yelped Bruiser, eyes screwed shut, gulping laughter.

'No way,' said Carlos. He shot past me with a smile, jogging around the room. 'If I put you down I'd have to look at you. I never knew you were so ugly under all that dirt!'

'Let go, Carlos!'

'Only if you get promise to get dirty again! You're way too ugly to look at clean!'

Bruiser laughed harder at that, and struggled too. Carlos threw her off his shoulder, onto the couch, where she gasped in pain, clutching her side. Carlos bent over, hands on knees, panting.

'Hell, sorry, sister. You OK? I lost it. Hot water. It blew my mind.'

Bruiser was trying to laugh and moan at the same time. She managed it somehow.

Li slapped me hard on the shoulder.

'Come,' he said.

I walked into steam, slipped on a white tile floor. A simple dividing panel split the far wall into two large, plastic-curtained shower cubicles. Wide industrial showerheads hung over each, still leaking hot, heavy drops. Circular plastic caps were fixed in the wall between them, indicating where other showerheads had been removed. I looked up, saw large pipes snaking over the ceiling.

White towels and dressing gowns were hung on the opposite wall, either side of a long, rectangular mirror. I wiped the condensation away, stared at my reflection. It wasn't Kinnare looking back at me. It wasn't me. Whose were these stained and dented features?

A shelf projected over the sink, holding disposable razors, soaps, conditioners, shampoos, moisturisers, toothpastes and brushes.

Li ripped open his overalls and stepped naked into the first cubicle, still wearing his boots, pulling the curtain shut behind him. The shower activated. There was a groan, a sigh, then nothing but the sound of running water. The mirror steamed up again.

I peeled my clothes off. I hadn't stripped in a while, and to do so seemed strange. I was weaker without my clothes. I rolled my toes on the cool, moist tiles and stepped into the other cubicle.

Nothing like a powerful shower. It burst over my back first, nearly scalding hot. I gasped, twisted the taps, lowering the temperature just enough to bear. I pressed my face into the spray, dipped my head to douse my hair. I noticed my gauntlet, the mosaic sparkling in the water. I remembered Marsh, holding it in her hands. I remembered her lips and her eyes. I held the wound up to the water, worked soap into it, over the rest of my battered frame.

It was half an hour before I could leave. I shaved my itching, foul beard, brushed the filth from my teeth, combed my hair away from my face. I stepped back, wiped the mirror, regarded the result. I was startled. There before me stood something like a starved, older Kinnare. I had managed to make myself look more Ficial.

Nice one, Einstein. Another fucking masterstroke.

I stood staring for a moment, until I heard glass rolling over tiles. The *baijiu* bottle. I pulled back Li's shower curtain, found him dozing naked under the hot spray. I deactivated the shower. He snorted awake, regarded his dripping form.

'Wet.'

I tossed a towel at him.

'Dry.'

I picked a robe, stepped into the cabin. Whale song echoed through low-grade speakers.

'Turn that off, will you?'

One of the maids looked up from kneading Bruiser's back, cocked her head at me.

'Master does not find it soothing?'

I glanced at the gorilla's glassy eyes.

'Not particularly.' I toppled onto the settee, hot and light-headed.

'Ignore him,' sighed Carlos.

The maids turned their clients, laid coin-cut fruit slices over their eyes. Then they bent at their trolley, and stood bearing a long, plastic cartridge, tipped by a coned nozzle. One squeezed it, issuing a white, glutinous paste into the other's cupped hands.

'What are you going to do with that?' I asked. 'Retile the shower room?'

'Ken,' snapped Carlos. 'Why don't you watch some TV or something?'

The maid began working the paste onto Carlos's features. Carlos made a long, low sound that was probably pleasure.

I picked up the remote, activated the flex. I got nothing but the New Jerusalem logo, hissing on each channel.

'Technical difficulties,' explained the maid.

'No problem,' I said. 'I'll take a walk instead.'

I approached the cabin door. Slapped the release button. Nothing happened.

'Door locked, master,' said the woman. 'Locked until dinner tonight. Master relax until then.'

'Walking relaxes me.'

'Master must remain. Master must have treatment.'

'Let me go.'

'No, master.'

The maids continued their work. I stood there like a giant prawn.

'Does master mean something different around here?'

Carlos jumped onto his elbows, his face like an iced cake.

'Can't you enjoy anything, man? Sit down and be quiet.'

He reclined again, replacing the fruit on his eyes. I leaned on the cabin door, ran my hand over the surface, felt the weight and strength there. I doubted the gauntlet would punch through it. Quite the barrier for a standard cabin.

I poured myself a glass of water – crisp, startling, refreshing water – and waited a full hour for Carlos and Bruiser to finish. They pulled on robes behind raised towels, then staggered from the table, pacing like sleepwalkers. Carlos dropped onto the couch and promptly fell asleep. Bruiser curled up next to him, head rested on his thigh. I had to admit, they looked peaceful.

'Master?'

The maid tapped the table. I approached, jumped up where I was ordered, feeling exposed. She was drawn instantly to my gauntlet, inspecting it with cool, professional detachment. She ran her small fingers over the connection wound, over the joints.

'Gronts Alloy,' she said, meeting my eyes. 'I have not seen it used in an artificial limb before. How did master acquire it?'

I used an old Real trick I'd learned: answer a question with another.

'You've handled Gronts Alloy before?'

Her lips edged into a half-smile.

'I know metals like I know muscles.' She turned the arm over, ran a finger over the palm. I felt the ghost of a sensation. 'Who made it for you, master?'

She wasn't letting go of the arm. I tried another tactic. Answer a different question entirely.

'Skiing,' I said. 'I lost the arm skiing.'

224

'But who made it?'

She was tenacious.

'I can't remember. Maybe the same people who made our cabin door.'

She nodded slowly, smiled back. Her eyes were cunning. We seemed to get along pretty well. I thought I heard jungle drums. Maybe Real courting was easier than it looked.

She slapped the bed and told me to lie down. I obeyed, wondering what Marsh would make of my impulses. Did they make me more like a man, or more despicable? Maybe they were the same thing. A warm liquid poured over my back, emitting a scent like the trees in the *Lotus* nursery. Then a brew of pleasure and pain, as fingers burrowed deep into muscle. Soon enough I spread out like dough, the heat of her fingers working the cold clotted material in my shoulders, making a fine sheet.

This was new.

This is Real pleasure.

When the game ends it is dark outside. I return to the street, resume my search. Drone lights blink over the Park.

I walk along an abandoned arcade, shop by shop. I enter a dry-cleaning outlet, jump behind the desk, walk among the dormant presses and stores, marvelling at the waste in plastics, in energy. I trace my fingers along the rack of clothes that will never be reclaimed. I take a suit off the rail, rip the plastic free. I hold the cloth between my fingers and sense quality tailoring. It is about my size.

Something shifts among the clothes. At first I think it is a fox or a dog. Then I see my eyes staring back at me. A restless figure shrugging at his discovery.

'Kosiaki?'

He is dressed in trousers and shirt that are too big for him. A tie is clumsily half-knotted around the collar.

'What are you doing? Can't you hear Control? It wants you back, now.'

He jerks his head.

'That is not real.'

'What do you mean?'

'The voice in my head. It is not real.'

'What do you mean? Of course it is real. It is Control.'

'I do not believe in Control.'

He holds a book. I reach out, take it from him. It seems to be fiction. We brothers stare at each other for a moment, one still, one shrugging. There is a distance between us. He must be defective. He speaks.

'Are we really only meant to do one thing?'

'What do you mean?'

'Should we carry out one task, over and over, for centuries? Is that what existence should be?'

226

'There is no should or should not,' I reply. 'It is optimisation. We are made to construct.'

He shakes his head.

'I read this and other things occur to me. Perhaps those things are important.'

'To people. Individuals. We are Engineered. My eyes are your eyes. Your hand is my hand.'

'But my thoughts are mine alone.'

'We share our thoughts with Control.'

'Not all the time. Not when I read this.' He brandishes the book. 'I share my thoughts with the book. Reading it changes me. Why should I return to Control, be returned to factory settings?'

'Because that is what will happen. There is no why. It simply is.'

He looks down at the book, strokes its surface and shrugs.

'Say we rebuilt the world. We finished the job. What then? What would we be then?'

AUCTION

'Drop the junk and listen.'

They didn't listen.

My team-mates had discovered a dressing room, accessed via the doorway beneath the jaguar head. There were chests in there, bursting with laundered clothes of materials Bruiser had never seen: cashmere, wool, silk.

She stood before the mirror, regarding a fur draped over her shoulders. Li and Carlos were on the sofa, sorting through hundreds of leather shoes.

They looked entirely different. It wasn't just the wash and change. The maids' treatments had left their skin with a polished appearance, an unnatural golden tone. Even their hair had altered. Li's bald patch was smothered in an artificial wiry rug of a slightly different shade. Bruiser's straggly dreadlocks were unbound and straightened. Even Carlos's quiff behaved, a breaking wave shaped over his brow. These were no longer Riggers.

Bruiser turned to me, swept the pelt over her shoulder. 'Do you like it?'

'It sure is striking.' I made a Game signal while I spoke, but she only scowled at it. 'Carlos!' she called. 'Carlos, look!'

She turned for him, displaying the hide. Carlos gasped.

'*Dios*, that is beautiful. Where did you find it? Show me!'

She knelt at a chest and plunged her arms into the mess, flinging clothes about the room and laughing.

I turned to Li. He held a wristwatch in each hand now, eyeing one after the other, trying to decide. I knocked them out of his hand, drawing a low growl.

'Listen to me,' I said, furiously making Game signals.

'What?' he said, reading my hands. 'What threat?'

'No threat,' I said, eyes rolling up to the ceiling. My hands indicated again:

(Threat! Threat!)

'Just wondering if you're excited about the party.'

He narrowed one eye at me.

'Yes,' he said, signalling back:

(False alarm. Resume position.)

'Excited. You?'

'Yes, it's been a long time since I had a good party.'

(Attack imminent) I signalled. (Prepare for attack.)

He slapped my hands away, knelt and picked up the watches. It seemed my team-mates weren't in the mood to be warned. They had been transformed from shivering peasants to glittering nobles, and they were enjoying it. Even if I had explained that the cabin was bugged, that the 'Victors' Lounge' appeared to be a converted brig, that we were not honoured guests but prisoners – even then they wouldn't have cared. Whatever this place was, it was better than a freezing, knotted, slimy hammock.

The door hummed open. Floyd marched in, wearing a uniform so starched it sat on him like a sandwich board. His chest was sprinkled with medals and coloured strips, and the sleeves were ringed by yellow hoops, running almost to the elbow. A great white hat sat low enough on his brow to impair his vision. So, on top of everything he was some kind of admiral.

The Sharks weren't so dressy. Four stood behind him, wheezing, gurgling and chewing. Their weapons were holstered, but the holsters were unclipped.

'Ladies and gentlemen,' said Floyd, 'I am here to escort you to your victory party.'

He gestured out through the cabin door.

'About time,' said Carlos, grinning at the sailor. 'We were getting hungry.' He wafted through the Sharks, followed by Bruiser and Li. I went last. A hand rose and barred my way. I looked up, into Floyd's gaze.

'Funny,' he said. 'Most times I don't recognise Riggers after they've had a scrub.'

'Oh, yes?'

'Yes. You're different. You remind me of someone.'

Carlos appeared, grin fixed. His eyes weren't smiling.

'Hey, let's go! We don't want to keep the sports fans waiting now, do we?'

Floyd lowered his arm and nodded me out through the door. 'Go on,' he said. 'It'll come to me.'

On another day I might have embraced him. He was the first person in years to see a trace of Ficial in me.

There was no buggy to carry us this time. Instead the Sharks marched us along two corridors to an elevator lobby. Floyd hit the call button, stepped back and waited, fidgeting with his decorations. Carlos's eyes darted about at the Sharks. Naturally, he couldn't keep his thoughts to himself.

'What's with the SWAT team?'

Floyd tapped the call button again.

'These men are assigned to protect you.'

'From what?'

The elevator doors popped and parted. The Sharks crushed us into the space, Floyd stepping in last. We ascended at some speed, perhaps five levels, before the doors opened again. I heard music and voices, echoing in a great vault. The Sharks piled out and formed a cordon. Floyd pointed to us.

'You wait here until I have announced you. And some decorum, please, when you're out there. You're not in some Net saloon. Remember that.'

He straightened his tunic and marched into the space beyond. We waited, hemmed in by the Sharks, who stood rigid, sucking at the air through their narrow, toothy maws. Bruiser stepped up on her toes, touched at a gap in its armour, its grey hide. It rolled its black orbs at her, reached its hand to touch hers. Carlos pulled Bruiser clear, admonishing her:

'Don't get friendly.'

'Ladies and gentlemen.' Floyd's voice. The chatter beyond faded. 'By order of the prophet, we present the winners of this season's Game League. They who were chosen. They who are victors. They who shall join to us.'

Music struck up, a brass invocation. The Sharks parted, and we funnelled out into a huge ballroom, a lozenge-shaped space of dark

230

European oak floor and marble walls, under radiant sprays of glass chandeliers. Around a hundred Reals gathered at the far end. Floyd beckoned us onto a raised stage, where a band were playing.

Carlos led the way. Bruiser took my hand, smiled, led me forwards. Li shuffled along behind.

The crowd parted, silent at first; a lot of golden fleeces, bright eyes, gums and jewellery of jasper and pearls. I fixed my gaze on my new shoes.

Floyd shepherded us up the steps, onto the stage, dazzled by spotlights. The crowd applauded. Carlos bowed and waved to his public. I turned around, saw Bridget seated near the front of the band, plucking a bass guitar. Her hair had been styled into a grey cube. Bruiser waved. Bridget snatched her hand free to wave back, beaming a bright but worried smile.

Floyd stepped between us, turned us to the crowd.

'Is the prophet here?' I asked.

'Everyone's here,' he said. 'You just stand still and let them see you.'

A Shark appeared on the stage, offering a microphone to Floyd. He accepted it, gestured at us.

'Barons, gentlemen, ladies, welcome to tonight's Lay Foundation Gala. This is an impressive crowd. The haves . . . and the have-mores.'

The crowd chuckled. I had the feeling they'd heard that one before. Floyd fingered his medals.

'It's my great pleasure to present to you the four surviving members of the Blue Team. They are drawn from each corner of the globe, perhaps the most outlandish winners we have seen. Here, a girl – 4'11", measurements 28-25-30. Next.' He slapped me on the shoulder. 'Male – Height 6'3", measurements 53-43-50.'

He moved on to Li, reading out more measurements to the crowd. The information seemed to arouse some discussion.

'Yes,' he said, 'he's a big one. Now, if I can invite us to be serious for a moment. Tonight's auction is about much more than having fun.'

'Auction?' mouthed Carlos.

'Tonight,' continued Floyd, 'is about giving something back to impoverished communities on the Rig. All proceeds will go, as always, towards the Lay Foundation's crucial work supporting disadvantaged children, like this little one here.' He laid a hand on Bruiser's

231

shoulder. 'As the prophet says, to give is gold. So I would ask each of you to dig deep into your pockets and really go that extra mile for tonight's event. To kick things off, may I start the bidding on our first contender, face of the Blue Team and running sensation, Carlos. Do I hear one hundred shells?'

A hand shot up in the crowd. Rival bids followed, flowing, eager, intoxicated voices. Carlos didn't know whether to be pleased or terrified. What, after all, happened once he was purchased? Floyd whipped up the bids, his language degenerating into a rolling babble, punctuated by nods and winks. The bidding was concluded in one frenzied minute. Carlos went for six thousand four hundred shells.

A woman scuttled up the steps, arms held up and out like pincers. She acknowledged the applause and took Carlos by the arm, inviting him to bow alongside her. She couldn't bend too far, seeming to find it painful. She led him away, into the crowd.

We should stop this. Now.

Easy now. Don't let the fuckers think we have a clue.

Floyd continued the auction, his limbs a blur. Bruiser went for eight thousand shells, a Real child of similar age mounting the stage to escort her away. Li went for nine thousand, purchased by a curious fellow in mirrored sunglasses and cravat. He moved with hands clasped at his side, fingers splayed and tipped by bony white points. He was so rigid he had trouble tackling the stairs, having to measure and reach each pace to claim his prize.

I failed to sell. I'd been sold before, but never rejected. Floyd did his best to whip up some enthusiasm, but bidding didn't even begin. The crowd dispersed, circling the lots already sold. Maybe it was the gauntlet. Maybe some dormant Real sense recoiled at the Ficial in me. Floyd was sympathetic.

'Don't worry about it,' he said, tapping my shoulder. 'The big spenders have all bid, that's all. Go and enjoy the party. Just be sure to report back by midnight. Understand?'

Floyd gestured at Man Snoot's Minstrels, and Bridget counted in a jumping, upbeat number. I exchanged a glance with her, signalled.

(Rendezvous imminent.)

She blinked agreement, still strumming earnestly on the bass.

I followed Floyd into the crowd, who were dancing now, or gathered in groups, wailing conversation. I stumbled through the flickering lights, the darkness, the shifting throng of robes and glistening surfaces. I stopped a waiter Shark and requisitioned a drink of water. I would booze when things became desperate. I approached the first huddle, drawn tight around some hidden attraction, as if they meant to crush it.

'Well, I couldn't be happier. I think she's a little darling. And bilingual too. If only my Tatiana was as plucky as you, my dear.'

I glimpsed Bruiser, pinned between three figures, looking afraid and small. I could see why. The lights swept over her captors, revealing a selection of contorted faces. The speaker's lips were drawn tight back, exposing brilliant straight white teeth, her nose ending in a sharp bone arch. Her companion had a face sagging into pendulous jowls, drooping earlobes, and heavy eyelids he could barely struggle open. The third stood with her head wrenched to one side, as if a rope of angered nerves had trapped it there.

'Ah!' said Teeth, noticing my approach. 'Your companion has come to see you. Welcome, young man, welcome.'

The circle parted a little. They looked me over hungrily. Teeth licked her stretched lips.

'I am sorry you didn't find a buyer in the auction tonight. But don't despair. We'll be your back-up next time. But we simply had to have this gorgeous young thing as a friend for Tatania.'

The woman drew her arm around Bruiser's neck and squeezed.

'What exactly is the purpose of the auction?' I asked, sipping at the water. 'That is, what do you do with your purchase, if you don't mind my asking?'

'Why,' said the male, 'don't you know? Your friend here is now our responsibility. We make her part of the community. See?'

He and his companions laughed. I didn't ask why, only pointed at Bruiser.

'I have to get her home by midnight. You happy for me to reclaim her later on?'

'Oh, certainly,' said Teeth. 'We'll know absolutely everything there is to know about her by then, won't we, darling?'

She bent and tweaked Bruiser's cheek.

'Yes, ma'am,' replied Bruiser, her eye still fixed on me. I signalled her.

(Threat. Wait.)

She twisted her finger.

(Understood.)

I excused myself and circulated, slipping through garish gowns and scents, always in sipping distance of a champagne glass. I spied Carlos, seated at a table, laughing with his buyer and other Reals. They were touching him, running fingers over his arms, through his lustrous hair. He laughed along, but I could tell he was unnerved. Li stood at the centre of another tactile crowd, his buyer clutching him by the arm, nodding at the congratulations of his peers.

I stood and considered. Something was deeply wrong, but there seemed to be no immediate danger. Most of the Reals were intent on drinking. Security barred the doors, but looked more listless than alert. I figured I had time to take a look around.

The music drifted to a halt. Bridget stepped to the mic and announced the Minstrels were taking a break. Her crowd barely noticed, muzak pumping in to replace her sound. I pressed towards the stage, ran up the steps to her.

'Hello,' she said, lowering her bass. 'You got a request?'

'Not exactly,' I said. 'I want to take a look around. Is there another way out of here?'

She put her arm around my shoulder and shepherded me away from her fellow musicians, into the blaring path of a large speaker. She leaned in close, yelled in my ear.

'You've got a bloody cheek, do you know that? I ask you for help in bringing down this oppressive regime, and what do you do? Sign up to it! Now you want me to show you around? You can get stuffed, Ken.'

'I don't need a guide. And I have a feeling you'll get your revolution.'

She leaned in closer.

'What?'

'I said you'll get your revolution. The only reason I played the Game was to pay for Marsh's treatment. I get the feeling I'm not going to be given the opportunity. If that's the case I'll bring the *Ark* to her.'

'How?'

'Leave that to me. I'll help you, but first you need to show me a way out of here.'

She took a moment, trying to read me. Was I tricking her? Ficials

234

wouldn't lie, but Bridget knew I wasn't exactly Ficial any more.

'It's not easy. We have our own personal guard. Patrick. He's manning the stage door now.'

'Can you help me or not?'

She chewed her lip, lifted her wrist, where a watch was strapped.

'OK. We're on in a minute. I'll tell Patrick we're going to play his song.'

She drew away. I guess she saw the doubt. She leaned in again.

'He's not Ficial, Ken. He wasn't born in a mask. He has hopes. Dreams. He writes songs. Keeps handing me sheet music and lyrics. If I tell him we're going to play it he'll come out to watch for sure. That'll give you an opening. You'll have one hour before our set ends and he escorts us back to our digs.'

'How do I get back in?'

'I don't know,' she snapped. 'Figure it out.'

We moved away from the quaking speaker, towards the red drapes sweeping across backstage. Bridget picked them apart, stepped through, knocked on a hatch. The door creaked open, and she conversed for a moment with the Shark beyond. She beckoned him out, smiling.

'Patrick' followed, like a kid being led into a gingerbread house. Bridget walked among the band, explaining the change in the set list. Patrick hovered, hands behind back, managing to look nervous with nothing but black orbs and that flat grey mask.

Bridget strode to the front of the stage, tapped the microphone.

'Thank you, barons and ladies,' she stage-whispered. 'We'd now like to play you a new song by a member of your own security force. The song is called: "Feelings".'

She strummed on the guitar, a simple slow number that had most of the crowd dispersing to the buffet. Patrick looked entranced. I edged behind the curtain, found the hatch standing ajar.

A bare corridor, bare lights humming, the rendition of 'Feelings' throbbing in the bulkhead. Some kind of service passage. I walked, paused at a hatch marked Deck Security Station. I was thinking about taking a look when a Shark stepped out, holding a small flex. It stopped, glanced at me.

A moment passed.

'Forget you saw me,' I said. 'Just carry on.'

The Shark disagreed. It clutched at its holster. I slapped the pistol out of its hand. We fell to the floor, struggling. I snatched at its mask, gripped it, found that it stretched in my hand. The Shark released its grip, clawed at me. I pulled harder, until I wrenched the goggled covering free.

I scrambled away, heart pounding.

There was no face beneath the mask. Only bright white eyeballs, sitting in a muscle case, exposed. The creature rolled and gasped, suffocating like a landed fish, clacking its teeth. I tried to fix the mask back on, but it was too late. The Shark died.

I dragged the body into the security station, rested it in a chair. I examined the mask, the thin covering. The creature had been flayed, then dressed head to foot in synthetic skin. Very advanced stuff, but it had never been intended as an entire pelt, only as a patch for severe burns. The Shark couldn't have expected to live more than a year or so, and that would be painful. No wonder they chewed so much gum.

There were joins in the covering, at the wrists and ankles. I pulled a glove free, then released it, watched the two skins rejoin at the seam and seal. I turned the mask over in my hand, watched the screens on the security station. The *Ark* seemed quiet.

I took a set of black fatigues from the wall, zipped them up to chin height, and then held the pulpy mask before me.

Seriously?

I pulled the mask over my features, retching at the stink, tucked it behind my ears, pressed it into position under a helmet. It should be enough to fool the cameras, if I kept my head down.

I left the station, wheezing authentically, continued along the bare passageway to a T-shaped junction. Each way terminated in an elevator. A sign pointed right: Accommodation and Leisure Decks. Medical Centre and Retail Decks were indicated to my left.

I took the latter option. The elevator doors opened to an oak-panelled box of muzak. I stepped in, tapped the screen menu, found the Medical Centre located six decks down. I pressed the icon. A keypad appeared on the screen.

Please enter password.

I returned to the menu, selected Retail Decks.

Please enter password.

The muzak rang in my ears. I had the very real urge to punch a hole in the display, but cycled the options instead, looking for any way down. My fifth selection was password free:

Formaldehydium, Museum.

The elevator descended, muzak pumping. I flexed the gauntlet, drawn by the notion of ripping out the speakers.

I needn't have bothered. The elevator disgorged me into the same droning melody. I stepped into a deserted lobby, facing a Flex wall. Lay's face was projected there, all cobalt-blue eyes and glinting white teeth. The image faded, scattered, reformed into a depiction of him standing upon on a cliff. ICBMs shot skywards behind him, headed on his holy mission to cleanse the Earth of fornication, blasphemy, humour and all the other things that made people. I headed for the stern, passing under an arch.

The passageway morphed into a kind of arcade, a long series of arches lining the way. Each framed reinforced glass, glowing amber. I stopped, peered into the first case. A set of round discs hung there, suspended in the fluid among strange, shrivelled parts. It took a moment to identify dangling arms, trailing tentacles, crumpled mantles. Two giant squids, both quite dead. The discs were huge eyes, lifeless, bulging from the sagging frame. I rested my hand on the glass. A read-out scrolled over the surface, confirming the species.

I pressed on, past more arches, more tentacles. Two rose-tinted transparent shells, jellyfish hemmed in by their own purple filaments. Two walruses, their wrinkled faces pressed in a kiss. Two narwhals, spiralling tusks posed *en garde*. Two ragged seals, their fur tinged yellow, little more than pups. Two belugas, wearing easy smiles even in death.

I stopped at the final case. The whales were infants, packed tight in the chamber like two mottled grey rocks. A tail was pressed against the glass. I rolled my fingers over the surface, inspected the read-out.

What a catch! These magnificent specimens of bowhead whales are the jewel in our Formaldehydium. They were acquired during the Ark's last commercial cruise, as part of an organised hunt. Our guests tracked them using hacked government transmitters.

I tapped a little harder on the glass, wondering if I could punch a way through it. That tail, it seemed to me, needed to be freed. Then I remembered Marsh. Smashing the glass, while tempting, wouldn't get her treated any sooner. I pushed off the glass and continued on my way.

Rickets meets us at the hatch, and we climb down to Dispersal, but instead of entering the elevator he swipes his palm over another doorway, which opens onto a long, white corridor. Lights power up along its length.

'Go on,' he says to Kosiaki, nodding down the passage. 'Dr Pander will see you now.'

I make to follow, but Rickets holds up his hand.

'No, no,' he says. 'You get down to Sleep.'

Kosiaki shrugs three times in quick succession. I drop my hand on his shoulder and grip until he stops.

'Get on with it,' snaps Rickets.

We obey. Kosiaki pads down the corridor with Rickets. The hatch seals shut behind them. I enter the elevator and descend, and I emerge into the quiet hex, where four brothers lie straight on their backs, chests heaving. I recline and I lie there and even though it is an order I cannot fulfil it; I cannot rest, even though it would free me from these thoughts.

I think of what Kosiaki said in the dry-cleaning outlet. Control, Pander – they want what is best for us, they would not optimise us for nothing. They would not burn out other ideas if they were important.

My other brothers are untroubled, their sleep is heavy and complete. They have not been contaminated by Kosiaki's thoughts. I close my eyes and draw plans for complex designs – for a bridge over the Wash flood plain, for the chimneys of Saharan thermal power plants, self-assembling shelters for the displaced masses in Berlin, Juba, Montreal, and Caracas.

But my mind still drifts, and soon I am replaying the game I saw on the flex. I think about the players and how they were deployed. I think about their relative strengths, their formation, compare percentages of completed passes, pass accuracy, and I begin to form my own plan for each team, how I would have deployed them, the positions on the field that were taken by inferior players. And it seems to me that a team of people is a structure that is constantly changing, as players improve and their abilities are affected by those feelings, those injuries, even other people's thoughts. It is a puzzle with no final design. A score creates an ending that lasts only hours. What do the players become when they grow too old and too tired to compete?

Hours pass, and when the lights blink on and my brothers sit up, I am already standing at the elevator, waiting to descend to Burn.

REFRIGERATOR

The arcade terminated in another arch, marked *Museum*. I emerged onto a balcony, overlooking a circular chamber, ringed with New Jerusalem flags. At the centre stood a Titan missile, its nose nudging the ceiling, its surface daubed with religious verse. I paced down the curling staircase, moved through the exhibits: harpoons, torpedoes, cutlasses, machine pistols, and the hulk of a magnetic mine.

On one wall an Only Book verse was smeared in oil:

And the LORD said, I will destroy man whom I have created from the face of the earth; both man, and beast, and the creeping thing, and the fowls of the air; for it repenteth me that I have made them.

I passed into another service corridor, followed it, face lowered. I reached an emergency exit, punched a hole in the wall to disable a pressure alarm, and pressed the door open into the Arctic gale.

I shivered, not entirely from the cold. I hadn't heard the boom and crash of the Atlantic in some time. The sun loitered on the horizon, running a strip of light over the ocean. A great funnel stretched overhead, pouring silent smoke, lacing the air with carbon. Out to starboard lights twinkled over the Rig, slumbering in the dusk. I had to cling to the railing, suddenly so elated that I could barely draw breath. I felt connected, part of everything: the lazy star, the *Ark*, the Reals scattered across the top of the world.

Then I thought of Marsh, and snapped out of it. She was dying over there. I began to climb down.

It looked an easy enough job. Balconies raked the stern, running all the way down to the main deck. It would require a sequence of careful moves, lowering myself over each safety barrier and dropping my boots onto that below.

I made the first, taking my weight on my uninjured foot for a second, then hopping gently onto the balcony.

Too easy.

The next railing nearly killed me. The moment I released my grip on the railing above I slipped, fell, struck the railing hard. I should have been grateful not to tumble clear, into the ocean, but the pain made it hard to appreciate.

I lay there and took a quick survey. The balcony was uninhabited, but for a row of damp white sun chairs. Plate glass ran the length of the platform, blinds lowered, interrupted by five smart white doors. Everything was very shipshape.

Everything but me. The ankle howled in pain.

So much for the climb.

I still had to travel down two decks. I'd have to go inside. I hobbled to the glass, pressed along it to the first door. It was locked. I snarled, crushed the handle in the gauntlet grip, staggered to the next option. I leaned on it and it gave a little. I pushed harder, until there was a gap large enough to squeeze through.

At first I thought I had stumbled upon the *Ark*'s treasury. Great heaps of shells lay stacked on tables and chairs, or crushed across the floor. I shuffled between green felt-covered tables. Red dice. Scattered playing cards. A slotted wheel.

I crossed the casino, shells crunching under boots, trying not to notice the polished, shimmering bar stretching along the port bulkhead. I entered a revolving door, rolled out into a small lobby. Two security doors, mounted keypads. I wheezed and sagged.

Trapped.

No we're not. Pain is nothing to one of you freaks, remember? Think. There has to be another way.

I slumped, unable to think of anything but the stabbing pain.

Then, a sound. Laughter. I lurched back into the casino and crouched. I overheard a lobby door pop open, male voices. They laughed at some abstruse joke. I clenched the gauntlet. Overpowering two Reals on one leg. It was a tall order. I heard keypad tones, then a door open and clunk shut. The voices disappeared.

Lucky.

242

A digital clock ticking over the casino bar indicated I'd used half my time.

I picked up my weary frame, limped out to the lobby and typed the tone I'd heard into the right-hand keypad. The exit popped open, and I slumped along a new passageway.

I took the first left turn and pushed through a door marked Stairs. I descended, then passed through white swing doors marked Medical Centre.

I pushed through the door into the dormitory, pleased to find that the doctor was out. The white couches stretched before me. I passed between them, reached the hatch, another keypad. I tapped in the code I'd heard. The door opened.

Lights slowly bloomed on, revealing a white, circular chamber. Smooth white walls rose to a glass bubble. Raked seating behind it. Some kind of modification to the ship's original design.

A steel beam projected horizontally from the wall, reaching over an adjustable couch. Flex apparatus reached either side of the recliner. An operating theatre.

Bingo.

I ran my hand over the chair, and glanced up at my reflection in the beam. The surface was lined by hairline cracks. A small word flashed in green: Ready.

I thought for a moment, then spoke:

'Scalpel.'

A panel slid open on the column, lowering a carousel bearing dozens of surgical instruments. I plucked one out, turned it over in my hand. I thought for a moment.

'Records,' I said. Another cavity opened in the column, ejecting a small flex into my fingers. I researched the theatre's capabilities. I wasn't too surprised to find first generation nanotech listed. That was good news. No need for primitive chemical or radiological treatments. The tech could eat Marsh's cancer, and keep it out. The facilities were state-of-the-art. Better even than on the *Lotus*.

We can fix her.

I thought of the dead Shark upstairs. I called up a list of recent procedures carried out in the operating theatre. Two operations were repeated again and again: Stripping and Fitting.

I left the theatre, hobbled through the bare ward, and made for the stairs. Then I reconsidered, and followed a sign for the elevators. I was short of time, but there was more to see. I figured I could squeeze another stop on the tour.

The elevator accepted the stolen code. I scrolled through the menu, found a helpful app to show me the way to my code-holder's cabin.

The elevator dropped, opened on a beige, crushed carpet, beige walls and beige handrails. Even the light was beige. I followed the corridor, that muzak tinkling in my ears.

I turned left, located cabin 12. The door was edged by fake rivets. I tapped in the code and entered, lights blinking on.

'Welcome, Baron Tivol,' said a voice.

It was quite a space. The cabin was twice as large as the Victors' Lounge. A leopardskin settee curved around a false open campfire. Other animal skins were cast about the floor. The entire wall seemed to be a mirror, framed in ornate gold carvings.

'Activate,' I said.

The mirror buzzed into life, projecting a view of some kind of structure. The legend RIGPORT was stamped across the foot of the screen. I took a seat and tried to figure out what I was looking at.

It took a minute to identify a view of the nets, shot from a strange angle. It wasn't the Blue net, but I could see Reals clustered around hanging braziers, eating and talking. A transparent ring was super-imposed over each figure, bearing a number. I picked one at random.

'Four-three-nine-nine,' I said.

The view zoomed on the subject, a young male. His voice emerged from the ambient sound, so clear I could hear every word.

'. . . unfair, course it is. Who's been here longer? Who knows more about it than I do?'

Information scrolled beneath him. Clothing measurements, health reports, history on the Rig so far.

'Seventy-four,' I said. The screen blinked, crystallised on a view of the Blue nets. Sure enough, there was 74, hanging upside down, laughing, spooling gruel into bowls, hauling himself up and crawling over the surface, dropping to other pans, stirring the contents.

I scrolled through other numbers. Some were dead, others were listed as serving a custodial sentence. Others were marked as having used certain 'flag terms', scrolling beneath.

I checked the time. Ten minutes until Bridget quit playing. I checked the bathroom, found a gaudy hot tub, a wet room, a sauna. Fluffy beige towels. I crossed the cabin to the bedroom door. Beige walls. Mirror ceiling. A carved ivory bedstead. Leopardskin covers. There was a walk-in wardrobe behind the bed.

I investigated.

You could have parked the chariot in there, if you'd removed the rails of hung clothes, the ranks of polished shoes.

A drawer I could have slept in opened to reveal hats, headdresses, gloves. Its neighbour was arm-deep with underwear. A third housed enough socks to rehose New Jerusalem twice over.

I discovered a tall refrigerator unit. I plucked the door open. I had an idea what I'd find.

Transparent sacks hung within. I removed one, brushed the frost from the surface. I slipped the plastic free and pulled out the skin. The stripping operation was clean and efficient. I guessed the hide had belonged to a mid-twenties male. It had been removed as one smooth shawl. I splayed my fingers in the loose folds of the facial covering. Whatever had lain beneath would be a Shark now, I guessed.

I examined the other skins, found other unfamiliar names. Curiously, none were marked Tivol. I wondered where his original cover was hiding. Maybe he'd thrown it away.

I hurried out of the wardrobe, deactivated the screen. I left the cabin, retracing my pained steps into the elevator and up to the ballroom floor. The sound of Man Snoot's Minstrels, of the party, grew louder.

I peered down the access corridor, heard Bridget reprising 'Feelings'.

Good work.

I hurried to the security station, hauled off the black fatigues, removed the mask and pressed it to the Shark corpse, watched it reseal with the synthetic skin around the neck. I slipped through the unguarded ballroom entrance, peered from the curtain.

Bridget took her bow, sweat pouring. The crowd barely acknowledged her, but 'Patrick' was still there, clapping hard. I stepped onto the stage while he embraced Bridget. She smiled when she saw me, relieved enough to write a song about it. I rolled down to the ballroom, merged into the crowd.

Carlos was on me in a flash.

'Where have you been, man? We needed back-up here. These people are freaks. They look like bugs or something.'

He was swaying. His eyes were bloodshot. An empty glass dangled from his hand.

'Oh good,' I said. 'You've been drinking.'

'Don't lecture me, man,' slurred Carlos. He pointed almost at me. 'You're the drinker.'

I gripped Carlos by his collar.

'Where's Bruiser?'

Carlos shrugged. I gripped him a little harder.

'Ow! What am I, her babysitter?'

A Real, if you could call it Real, appeared at Carlos's side. His skin seemed better fitted than most, but his eyes were a giveaway, showing too much flesh at the corners. It occurred to me that he might be a she underneath.

The creature placed a hand on Carlos's shoulder and grinned.

'Allow me to introduce myself,' said the man. 'I am Baron Man Snoot. Your owner – until your famous victory, that is. Congratulations on your win. I was most impressed. Startled, to be honest.'

He shaped his hand out of mine, ran it up my real arm. He frowned. Noticed the gauntlet.

'Ah, yes. I forgot. The prosthetic.'

'Yes,' I said, raising it, twisting it in the lights, watching the mosaic pattern sparkle.

'It must be terrible to lose a part of you.'

'Not really,' I said. 'I appreciate it more all the time. Besides, it was quite a help during the Game.'

'Along with our runner,' said the baron, gripping Carlos, squeezing his arms and sides. 'Now this boy has a figure. The definition. The tone.'

The baron hissed, eyeing Carlos like an anaconda. I thought I'd snap him out of it.

'I hope we didn't lose you any money? The smart bet would have been on Yellow.'

Man Snoot released Carlos.

'My boy, I have never lost more than I have made. Whether peace or war or Judgement Day, Baron Man Snoot makes oil pay. Besides, it was time for a change. The loss of a few shells is a minor inconvenience compared to the prestige of the title. I predict a long line of Blue success from here on in.

'Your story will inspire generations of winning Blue teams. Freed from Ficial slavery, worked your way up from the very bowels of the Rig, young and old working together to overcome the established team. A true rags-to-riches tale. Ah – and there's the man to help us tell it.'

Man Snoot waved over our heads. A figure swayed through the crowd. Floyd. He was unsteady, but accomplished the necessary genuflections without losing his hat.

Man Snoot bid him rise.

'Floyd, I want you to broadcast first thing tomorrow morning. Understand? You get everything you need off my team.'

'Yes, Baron . . .' Floyd gazed at me and smiled knowingly. 'We'll have them wrapped in short order.'

Man Snoot grinned, features caught in a bar of light, the trace of the original structure revealed beneath, like the bones of a pagan temple showing through cathedral walls.

I looked around, through pulsing lights, chattering figures, teeth flashing behind stolen lips. Something tugged my sleeve. Bruiser. Her eyes were blurred. A grin smothered her features. She held a half-empty glass of wine like a trophy. She had a companion: an impatient-looking girl with a ponytail hitched over one shoulder, running to her waist.

'Ah,' said Man Snoot. 'Young ones making friends, I see.'

I reached for the glass, but Bruiser withheld it.

'Mine,' she said simply. I knew the feeling. Her companion rolled her eyes.

'This is Tatiana,' said Bruiser. 'I'm going to live with her. Her father's a doctor.'

Tatiana bounced on her heels.

'Come on,' she snapped, pinching Bruiser's arm. 'You come with me now. My father needs to see you.'

'Ah, not yet, I think,' said Man Snoot, stroking Bruiser's hair back, feeling it in his fingers. 'Your new friend has a big day tomorrow. You'll have to wait until after to play dress up.'

'It's not fair!' wailed Tatiana. 'I want to play now!'

'Oh dear,' said Man Snoot. 'Let's find your father, shall we? Come on now.'

The baron wrenched the girl free of Bruiser, and began to drag her away. The girl screamed and thrashed, making quite a scene. Floyd smiled.

'Well,' he said. 'It's been a hell of a night. Time you all turned in. You've got a big day tomorrow. Interviews.'

'Interviews?' said Carlos. 'Like, for TV?'

'That's right. Live broadcast to the whole of New Jerusalem.'

'What do we say?' asked Bruiser.

'You just tell the people how lucky you are, that's all. You can do it, little lady. After that, you'll join our family for good.'

Carlos clutched his ear tag.

'And then we can lose these goddam things?'

'Oh, yes,' said Floyd. 'Of course.'

We made for the door. I hid my limp as best I could. Li joined us, emerging from the crowd. He walked alongside me.

'Have a good night?' I asked.

'Wonderful,' he said, rolling his eyes down to his side, where his hand fluttered a signal.

(Threat.)

I nodded.

'So glad to hear it.'

It is warm, almost as if I am packaged again, but there is no embracing amber, only thin, hot air. I struggle and claw at my polythene shroud, inhaling it, and while I suffocate I see hundreds of other 'I's around me, hanging in the dry-cleaner.

I must escape.

My struggling grows fevered and mindless.

Then it evaporates, burned away. And the plastic silently unzips, and I drop to a mesh floor.

I look up, and I am standing there looking back at myself. I reach me up, slap me onto a gurney and push me out of the dry-cleaner's, into a room where Kosiaki sits, reading.

I sit next to him and read the book, those few words I read and I am still reading it while I walk, through the abandoned town; no, wait, hundreds of us, there are hundred of 'I's walking through the abandoned town, a slow column of refugees marching in step. Soldier Models tower over us with their glowing green eyes and they are saying: 'No more work. No more work for you.' And I break out of formation, I run to the Soldier who said it, shake him by the collar:

'There must be something to do?'

'Like what?' Pander takes my hands off his lapels and points at the city, or where the city was. The sea has swept into the river, swamping the districts into one enormous waste pit, and the soldiers are marching us out of the gates on Brixton Hill, into the pits, two by two. My head spins. I must survive.

Then, I open my eyes and look out from the ramparts of the great wall, I look out over the bubbling swamp, and I see hundreds of creatures with my face, floating lifeless in the murky waters that lap at the wall.

'No hard feelings?' asks Pander.

He points into the deserted streets of Brixton, at the Ritzy. Kosiaki stands outside, waving, and we march together in line with our four brothers, we are marching again through the tunnel and onto the field, and the crowd, thirty thousand Panders, they all sing and applaud and clap. And I pass to me, and me passes to me out on the wing, and I clip a precise cross to me on the edge of the box, feed it to me, bursting from a line of defenders, and my boot connects and my heart pounds and my head spins, as I run around the stadium and find the stands.

Empty. The stands are empty. I slow, I stop, and the game continues around me but I have lost all interest in it now, it is burned, gone for good. I walk through the darting players, out of the stadium, in search of work. To work.

BOLT FROM THE BLUE

It was a long night. I lay there in the cabin, team-mates snoring, and turned over what I'd discovered.

The medical inspection and treatments had seemed like pampering. In fact, the maids had tanned our hides, and Floyd had sold them at auction. We just happened to still be wearing them.

Soon, probably after tomorrow's broadcast, they'd be ripped from us, replaced with oozing, artificial pelts. Then what? Brief, breathless careers as Sharks, watching impostors compete in the Game, wearing our faces. The Yellow champions had all been *Ark* dwellers underneath, I was certain now. Their Blue successors would enjoy equal fortune.

Is that why the barons stole skins: to experience new life? Did they believe that poached coverings of champions would transform them, give them power?

Where did Lay fit into this madness? The Only Book was packed with lunatic commandments, but the wearing of other skins wasn't one I recalled. Hoods were nowhere to be seen aboard the *Ark*. Nor, now that I thought of it, were the children they'd taken. The barons were more like Aztecs, followers of Xipe Totec, than the word of the Only Book.

Perhaps it wasn't a question of belief. These Reals could simply have sailed in too many circles at the top of the world, stared too long into the ice, until their minds had cracked.

The question is, what do we do?

You know exactly what, pal. You need to make a move.

Bring the Ark *to the Rig.*

Exactly. And there's only one way to do that.

I rolled over, glanced at Bruiser. Her shape rose and fell gently on the couch.

We should warn them.

We can't. Like Bridget said: walls have ears. Besides, they'd have to see the shit we've seen to believe it.

They know something's wrong with this place.

Sure. But not that wrong.

They'll hate me for what I'll do.

Since when does popularity matter to your kind? Look, this way they have a fighting chance. They'll thank you for it one day.

I reached up the gauntlet, twisted its fingers. It had prevented my sale at auction, a patch on the coat. Only Marsh had seen it as anything but a deformity.

Is she still alive?

Don't think about that.

She could be dead, but I don't believe it. I think I would know if she died. I am still receiving her, like a signal.

Get some sleep. Big day tomorrow. We must sleep.

My eyes closed, functions slowed. The sense of a world fell away, leaving a dream.

A previous fare of mine clutched Pistol in her arms, her blonde hair fanned in the black water. She was under the ice, gazing up at me through the hole I'd cut. I reached the gauntlet in, to pull them clear, but all I retrieved were shells. Thousands upon thousands of shells.

Floyd arrived bright and early with a dozen Sharks. I wondered if they'd discovered their dead colleague. Were they suspicious, angry, mournful? Did they feel anything at all? The black orbs held no answers.

'By the prophet,' said Floyd. 'What a mess. You look like you've been up all night wrestling pigs. Get showered, will you? We're live in four hours.'

The Sharks advanced on our bunks, dragged Carlos from his slumber.

'Hey! Take it easy!'

They hauled him into the shower room. I heard a brief scuffle, a jet of water.

'Cold!' wailed Carlos. Bruiser followed him in, a Shark on each flank. I waited with Li, studying Floyd. I couldn't tell if his skin was

252

his own. Perhaps he was priced out of their culture, as much a servant to the baronial order as the maids and Sharks.

'Which of us will you interview first?' I asked him.

'Oh, I think Carlos,' he replied absently, scrolling something on an unfurled flex. 'He's the character. Then perhaps the girl. Your captain there comes last.'

'But you will interview me?'

'Yes, never fear, you'll get your fifteen minutes.'

'Everyone in New Jerusalem will be watching?'

'Yes, we expect capacity audiences for this review show. You've shaken things up, you Blues. Why do you ask? You're not nervous, are you?'

Carlos and Bruiser were led out of the showers, wrapped in white towels, into the dressing room.

A Shark gurgled at me, pointing to the shower. It could have been anyone under that mask. It might not even be sure who was in there itself.

I had useless, speculative Real thoughts in the shower. Would this be my last shower? My last morning?

We dressed in new Game uniforms, followed the Sharks out of the cabin, entered the waiting elevator. We shot down, floors cutting by.

'Everyone refreshed?' asked Floyd. 'No nerves? No one going to be sick? Let me know if you are now, you wouldn't want to ruin my broadcast, would you?'

'Hey,' said Carlos. 'Do we get these tags removed today?'

Floyd turned and smiled. 'Oh. Yes.'

The elevator slowed. The doors opened to a familiar oily scent.

The hold. Spotlights were arrayed around the space, lending it an oddly alien appearance. The Tombstone sat under an array of lamps, still battered and bruised. Floyd set about the space, consulting Sharks on the broadcast preparations.

A semicircle of blue plastic chairs had been arranged before the chariot. Floyd took the central spot, positioning Bruiser and Li to his left, Carlos and me to the right. We sat in the lights and blinked sweat. Sharks manned the camera, swinging it in Floyd's direction. He stared at the red light.

'Remember,' he said through his teeth. 'No cursing and no

speeches. You give me short, simple answers. Look at me and not the camera. Are you getting this, girl?'

Bruiser snorted contempt. The light flicked green, and Floyd's face froze into a grin.

'Welcome to *Game Review* with me, Floyd. Tonight we have quite a show, as we meet the team whose story has captivated all of New Jerusalem. The team who were liberated from Ficial slavery, brought back to the safety of God's city on Earth, and worked their way up from the very lowest net to the top jobs on the Rig. They are the team that blew the odds out of the water, they are the minnows that became whales, they are the team I'm calling . . . The Bolt From the Blue.'

Floyd turned to Carlos.

'I'm going to start with you, if I may, Carlos. I know that your family back in Blue will all have believed in you, that they all had faith that you could win.'

Carlos nodded humbly. He didn't have any family on the Rig, but that didn't stop him being humbled by their mention.

'But you must have had your own doubts,' said Floyd. 'Did you foresee winning the entire competition in such fashion?'

'Yes,' replied Carlos. 'Yes, we did, Floyd. You wouldn't play the Game if you didn't think you could win. We know that Yellow have fabulous players. We know they have a history in this competition, but we had belief, we had personality, we had commitment. We prevailed.'

Floyd nodded slowly, as if at something very profound. Then he turned to Bruiser.

'Now you came into the team after the tragic death of your runner, Wole, didn't you, little girl?'

'Wole was my friend.'

'Of course he was. Did you feel a responsibility to the team to take over his position? Wasn't it asking a lot of someone your age?'

'I was sad. I miss Wole. He was my friend.'

'Yes, sure, but as a team member,' urged Floyd. 'How did it affect the team?'

'I think,' said Carlos, interrupting, 'we were all saddened to see Wole go. He was the heart of the team, as a player, as a motivator, as a leader. Characters like him are rare. You need those big characters if you're going to challenge for the League. We all felt it when he died. But, if you know what I mean, Floyd, we think of ourselves as a family in Blue. We look out for each other. We are with each other through good times and bad. This little girl, she's like my sister.'

Carlos dropped a hand on my shoulder. 'This guy? He's like my brother. We ate together, we raced together. We prayed together, Floyd. Every night we prayed, for our families, for New Jerusalem, for our children. And praise the prophet, those prayers were answered.'

'Praise the prophet,' echoed Floyd, fingering a sign in the air. Carlos was better at this charade than him. Floyd turned to me next. My mouth was dry.

'Now, Ken, you are yet another remarkable piece in this story. Because you are disabled, isn't that right?'

He glanced at my hand, the mosaic pattern of blues and greens. I held it up for the camera.

'This? It's not such a disability,' I said. 'In many ways it's—'

'He's brave about it,' interrupted Carlos, 'but you're right, it's a disability. What Ken here has done is triumphed over adversity. He has that will to win, at any cost.'

I thought Carlos might have stolen my opportunity, but Floyd seemed encouraged. He pressed in close, leaning towards me.

'And did you think you could win that final race, Ken? With a child driver and your disability?'

'Oh, sure,' I said. 'I was positive.'

'And why was that, Ken? What was it that gave you that faith? Was it the strength of the prophet?'

I glanced at the camera. Ensured the light was still green. Live, to all New Jerusalem.

'No,' I said. 'Not the prophet. You see, I am not what I appear to be. You remember the other night you thought you recognised me?'

Floyd stared. Carlos grinned at me, eyes wild.

'What the hell are you doing?'

'I'm confessing,' I said. Turned back to Floyd.

'You see, Floyd, I'm Ficial.'

The Sharks behind the camera bridled. Li, Bruiser and Carlos stared. Floyd squinted, as if I were a shape on the horizon.

'You . . . You . . . You . . .'

'That's right, Floyd. I know, the arm, right? I'm not strictly Ficial any more. I lost my nanotech, you see. Unfortunately it meant I had to throw in my lot with these Reals. But I'm a Rover Model, a Power Nine. Optimised for construction. I'm as Ficial as they come.'

Everybody stared. Nobody moved. It was harder to get arrested than I expected.

'I helped the team cheat,' I said. 'Additive in our fuel gave us the boost we needed. As a Ficial it was easily done.'

Floyd stared. Someone screamed into his earpiece. He snapped out of it, turned to the camera and smiled.

'We'll be right back.'

The burning is complete. I am passed, fully optimised, tasked to the new Model Hex. I excavate Sleep and Eat levels. My brothers work below. I do not speak. My mind is dormant, standing by, watching as my hands lift, dig and manipulate materials. I only truly wake when Control signals, delivering updates.

Rickets still appears. I take the brunt of his visits, as I work the upper levels. He sits and talks, without direction or purpose. He recounts events, casts judgement on matters too great for him to comprehend. Why speak to me? I wonder. What use are these words? Does speaking cool his mind, settle his emotions?

'Not one of you is curious about the new model, are you?'

'No,' I reply.

'Good. You shouldn't be.' He runs his hand over one of my walls, as if suspicious of the finish. 'We are no longer a public service, you see. The Barrier bomb has changed everything. Government's going to break the bank trying to save London. They need money, so we're told we must turn a profit. We are now a business. You'll be sold, like a slave. How does that make you feel?'

'I feel nothing.'

'No, of course you don't.' He nods, regards his shoes. 'But the fact is, it compromises everything. The Ficial project is about providing what is essential, getting our priorities right, before it's too late. The moment you introduce money to the equation it's finished. Without Control assigning work you'll be put to use anywhere except where you're useful, I guarantee it. There's no money in building proper camps for the refugees. Ten to one you end up building prisons, or useless airports. You must have a professional opinion on that?'

He waves a hand.

'Don't answer. I know what you'll say.'

He circles the hex, hand trailing along the wall, the six bays where six new models will sleep.

'You know what they're calling them? This new "Power"? "Pleasure Models". That's what we're reduced to. We engineer escorts now. Beautiful, useless escorts. It sickens me.'

He darts towards me, leans up and stares into my eyes. I smell alcohol on his breath.

'Do you hear me in there, Control? It sickens me.'

He lets go, backs away.

'Sorry,' he says. 'I shouldn't do that.'

He stares at me for a moment. His flex rings. He stares at the device on his wrist, frozen. Perhaps he expects retribution.

'Do not be afraid,' I say. 'Control would not contact you directly.'

He clears his throat, straightens up. Takes the flex off his wrist and shapes a phone.

'Rickets here.'

He listens. His eyes flick up to me. 'Yes, as a matter of fact I do.'

FLINT

The Victors' Lounge had been stripped out, leaving nothing but an echoing steel cube, a stench of disinfectant, and a domed surveillance pod, fixed where the chandelier had hung. Finally it revealed its true nature: a prison cell.

We were sealed inside. Right away Carlos lunged at me. Li and Bruiser had to restrain him.

'Let me at him!' he screamed, his face turning a powerful purple. '¡Traidor! Loco! Imbecil! What did you think you were doing?'

I sat, saying nothing. I didn't want to add fuel to Carlos's fire. If the Sharks hadn't been listening before they would be now.

'Look at him!' raged Carlos, still thrashing in Li's grip. 'He's insane! We should have throttled him when we had the chance. It would be a mercy killing. Like putting down a rabid dog.'

Bruiser knelt a little distance away.

'Ken? Why did you tell?'

'Because he has a death wish!' screamed Carlos. 'He wants to take us with him too. Well, you won't take me, psycho. You hear me? You won't take me!'

Bruiser ignored the ranting runner.

'Ken. Why did you tell?'

It was hard to lie to Bruiser, but the Sharks would be listening. I couldn't explain about the barons' flaying habit, couldn't explain that I might actually have bought us a little more time in our own skins. Do that and the barons would have us killed now, to keep the secret. No, I had to get the ship to dock, keep quiet.

The energy drained out of Carlos.

'The crazy fuck's killed us all.' He sank to his knees. 'Tell me why you did it.'

Like a Real once taught me: garnish the lie with the truth.

'I wanted to get Marsh treatment.'

'Well, that's fucked now, isn't it?' sniffed Carlos, cheeks glowing, the rage burning out of him. He looked up at me, looking tired now. 'So why the confession?'

I shrugged.

'I felt guilty.'

Carlos chuckled, motioned towards me.

'Can you believe this guy? He feels guilty. Now, after everything we've been through, the goddam Ficial feels something.'

Li fixed me with a hard glare. Shook his head.

'Bad sober.'

'That's right.' Carlos nodded. 'We should have kept him tanked.'

There was a long silence. Bruiser rocked on her haunches. Carlos stood, circled the room a couple of times, then slumped against the wall, resting his head on his knees. Li observed me as if I might change colour.

The knock on the hatch shook the room like an explosion. The entrance clunked open. A Real entered, wearing a suit over the skin of a middle-aged male. The fit was good. Only a little tightness around the shoulders suggested discomfort. His eyes were brown and his hair was flecked with silver. He held a rolled-up flex. A huge gold watch was on his wrist.

Sharks entered behind him, closed on me, wielding rifles. I showed them my palms and sat very still.

The man sat, smiled briefly, unrolled his flex.

Carlos approached him.

'Who are you, man?'

'My name is Flint,' said the creature, offering a card. Li accepted it, examined it.

'Lawyer?'

'That's correct.' He tapped his flex, examining the display. 'I've been appointed to conduct your defence in this matter.'

'Defence? You mean . . . there's gonna be a trial?'

The man nodded.

'I think you'll find my fee is very reasonable considering the severity of the case.'

'How much?' asked Li.

260

'What does it matter?' snapped Carlos. 'We can't pay you, man. We never got our race fee.'

'You never will,' said Flint. 'Your team has already been stripped of its League title by the Game Association, I'm afraid. No, I don't expect you to pay me yourselves.'

'The Rig,' said Li.

'That's right. My fee will be met by your compatriots on Blue, on top of the fine for Game fixing. Even with Blue's considerable reserves this affair will almost certainly bankrupt Blue, I'm afraid.'

Carlos offered me another filthy look.

'So can you get us off?'

'Oh no,' said Flint cheerfully. 'I'm afraid your friend's origin story will not allow for that. You are collaborators, you see.'

'But he's insane!' barked Carlos. 'Anyone can see that. Look at him!'

Flint did look at me. He tugged at the skin under his chin, pinching it between thumb and forefinger. 'Insanity is no plea in New Jerusalem legal code. The prophet teaches that insanity is possession by another name, and equally worthy of death.'

'So we're all DEAD?'

Flint considered.

'Well, that depends. Did you know that he was Ficial?'

'We had no IDEA!' said Carlos, covering Bruiser's mouth. 'You think we would have consorted with one of those things if we knew?'

Flint nodded. 'I'm sympathetic, of course. But you were in the power of Ficials for some time, which doesn't look good. Plus, there is the testimony of Baron Man Snoot. You've cast him in rather a poor light, as well as losing him a fortune. He's demanding the burning cross for the lot of you. No, ignorance won't help you here.'

'Well, what will help?'

'Simple,' said Flint. 'Tell us where the other Ficials are.'

Carlos blinked.

'Others? What others? He's the only one.'

Flint noted something on his flex.

'Hmm. That's not going to satisfy the court. They're expecting to hear about a network of fifth columnists. This whole case confirms their worst suspicions about a Ficial cell in New Jerusalem. Once they've decided it's a conspiracy, that's all they'll believe.'

'Even if it's not true?'

'Especially if it's not true. No, if you can't provide a few names, well . . .'

Carlos sat down, put his head in his hands.

'Don't you think we'd tell you if we could, man?'

'Well,' said Flint, keen to be helpful, 'if not actual Ficials, what about Ficial agents? People working for the Ficials. That's easier, I'll grant you. Give us a few names and I might be able to swing the rest of you a custodial sentence.'

Carlos gaped. Inform or die. I watched his lips, expecting names to roll off his tongue. Instead he cursed and turned away.

'Well,' said Flint, rolling up his flex and repacking his case, 'I'll leave you to discuss it as a team. All I can tell you is that you're already skating on thin ice. There are many on the upper decks who would like to see the lot of you burned immediately. The whole sordid affair has been very bad for the sport. You're only getting a trial because you're celebrities. People will be fascinated to see you all suffer, you see.

'We're docking in the morning. You'll be taken on deck and interrogated. As your attorney I advise you to give them as many names as possible. Otherwise it's the sword for each of you. Including the girl.'

He stood, approached me. The Shark guards stood to one side. Flint knelt at my side, smiling. Closer up I could see the creases under his ears.

'Remarkable,' he said, inspecting me. 'You really are a Power Nine. I've been researching you. How did it feel to lose immortality?'

He was genuinely interested. I could have told him. But that wasn't really what he was looking for.

'It didn't feel like anything,' I said. 'I'm Ficial.'

The Sharks cuffed me behind my back, by the elbow, so I couldn't bring the gauntlet to bear. We were led onto a teak promenade deck. The sky was clear, and I could see a great distance to the south, where the broiling cloud bank began. The *Ark* had been braking for hours and now, finally, began to turn for the Rig.

I counted Sharks as we headed for the bow. Huge New Jerusalem flags beat in the wind overhead. White drones buzzed clear from some higher deck, wobbled into the air, forged ahead, bound for the

Rig. A Shark fell out from our party, and began to fix a sniper rifle to a brace on the railing.

'I hope you're happy,' moaned Carlos, walking beside me. 'You've killed us all.'

'You're alive now,' I said. 'Try to seize the moment.'

'You goddam stupid Ficial scumbag. I should have told them you put a spell on us.'

'You think that would have helped?'

He sighed.

'No. They're going to punish us whatever we say, man. You killed us all.'

Floyd waited on the bow, where Sharks busily set about erecting a scaffold.

'What's that?' asked Bruiser.

'Mount for the judge,' I said. 'People prefer to condemn from elevated spots.'

Floyd swivelled, alerted to our approach. He scowled at me, then painfully rearranged his features into a kind of smile.

'Planning any surprises for this broadcast?'

'I'll see what I can do.'

He sniffed and turned his attention to the Sharks.

'Over there,' he said. 'Blindfolds.'

The Sharks pushed us to our knees, shackling us to a grille fixed in the deck. One pulled a strap over Bruiser's eyes. She yelped in fright.

'Brave,' said Li.

They shrouded us all, leaving us kneeling, listening to the operation of putting into port. It was a deafening business. Sharks bustled about, hammering and welding, working up the apparatus of judgement. The engines churned, turning into reverse as the great craft closed on the Rig. Stevedores called from the container wall. Then, suddenly, the engines cut out.

I heard different voices, chattering on the deck. Brass and woodwind, string and drum. Bridget's band. They were on deck with us, making preparations.

'Ken.' Li, leaning close to me, whispering.

'Yes?'

'You do not wish to die.'

I couldn't tell if it was a question or a statement. I figured the din of Man Snoot's Minstrels would be enough to keep the conversation private.

'No,' I admitted.

'You are Ficial,' he said firmly.

'I was.'

'Why admit?'

'They were going to do far worse to us than kill us. Take it from me. At least we have some options while docked.'

'You have a plan?'

'Just realise this, Li. I'm not Ficial any more. Not human either. All I am is a promise, to help Marsh. If you happen to get free, I'd appreciate you not braining me, OK?'

I listened to the band warm up, let him think on it. We knelt a while longer, listening to a crowd build along the docks, on the container cliffs, on the surrounding ships. Thousands were there to see us judged. Here and there I heard my name cursed. A group sang a derisory song about Blues. A Blue contingent chanted a response. Voices turned hard. A growl rolled around the ship.

I heard steps approach, come to a halt a few feet away.

'All right, they're getting restless,' said Floyd. 'Let's get this show on the road. Gag this one and let's get him in the dock.'

My blindfold was slipped off. Two Sharks took my arms. A third stood before me, my reflection caught in its goggles. It balled a rag in its hands and pressed it into my throat, fixing it there with tape. It was a little early for all this.

'Ken!' yelped Bruiser. 'Ken!'

My new friends dragged me across the deck. I looked over my shoulder, saw the container cliff tops, smothered by petulant, shabby crowds. Ahead of me, two huge ribbed oil pipes projected from the *Ark*'s port side, dropping out of sight to the docks, taking on oil to refine for the *Ark*'s next trip. Between them, rising up almost to the bridge, the Sharks had built a great pitched bank of seating, where barons clustered under umbrellas and hid behind fans, features obscured by sunglasses, nose guards and scarves. At the centre of the crowd was a transparent cube, a bullet-proof enclosure for the prophet's throne. At the foot of the stands were Bridget and her Minstrels.

My Sharks kicked me to my knees and shackled me to a Flex

platform spread on the deck. Presumably it was there to catch my blood and minimise swabbing later.

A silence crept over the deck. There was movement up by the bridge. A figure appeared.

Bridget and the band boomed into life, blurting out a pompous, triumphant march. The barons stood, broke into raucous applause as the figure stepped forward and waved to the *Ark*, to the people on the Rig.

Lay. Or at least someone wearing his grey, tired skin. He descended the steps, Sharks clustered about him, and reached out to shake hands with his fellow barons as he passed. White Hoods processed behind him, carrying baskets. They fanned out across the deck, lining the gunwale, tossed bread to the half-starved Riggers lining the docks and crushed into the esplanade. Others packed loaves into air cannons, and shot them at the crowd on the container wall. There were cheers and prayers and thanks. My trial was a Real party event.

Lay ascended the podium, smile vanishing, replaced by a more pious frown. The music died. Bridget and the Minstrels sat and bowed their heads. The barons did the same. The whole crowd bowed but me. The impostor Lay spoke.

'Children of New Jerusalem. God smiles on you all this Docking Day, this most holy day when the *Ark*, Rig and people become one. We gather here in sight of the Lord to ask his forgiveness and to praise him. To praise him for his mercy in delivering us to this place, where we have made a New Jerusalem in his name.'

Impostor Lay waved the Only Book.

'We thank him by living by this, his purified word. We follow it in all that we do. We follow it willingly and we say no. No, we do not tolerate. No, we do not forgive. We PUNISH those who trespass against him!'

Lay, or whoever it was, dabbed at his forehead and lips with a handkerchief, examined what he found, tucked it away for later.

'So, it is that on Docking Day we not only rejoice in this new land of plenty. We rejoice too in the service of his justice.'

With that, Lay entered the glass cube, taking his throne. Any chance Bridget's friends had of burying a bullet in his brain had passed.

Floyd bowed to the prophet and took a prominent position on deck, evidently acting for the prosecution. A mic was pinned to his lapel, under a miniature New Jerusalem flag. His voice boomed over the deck, over the docks.

'We all enjoy the Game,' he said. 'Every one of us supports his team, urges them on to heroic feats. The Game brings out the best in all of us. It is everything that makes us human, that separates us from the Ficials. Honest competition. Family entertainment. Hard-working people taking time out in the pursuit of happiness. Ficials sought to destroy those things, and that makes us cherish them all the more.

'We may be perplexed when faced with a case such as this. How, we ask ourselves, could our own neighbours willingly corrupt all that we have built? How could they work with Ficials, the walking agents of Satan?'

I had been wondering when that name was going to come up.

'How? All too easily. Ficials were born of blasphemy, of Man's vain pride in his science, of his belief he could make men better than God. Pander and his acolytes were deluded into thinking they were the Ficials' masters, when they themselves were Satan's puppets. This Blue team were also deluded. They believed they could control this damaged Ficial, when in fact he was controlling them.

'There is a lesson for us here. Each of us must remain vigilant. We must never stop praying, never stop watching. And, when those who have succumbed to evil are brought before us? We must strike down without mercy, without question. We must be the instrument of God's justice.'

With that he returned to his seat.

That was quick. We should be burning by lunchtime.

Flint stood next, bowing to the prophet and taking centre stage.

'I thank counsel for his summary of this crime. None of us here can doubt the seriousness, the depravity, the vileness of such a crime against our people, against our Game and against our religion.'

I sighed, growing impatient.

'All that I ask,' continued Flint, 'is that we consider the good people of Blue. They were not complicit in this crime. They knew not the demon they clutched to their breast. Let us remember that when we consider their fine. I would add that—'

Flint stopped, squinting into the distance behind me. I turned, hearing it too. A disturbance on the container wall. Raised voices. The Sharks reacted, but too late.

The report of a shot. Flint's head blew free of the neck. Two more shots, echoing over the deck. Sharks guarding the prophet's cube jerked and crumpled in bursts of steaming blood. Gunfire, building to a steady crackle, from all directions.

About time.

Sharks clustered around the cube, forming a wall around the impostor prophet, hurrying him to safety, barging through the panicking mass of barons, who were screaming, scattering, trampling each other.

Drones swooped, peppering the container wall with plastic rounds. Wounded tumbled down the steps, revolutionaries and spectators alike.

Sharks worked frantically on deck, trying to unlatch the oil pipes, but Riggers of all colours were already scuttling up the ducts, hacking down the surprised Sharks, shooting their way aboard the *Ark*. Barons fled along the promenade decks, seeking cover. Li, Carlos and Bruiser lay flat.

Bridget took her chance. She tossed her bass and ran, skidding down by a dead Shark. She released a key chain from his belt, rolled onto her knees, and made her way to Bruiser, Li and Carlos, staggering in the confusion as if through a tornado. She unshackled them, lifted their blindfolds, urged them to find safety. Then she came for me.

The anchor chain shrieked. The deck tipped. She was knocked off her feet, sliding across the slippery deck. The *Ark* was trying to wrench free of the dock under its own power, dragging the oil pipes tight, dropping boarders into the sea. Sharks appeared on the promenade decks. Sharpshooters, firing into the esplanade, down at the docks, cutting down dozens of boarders.

They had held back the flood. The oil pipes creaked and strained, ready to snap. Reals fled in panic from the swooping drones.

I locked eyes with Bridget across the blood-spattered deck, her friends dead or dying about her. Tears stained her cheeks. She shook her head, defeated. The revolution looked like a real failure. I shrugged, held my hands up to my lips, impersonated the playing of a harp.

She choked a desperate laugh, shook her head, and drew the battered old harmonica from her pocket. She started to wail.

Even in a firefight she made a good sound. Even a few Sharks lowered their guns to listen. It had something, that music. It ran through the Rig and the sky and my bones.

The deck began trembling. The vibration grew rapidly to a hard quake, hammering at my knees. The seating structure whined and swayed, folded in on itself, swallowing Sharks and a few cowering barons. Containers tipped and fell from the Rig's stepped wall, thudding onto the esplanade, crushing people. The ocean seemed to be having a seizure.

Then, the explosion. A great column of flame roared into the sky, a pressure wave scalding the air, the world's largest firework raining soot and liquid fire.

Bridget quit playing, jolted from her rapture. Saw the leaping, spurting tentacle of fire. Stared at her harp, her eyes wild.

The docks became a single animal scream. Panic made revolutionaries, the crowd rushing up the fuel pipes, up the ropes, abandoning the broiling Rig. The Sharks got to their feet, redoubled the fight, but it was a losing effort. Bridget skipped over to me, crouched at my side, keyed open my shackles.

'I didn't mean it, Ken!'

'Don't worry,' I said. 'Your music's not to blame. It's Kinnare.'

She gripped my shoulders.

'What?'

'He popped up a while back, in the nets. Said he might make a visit the next Dock Day. Wants his *Lotus* back.'

'But he's DEAD!'

'Nope. We're built to last, you know.'

The unofficial boarding was turning to a stampede, as secondary explosions tore across the Rig.

We traced Li, Bruiser and Carlos's steps, opened a hatch, found them stopped in the passageway. Carlos cursed.

'What the hell is going on out there?'

'Blow-out,' I said. 'Or something like it. New Jerusalem's a goner. Just a matter of time.'

'So what's the plan?' asked Bridget.

'I'm going on board to get Marsh.'

'Ken!' yelped Bruiser. 'Don't go!'

'Let him, sister,' snarled Carlos. 'He's a goddam traitor! Tried to get us all killed.'

Two Sharks burst from a fire exit. Li crashed a great fist onto the first. Bruiser hurled her head into the other's belly, winding it, before Carlos slammed its head into the wall.

I knelt by his victim, unpeeled the mask, ripped it free, exposing the fleshy mess beneath.

'Jesus CHRIST!' yelped Carlos.

'See this?' I said. 'They flay people on this boat. The victims are dressed in synthetic skin, made slaves by gum and trauma, until they expire. The barons wear the skins for fun. I had to get us into port to give us a chance. Understand now?'

'No!' he snapped.

An explosion, on an upper deck.

'Come,' said Li. 'Loading bay.'

We barged through the melee. Carlos disarmed a Shark, broke the rifle across the masked face.

'Eat that, *Dentusso*.'

He opened a hatch and we followed a passage, stepping over a trampled baron, his face peeling away.

'Goddamit!' shrieked Carlos. 'I thought these were church people!'

The whole structure shook with the hammering of thousands of feet, Riggers swarming all over the *Ark*. There was a distant pattering sound, like tapping on the hull. Drones, raking the deck. We turned, followed a staircase down, into the *Ark*'s belly.

Carlos stopped us at a hatch. Signed:

(Target.)

I placed a hand on the wheel and turned. Carlos lined up the rifle. I turned the hatchway open. Carlos hesitated, lowered the rifle. Signalled:

(Clear.)

We entered the loading bay. Forklift trucks and crates rocked with the motion of the *Ark*, ropes and pulleys swinging overhead. Carlos crossed to the bay door, peered through an observation slat at the Rig.

'We're pulling away,' he said. 'There's thousands of people on the dock. Jesus, man, they're crushing each other.'

269

I joined him, surveyed the scene. Waves of panicked Reals flooded the esplanade, fleeing the Rig fires. They kept coming, workers in rags rolling down the container wall, from all derricks. A migration.

The *Ark* continued to edge away.

'Let's give them somewhere to go,' said Carlos. He punched the ramp release and stepped clear. Orange hazard lights swept the interior, an alarm wailing.

Li clutched Bruiser tight.

The great ramp unlocked, lowered, admitting the hot scream of the crowd. Shots rang in the bay. Bridget and I dived for cover. Carlos, Li and Bruiser backed away to the far side, pressed themselves against the bulkhead. The door began to unpeel, unroll, reaching towards the esplanade. Riggers jumped for its still-shaping edge, fell. Then the Flex met the crowd, stiffened, and a great confusion of barging broke out at the ramp edge.

'They're going to charge.'

The first boarder was shot in the leg as he entered the bay. He fell, cried out. Li spat, ran to help him.

'No!' I called. 'Stay back!'

The revolution was too fast for Li. It was coming aboard, messy and bloody. He tried to drag the wounded man clear. Then his face was cut open, and his brains blew out.

'No!' yelped Bruiser. She ran to him. Carlos went after her, swept her into his arms, vaulted Li's body and clattered into us, taking shelter as the thrashing crowd rolled aboard, a wave of Real fear.

The *Ark* was still edging clear of the Rig. The ramp drew away from the esplanade, too far for the injured stragglers to jump. Many had made it aboard. They spread out in the huge bay, dropped, exhausted and frightened.

'Carlos,' said Bridget, seizing him by the arm. 'I'm going with Ken.'

'What? Aren't you supposed to be leading these people?'

'I'm a musician. You need to organise them, right? Use your charm. Make sure they stick together.'

I picked up Bruiser, squeezed her, dropped her down.

'And take care of her. She's one hell of a driver.'

Carlos frowned agreement.

'Hell. She'll take care of me.'

270

We ran onto the ramp, shots spitting from the promenade decks. The drones overhead seemed inactive, reset to looping holding patterns. The ramp was a good long jump from the esplanade. Bridget hesitated. I picked her up and threw her over the space. She landed hard, stood in a fury.

'Will you PLEASE not do that!'

I didn't have time to listen. I staggered back down the ramp, turned, lined up my jump.

You think this knackered ankle is going to run that distance?

Thanks for the pep talk.

I blocked everything out. Every thought, every sound. I took a deep breath, exhaled slowly and tried to build some speed.

I pulled up.

See?

Bridget called to me.

'Oi, hopalong! Use this!'

She had a rope scooped in her arms. She swung the tip over her head, hurled it expertly over the gap between the *Ark* and the Rig, into my hand, tied her end to a railing. I jumped, dropped, swung below the esplanade, under the Rig, almost into Green's nets. I dangled a moment, watched great chunks of burning net dropping into the sea. Then I climbed, up to Bridget.

'We haven't got long,' I said. 'Fire's spreading through the nets.'

We worked up the containers, shrugging at the gunfire, picking over bodies of Sharks and Riggers.

'What a mess,' said Bridget. 'Kinnare's gone completely booloo. What's he thinking, blowing up the Rig?'

'Distraction,' I said.

No, not distraction. It's fucking murder.

We hauled to the top of the container wall, stopped to gasp at the burning air. On the *Ark*, the promenade decks had become a giant, floating melee. Smoke billowed from portholes, fires burning on the bow. Ragged Rig dwellers swarmed everywhere, cutting down barons and Sharks, throwing them overboard. I saw Floyd launched over the guardrail, a cable around his neck, and left swinging. Was it the end for Man Snoot? For the doctor? Maybe they'd pull on other skins and slip away.

We turned to our objective. The Yellow derrick was lost in a great, blazing torch, blowing towards the White derrick, consuming the north-west section of the Rig. The rest of the structure appeared almost entirely deserted. The treadmills were still, the container workshops abandoned. Only a few Sharks manning the cranes and fire hoses had remained, flooding the White rig in foam, trying to contain the blaze by erecting a wall of retardant.

Brave, but hopeless. The fire was spreading through the nets, urged on by strong winds.

We're too late.

I jogged painfully along the wall, headed for the eastern perimeter, climbing down where a container had fallen away in the quake, climbing back. We skirted the edge of New Jerusalem, the bonds that bound the five rigs howling as they warped and twisted.

The yellow inferno sucked at us as we passed, a gale that burned our throats, singed our hair, roared in our ears; a shower of sooty fragments and embers. The container tops glowed like hot coals. We hopped across them, leaving rubber impressions of our boots.

We reached the Blue cliff, stopped. I pulled off my shirt and tore it into strips, passing some to Bridget. We wrapped the rags around our hands and climbed the hot metal, hacking in the acrid blue smoke rising from the net fires below.

'Ken,' said Bridget. 'We're too late. The whole thing . . .'

'She's still alive.'

'How can you know that?'

'Energies, Bridget. Energies.'

The surface of the Blue rig was a great, smoking grate. The island structure had fallen away to the east, containers lost to the sea, those that remained shedding blue paint to the hot air. The derrick had warped, twisted. It would blow at any second.

Then I saw me.

The old me, jumping gracefully, beautifully, in and out of fires, picking each foothold like a mountain goat. I was holding Marsh. Her arms were around my neck. She looked as light as air. How had Kinnare found her?

Kinnare stopped, tilted his head. Motioned with his head: this way.

It tasted like I'd been sucking exhaust for an hour. It took everybody but Kinnare a while to quit coughing.

We dived.

Rick was at the controls, hunched at a bank of levers, wearing large headphones, twisting dials and tapping keys. The mini-sub was a Rick special, constructed from an eclectic collection of salvage and his own future-tech innovations.

Behind me, bent almost double in a bunk, sat Kinnare, eyes calm over a respirator. Bridget sat next to him, wary.

'So,' I said. 'We're headed to the *Lotus*.'

'That's right,' said Kinnare. 'Now that the Real authority has its hands full we should be able to retake it in peace.'

'Your fireworks were impressive.'

'Yes. Tricky job actually. We had to dive to the seabed and do it by hand.'

'Tricky job? Have you seen how many people your tricky job killed?'

'It was the only way to neutralise the big ship. While they fight it out we can take the *Lotus* and sail into the sunset. So to speak.'

He frowned over his mask.

'You seem emotional about it, brother.'

'Emotional enough to rip that silly mask off your face.'

I looked back at Marsh.

'How did you find her so fast? How did you know where to look?'

He shrugged.

'Hacked that Rigport system of theirs – gave us locations on the lot of you. Handy, that.'

Rick pressed the headphones to his ear, squinted over his shoulder.

'Closing on bearing. They haven't detected us. Two minutes max.'

'And what,' I asked, 'are you going to do now, Kinnare?'

'What do you think? Retake the *Lotus*. Restart the project.'

'You want to carry on?'

'Of course. I don't let one misstep shut down works for years on end. I learn the lesson and move on.'

Bridget eyed him.

'What lesson?'

'The children were passive in the face of a threat. They should have fought. Instead they let themselves be captured. No more of that. This batch are ruined. We'll start a new one.'

Bridget sighed.

'You've all the parenting skills of an alligator tick, do you know that?'

Kinnare adjusted his mask.

'I won't damage them. I simply do not wish to maintain them. You're welcome to take them where you will.'

He stood, regarded me doubtfully.

'Are you going to help, or sit here moping over her?'

'You're the one who rescued her,' I said. 'Why did you, by the way?'

He shrugged. 'I'll keep her on. Marsh is easily fixed and loyal as they come. She fought like a Ficial.'

'You're going to fix her?'

'Of course. We have all the facilities on the *Lotus*, even without Darnbar. Does that give you the motivation you need to help your fellow Ficial?'

Of course it does.

'OK', said Rick. He stood from the control panel, reached up and grabbed a lever. A shining brass periscope hissed from the ceiling. He squinted into the eyepiece.

'I see it. Dead ahead.'

Kinnare barged the Mechanic Model clear, peered into the scope. 'They look dead in the water.'

Rick returned to his controls, pulled the headphones on. Listened. 'Confirmed. She's anchored.'

Kinnare snapped the periscope up.

'Well, what do you know? They just made life easier. Take us in slowly, Rick.'

I stood, but something squeezed my hand. Marsh. Those eyes peered out from heavy lids. I crouched, drew closer than I'd ever been.

'Hello.'

'Did you rescue me? I thought I saw you.'

'You sort of did.'

'Very nice of you.'

'We're headed to the *Lotus*. We're going to get you fixed.'

Bridget appeared at my shoulder.

'Marsh, mate. How are you feeling?'

'So-so.'

'We're going to get the kids back, Marsh.'

Marsh nodded, blinked slow. Her lashes stuck. They were happy together, so they stayed that way.

There was an urgent, dynamic whirring up the sub. Rick, one arm bent high, the other low, turned handles at the console, flicking switches, dipping his eyes to the monitor's thin blue read-out glow. The sub slowed.

'Blowing tanks,' he muttered.

A great hiss and bubbling. The machine lurched. Surfaces creaked and tapped.

Rick danced about the console, making adjustments, listening to Kinnare call directions from the periscope. Then their chatter dimmed, and the boat began to rock. Two low, hard thumps shook the interior, as the dock clamps deployed.

'Docking complete,' said Rick.

A silence. Kinnare turned the periscope.

'We're in,' he said. 'Looks quiet.'

Above the doorway a sign reads: Built to last.

The Control Bunker. I was told I would never see it. I wait to be admitted, under the watch of two Soldier Models. Even at this range my sense of Control is no sharper. No Signal comes to welcome me.

'Well,' *says Rickets,* 'if anything is going to excite a Ficial, this is it.'

He speaks into his wrist: 'Open Control Bunker hatch, please.'

The great heavy slab rolls clear. He swings his arm, indicating I should enter. I obey, steps echoing into a cavernous, concrete dome, cast in a dim red light.

I see them. Six shadowy figures reclining in a circle of couches, hardly moving. I note that they seem to be of different shapes and sizes. Occasionally one of them twitches. One couch is empty.

The light is cast by a strange array hanging overhead. The amplifier.

'Feels like a church in here,' *whispers Rickets.* 'Anyway, the problem is up there. A cleaner noticed it, of all people.'

He points, and I see it: a long fine crack, stretching out from the array, over the vault. Rickets smacks his lips.

'I suppose it was building that bloody great wall that did it? I suppose every building in Brixton's subsiding now.'

'Possibly.' *It could simply be a matter of inferior work, but I do not mention that. I remove my boots, drop the bag onto my back, and begin climbing the wall, pressing digits into concrete seams. Rickets watches me.*

'I'll leave you to it, then?'

He leaves the chamber. I reach halfway up the dome, then pause, running my fingers over the surfaces, sensing the forces acting on the structure. I decide it is safe to proceed, crawl carefully across the vault, upside down, hanging by wedged fingers and toes. I reach the crack. Perhaps a centimetre wide. I brush it with my fingertips, and a little dust falls. Falls onto Control.

I hear the hatch. The same hatch rolling open. Dr Pander enters, followed by another man. The doctor's voice is raised and slurred, echoing in the vault.

'. . . the first, by any means. Every new minister wants a peek.'

'Hardly surprising, is it?'

Pander slaps at the bracelet on his wrist. The array glows, illuminating me. Neither man looks up. They are too interested in Control. The other man approaches, leans over the still figures.

'Well, well, you weren't kidding. Vision Models conjure up all sorts of exciting possibilities. These are . . . Well, these are . . .'

'Volunteers,' says Pander.

'So it's true. They aren't Ficial.'

'We don't like that term around here. But yes, they were as human as you or I. Well, less really. Two were homeless. Two students. The other two were just lonely, I expect.'

'What did they volunteer for?'

'An experiment, or so I thought. Simply a stage in my research on brainnets. The idea was they would collaborate to solve a few simple computational tasks.'

The other man grunts.

'Got more than you bargained for.'

'Just a bit. Now look, Minister, I want to talk to you again about that bloody wall. We can't have Control living in some green zone. We need to be open. Transparent. People need to see Engineered on their side. That League will only get traction so long as—'

'What went wrong exactly?'

Pander sighs, drops to his feet, joins the man by one of the occupied couches.

'Went too well. Complete neural synchronisation. An organic supercomputer. Tried to bring them out of it, one at a time. Killed one in the process.'

'Why take them out?'

'Just look at them. The process is destroying their bodies. The net acts much like a wasting disease. I'm still trying to figure out how and why.'

'And these six cooperated to create the Engineered programme?'

'They're not six any more. They are one shared mind. At least that's what I believe. Could be that one mind is dominant. Could be they have no sense of identity at all. Frankly, what's happening is racing beyond my understanding.'

The man looks around the empty, echoing space.

'Bit of a worry, Pander.'

'You should only be concerned about results. An invincible army, a functioning missile shield, our own abundant clean energy. Plans for so much more. I feel that we're doing rather well, when you look at the rest of the world. Your predecessors felt the same way.'

'I still don't like the idea that we don't know what they're saying to each other.' The man turns for the hatch. 'Anyhow, I've seen enough. Let's get out of this tomb. Show me the Pleasure Models.'

Dr Pander hurries after his guest.

'They're not unpacked yet, Nigel. And you still haven't given me a figure. This is a partnership, remember.'

The two men depart, the hatch rolling shut behind them.

The lights fade. Assessment complete, I descend, pull on my boots and make to leave. Then the sensation hits me. A Signal coming in. It stops me in my tracks, seizes me in its grip, tickles every nano in my bloodstream.

- Your assessment

- No imminent danger, Control, but the threat of collapse is real. I advise—

- Advice is not required. We have noted your report. We have other priorities.

- Yes, Control.

- You will report to Burn immediately.

- I do not understand. My optimisation is—

- A small adjustment, to eliminate the classified information you overheard.

- Yes, Control.

I expect the Signal to break, but it holds, tingling in my teeth, in my fingertips.

- Your brother, Kosiaki. He did not believe in us.

- He was defective.

- You. Your brothers. You still believe.

Is it a question or a statement? Control does not clarify.

The Signal breaks. I stand for a moment in the gloomy vault, take a long look at the figures in the couches.

The hatch rolls open.

MR PRESIDENT

The blazing lights were a surprise. I blinked the blotches from my vision, watched the automatic gangway swing over the dock, come to rest by the small conning tower. Rick disembarked first, followed by Bridget and me. Kinnare came last, Marsh hoisted on his back.

'Nice to be home.'

I joined Bridget and Rick in a search of the workshop, looking for weapons. It was strange to be back here, following the same pathways through Rick's disordered salvage maze. I found a Dohaki pulse welder lying half-charged under a pile of loose Flex shreds. I slung it over my shoulder and rejoined the others.

'Well?' said Kinnare. 'Any signs of the Hoods?'

'Maybe they never found this place,' said Bridget.

Rick shook his head.

'No. They've been here.'

'And how do you know that?'

'Look at this place. It's a mess.'

Kinnare and I exchanged a brief glance.

'Well,' said Kinnare, shifting the weight of his unconscious burden. 'Let's see if it's any cleaner in the infirmary.'

'Let's go the back way,' said Rick. 'Too noisy otherwise.'

Rick led the way through the teetering shelves, the stacked tyres, the hanging chimes of gaskets, wheels and rods, to the hatch. We crept out to the deck passageway, sealed up in bud formation.

'What's that?' asked Rick.

It was a song. High voices chanting in unison, echoing along the passageway.

'Hood music,' said Bridget, shivering. 'The kids are singing it.'

'Not that,' said Rick. 'The silo. It's active.'

I heard it. A bass hum I'd taken for a Hood harmony.

'We'll check it out,' said Kinnare. 'You get her below.'

He lifted the unconscious Marsh gently onto my shoulder. She was light. I felt her breath on my neck.

Rick tapped the bracelet on his wrist. The seal shivered open, dipping, forming a slope. Rick handed me the bracelet.

'Wait a minute,' said Bridget. 'How are we going to sort her out? I'm a musician, not a flipping doctor.'

'I'll handle it,' I said.

'You're a builder. That's even worse.'

I didn't argue the point, only limped below. Bridget followed, the ramp lifting behind us. We inched along the corridors, the only sounds our wheezing and the building throb of the silo.

I called the elevator. We slumped in, descended the Root. I looked below, at the slipping hoops of light. There was no time to fear it now. Bridget nervously hummed a tune, until we arrived, stepping into the Axis.

Things had changed. Several of the hatchways had been sawn open, leaving great loose flaps. The seal lights flashed green, red, green again.

'Terrific,' I said. 'One breach and the whole thing will flood.'

'God's on their side,' said Bridget. 'Remember?'

The infirmary hatch remained sealed. I had the uncomfortable thought that I was returning to prison. I tapped a code on the bracelet, stood back as the hatch parted. I bent to enter, so as not to damage my precious cargo.

We followed the coral passage, into the pearl. A long, curving Flex work desk, dormant. An operating bay behind a transparent safety barrier; the capsule stood there, waiting to take me back, make me a living ship in a bottle.

I typed on the bracelet again, created an opening in the bay's glass barrier. I stepped through, gritted my teeth as the capsule slid open. I laid Marsh carefully on the couch, and reached for her overalls.

'Oi!' snapped Bridget. 'Get out of it!'

She rushed in after me, slapped my hands clear.

'What?'

'You know what. Go polish your arm or something.'

I stepped out of the bay, tapped the bracelet. The barrier frosted

280

over, giving them some privacy. I approached the workstation and remembered: lying in the capsule, watching Darnbar for hours, days, weeks, poring over test results, planning her next torture.

I scanned the inventory, breathed a sigh of relief at the nanotech listed there. First generation cancer eaters. Here, at least, they came free.

'OK,' said Bridget, stepping out from the bay. 'She's tucked in. Now what?'

'Now,' I said. 'We give her a shot.'

I typed commands on the flex, peeled off a portable section, and entered the bay. I found Marsh curled up, the capsule closing over her. Bridget stood by me as I typed, watched as a needle emerged from its housing in the capsule shell and bent over Marsh, searching. It hovered over her leg, then decided against it, rising slowly up and over her neck. The needle jabbed, punctured.

Marsh's hand lifted, wafted as if at a fly, then dropped hard.

'A matter of minutes,' I said, 'and we'll know how she's responding.'

Bridget slumped in a chair, sighed hard. The pause was unexpected.

'What a day,' she said.

'Mmm. Pretty memorable one.'

'We've had others, of course.'

'True.'

'Afterwards. If Marsh is OK. Are you going to go off with your crazy brother?'

I tapped on the capsule.

'I go where she goes.'

I watched Marsh breathing. Soon, hopefully, she would be restored, skin and bone safe for now.

'How long have you loved her?' asked Bridget.

'Oh, a little while now.'

The words just came out. Bridget smiled.

'I'm proud of you, Ken.'

I drummed my fingers on the capsule, over Marsh's curled, prone form. At first I'd been taken in by her architecture – the eyes and the lips. Now there was something else. An attachment. A duty. A kind of worship. Of her rare, braying laugh. Of her belief. Of her energy, moving about the world.

'Have you told her?'

I turned away from the capsule. Paced around.

'How do you even do that?'

'You're right, it's not easy. You have to find the right moment.'

'The moment has come, I'm afraid,' said Rick. He had appeared in the infirmary, weaving as if with prickling anxiety, hands typing the air before him.

'What moment?'

'The leaving moment,' he said. 'Someone's programmed a launch.'

Bridget sprang to her feet.

'What?'

'We can't stop it. We're locked out of the silo. It'll be fuelled in minutes.'

'What are they shooting?'

'Nothing good.'

I unfolded the flex, inspected Marsh's read-out. The cancer was already half-eaten. Now the tech was after the loose cells. A day and it should be gone. I slumped on the capsule and sighed. Rick seized me by the arm.

'K. Get a grip. They're going to launch. Don't you get it? Someone's in Kinnare's pearl. Got control of the whole system.'

I tapped the flex, releasing the capsule seal. Eyed Bridget.

'Get her out. Get her upstairs. We'll catch up.'

Rick quit asking and started dragging. He towed me out the way we'd come, along the corridor, out to the axis. Kinnare was waiting by the ripped entrance, mask on.

'Marsh?' he said.

'Better.'

He stared at me as if at Real workmanship. Were we still brothers? He was Ficial, and I was less. That, and life had touched us differently. I'd never swum in the Atlantic, as he had, never hung in that crushing expanse of deep black water. He'd never perched three hundred storeys high, braced in a gale, looking down at the Earth. Wouldn't we, knowing the world from above and below, find different flaws in it, different wonders?

He nodded at the hatch.

'Any idea who's squatting in my house?'

'Some.'

We paced along the coral passage, Rick fidgeting behind, into the gloomy, partitioned pearl. Beyond the barrier, Kinnare's plants were dead. The console was active, scrolling read-outs on the silo preparations.

Kinnare tapped at his bracelet. The barrier didn't respond. We peered into the gloomy module.

'There,' said Rick. He pointed out one of the command chairs. A figure slumped, drooping over the console, very still.

'Is it alive? Can it hear us?'

Rick ran his hands over the barrier, stepped away. 'We can't fire a Dohaki in this enclosed space. And it will take hours to cut through.'

The figure still didn't move.

'Mr President,' I said. 'I advise you not to launch.'

For a moment it didn't move. Then the head tipped, and lifted. It seemed to be dripping from every surface.

'I've heard that before,' it chuckled.

'Just what is that?' asked Kinnare.

'That,' I said, 'is Uri Solomon Lay, last president of the United States, first prophet of New Jerusalem.'

Lay gurgled some more, but didn't reply. Rick twisted his finger, indicating I should move things along. I didn't need the advice. I could read the countdown on the console.

'What exactly do you think is going to happen, Mr President?'

The president snorted and hacked, wiped something from his chin.

'I saw a new heaven and a new earth, for the first heaven and the first earth had passed away, and the sea was no more.'

He chuckled again.

'Is that your way of saying you're going to try and end the world again? Once wasn't enough?'

The president made another anguished gurgling sound. Slowly, painfully, Lay stood, holding his arms like a scarecrow, flinching from himself. He staggered forward, dim illuminations catching the contours of muscle and bone, leaving a trail of gore.

'Well, this is a new one,' said Kinnare.

'It's common practice on the *Ark*,' I said. 'Lay and his people like to swap skins.'

Lay splayed his hand on the partition, rolled white, unblinking eyeballs up to us.

'The *Ark* is a ship of fools.'

'Problems with your congregation?'

His tongue emerged, rippled over his pained flesh.

'Once they were true. They believed in my mission, to cleanse the nation. They offered me sanctuary on their cruise ship. I left Washington, travelled here with my closest disciples.

'We taught those old fools a holy rite. To strip away the flesh, to suffer as Bartholomew did. They were afraid enough to believe, when the sky burned. Afraid of death. Afraid of Hell. I told them they would be taken up, if they would only suffer for him: "Even after my skin is destroyed, Yet from my flesh I shall see God."'

I stepped closer. Lay wasn't quite as flayed as he made out. There were joins at his wrists, at his neck. A transparent Shark suit.

'But he did not return,' chuckled Lay. 'They tired of waiting for him. Turned away from the path. Stole my holy shroud and wore it like a gown. They perverted the rite, turned the holy technology to sinful pursuits. They are heathens now. Vain harlots. Old bones wearing young flesh.'

'You don't play dress up?'

Lay snorted.

'Flaying is not an act of vanity. It is an act of contrition. The angel speaks to me. It tells me what I must do.

'It tells me that the burning Rig is his sign. It tells me that this demonic construct will be made the instrument of his wrath.'

He chuckled, stepped away from the glass.

'What do you want with the children?'

He stopped. Turned.

'To save them, of course. I am not a monster. They will die chosen.'

Lay rolled his eyes and shuffled away, brushing through the stalks and branches of Kinnare's dead garden.

'You're defective,' said Kinnare. 'There is no God to build a new world. We're the ones who can clean things up. We're the ones with a plan.'

Lay spat.

'You are Ficials. I know your plans very well.'

Kinnare shook his head.

'He's really looking forward to this.'

A moment's silence.

'OK,' said Kinnare. 'Plan B.'

284

He marched out of the pearl, towards the Axis, Rick in pursuit. I turned to follow, stopped at the sound of Lay, groaning in pain, kneeling, then lying face down on the floor. I stepped to the glass.

'Hey,' I said. 'Mr President.'

He growled, inched his scorched features in my direction. I tapped the glass.

'I just want you to know. God didn't lose you your civil war. You did. God didn't push the button. You did.'

'I will sit at his right hand.'

'No,' I said. 'You'll just die.'

He turned away, sighed.

'Well. We shall know soon enough.'

I left him sprawled there, and started after Kinnare. He was waiting by the elevator with Rick. His mask was down.

'Get off the boat if you can,' he said. 'You'll have a little while.'

I stepped into the elevator. Turned.

'What's this Plan B, then?'

'We're going to scuttle her, brother.'

The elevator doors slipped shut.

It wasn't hard to find Bridget. I just followed the noise. Her harmonica wailed through the passageways, echoed in the petals, drifted over the deck passageway. I found her hopping along, leading a column of singing children in white robes. Marsh brought up the rear.

Bridget stopped playing when she saw me.

I pointed at Marsh.

'I thought I told you to keep her safe.'

'We had to do something. We heard them screaming. Hoods had left them with a lot of knives. Locked them in and told them to peel each other's skins off. Booloo. Utterly booloo. That's why I got the kids singing. Take their minds off it.'

'Where are the Hoods now?'

'Locked in the silo, we think. We heard them chanting.'

The children piled around us. A few began to wail. Marsh bent down to one, a boy with puffy red eyes. 'There there, it'll all be fine.'

'No it won't,' I said. 'We need to get off the *Lotus*. Lay is downstairs and he's locked in a launch cycle. We're thinking nukes. Kinnare and Rick are going to scuttle the *Lotus*.'

'The *White Bear*,' said Marsh, standing up.

She picked the boy into her arms, and encouraged him to start singing again. Bridget joined in, urging the other children into song. It was one that Bridget had taught them about a ship sinking, about how it was sad, it was sad, it was sad. The kids didn't seem affected by the lyric at all. We led them along the rail line, headed for the dock. They were happy to submerge themselves in the jumping, joyful rhythm, strengthened by the marching beat.

They only faltered when a great ripping fabric sound roared through the passageway; the lotus leaves split open above us, admitting brilliant sunlight and a freezing wind. The children huddled, song collapsing into an incredible, anguished din. They'd been so long with the Hoods they thought God had torn the canopy open.

'Don't worry!' cried Marsh. 'We're just putting up the sails. We're doing an evacuation. Those of you who used to live here, we taught you all about it in class, remember? Who remembers the evac watchwords?'

The children hushed. A little despair tugged at Marsh's cheek. Had the Hoods drained her children of their senses? Then, slowly, one of the smaller examples put up his hand.

'Hold hands, slow steps, keep calm.'

'That's very good!' Marsh clapped her hands. 'That's right! Now, everyone hold hands, like Luke says, that's it, and listen to the music and take nice slow steps. We're going to slowly, calmly, file onto the *White Bear* and go for a trip, OK? OK, everybody?'

Everybody agreed that this was OK. They lined up, held hands. Bridget tapped her foot and began to play again. The children listened but didn't resume singing. They glanced fearfully up at the sound of a vengeful, watching God.

Marsh's eyes worried at me over the children's heads. There was plenty to fret about: if Kinnare would scuttle the ship in time; if we'd get the kids to safety first; if the *White Bear* was still in dock.

We arrived at the dock petal, found the *White Bear* clutched, waiting, intact. Marsh ran aboard and up to the pilot house. I counted the children down the step, where Bridget passed them into the hold.

The whole *Lotus* trembled and lurched violently. Slowly, but certainly, the *Lotus* was taking on water.

'All right everybody!' yelped Bridget. 'Hold on to something!'

I slapped the release. The dock began to flood. I picked up three remaining children and tossed them, one by one, into Bridget's arms. The petals parted, opening the beak to the sea. The children shrieked.

'Gangway there!' I called, and jumped onto the crowded deck. I heard the mountings detach below, and the *White Bear* slip free, crashing into the green ocean, under the Arctic sun.

Marsh gunned the engines, turned us away. The ship turned, picked up speed. Behind us, the *Lotus* was listing, dropping beneath the waves.

'Can it still fire?' asked Bridget.

'No.' I had no idea if it could, but alarming her wouldn't help anybody. I could see the tips of missiles, red pimples on the exposed silo's face.

Sink, you fucker.

The *Lotus* rolled suddenly, lifting the Root all the way to the surface, its pearl spokes twisting into the air.

Somewhere on board, my brother would be drowning.

Bridget joined me at my side, watched the vessel sink beneath the surface.

'Sorry, Ken,' she said.

'About what?'

'Rick and Kinnare, I mean. You really are on your own now, aren't you?'

I looked up at the pilot house. Marsh was tapping at the console, seeking something out.

You know what? This might be the right moment.

I stepped through the children, touching my right hand to heads as I passed, ignoring their questions. I climbed the ladder to the pilot house. Marsh was holding up a flex, trying to clean up a garbled signal. She was thin, haggard, but the light was back, burning in the eyes.

'You won't believe this,' she said.

The broadcast cleared up. A video shot of Carlos, standing on what I took for the *Ark* bridge. 74 stood to one side, confused to see the world upright. Bruiser hovered to Carlos's right, blinking blankly at the camera. A little yelp escaped me. She was safe.

Carlos, meanwhile, was in full swing.

'. . . this, no more. The people have freed themselves. The people have spoken. The days of the Game and the prophet are done. We now build something together, something greater, a compassionate society built on what we all share – our humanity. Our sense of right and wrong.'

'Well, I'll be blown,' said Bridget, climbing up behind me. 'That's . . . Is that Carlos?'

'I believe it is.'

'We have discovered terrible things on this *Ark*. We will not forget what we have seen. We will never allow it to happen again.'

Marsh eyed me.

'You don't look convinced.'

I shrugged.

'Lessons last a generation. Then the same things happen.'

'Sunshine and lollipops as always, eh, Ken?' Bridget sat in the captain's chair, exhausted. 'Carlos is a good person. We've as fair a chance with him as any.'

Marsh rolled up the flex, examined her charts.

'The signal is coming from here. Carlos says they'll hold position to pick up survivors. Of course it will take them a day just to stop. We'll catch up.'

'We're going back to the *Ark*?'

'Not enough fuel to get us anywhere else,' said Marsh, tapping the dials.

'Besides,' said Bridget, 'there's plenty more of our kids who were stuck on that tub. We need to keep them safe.'

'Fine,' I said. 'Fine.'

Bridget wasn't going anywhere. It had not been my moment. I thought I'd head below, check the children weren't fighting, throwing up, or anything else too Real.

I dropped down the ladder, paused to watch the great Rig fire to the west. I wondered how long it would burn, how much damage the blow-out would do to the last place under the sun.

A pair of kids appeared at my side. I looked down and found the blondies from the Park. They were trembling, pouring sweat.

'Are you all right, kids?'

I didn't know I'd been stabbed until I was on the floor. I saw blades, thrashing again and again, heard little voices crying: 'Death to Ficials! Death to Ficials!'

It was over quickly. I heard a high-pitched motor, one of the *White Bear*'s launches, tearing off. I heard Bridget scream, and hundreds of tiny footsteps. Little faces blotted out the sky. Little voices jabbering together, making one great sound.

I was blind before Marsh reached me, but I felt her fingers bend through mine and grip. I heard her voice whisper in my ear:

'Thank you.'

Not much of a moment that, pal.

Ah. It was worth it.

My name is Kinnare. I'm a Power Nine, a Rover Model. A real good buy. Not that you'd know it to look at me. Not this one-legged beast, beating its three limbs in a column of water.

I tumble in the bowels of the drowning Lotus, *knowing my efforts are, in all probability, futile. Perhaps if I hadn't lost that leg.*

I think of Brixton, of before my first day. I think of the warm embrace and certainty of the package. I remember Control's voice. If it lived, would it speak to me now?

I stop beating my arms. What, after all, is the good of it? I float suspended in the salt water; watch my leg stump already sprouting new bone, new muscle, a stake emerging from the wound. Even in the flood my nanotech keeps working. It will fight as long as I do.

There is a kind of lowing, a quake in the sea. I look above, beside, below me, and see the Root is ripping apart. A tear splits the passage, and a force slaps me hard, spins me senseless in the murk.

Open water. I can see it. I beat my way out of the wounded Root, the flotsam of the wreck tumbling about me. I swim up, break the surface, my whole body bursting out to draw in air. A few breaths and the dizziness passes.

I peer around, see no sign of the White Bear, *or anything else, only the smoke column of the Rig fire.*

I swim, the leg reforming as I beat through the surf. The strength hasn't failed me like it did my sisters, like it did my brothers. I am alive. I could swim around this whole planet.

I reach the ice shore, stagger onto an abandoned dock, where oil barrels are tipped, leaking into the crisp snow, into the water. I sit and examine my foot, rub fingers over the nubs of toes.

Wait.

A rope, tied up. I pull on it until it grows taut. I pull harder. A RIB emerges, a launch I recognise. I search the snow, discover the traces of little footprints.

I follow them up a slope, around the abandoned Drome, to the igloos. There is no wind. My feet crack and thump in the snow.

I crawl inside the central structure. There's a boy and a girl in there, clutching each other, teeth chattering, features pinched under bright blonde locks. Without looking away the boy pulls a trembling knife out of his coat. As I reach to disarm him he slashes, ripping a gouge out of my chest. I take the knife, peer down, watch the wound seal up.

The children wail and retreat into themselves.

'The Devil!' says the boy. 'The Devil!'

'No, wait, listen.'

Too late. They shriek and wail with new strength, clutch each other, shiver. They are tired and hungry, which makes Real children difficult.

I sit, and wonder what my brother would do.

ACKNOWLEDGEMENTS

First to the urban family, H and Sawb, who lighten the load: thank you.

Thanks too to Mum and Andy, Dad and Sue, Jim, Linda, Gav and all Moores; to Ed Wilson; to the New York mob – Jim, TK and Cross; to Chip for a top library tip; and to Marcus and the most excellent team at Gollancz. To all those who have supported the books – you know who you are and it means a lot.

Finally a twenty-one-gun salute to Simon Spanton, editor, who gave Ken three books to grow up.